ROSEMARY ROGERS

MIDNIGHT LADY

AVON BOOKS NEW YORK

AVON BOOKS
A division of
The Hearst Corporation
1350 Avenue of the Americas
New York, New York 10019

Midnight Lady

Prologue

England, 1799

It was so *dark* in the hallway, even with tiny, wavering pools of light from the lamp high on the wall. Shadows crouched low along the wainscoting and squatted in corners like ravenous beasts waiting to swallow the unwary. Though it was forbidden, Kyla could not help putting her thumb in her mouth and sucking hard. Slowly, she moved down the hall toward the thin ray of light that shone in a tiny beacon of comfort around her mother's door. The door was open a little, and she hurried before it closed against her, as it often did at night when she only wanted Maman to hold her but was held back by Marie. Where *was* Marie? Her nurse had gone out again, and would come back smelling of wine and all giggly, hissing at her to go to sleep and not to tell or *le cauchemer* would get her.

A soft whimper rose in her throat at the thought. Would the nightmare come *here* to get her? In the hallway outside her mother's door? She splayed her hand against the paneled wainscoting that felt rough against her fingers, the other hand still to her face with the comfort of her thumb in her mouth. Fear surged through her, but she forced herself forward a step, then another, until she stood in the faint splinter of light that shone through a crack where the door was ajar. She blinked several times.

What was the matter with Maman? She could hear voices. It sounded like that man again, who came now at night to see her. Her lower lip thrust out, and the funny feeling came back. She did not like him. He was not a nice man, for sometimes she heard Maman cry out when he was there, and it was always such a queer sound, as if she was being hurt. But later, when she saw her, Maman did not seem hurt. No, then she would smile softly at her, though she could tell that she was not really paying attention, even when she was naughty and spilled her tea, or when she deliberately crumbled a biscuit on the floor so that Maman would *have* to look at her—*really* look at her instead of just nod and smile in that distant, faraway manner. . . .

But now he was here again, and she did not like it. She pushed at the door, her bare feet making no sound on the wooden floor, and peered around the doorframe. Her hair strayed into her eyes, but she could see through the pale tousled strands into Maman's dressing room. Her eyes widened.

Maman wore only her red dressing gown, and it was open in the front, leaving her bare from the neck to her ankles. Her pretty light hair, always worn in a neat coil atop her head, was loose and hanging down in wispy ringlets around her face. She was staring up at the man, not protesting even when he touched her *there* in the place where Kyla had been told *no* one should ever touch . . . why was he doing that? And why was Maman letting him? But she was sitting still in her chair, unmoving as the man's hands stroked and caressed her, pinching her at times so that she moaned a little.

Distressed, Kyla stepped into the room. Her bare toes curled into the warm thickness of the carpet. No one noticed her, and she stopped, uncertain. She had been told she must never come into Maman's room at night, always to call for Marie instead, but Marie was gone. The night candle had gone out, and the dark surrounded her bed with huge, monstrous shadows.

The man was in front of Maman now, so she could not see her mother, only his back. His white powdered hair was tied back in a queue, and he bent forward, pushing Maman back in the chair, shoving apart her legs to kneel between them. Now Maman cried out again, a soft sound, and the dressing gown slipped to the floor in a puddle of crimson.

Watching them, Kyla whimpered. Something was wrong. Maman would not let *anyone* see her without her clothes! Now the man was touching Maman again, his hands pulling at her and at his own clothes. Kyla tried not to, but began to sob as her mother made that queer sound again, a sort of moaning sigh as if she was hurt.

"What is that?" Maman sat up, pushing the man away as she reached for her dressing gown. And then she saw her there, and her face went pale and she said in French, "No, no, good God— my poor baby. . . ."

The man turned. He seemed so annoyed Kyla

did not dare look at him closely, though she was aware that he was staring at her with fierce intensity. "Who is this child?"

"My daughter, my lord. Please. Allow me to take her back to bed—"

"No. Bring her here. Your daughter, you say. Sly baggage, you never let on. God, she is a pretty thing. Like her mother, what? Come here, child— what is her name?"

Maman hesitated, pulling her dressing gown tight around her, then said softly, "Kyla."

"Kyla ... An unusual name, yet so familiar. Have I not heard it before? Ah, no matter. It suits her, for she is unusually pretty. I said come to me, Kyla. Here ... yes, you shall sit on my lap, and I shall stroke your pretty blond hair."

Kyla hung back, but he took her hand and pulled her to him, lifting her to seat her on his thigh. He crooned to her softly, and held her much too tightly. She did not like it. He smelled of sour wine and other things she did not know or like. Yellow silk covered his thighs, tied at the knees with scarlet ribbons and diamond buckles. She dared not look at his face, and focused instead on the glittering buckles.

"Pretty child ... so blond and pink and perfect." He held her so tight, his hands crumpling her gown around her waist, and his fingers were fat, all white and soft as they stroked her bare thighs where the hem of her nightgown rode up. She squirmed and looked up at her mother anxiously.

Maman's face was pale. Her fingers tightly clutched her dressing gown closed. "My lord— she is not even four years old. Please."

"A lovely child. So young and innocent. Untarnished by life." His voice had grown hoarse, and there was an odd note in it that must have been bad, for Maman grew quite agitated with him.

"Put her down at once, my lord! I will not have it." Maman came forward, and pulled her from the man's lap to hold her tightly in her arms. Kyla had a brief, blurred view of a face all pale and plastered with black patches. His eyebrows were dark and bushy and bristled like fur over pale eyes that were half-open almost like a cat's as he glared at her mother.

"*You* will not have it?" The man sounded soft and suddenly dangerous. "You, madam, are in no position to say anything about what I do."

Kyla put her arms around her mother's neck and breathed the sweet scent of perfume that took away the clinging smell of sour wine. She pressed her lips against her mother's ear. "Maman, I do not like him. Take me to my bed. Marie is gone, and there is no light in my room."

"Shush, my precious. I will make it all right. Be still a moment, and go wait for Maman in the hall. Be a good girl now."

"Yes, Maman." She did not protest when her mother put her on the floor, but went to the hallway just outside the door. Only one candle burned, and it was so high upon the wall, dim and making scary shadows down the corridor. Kyla clung to the doorframe. Maman would come for her in just a moment.

In her dressing room, Maman was talking softly, but some of her words were loud enough to hear: "No! She is a child . . . not to be used like . . ."

"But such a lovely child . . . pay well for her . . . you are a fool not to see what lies ahead . . ." Laughter. *Mean* laughter, not nice and jolly but sounding all harsh and cruel.

Kyla shut her eyes tightly and put her hands over her ears. She thought of the park, where flowers grew and the trees were shady, and ducks floated on the water and quacked loudly at her when she took them crusts of bread.

In a moment, the man came out into the hall. He was angry. His face was all red, and his voice was loud. "You are making a mistake, my dear. You will not be so well treated in London after this night, I assure you. Perhaps you should reconsider my offer. After all, what else can you do? Do you think you will always have such soft skin and a pretty face? Once your looks are gone, so will your money and protectors be. Keep that in mind."

"Leave, I tell you . . . there is nothing you can say that will change my mind!"

"Oh, I think differently." There was a grating softness in his tone, like a large purring cat, all smug and satisfied. "You will change your mind. You will have no choice, m'dear. I will see to it."

"Get out!"

Kyla had never heard her mother speak in that voice, a shrill, almost frightened tone that made her begin to cry again. Maman came to her at once, shielding her from the man with her own body, her voice calmer now.

"Leave, my lord. I will do what I have to do to protect my child from men like you."

"You'd best try to protect her from becoming what you are, madam. But I fear that is impossible. She will be what you are one day, for there is no other life open to her."

"You are wrong!" Fiercely, Maman gripped her so tightly she could scarcely breathe. "My daughter will have what is hers by right one day."

"No doubt, madam." He sounded amused. "But you have yet to embrace the truth of what that will be."

"Get *out*, I tell you. Get out of my house!"

"Yours only as long as you can pay for it, do not forget. Without my money, that will not be long. Do not think I will allow you to leave until I am ready to be rid of you, m'dear. I will not." His laugh was unpleasant. "I will be back tomorrow, never fear. And the *three* of us shall have a nice visit, what?"

Kyla buried her face in the curve of Maman's neck and shoulder, and was intensely glad when she heard him leave and the door shut behind him. Now she would have Maman to herself again.

"I do not like that man, Maman."

"Nor do I, my precious, nor do I." Maman's voice was all shaky, as it was sometimes when Kyla surprised her in the small garden with a damp handkerchief and her eyes all red. But she sounded more cheerful at once. "Now come, my sweet, precious girl. I shall tuck you into bed and tell you a story, of a place where the sun always shines, and there are flowers and trees like you have never seen, and huge gray beasts that are bigger than coaches, with long noses that drag along the ground. . . ." Her words ended in a faint sob, and she clutched Kyla so tightly she began to squirm with alarm and sudden dread.

"Will we be all right, Maman?"

"Oh my sweet little girl . . . I pray that it will be so. I will do it. I will write him back at once, and perhaps he will send for us . . . oh God, I have no other choice. There is nothing else I can do now, for he is right . . . but the risk here is greater than there. Yes. For you, I will do it. I will leave this country tomorrow if I can!"

Kyla peered at her mother's face anxiously, still not certain, still afraid. "Maman? Are we to leave England?"

"I hope so, my sweet girl, I hope so. . . ." She paused, and sounded so tragic and forlorn when she added in a soft whisper, *"Edward, Edward— why did you leave us to this . . . ?"*

"Who is Edward, Maman? Is he a bad man?"

Maman looked startled, then hugged her again, smelling of gardenia flowers. "I shall tell you one day, my precious. But do not think of tonight again. Put it from your mind, for I shall keep you safe. Now come. Let us tuck you into bed, where I shall stay with you until you are no longer frightened."

But it was hard not to be frightened, when Maman had tears on her cheeks and wetting her dressing gown. Kyla hoped that bad man who made her mother cry *never* came back again.

Part I

London, 1816

One

Fog drifted over the Thames in thick layers that shrouded the other ships with a spectral haze, blurring the dark outlines of buildings that loomed up from the mist like the ravenous monsters of her childhood fears. The fog was damp and quiet, muffling the sounds of creaking boards and flapping canvas, muting the noise of the harbor. Kyla Van Vleet wrinkled her dainty nose as the *Sea Lady* nosed its prow through the maze of ships and currents and down the wide, winding ribbon of dirty water. What a fetid smell London had, with floating debris and sour refuse bumping alongside ships and smaller craft. In the tattered shreds of mist she could see gaily colored barges weighed down with the gilt ornament of wealth floating next to shabby merchant barks. Hundreds of small boats darted about like tiny insects skimming over the surface.

After passing under high, wide arches of the London Bridge that spanned the Thames, long rows of ships formed watery channels filled with French, Dutch, Spanish, and countless other vessels. Kyla peered at this exciting array through a mist made thick with tiny black flecks of soot. Chimney pots poured dense black smoke into the sky and thickened the haze until it stung eyes and nose with acrid odors and gray ash. No one had mentioned how *dirty* London would be, but after all, she was accustomed to the markets of Poona in India, where the teeming masses and crowded marketplaces were noisy and polluted. Why had she thought London would be different? Yet it was. Even from the river there was an air of excitement that infused her with anticipation—and dread.

Kyla stood at the ship's rail with her gloved hands tightly clutching the smooth wood. What would they say? How would they greet her? Oh, *why* had she come back here? But she knew the answer to that, knew that there was no other choice. It was a decision that she would have made in time even if Papa Piers had not sent for Tante Celeste to come to India and escort her back to London.

A gust of brisk wind caught Kyla's blond hair and the blue ribbons of her hat, whipping them across her face to tickle a cheek burning from sharp winds whisking over the ship's deck. One of the crew—Mister Rand, the first mate, who had been *very* attentive—cast her a sidelong glance as he went about his duties, but Kyla pretended not to notice. He had been a pleasant diversion on the long voyage, but that was all. A mild flirtation on her part, though Tante Celeste had scolded her for being cruel.

"You *know* that this will lead to only frustration on his part, *ma chérie*, so do not give him hope."

"I have said nothing, Tante, to give Mister Rand

cause to think of me as more than a shipboard passenger."

"It's your eyes, my dear. They are so unusual, with such long lashes like graceful wings—yes, your eyes speak volumes, make promises of paradise without your knowing it. You cannot help it, for even your dear maman had the same unaware way about her, but there you have it. So do not be cruel to the poor man."

And so she had ignored him the rest of the voyage, but still he looked at her with longing in his eyes, as he did now from the foredeck, and she turned away. The *Sea Lady* edged slowly up the Thames to nudge into the docks of London's East Side, churning through brown water thick with refuse and pungent scents as the prow nosed toward the dock.

"We're almost there, Kyla." Celeste du Bois sounded brisk and matter-of-fact, but beneath her outward complacence could be heard a faint quiver in her voice. Excitement? Anxiety? It was hard to tell, for Celeste prided herself on remaining composed in any situation, and now she was efficiently tugging on expensive velvet gloves made on London's Threadneedle Street, each finger measured and sewn to tailored perfection just for the comtesse du Bois, who was—even though the revolution in France had destroyed so many lives—the essence of French nobility. The elegant, patrician Celeste had been Faustine Auberge's very best friend, right up until Faustine had succumbed to a fever.

Poor Maman. Kyla thought of her often, of her fragile mother who had seemed so out of place in the sun and heat of India with her delicate beauty.

Faustine may have appeared frail, but her golden hair and ivory skin masked a resilient nature. How else could she have survived the horrors of the French Revolution, then abandonment by her aristocratic husband? Thank God for Piers Van Vleet. The wealthy Dutch merchant had fallen deeply in love with Faustine, and become genuinely fond of her daughter.

But now, all that Kyla had known was gone. Her mother was dead, the only father she'd ever known forced to send her away from India for fear of what might happen to her once he was gone.

"*Ja*, you need more den I can give you, *engel*," he'd said in his thick Dutch accent, "so I tink it best dat you leave India and go where you will haf a better life. Marry someone good for you."

Marry? Kyla had almost laughed at that. She was near twenty-one, past the prime as far as most were concerned. Not that she had not had her share of attention from the English army officers stationed in India, for of course, she had. But none had ever interested her, being far too eager, or far too interested in the income from Papa Piers's investments with the East India Company, and his burgeoning plantation. But what did she want with some fresh-cheeked lieutenant swelled with his own importance? Or even the grizzled old colonels who had paid calls, all with that same look of lust and desperation in their eyes . . . no. She would rather end her days as a spinster than as the discontented wife of an army officer.

It was her own decision. She preferred to while away long hours with her books, or riding a horse over the seared plains as fast as she could go, with the wind in her hair so hot and hard that she could barely catch her breath—and at night, when it was dark, she had loved to slip from the house and down to the deep, murky waters of the small tributary to the Godavari River that sighed past the sprawling house set beneath towering jakfruit trees. There, she loved to remove all her clothes despite the wailing protests of her *ayah*, and slip into the cool waters to bathe. It was one of her few refuges from the world, where time was suspended and there were only the wet dark waters of forgetfulness around her. Her Lethe, her sanctuary from the sorrows that she could not escape.

But now she had left India behind, the warm sunshine and her beloved *ayah*, who had raised her since childhood. India. She missed it already, the whitewashed walls glowing almost pink under the hot sun, the opulent greenery of mango and jakfruit trees, glossy leaves and enormous fruit, the huge spreading roots of the banyan tree like the snaggled teeth of a broken comb—all left behind to come to this chilly land of gray sea and barren skies that she barely remembered.

A drizzling rain seamed the horizon of sea and sky together quite efficiently, so that it would be impossible to tell where one began and the other left off if not for the misty warehouses of the London dock district that sprouted up from the fog like mushrooms. Flashes of color melded into gray chunks of stone buildings, appearing like great specters for only a moment before disappearing again into the mist.

Kyla tugged her cloak more closely around her, grateful for the warmth. She had almost packed the garment, insisting that she would be warm enough. Celeste was right, as usual, but then, she was more accustomed to English climate. London had been Celeste's home for the past twenty years.

"*Mon Dieu*," Celeste said fervently as the ship moved sluggishly in a slow arc. "We're finally docking. This old tub wallows most disgracefully, I think. But, it is over. We are arrived!"

Sweeping an arm out in an elegant gesture, Celeste smiled her brightest smile, only for her godchild's benefit, Kyla was certain. After all, it had been Celeste who had been most miserable on the long sea voyage, tucked into her damp cabin and moaning of *mal de mer* most of the way, while Kyla had strolled the upper decks and enjoyed the fresh air and sea breezes. Even now, there were faint smudges under Celeste's bright brown eyes, vestiges of her recent travails and vows never to board a ship again, not even to save her only goddaughter, no, not her!

Kyla hid a smile at Celeste's dramatic gesture, and asked the question that had been on her mind since she had first learned the truth of her birth. "What will they think of me, Tante Celeste? These people have never met me, and may never have heard of me."

"How could anyone not love you, *ma petite*? You are so beautiful, so much like your maman, with the sweet face of a madonna, fashionable pale hair, but such *unusual* eyes—like the waters of the Mediterranean, changing from blue to green and back again. No, it would be impossible *not* to love you."

"But will she accept me, do you think? This woman who married my father?"

A frown knit Celeste's brows together. She

looked away, over the dipping rail of the ship to the murky outline of warehouses and the city beyond. After a moment, she looked back at her, a faint sad smile on her lips. *"Non, petite.* I do not think she will accept you gladly. You understand, of course, that the dowager duchess of Wolverton will not be excited to learn that there is another claimant to the estate of her late husband—your papa. Nor will the new duke, I fear. But, the barristers will see to the details, I am most certain, and soon you will be able to claim that which should have been yours long ago." Celeste's tone hardened slightly, and the brown eyes which were usually so lively and merry, darkened into brittle hardness like glass. "It should have been given to my Faustine as well, but those—those *canaille!*— who were your papa's parents, they did not agree."

Kyla gripped the ship's rail tightly, and leaned against its smooth curved surface to steady her balance as the ship swayed in the current. She gazed out over the wide ribbon of water toward the shore, close enough now that the buildings were distinct in the turbid light. The memories were so vague, seen from a child's perspective, hazy and unformed, only a jumble of impressions that held little truth in them.

Uneasy at the press of disturbing memories that were more like bad dreams than reality, she turned away from the rail to face Celeste. "If not for Maman's journal, I would not have known the truth at all. Would you have told me of it?"

There was a small hesitation, and Kyla could almost feel Celeste's reluctance before she shook her head. "No, I would not, *petite.* It was not my story to tell, you see. It was your dear maman's, and if she had wanted to tell you ... but perhaps this is the best way after all. It is as if she *is* telling you, *n'est-ce pas?''*

Yes, that was so. The small casket of carved teak wood and velvet lining, that had stood for so many years on her mother's bedside table was given to her by dear Papa Piers only a fortnight before she left India. Nestled inside with the important marriage lines was a journal, detailing so many things, so many years and betrayals, hopes and dreams and crushing disappointments, that for a short time, Faustine had been alive again, in the dried ink and scented pages of her journal. Weeping, Kyla had vowed to claim her rightful legacy, to take the place in life her mother should have occupied. After all, it was her right, was it not? And it had been Faustine's fondest wish that her daughter be acknowledged by the man who had fathered her.

There was only one man she could remember seeing with her mother other than Papa Piers, and he was a vivid memory of sound and formless impression more than sight.

Had that man been her father? She shuddered. It was unthinkable. He could not have been her father, not a man who would hold a little girl so tightly, and make her feel so uneasy, so—*dirty*. If only she had looked at him more closely, but she had been so frightened then, unsettled by the silky heat of his voice, that purring sound that grated on her like rough nails. The memory had been pushed away, to the deep recesses of her mind, hidden with all the other childhood fears like banshees and thunderstorms.

Now she was here, in London, where the duke of Wolverton had first met Faustine Auberge when she was a beautiful young girl fleeing from the horrors of the revolution in her native France. The details of their affair intrigued Kyla even while she wept for her mother's grievous betrayal. The duke *had* married beautiful Faustine, defying his parents and their protests, for the certificate of proof was in the teak casket, waiting after all these years to be given as evidence. And now the duke was dead.

Kyla drew in a deep breath that smelled of sea air and river tang. *I am an heiress. A deposed heiress, perhaps, but linked by blood to one of the oldest families in all of Great Britain. And I fully intend to claim my rightful inheritance from those who denied it to Maman!*

"You know," Celeste said when they were bundled into a handsome coach with all their baggage piled atop the swaying vehicle, "that my poor Faustine kept the proof of their vows not only because of what came after, but because she wanted you to have what is yours by right one day."

Rubbing her gloved knuckles against the dingy glass pane of the hack's window, Kyla nodded. "Yes. But she was not . . . not *wicked*, I do not care what others may say." Hot tears suddenly stung her eyes and made her throat ache. She looked back at Celeste, whose face reflected the same anguish.

"It was not pretty, what happened to my poor Faustine, *petit chou*, but how else could a woman whose very reputation and life had been shattered through no fault of her own make her way in this world? She had no other choice. Do not fault her for what she became, for inside, she was still the sweet, pure girl she had always been."

"I know that." Kyla cleared her throat of the sudden huskiness that made her words come out all hoarse and thick. "I know my mother was not what some say, for Papa Piers told me how she arrived in India as a crushed, fragile butterfly still battered by the storm around her. If not for Papa Piers—" She drew in a ragged breath. "If not for him, my mother would have died long before she did. I will never be able to repay him for what he has done for her, and for me."

"Piers Van Vleet is a decent man, *ma petite*, and there are few of those in this world, I fear." Celeste's voice hardened a little. "Do not let others tell you that you have no rights. You do. Wolverton may not have given them to you, but by all that is holy, you shall one day have them. It is your birthright. And there have been so many of late who have lost their birthrights through the selfish, heedless actions of others . . . so many. . . ."

Celeste's voice trailed into one of the sudden silences that came on her when she spoke of those times of the Terror that had overcome her beloved France. So many killed, the nobility nearly eradicated, and even the king and queen slaughtered as if animals. Faustine had spoken of it only once, when she had a fever, the babbling words and cries chilling Kyla until her *ayah* had come to lead her away. If the transferred fear had been so great, what must those poor souls like Faustine have suffered?

Celeste's face looked pale in the wan light streaming through the small window. Faint lines gathered at the corners of her brown eyes, and her glossy dark hair bore a trace of gray, barely visible beneath the stylish hat atop her elegant head. Marks of suffering still etched her lovely face, visible only when the light caught her just so, and then the tiny white scars could be seen, mementos of a past too horrible to express.

The comtesse du Bois had barely survived those times, the comte having met his fate at the guillotine and leaving her a young widow fleeing for her life to England, as had so many of the French aristocracy. There, pretty Celeste had survived by meeting a man who had snatched her from penury and married her. An elderly English baron only, but a good man, and Celeste had devoted herself to him until his death. As had Faustine been devoted to Piers until her death.

Leaning forward, Kyla put a hand atop Celeste's knee. "Forgive me, Tante. I did not mean to dredge up painful memories."

Celeste patted Kyla's hand fondly. "The memories are always there, *ma petite*. They will never go away. I hold them at bay as long as I can, like ravening wolves. But, I just thank *le bon Dieu* that I have my health and widow's portion now, though dear Reginald's children have inherited the estates. Still, they are good children, and have been quite kind to me." She sighed pensively. "If only Faustine had—"

"No, do not be sad for Maman. She lived her last years happily." Kyla sat back into the velvet squabs of the coach. The huge wheels rumbled loudly, occasionally dipping into a hole and jolting them hard against the interior so that they had to cling for safety to the leather straps dangling from the ceiling for just that purpose. She peered outside as the vehicle rocked sluggishly from side to side over the cobbled streets.

London bore an air of vigor beneath the tawdry trappings of dirt and smudged skies. And despite the uncertainties of what lay ahead, she could not help a greater sense of anticipation. Whatever came, she would manage it.

Two

Kyla gazed at the elegant woman seated before the fire. Yellow-and-orange flames were reflected in the polished sheen of brass firedogs and the heavy silver teapot on the table. Embroidered napkins of Belgian lace draped over the table and foamed in stark white froths from the dowager's lap. A formidable grande dame with inbred arrogance regarded Kyla from over the rim of a delicate white teacup embossed with exquisitely painted pink roses. She sipped at her tea with a remarkable composure that was broken only by the slightest tremble of her hand.

"So exactly what is it you wish of us, Miss Van Vleet?"

The question, so cold, so aloof, as if Kyla was there for the return of a borrowed silver tea service instead of the rights long denied her, raked across Kyla's strained temper and made her voice tart. "Nothing that is not due me, Your Grace."

The duchess stiffened slightly, but her composure did not crack. Not a flicker of an eyelash, not the faintest glint in her eyes nor twitch of her lips betrayed any emotion.

"Then we are of like mind, Miss Van Vleet. For you are due nothing."

Kyla stared at her. "Nothing? You mistake me if you think I will not pursue this, Your Grace. I have nothing to lose by it."

The teacup rattled slightly in the wafer-thin saucer as the duchess leaned to place it on the tray. "My dear Miss Van Vleet, you have nothing to *gain* from it. What do you think I should tell you—that your claim is valid? I will not, for it is not. As your barristers have been informed, your mother was not wed to my late husband, and even if she had been, it does not follow that you are his child."

Though Celeste had cautioned her that the dowager duchess would not bend, Kyla was unprepared for the fury that raged through her at the cool confidence and shrugging denial. She took a step forward.

"With all respect, Your Grace, I have the necessary papers that prove my claim. When the duke's parents forced him to repudiate my mother, they could not take away the legal documents. She hid them, and I have them."

At last the duchess's eyes flickered with reaction, but her voice was coolly composed. "Show them to me, Miss Van Vleet, and I will be able to tell you if they are valid."

"I am not so big a fool that I will surrender documents to you, Your Grace. They are safely hidden. All I ask from your family is my portion of the inheritance, and the acknowledgment that my mother was indeed wed to the duke. I want my birthright, and her name cleared."

"Your mother was nothing more than a lady of

the night, my dear, little though you may want to hear it. Do you think anyone would ever believe anything else?" The hooded eyes glittered. "Not after she spent so many years as a demimonde in London, they would not. A well-known demimonde, I might add. No, I do not think your claim will earn even a moment's notice from any magistrate, much less a qualified judge."

"Do not dare talk of my mother in that way. She was not what you pretend. Her lineage was as aristocratic as any in England, and I daresay, more so than yours, madam!"

It was *true*. Beatrice Hyde Parker Riverton might be the daughter of an English viscount, but Faustine Auberge had been the only child of a French marquis. And for *that* matter, Kyla herself was the daughter of a duke, so this arrogant harridan need not treat her as if she was some strumpet off the streets.

Ah, Tante Celeste warned me, but I did not think it would be so difficult to ignore such insolence and innuendos . . .

Lady Beatrice rose slowly to her feet, drawing herself into a silk-clad knot of dignified fury. She stared down her long nose at Kyla. "Faustine Auberge was a blue-blooded tart. She may have been born into aristocracy, but she fell lower than any street harlot in London's East End. Now get out. Take your preposterous claims and do what you choose with them. I assure you, I have a vast stable of barristers who will know how to deal with your fraudulent claims."

Trembling with fury, Kyla took a step forward, her feet cushioned by a thick Turkish carpet. A mantel clock of fussy ormolu curves ticked loudly, and the fire hissed in the grate. Her hands clenched tightly on her reticule.

"Do not think for a moment, Your Grace, that I will be intimidated by your threats. I will not. I came here to get what is mine, and by all that is holy or unholy, I will get it. You will have to share what you have gained from the duke's death, whether you wish it or not."

"What do you think you can do?" The duchess laughed, but it was a brittle sound. "There is nothing. You were not mentioned in his will."

"As a child and heir, I am entitled to that recognition which was denied me. A portion of your estate is mine, Your Grace."

A faint smile curved the dowager's mouth. "You little fool, you should have talked with a knowledgeable barrister before coming here like this. Ashleigh is not mine, nor does it belong to my daughters—Edward's *legitimate* children. It is entailed. Do you know what that means?"

"Of course I do. The lands have passed down to the next male heir. I am well aware of that."

"Then you should also be aware that Edward's four daughters have a legitimate claim that would far outweigh any spurious claimant such as yourself."

"Not at all." Kyla smiled. "I am, after all, the *eldest* child of Edward Riverton. But I am not greedy. I only want my share. If I must divide it with four sisters, then so be it. But remember, Your Grace, that I do have rights that the heir to Wolverton will have to recognize. He must then yield to me that which is my just due."

"Ah yes, I very much look forward to you managing what I have not, though I do not think the veriest of chits will be able to do it. Certainly. Go. Ask the duke yourself, if you can drag him from the kennels and his infernal hounds and horses." The duchess rattled her ivory-and-lace fan, shutting it with a decisive snap. "I anticipate greatly his response to this ridiculous claim, and only wish that I could be there to hear his answer myself."

"Your wish is granted, Aunt Beatrice."

Kyla turned. Her breath caught in her throat, and her lungs emptied of air as she caught the hard gaze of the tall man looming in the open door. How fierce he looked! Light-tricked gray eyes beneath heavy-lashed lids glittered like shards of splintered glass, and were as sharp, piercing her to the marrow so that she shriveled inside. Black garments lent a sinister appearance to a man who certainly needed no such embellishment. He reminded her of a pirate, with high cheekbones and a well-cut mouth, a nose as straight as an axe edge, and beard shadow darkening the square line of his jaw. What a frightening man!

He moved forward, graceful and dangerous at the same time, and she thought at once of the black panthers of India prowling through the tall grass with innate confidence and assurance. Dear God—this could not be—but was it? Was *this* man the new duke?

It was no surprise to hear the dowager duchess make the introduction with malicious delight: "May I present Miss Kyla Van Vleet to you, Your Grace. She has come to make a claim on your inheritance."

The gray stare like demon-smoke evolved into

a cold, dark assessment, and his symmetrical features arranged into such chill hostility that she forgot all she had intended to say in her behalf. The duchess waved a negligent hand.

"Miss Van Vleet brings most interesting information, Brett. You should listen well, for it will be quite entertaining, I assure you."

"No doubt." The duke's cold eyes did not leave Kyla's face, and she found it difficult not to quail under that fierce glare. "Another fortune hunter, Miss Van Vleet? Tell me, did the duke sleep with you as well? Perhaps leave you with child? Come. Don't be shy. Tell me what amount will satisfy your sudden discovery that you cannot go on without a portion of my cousin's inheritance."

"I . . . it is not that way, Your Grace." She stiffened her spine, though there was a curious crumbling at the back of her knees that threatened to collapse her at any moment. "My mother was married to the duke."

His dark brow winged upward. "How refreshing. A new claim. So you maintain you are his child, then."

"Yes. I am."

It was said quietly and firmly enough that he looked at her for a long moment. He was so close she could have run her hand over his immaculate sleeve, reached up and touched his face. Lucifer's face, devilishly handsome, with hellfire burning in his eyes and drawling voice.

"While I admire your initiative, Miss Van Vleet, I must disappoint you. I am aware of no former wives with valid claims. And in any case, my cousin would have settled fairly on a child of his."

"But he did not. He was forced to repudiate my

mother. As the duchess knows of this, then you must also know that it is true. And I have the papers to prove it."

"Your mother was Faustine Auberge."

Hope blossomed at his sharp comment. "Yes, Your Grace. So you do know of their marriage?"

"I know that it was annulled, and that your mother was paid a great deal of money to disappear. As far as the law is concerned, Miss Van Vleet, there never was a marriage, and I have certainly never heard of a child from it. Perhaps your mother . . . ah . . . miscalculated the father's name."

The last was said so cynically, the inference so patently insulting, that Kyla did not stop to think. Her arm swung up and out, her palm crashing against the duke's cheek with a force and suddenness that surprised them all. Before she could step back, he grabbed her wrist in a painful grip, his fingers biting into the tendons so deeply that she cried out.

"A warning, Miss Van Vleet—I am no milksop who will tolerate being struck by anyone, male or female. If you should ever try that again, I will retaliate in kind."

As he released her arm with a slight shove, Kyla regained her composure. "How manly of you, Your Grace. I will keep in mind that you have a proclivity to strike women."

"Only those women who are foolish and base enough to strike me first."

There was a harsh glitter in his eyes that warned her he would not be pushed, and Kyla drew in a deep breath, more to purchase time than to fill lungs sadly depleted of air.

"I see that this interview is futile. My barrister will be in contact with you again on this matter."

"Save your money, Miss Van Vleet. If you think to share the duke's fortune, you will be gravely disappointed. When he died, there were only house and grounds left, and those in very disreputable shape. Any monies there are now, are mine. So you see, you will get nothing if you cause trouble and stir up old gossip. All that will do is smirch the family name and remind people of what your mother was—"

"My mother was a lady. Do not slander her again."

"May I offer you the same advice. If you think to malign this family, you will regret it."

"A threat, Your Grace?"

"A warning, Miss Van Vleet." He stalked past her to the door and opened it, and she could see the butler waiting in the hall. He must have been listening at the door, for he stood there waiting when the duke bade him show their visitor to the door. "And do not allow her in again, Reade."

"No, Your Grace." Reade stepped back to indicate she should accompany him, and Kyla had little choice but to go quietly if she wished to retain any semblance of dignity. At the door, she turned to regard the duke with a gaze she hoped was glacial and haughty.

"You have not heard the last of this, for I shall not rest until I have my legacy."

It was a parting shot, futile but enough to allow her to leave with some sort of pride intact. She swept past the duke with her chin held high, achingly aware of his narrow regard, his rakehell features as cold as a death mask as she left him in the open doorway of the day parlor.

Her legs were shaky, her hands trembling with anger when she stepped up into the hired hack that waited at the foot of the elegant front steps. As she sat back into the seat, she glanced up and saw the duke at the Palladian window over the double front doors. Leaded glass panes diffused his silhouette, but she recognized that tall, lean frame, the predatory stance as if he scented prey. God, that was how he'd made her feel, gazing at her with such rich contempt, the dangerous look of a panther in gray eyes like steel.

For an instant, she had the thought that he was watching her, but the impression disappeared as swiftly as his shadow from the window. Empty glass stared back at her, reflecting gray scudding clouds and greening trees. Like vacant eyes, diamond-shaped glass panes that held no hint of emotion gazed serenely over the parklike grounds as if Kyla did not exist. Doric columns soared across the front with stately elegance beneath the windows, and she saw now what she had not noticed before: the evidence of long neglect in crumbling stones and chipped brick, weeds straggling up through paving stones, and walls newly plastered with stucco and Coade stone.

The vehicle lurched forward, dipping slightly as the boot boy took his place on the running board. Wheels rolled with a loud rumbling sound over the finely ground gravel of the curved drive that swept in front of Ashleigh Hall. She sat back. Her throat burned with disappointment and grief. They would not acknowledge her. Celeste had warned her, had said after they left the barrister's offices that perhaps it would be best if Kyla found another way to approach the family.

But why should I? she thought rebelliously. *Is not Ashleigh Hall my legacy as well? Did my mother not stay there, however briefly? Ah, poor Maman, what she must have endured from such stiff-necked, arrogant people in that magnificent, cold mausoleum of a house.*

Slowly, anger began to replace her distress at being rejected so brutally. So. They did not wish to acknowledge her, wanted to say that Faustine was a whore and worse. No, and no. It would not be tolerated. Kyla picked at the muddy stains still on her skirts with idle distraction. She would find a way to fight them, though she did not know yet how.

Celeste had no such faith when Kyla poured out the story of her disastrous visit. Instead, she regarded her goddaughter with a steady, thoughtful gaze and said the outlook was grim.

"The duke wields much power, Kyla."

"But all is not yet lost, Tante Celeste."

Celeste heaved a soft sigh. Poor child—she so greatly resembled Faustine, it was almost painful at times to look at her. But beneath the ethereal beauty Kyla had inherited from her mother was a strong thread of resilience that Faustine had lacked. Perhaps her dear friend had once had it—of course she had, or she would not have survived the rigors of the Terror—but the events that followed had slowly drained her strength and left her a shell of the former, lively girl Celeste had known in France. Edward Riverton—that *cowardly* duke of Wolverton—had near killed her with his betrayal. Worse, the money she had been promised to sign those damning papers had never been paid her, leaving her in penury and dire straits. It had all been a trick, a lie to have her sign away her life, have her renounce the heir to Wolverton and even their child. . . .

If not for that Faustine would never have had to leave England, to go to India as an *indentured servant*, for God's sake! Thank God for Piers Van Vleet's innate goodness, for he had taken Faustine in even when she had arrived in Bombay on a litter, so sick it was thought she would die and leave her little girl orphaned. It was Piers who had nursed her back to health, and fallen in love with the fragile beauty—enough to marry her, and take her small daughter into his heart as well.

Long ago, Celeste had made Faustine Auberge a solemn promise, a vow that she would do whatever was within her power to safeguard her small daughter, and that she would do. Had she not left England immediately upon receipt of Piers Van Vleet's letter, despite her great fear of the water? *Nothing* was too great for Faustine's daughter, for the beautiful Kyla who looked so much like her maman. Yes, she would do what she could for Faustine's daughter, despite the great odds that favored Wolverton.

"Tante Celeste, what do you know of this man who is the new duke?" Kyla sounded agitated, moving about the parlor with abrupt steps, lifting and setting down various objects with restless, nervous motions.

Frowning a little, Celeste related what she had heard about Wolverton: "He is a brash rogue from the Colonies, a man who was born in England yet abandoned this country in favor of his adopted land. Or, more correctly, I should say that his father deserted England for America. Ah, but then Colby Banning did not know that one day he would actually *inherit* the Wolverton title and estates, for he was only a distant cousin. And then, of course, the duke, your father, was still young enough to produce a male heir when Colby left England behind. It was only after it became apparent that Edward Riverton would produce only daughters that Colby must have at last realized he would most likely one day inherit the title and estates. Then, I am told, he groomed his young son as his own heir, educating him in England, sending him on as much of a Grand Tour as was possible with Napoleon running amuck all over my beautiful land—ah, poor France, how she has suffered."

Celeste fell silent as scenes from the past rose to haunt her, then shook her head. Enough of that, or she would yield to sorrow again. She shrugged lightly, and sipped her tea before continuing: "Colby Banning did all the things that English gentlemen did for their sons."

She paused, thinking of another preposterous rumor she had heard, and leaned forward, her voice low. "It is said—but of course I do not know how true it is and it seems quite impossible—that Brett Banning's mother was one of those brown-skinned natives, but I do not know if I believe it. I mean, Colby Banning was wild and a rogue and quite unconventional, but I do not think even *he* would go so far as to marry a native girl! It *is* true that there was some talk about it, since he brought her over here, and I understand she was *quite* beautiful and exotic—rather Spanish-looking, I believe. It was because she was so unhappy here that they returned to America, you know. That was before I came to England, but Lady Pemberton told me about it, and Alice is rarely wrong. She met her, however, and said she was very shy and spoke with a strong accent, but pleasant enough. Her manners were said to be unpredictable, but then, what can one expect from a Colonial? Ah, that is all conjecture, I fear. Colby went back to America, and as it turned out, he did not spend even one day as duke, for he died before Edward, and it was left to his only surviving son to take up all the responsibilities."

"Which he seems to have done most gladly." Kyla's tart comment barely masked her dislike. "I can well believe the man is the son of a barbarian, for he is most uncivilized."

And yet . . . Celeste smiled. And yet it was said that Breton Colby Banning was a most reluctant duke. It was no secret that his recent succession to the title was not his first preference. Like his father, he had made it clear to certain parties that he preferred America to England. All he wanted was to marry off his female cousins in quick order, then return to see to his lands in the Colonies.

A germ of an idea sprouted and began to take flower. This reluctant duke—this American upstart—perhaps he would not care for the notion that the marriage chances of his young cousins might be greatly damaged by gossip, for that is how it was in society. Did *she* not know that well enough herself? English society had embraced French refugees only if they were aristocratic, adopting French mannerisms, fashions, the exquisite habits of those who had once ruled in France as if they were their own. It was what had saved so many of the aristocracy, like herself. Dear Reginald, he had done much for her by marrying her and leaving her with a comfortable pension when he died, but it was as her title as comtesse du Bois that the English referred to her, not the lesser title of English baroness.

Titles meant a lot, but even a hint of scandal was enough to sink many a young lady's hopes and aspirations to a good marriage. *Yes . . . it will do very nicely, if only I can persuade Kyla to agree— but why would she refuse? It is, after all, to her advantage. . . .*

Celeste rose from her chair by the hearth and crossed the parlor to where Kyla now stood gazing out the window at the street below. *"Ma petite,* I have an idea."

"Do you, Tante?" Kyla turned away from the window, and gray light slanted across her face, gilding her long lashes with a faint sheen, brightening the blue-green depths of her eyes with diffused light. The straight line of her brows lifted slightly, and there was a faint flush on her high cheekbones that lent her face charming color. "What have you thought of that will help my grave situation?"

"I have a friend—Ondine, Lady Rushton, as she is known now. She is married to a most charming man, the earl of Rushton, and is quite well fixed in society. If Lady Rushton approves of one, that person is accepted."

"Do you intend that I shall enter society? I have no name, no position—"

"Ah, but that is untrue. You are—let us see— the daughter of a marquis who died in the Terror, perhaps, which is not so very untrue, as your grandfather was a marquis and your real father a duke. And your mother's birth was impeccable, even if that vile Riverton managed to befoul her good name later."

"Am I supposed to relate the sordid details of my birth to those curious enough to inquire?" Kyla's smile was a bit crooked, and she shook her head so that pale blond ringlets on each side of her face tickled her cheeks. "It would not do, Aunt, though I know you are only trying to help."

"No, no, you misunderstand!" Celeste wadded her lace handkerchief between her fingers, knotting and unknotting it into a frayed rag as she paced the floor in intense thought. "Do you not see the potential here? This duke, he would not like scandal, am I correct?"

"I think he would be most averse to it, yes," Kyla replied dryly. "He as much as threatened me if I breathed a word of my situation to anyone."

"Then he would be most perturbed were word to leak out that a certain, beautiful newcomer to London is the mysterious daughter of an unknown duke, with enough clues hinted about to leave one wondering—*could it be Wolverton*?"

"I still do not see—"

"Leave it to me. I have a little idea that just may work. Of course, we will exhaust all possibilities before we do something too drastic, but that, you see, is our trump card. And we shall hold it over Wolverton's head until he yields."

"The duke does not seem the kind of man to surrender easily, Aunt. I found him most formidable."

"Yes. We will see. I think if we can be clever about it, we may yet succeed, *ma petite*."

Kyla smiled, but she did not look at all convinced, and Celeste privately admitted to her own doubts. But what else was there to do?

Three

"*Intolerable, I* tell you!" Beatrice, dowager duchess of Wolverton, drew in an angry breath, her bosom quivering beneath layers of Bruges lace and Chinese silk.

Brett eyed her briefly, then turned back to the letter he was reading. "I will see to it, madam."

"Ah God, to think that she *dares* imply . . . did you know that Lady Rushton actually hinted that Miss Van Vleet is the daughter of an English duke and a French marchioness? It seems that she has heard certain talk . . . Brett, are you listening to me at all? Do you not care that my daughters—Edward's *legitimate* children—will be gravely affected by this . . . this *creature's* efforts to malign the family and ruin our good name? We will be the laughingstock of all London if she publicly claims Edward was her father, I tell you, and will be unable to show our faces in any respectable house—the Season begins in only a few weeks, and Arabella and Anna are to be presented for the first time. How will I ever make a suitable match for them if we are gossiped about? I daresay none of the patronesses—even Lady Cowper, who is my friend—will extend any vouchers for them to attend Almack's if it is believed that they are somehow connected with this despicable, infamous, dreadful girl who dares to . . . I feel giddy. I may swoon."

Brett eyed her darkly. It would be too much to hope that she would actually succumb to a fainting fit and give him a few moments of blessed peace. He stood up, flinging down the letter to shove an impatient hand through his hair.

"Good God, Aunt Beatrice. People cannot be so foolish as to give any credence to what Miss Van Vleet may say."

"Oh, you do not know." His aunt sounded pitiful. She moaned slightly, and sagged to the reclining chair with a flutter of her lashes that left him unmoved and not at all disposed to help her. These irritating swoons were only for his benefit, he noticed. Any other time, she was as formidable as a pugilist. After a moment, she opened her eyes to peer at him with some annoyance. "But how could you know, Brett? You were not reared in England, so you cannot be fully aware of the significance of one's reputation. A simple *rumor* can destroy one's life. A snub from significant people can shatter the marriage hopes of a girl."

"I find that as asinine as I do irritating. But then, I'd forgotten that there are so many of your acquaintances who have nothing better to do than discuss the lives of others."

Rather tartly, the dowager said, "It is a trait you might do well to cultivate yourself, Brett. After all, Arabella and Anna are to make their debuts this year, and do not need to be thought rude Colonials like—"

"Like myself?" he said softly when she jerked to a halt and flushed with the realization that she had just insulted him. "Never mind, Aunt Beatrice. I won't call you out for it, as you did not add a clarifier as to the particular kind of rude Colonial."

Her flush faded to pasty white, and she fumbled with the choker of pearls at her throat. "No, no, of course you would not—and I understand completely why you felt compelled to engage in such a horrible act—it was so very fortunate you did not kill him, after all, but only wounded him . . . a providential shot, indeed."

"If I had meant to kill him, madam, he would be dead. A little blooding might make Iversham a bit more cautious about whom he insults the next time. It doesn't hurt to provide warning to any others who may feel the same need to discuss my parentage in less than flattering terms, either. Wouldn't you say?"

Faintly amused by her retreat into stumbling dialogue that *she* did not think that of him at all, Brett barely listened to her efforts to retreat gracefully: "I know you have been reared properly and attended polite schools and received all the education necessary for a young man, but, after all, there are those dreadful people who are not as well acquainted with you, and, unfortunately, they are often influential and could harm your cousins' chances of making a proper marriage— Brett, are you even listening to me?"

He gave Beatrice—his third cousin's widow—a brief glance. "I am well aware of the situation, madam. Your daughters will have their Season, and no doubt, enough vouchers to Almack's or wherever it is they think they must go."

Beatrice sniffed. "It is the least that can be done for them, poor lambs. Imagine, having spent all their years with such expectations, only to have their beloved father die and all the promise in their lives become so precarious. However Edward could have done that, I mean, to leave us in such *dire* straits, when he knew he must die one day—well, I just cannot imagine why he did not provide better."

"Your husband was a wastrel, ma'am." Brett lifted a brow at the shocked outrage in her eyes. "You know it, however much you pretend you do not. If he had not gambled away your children's inheritance, no doubt I would not have had to sink so much of my own coin into this vast museum of a house. I should have sold it first thing, instead of allow you to talk me into keeping it. It's a damned expensive monstrosity, unlike Ridgewood."

The duchess paled. Her hands quivered slightly as she lifted a lace-edged handkerchief to her nose. Some of her usual spirit surfaced as she snapped, "It is our home! Robert Adam designed the last additions, and before him—"

"Please. Spare me the interminable list of architects who created this horror."

"I suppose you much prefer squat, ugly buildings of mud and wattle, with cows ranging about the park and . . . and kites baying at the moon."

Brett's lips slightly curled. "Coyotes, madam. Four-legged predators. And it's not mud, but adobe. And yes, as a matter of fact, I do prefer that kind of house. It's not as drafty and austere. But that is not the point. It is my money that is allowing you to live here. Believe me, I want as much as you to see your daughters properly wed. I have no desire to support them interminably."

Beatrice regarded him with an assessing gaze, her eyes shrewd behind the giddy facade she insisted upon posing with him. "Whyever did your father insist upon going back to America to live? It seems to have had an abominable effect on his son. Of course, no one knew then that *you* might be heir one day. Ah well. I suppose it is because you are accustomed to being blunt, Brett, but I find it most disconcerting when you say such things."

"What? That I do not want to be doling out pin money to four spinsters the rest of their lives? That should not disconcert you near as much as sharing my money with some gypsyish hoyden with illusions of fame and fortune. And yes, to answer your earlier question, I fully intend to deal with Miss Van Vleet at the first opportunity."

Just her name conjured up an image of blue-green eyes gazing at him with uncertain arrogance out of a perfect, oval face. Well-defined light brows had arched above her heavily lashed eyes, like the furry markings of some fey woodland creature. It was an odd impression, the mixture of patrician and earthy features, for though her oval face was perfect, as were her nose and mouth, her eyes held sensual, provocative secrets, as if she knew the answers to all the mysteries of life and legend. The face of a saint and the eyes of a whore . . .

Curse her. Tempting visions of Kyla Van Vleet had returned with annoying frequency since she

had appeared on their doorstep with her preposterous claim.

Beatrice settled back against the brocade cushions of the reclining couch with a satisfied smile.
"Excellent, Brett. I am elated that you will take
steps to rid us of this pariah before the Season
begins." She shuddered delicately, yet there was
a steely note to her voice when she mused aloud,
"I wonder, just *how* did she manage to catch Lady
Rushton's ear so quickly?"

It was not a pressing concern of his, not when
he had more important things to worry about, and
the problem of Kyla Van Vleet was put aside
while he focused on a much more urgent issue.
He reread the message that Reade had delivered
to him an hour before.

One of his bullion ships from America had been
taken by pirates as a prize off the coast of Cuba.
Not unusual, but damned inconvenient most of
the time—this time, however, the vessel also carried important documents. And he was damned
if he knew why a vital document such as the deed
to his most productive silver mine would be
aboard one of his ships. The Santa María Mine put
out two tons of raw ore a day, a good investment
by any standards, and one that would certainly
attract attention from unsavory characters. His father had discovered the mine years ago, but only
in recent years had the mine produced such high-
grade ore. The deed normally rested in the safe-
keeping of a local registrar's office—what the
devil was it doing aboard one of his ships? Even
more important—where was it now?

No, he had much more important things to
worry about than a fortune hunter like Kyla Van

Vleet, but he was damned if he intended to allow the little adventuress to get even a penny. He'd squash her aspirations quickly enough, and focus on what was really important.

Kyla gazed out the upstairs window of the house on Curzon Street. Below, carriages rolled over paved streets and neat fences enclosed tidy gardens that fronted elegant mansions. Only a few blocks away, London became the bustling, dirty city she had first seen, but here it was quiet, with small pockets of an almost countrified atmosphere. It would change quickly enough, as new construction began every day, the city reaching out like a giant bird of prey to swallow eventually the serene residences of the wealthy. She pressed her face against the thick, cool glass, and her breath frosted the pane.

"Ah, *ma petite*, did you enjoy your ride in Hyde Park today with Lady Rushton?" Celeste chirped. "She knows most of London! What good fortune, that I am such excellent friends with Ondine, for as wife of the earl, she is one of London's influential social stars. Our alliance is most fortunate, do you not think?"

Kyla turned away from the window with a faint smile as Celeste bustled about the room with exquisite laces and material draped over her arm, looking more like a seamstress than an aristocrat. "Yes, Tante, it was a lovely day for a ride in the park, and we did meet many interesting people, but I was reflecting on how everything changes so quickly."

"Ah." Celeste gave her an odd look, so that Kyla did not expound on the subject, but allowed herself to be drawn into a deep discussion of the merits of colored silks over muslin, and even satins and velvets.

"Bishop's blue," Celeste announced at last, "in silk, of course, so it will drape quite beautifully over your most pleasing attributes. You have such a lovely shape, slender but still possessing enough curves to entice gentlemen's eyes . . . ah, do not blush, *ma petite*. You know it is true. And we want you to look your very best, *n'est-ce pas?*"

Standing still while her godmother draped a length of blue silk over her shoulder, Kyla could not hide a trace of bitterness when she asked how it would help. "I will never be received into the best homes, never be able to claim my true legacy. I am an outcast."

Celeste looked up with a pained expression. "But, *ma petite*, that is not true! Your father was a duke, your mother the daughter of a marquis. Your lineage is quite impeccable."

"You know as well as I that if even a hint of scandal is attached to my name, I will be *de trop*. A pariah. No one of consequence will receive me."

Celeste drew in a deep, unhappy breath. "Yes, it is true. And there are those with long memories, I fear, who would recall not that your mother was once a duchess, but only that she was put aside by her husband, then . . ."

"Then became a *fille de joie*. Yes. That is what will be remembered about my birth, Tante Celeste, if it is revealed. Why do we bother with this farce?"

"I told you. It is to pressure that devil duke into giving to you what is yours."

"Even our barristers hold out little hope that he

will agree. He is from America, they say, and does not care for convention or propriety. I can well believe that he is a barbarian." She shivered slightly, recalling steel gray eyes and a mouth curled into a predatory snarl. No, he was not a man who could be pressured, not as Tante Celeste and Lady Rushton hoped.

"Perhaps the duke does not care, but the duchess most certainly cares." Celeste flipped the silk from Kyla's arm with a deft curve of her hand. "She will torment him until he knows he must do something to stop you. And it is then, *ma petite*, that you will give to him your ultimatum. If the timing is just right, he will yield."

"And declare me a legitimate heir?" Kyla's mouth turned up in a wry smile. "I doubt he will care what is said."

"It is no longer about that. Now, it is about the money you are due, the funds that were to have been paid Faustine that she never received. Ah, poor girl, left to fend for herself, pregnant and destitute, at the mercy of men like—but that is enough. You are acquainted with all this, and it does not need repeating."

Celeste looked down, busying herself with the length of blue silk as Kyla frowned. There were times her godmother kept things from her, not out of spite, but kindness, yet often it was disconcerting later to learn facts that it was supposed she knew well.

"Tante Celeste, who took Maman in when she was left so brutally without shelter after she was turned out?"

"That is best left unsaid now, my pet. Come. Let us try this shade of Clarence blue against your eyes—no, I do not think it will suit. It is too faded against the brilliant color of your eyes. . . ." She bit her lip at Kyla's steady gaze and looked back down at the basket of silk scraps, her tone irritable. "Read Faustine's journals."

"I have. She does not use names, but only initials. It was as if she wanted to forget them—do you know? I have memories, but they are so vague, and—I know it could not have been Papa Piers who took her in. Not at first."

Celeste heaved a great sigh and replaced the silks into the wicker basket, then rose to her feet. Faint lines fanned from the corners of her soft brown eyes like tiny sunbursts, and when she frowned as she did then, deeper grooves appeared at both edges of her mouth.

"I shall ring for tea, and we will discuss this. There are things that you should know, perhaps, but it has been so long, and I had hoped they were forgotten."

Kyla sat down woodenly, her throat feeling suddenly tight. Always, there was something else about her past, when she recalled so little. Oh, there were some things—walks in the park, skipping beside Faustine and laughing when her hair ribbon came undone and floated away in the wind; riding in a carriage with one of Maman's friends, always a man, it seemed, who would laugh and smile with admiration at her most beautiful mother . . . then another man, who was not so nice, but made her feel funny inside, all frightened and anxious. But it was so long ago, the images melding into one another in such a confusing array of jumbled impressions that often she could not distinguish one from the other. She recalled the ship that had taken them to India, though, and how Maman had been so sick, like Celeste always became on the water. And then there were the vague memories of tumultuous noise and men in turbans, that had at the time seemed so strange . . . heat, of course, and a searing sun and Maman growing more ill . . . and then Papa Piers, his kind face strange at first, then so dear and familiar.

She looked up as Sally brought in the tea things and set them on a small table. After the maid had departed, Kyla leaned forward. "Maman did not meet Papa Piers in England, did she."

Celeste stirred uneasily. "Not precisely. She was introduced to him by way of the *Daily Times.*"

"The newspaper?" Kyla stared at her godmother. A growing suspicion lurked at the back of her mind, yet she could not bring it to light, as if saying it aloud would give it substance and make it real. But then there was no use in pushing it away, for Celeste was telling her quickly, the words tumbling over one another like the waters of a brook over flat stones, swiftly and clearly:

"She was purchased, you see, by Piers, who needed a woman to manage his household. He placed an advertisement in the *Times* . . . She was so desperate, and I had not yet met dear Reginald and was in no position to help her . . . you were not yet four, Kyla, so small and she feared that you would be left in the streets, or worse—taken in by men like . . . like those who frequent the procuresses in Covent Garden. There are men who prey on small children for perverted purposes . . . Faustine could not bear to think of you left to the uncertain mercies of men like that, as she had been left, and so she did the only thing she knew—she indentured herself to Piers Van Vleet when she read his notice in the papers. Only when she arrived at last in India, she was so ill, and he is such a kind man, but I think he fell in love with her so that he did not mind . . . and she did do what she promised to do, managing his household, and he swore to see that you would be taken care of—he did take care of you, Kyla, until—"

"Until his company began to fail, and he ran out of money." She drew in a deep breath. "He told me that he thought I should read my mother's journals, that I should have what was mine, because he could not promise me a better life than I might find here."

"Yes. He wrote me of his situation when he sent for me to bring you back with me. I had always promised Faustine that I would watch over you, as well."

"I have so many guardian angels, why should I ever lack for anything?" Kyla rose abruptly to her feet, sloshing tea from her cup and saucer onto the floor. She hadn't meant to sound so bitter, but it seemed as if every good thing in her life turned sour. Poor Papa Piers. He had been so anguished over his failure, caught in a failing business venture and uncertain of the future—he had done his best for her, giving her what monies he had available and sending her with Celeste. And now she was here, and the hope that she had nurtured so briefly was ashes in her mouth, dry and dusty and barren of promise.

Extinguished by the drawling, sardonic refusal of the duke of Wolverton to countenance her claim.

She looked up at her godmother and smiled faintly. "You are right. Forgive me. It was temporary doubt. I cannot give up now. I will do what I must to force this odious duke to recognize my mother's rights and give me what is mine."

Relief flooded Celeste's face. "It will be your only salvation, *ma petite.*"

"How well I have learned that of late. One's character is not as important as the character of one's family. It seems odd, to be judged by the actions of others instead of your own." Kyla's smile felt ironic. "Yet I must admit, it was much the same in India, especially among the English. Proper society is not at all sociable."

"Most of the time, no." Celeste lifted her shoulders in a characteristic shrug. "But it has not changed, whether in England or in France. In France, ah ... the beauty that was the French court, *ma petite*, the elegance and style that cannot be duplicated ... it has been forever vanquished, drowned in the blood of my friends and family. ..."

Sudden sorrow carved lines in her face, and Kyla knew then that her godmother would be morose the rest of the day, as she usually was when remembering the days of glory, of the French king and his beautiful, tragic, reckless queen. All those stories she had heard before, related to her when Faustine was ill in bed, trotted out with sighs and smiles and sweet remembrances. Only once had Faustine mentioned the time of terror and the guillotine, when her world had come crashing down on her and been shattered forever. It had been after that Faustine had come to England, and met the man who had ultimately destroyed her, though never once had she spoken of him. Not once.

Until Piers had given her the teakwood casket, Kyla had not known of James Edward George Riverton, duke of Wolverton and her father. Poor Maman. How she must have suffered. First from rejection, then utter betrayal and desertion. Yes. It would only be fair to recoup what she had lost, even so late. It was time and past that Faustine was vindicated.

Four

Night had fallen, and outside the house on Curzon Street the evening lamps had been lit. Rosy pools of light gleamed cheerfully along the street like fireflies, reminding Kyla of happier days in India when her mother was still alive and disaster happened only to other people.

Seated by the fire, humming to herself a French ballad, Celeste gazed morosely into the flames and sipped tea that Kyla strongly suspected was heavily laced with brandy. One of Celeste's moods had come on her. On nights like these, they stayed in their rooms and received no guests, for neither Kyla nor Celeste dared risk uncomfortable questions.

Kyla wandered aimlessly, picking up and putting down a novel, too restless to read, too distracted to keep her mind on any one subject. So many things came to her, the memories, the hopes, the fears—*why* had she ever thought it would be possible? She feared it was not. The duchess was so coldly haughty, the duke—*bon Dieu*, the duke. She thought of him sometimes at night, when she was supposed to be sleeping but the sweet oblivion would not come, and suddenly he would be there, his eyes not hostile as she had last seen him, but warm with admiration and acceptance. A dream only, of course, for he was not the kind of man who would change his mind and accept a young woman he considered an adventuress.

Pausing at the window, she shoved aside the curtain and looked outside again, surveying the street now shiny with rain. Drizzle formed radiant halos around the streetlights, rosy and golden and shimmering. A carriage came by, and light reflected off the tooled black leather of a Town coach. She watched idly as the vehicle slowed, then came to a stop in front of the house. A liveried footman dismounted, and opened the door of the coach for its occupant. There was a coat of arms emblazoned on the door, visible even in the dark.

Wolverton. He stepped out with lazy grace, his tall frame easily recognizable.

Kyla dropped the curtain and pressed back against the wall, suddenly panicked. Her heart thumped madly against her ribs, and she glanced toward Celeste, lost in her private world. Ah God, what a time for her godmother to succumb to the past . . . *but why am I so nervous? Is this not what I want? Yes, of course! If he has come to visit, then it means he is, at the very least, considering my demands, and at the very worst—infuriated.*

But that was none of her concern. What she demanded was only her just deserts, was it not? Of course. And if he even *hinted* that her mother had been less than nobility, she would show him the door at once, just as he had done her.

Oh God—how must she look?

Kyla flew to the mirror. Her hair straggled from the neat knot on her crown, lying in pale wisps about her face, and she looked so pale—she pinched her cheeks and bit her lips to give them color, and smoothed the folds of the day dress she was still wearing. She would not give him the due of changing into a more elaborate gown, or he might think she attached some importance to this visit. *No, he will see how little I care for his opinion,* she thought suddenly. *Let him know that he is of no consequence as far as I am concerned.*

A gentle tapping on the door jerked her attention from the mirror, and she turned with only a brief glance at Celeste, who had not seemed even to notice. Sally entered at Kyla's command, her pretty round face flushed with color and excitement.

"Miss, you have a visitor—a *duke!* It is Wolverton, m'lord said to tell you, and he requests the pleasure of your company in the downstairs parlor."

"Inform the duke that I am indisposed, and cannot be disturbed."

Sally looked horrified. "Oh, miss, are you certain? Shall I say such a thing?"

"Yes, of course you shall. He will insist upon seeing me when you do. Then you come back up here to tell me. Now go on. Do as I say, and don't be such a goose. He won't eat you."

There was no certainty of the last, Kyla thought as she moved to the armoire and took out a Kashmir shawl. It was soft and warm and covered her from shoulders to ankles, as if she was settled in for the night. She smiled slightly. If she read him correctly, he would not take no for an answer, and so she waited expectantly for Sally to return and fetch her downstairs to the parlor.

In only a few moments, there was another knock at the door, a forceful rap that made her frown at Sally's nervous foolishness. Before she could give permission to enter, the door swung open, and to her shock, the duke stood in the opening, his gaze raking over her with a critical lift of his brows. Lamplight flickered over his dark hair and face in subtle illumination that gave him a sinister appearance.

"You do not look very indisposed, Miss Van Vleet."

"How . . . how *dare* you, sir!" She clutched the shawl to her throat, staring at him with anger and apprehension. In the open doorway, Kyla glimpsed Sally bobbing about in the hallway, wringing her hands and making small chuffing noises like that of a winded hound.

Leaving the door open, Wolverton strode across the room to Kyla, and stared down at her with a faint curl of his lips. "I do not like being lied to, Miss Van Vleet."

"Really." Her chin came up. "Neither do I. Pray, tell me again how you know of no child born to Edward Riverton and Faustine Auberge."

"I said there was no proof of it. There is not."

"And again, you lie, sir. I stand before you."

A dangerous light glittered in his gray eyes, turning them from smoke to soot, dark and ominous. "If you have proof, Miss Van Vleet, produce it. If not, stop this charade before you find yourself in dire straits."

Kyla stepped away casually, as if only moving

to trim the wick on a guttering candle. Tante Celeste gazed into the fire without indicating she heard them, apparently still lost in her thoughts and brandy. With a steady hand, Kyla lifted the tiny scissors and trimmed the wick, then looked up at the duke over the bright oval flame as it steadied.

"Your Grace, you must forgive me if I do not find your threat very intimidating. It is far too vague, when I have endured much to humble myself enough to ask for your legal recognition."

"Too vague?" Wolverton stepped close again, until she could feel the heat from his powerful body, catch the faint scent of leather and whiskey—a potent mixture. "Let me elucidate for you—leave London at once, and you will suffer nothing other than the knowledge that you have failed in your scheme to swindle money from me."

"And if I choose to stay?" She smiled at the narrowing of his eyes, too angry at his high-handed attitude to care what she said or did. "I have made friends here." She waved an arm to indicate the street outside, and the fringe on her shawl fluttered. "Already, I have been invited to several affairs. Of course, you could damage my reputation if you choose."

"Madam, that is the least of what I will do if you persist in this scheme."

"Really?" Kyla's laugh was brittle, her face hot with anger as she affected a careless shrug. "Then I suppose I will be a pariah in polite company. How dreary. But of course, if you choose to be so unkind, I will have to tell certain people how my father was the late duke of Wolverton, and how he debauched his poor wife and abandoned her to starve with their child in the London streets. Poor Maman. I do have the proof, you know. The marriage lines are quite legal, Your Grace, though you may not wish to credit it."

"The marriage was annulled, as you know well enough. Money was more important to your mother than my cousin, apparently, for she was quick enough to take it when it was offered. But then, what else could be expected from a whore? The family was well shed of her. She was an embarrassment."

His brutal assessment brought heat to' her cheeks, and filled her with reckless fury that she managed to hide under a light shrug of indifference. "Do you think so? Then it may be most distressing for you to learn that your cousin's daughter should choose to become a Cyprian— that is what you call loose women here in England, is it not, Your Grace? Cyprians, Impures, demi-reps, *filles de joie*—ladies of the night. Yes, perhaps there is a lesson in that for me. Maman was much sought after, I understand. She was, after all, a French marchioness, born into the nobility and wrenched away through no fault of her own—what a charming story that will be for you to hear when you play Hazard at White's, do you not think? The daughter of the late duke of Wolverton and a French emigrée, sharing my favors with those who can afford me—Perhaps they will wager who is to have me first, for my price will be quite, quite high, I can assure you."

As she talked, Wolverton's eyes grew darker, his mouth more taut, and there was a visible throb of muscle in his lean jaw. Kyla laughed angrily.

Her laughter swiftly changed to a gasp of pain as his hand clamped down on her wrist in a tight grip. He dragged her to him, and she would not attempt a struggle when she knew she would lose. Instead, she stared up at him with all the arrogance she could muster, as the heat of his thighs transferred to her even through the Kashmir shawl, petticoats, and muslin skirts.

"Women like you come six a shilling. Do not threaten me, Miss Van Vleet. Nor do you want to challenge me, for I do not retreat easily."

Stung, she glared up at him, refusing even to try to twist from his painful grip on her wrist. "Release me at once, or—"

"Or what? You will scream?" His hard mouth quirked up at one corner into a hateful smile. He was holding her so close against him that the pressure of his body was like a searing flame, his lean, masculine frame a harsh force against hers. He smelled of rain, and tiny sparkling drops glittered in his black hair.

"No, I see no use in screaming, Your Grace." Her voice was much more composed than she felt on the inside, all hot confusion and simmering emotion. "There are other ways to combat a man like you."

"Ah, and you no doubt know them all, little cat." His hand slipped up her arm, bunching the thin material of her puffed sleeve in his strong fingers to grasp her more firmly on the shoulder. "I have dealt with women like you before."

"No doubt you have dealt with women before, but not like me, Your Grace."

"There, you are wrong."

Before she could guess what he intended, his

head bent, and his mouth came down over hers like a swooping hawk on prey, capturing her lips and plundering her open mouth with his ravaging tongue. One of his hands moved up to tangle in her hair, loosening the braid on her crown, pulling it free so that her hair tumbled down her back and pins scattered over the floor. Her hands were trapped between them, and she tried to push him away but it was useless. He held her still, his hard body pressed close to hers, his mouth crushing hers until she felt a peculiar lassitude begin to steal through her limbs, rendering her incapable of struggle or resistance. She felt so weak, while inside there was a heated turmoil that swept through her veins in a fiery rush that left her flushed and trembling, clinging to him with her fingers curled into the front of his shirt, aware of the strong beat of his heart against the backs of her fingers and the loud thunder of her own heart in her ears. *Mon Dieu*, what was he doing to her? It was bewildering . . . nothing had ever happened to her like this, leaving her so . . . so *breathless*, and with such an odd, aching throb in the pit of her stomach and between her legs, a most peculiar sensation that was frightening and tantalizing at the same time.

When he released her at last, she had to cling to his arm to keep from falling. A gleam of triumph lit his eyes, and his mouth curled into a smile of satisfaction. "You see, Miss Van Vleet, I know you better than you think. Give up your wild demands and leave England quietly."

Anger and embarrassment made her voice sharp as she steadied herself and wiped away the feel of his mouth from her lips with the fringed edge of her shawl. "Your family had no compunction about putting my mother out without a penny to her name. Why should I take such risks? A duke's daughter should command a large fee for her favors, do you not think so, Your Grace?"

"Damn you."

Behind him Kyla could see the anxious faces of the housekeeper and a footman peering into the room. Sally must have fetched them, fearing there would be trouble. Now Wolverton turned, raked them with a contemptuous glance of dismissal, and stalked to the door. He turned in the opening, his expression so ruthless that for a moment Kyla's knees weakened so that she had to grab the back of a chair. "You have not heard the last of this, Miss Van Vleet."

"Nor have you, Your Grace."

Wolverton pivoted on his heel and pushed past the uneasy footman. Kyla stood silently, unable to move as she listened to the sound of the duke's boots on the stairs, then the slamming of the front door behind him. Her gaze shifted to Mrs. Peach, the housekeeper, who clung to the doorframe with wide eyes filled with apprehension.

"Are you all right, Miss?"

God, how much did they hear? She nodded. "Yes, I am fine. Please forget the scene you just witnessed. I am afraid that the duke mistook me, and so I made empty threats intended to anger him."

"You have made an enemy, I fear."

She nodded again. "Yes. But it was his choice."

From her chair in front of the fire, Celeste looked up from her empty teacup. Her voice was quavery. "He will be a dangerous enemy, *ma petite*. Perhaps we should not pursue this."

"No. *No!* You said earlier that it was my mother's right, and so it is. I could never forgive myself if I *allow* them to bury her good name with lies." Shivering, she bent to pick up the shawl that had dropped from her shoulders, and went to kneel in front of Celeste. Brown eyes gazed back at her, misted with a slight sheen of tears, but not as hazy as she had thought they would be. "Tante, I must not surrender now. Since he troubled to come here, he is worried."

"He came here to warn you, child." Celeste sighed, and with a slightly trembling hand that made the china clatter, placed the empty teacup on the table beside her chair. Brandy fumes enriched the air, potent and dense. She reached out to cup Kyla's chin in her palm. "You are very beautiful, like Faustine. But you have a strength she did not. Do not mistake that strength for power. The duke wields much power, and he can crush you. Ah, we should never have begun this." Her hand fell away, and she leaned back in the chair, closing her eyes.

Kyla took her hand and held it between her palms, stroking the soft skin with her thumb, making tiny circles on the thin, blue-veined flesh. "But it *has* begun. And there is no turning back now. We can only go forward."

Five

Late-afternoon light stretched across St. James's Street, the sun emerging from behind a cloud to cast long misshapen shadows like bony fingers into alleyways and curling up like cats on windowsills and in doorways. Brett took the steps into White's two at a time, his mood as foul as Kyla Van Vleet's threat. Curse her. The past two days had been spent badgering Edward's barrister into finding out all he could about her ridiculous claim that she was his first child and legitimate daughter. Worse, he had just left the barrister's office, and the fool had admitted that he'd known of her claim, but not thought it worth mentioning because Faustine had signed papers relinquishing any rights.

Brett swore softly under his breath. Why the hell was he still in England anyway? He'd much rather be in America where he belonged. He was comfortable there. The unclaimed territory beyond the Mississippi River was new to the United States, having been acquired through the Louisiana Purchase in 1803 and still largely unsettled. Only lately had the border area been in dispute, claimed by the Spanish yet nudging Mexico, and increasingly explored by American adventurers intrepid enough to defy both Spain and Mexico.

Tejas. It suited him. Brash, sprawling, wild— there was a future there for a man willing to stand against the odds. He missed it, missed the hot, searing days and dry heat. It rained almost every day here, with blue skies a rare treat that barely dried the damp air before it rained again.

By the time he reached White's gaming room— damn her for knowing he frequented the place—his temper had not improved. Barry Baylor—Viscount Kenworth and fourth son of the third earl of Montgramercy, greeted him with a lifted brow and a cocky grin.

"What ho, Wolverton. Some jade got you in a pet?"

"As a matter of fact, yes." Brett found the young buck witty and amusing most of the time, though there were the moments when he was more irritating than entertaining. Barry possessed the urbanity of his class, but without the pompous arrogance that usually attended it, a definite saving grace in Brett's opinion.

Barry laughed softly. "I should like to meet the woman who has managed to unsettle the dangerous duke, I think. Or does she still live?"

"Your levity is out of place, Kenworth." Brett lifted his hand to signal a waiter, and took a small snifter of brandy with him across the room. Smoke drifted in layers, and numerous dandies peopled the huge chamber, sitting at green baize tables, lounging on leather settees, or—if one of Beau Brummel's famous inner circle—seated in the bow window that looked out over St. James's Street.

"No doubt I am a bit premature," Barry agreed cheerfully, his humor no less for having admitted it inappropriate. "Yet it has been well noted that you do not tolerate the whims of even the most prime article, a fact envied by several gentlemen who have found themselves in the sorrowful state of suffering the sharp side of a pretty female's tongue."

"And yet you refer to them as men." Brett lifted a sardonic brow, and Barry grinned.

"As usual, you have put your finger right on the heart of it, Wolverton. I daresay, there are those who will not agree with you, however. Do you play tonight?"

Brett shrugged, sipping at his brandy and exchanging a cordial nod with Brummel's great friend Lord Alvanley, who paused beside them.

"Wolverton. Brummel indicated he has an empty seat in the window." Alvanley's brow lifted in a mute comment on the Beau's offhand invitation. "I believe the cut of your coat is greatly admired."

"Is it? I wear it for comfort more than style, but I am gratified to hear it meets with approval." Amused, Brett turned and gave a nod in Brummel's direction as Alvanley moved past on his way to one of the gaming tables. Not a bad lot, but a bit too dandified for his tastes. He appreciated Beau Brummel's sharp wit, and approved of his passion for cleanliness, even if he thought him a bit pretentious and overdone when it came to being the arbiter of fashion. But then, it did not really matter to him if his attire met with approval, or even if he met with approval. Barry had once remarked that it was Brett's attitude of indifference that no doubt appealed to some of the *ton*.

"They are just arrogant enough to appreciate someone even more arrogant," Barry observed with an ironic twist of his mouth and that engaging grin that had so far kept his creditors from hauling him off to debtor's prison.

Now Barry gazed ruefully around the room, and admitted that his pockets were to let again. With a careless shrug, he remarked, "I'm afraid I was cup-shot, and lost my purse to Hayworth last night. Leaves me out tonight, I'll tell you."

"I've told you before that you play too cautiously. If you must wager, play as if you've all the money in the world to lose."

"Easy enough for you to say, when you most likely do have all the money in the world," Barry retorted. "Damme, but it's deuced unpleasant to have to go with hat in hand to m'father to beg for an advance on my allowance. The old tartar sits on his money as if waiting for it to hatch—" Barry paused, frowned a little, and glanced up at Brett with obvious curiosity. "Tell me the truth, Wolverton. Did Prinny really approach you for a loan? It's whispered over most of London that he sent someone to ask you for money."

Brett took another sip of brandy. His brow lifted and he gazed at Barry over the rim of the snifter until he flushed and muttered that it was really none of his business, but he'd just heard the rumor. . . .

"You're right. It really is none of your business. But you know the prince and I are acquainted, since he was most eager to hear about certain activities in New Orleans that caught his interest. As for a loan, it was only a donation to help finance improvements in the fair city of Brighton."

"Not the Pavilion! That eyesore? Looks like Saint Paul's went down to Brighton and pupped, I heard it said. And work has just started on it. He must have got to you on one of your better days."

"Actually, I had the devil of a hangover and would have given twice as much just to get his ferret-faced secretary out of my parlor."

"Still, it's not like you don't have the blunt to spare, Wolverton. If I had a silver mine in the Americas, damn if I would invest it in a Chinese pagoda in Brighton, though."

Brett said softly, "The investment is in the prince, not another architectural anomaly."

Struck by this, it still took Kenworth a moment to absorb all the implications, then he grinned. "You're no cully, by God, you ain't!"

"Damned with faint praise again." Brett smiled slightly as he regarded Kenworth. They were near in age, he being older than Barry by four years, but decades apart in experience. "Your grammar is deplorable. Be careful, or it will be said that you're becoming too much like the company you keep."

"I won't be a cat's-paw, Wolverton, don't think it for a minute. Couldn't be in finer company, in my opinion."

"Don't let that get around. You might be mistaken for a rustic as well."

Kenworth shrugged. "I've had worse said about me."

"So have I."

"Not to your face, not after that set-to with Iversham. He certainly came away with the worst of it, though I've heard it said he was damned lucky. An inch in the other direction, and he would be cold meat."

"An unpleasant thought—but of course, highly unlikely. A shoulder wound is usually not fatal if properly tended."

Kenworth looked at him curiously, then away, nodding acknowledgment to one of his hunting companions before turning back again. "You're a sharp shot, but what would you have done if you'd missed? If you'd killed Iversham?"

"Accepted his death as satisfaction, no doubt. What would you expect me to do?"

Shrugging, Barry looked a little perplexed. "You're a cool one, damme if you aren't, Brett, but dueling is a serious offense now, you know."

"Any man who thinks that shooting at another man isn't serious is a fool. Iversham gave me little choice. I tried to warn him, but he chose not to listen. Shall we go to Arthur's or Graham's for decent sport?"

Barry looked startled, then grinned. "I suppose it's time to change the topic of conversation. Arthur's would be best, though I've not much of my allowance left and will probably be put out of the game quickly."

To Barry's chagrin, he was right, and was out of funds and the card game quickly. Brett found that fortune was with him, however, and played until well into the night, quitting only when he grew bored and one of the other players grew too drunk to be rational.

He found Barry waiting for him in a comfortable chair, and was faintly surprised. "Napping, Kenworth?"

Looking slightly sheepish, Barry shrugged and rose to his feet. "It's a little late to get a chair in this part of town, and thought you might give me a ride back to my house. Unless you have other plans, of course."

"Nothing that can't wait."

"Gad," Kenworth muttered, looking past him, "if it isn't the old reprobate himself—Lord Brakefield, earl of Northwick. What's he doing *here*? Too tame, I'd think."

Brett glanced up. He knew Brakefield, had met him years before, and liked him just as little now as he had then. It was rumored he dabbled in unsavory affairs, and the evidence marked his face with lines of dissipation.

Barry groaned. "He has seen us—look, he approaches. How the devil can I avoid him?"

"Claim illness. I hear that Brakefield has a dread of any kind of sickness."

"You mock me, but damme, the man is unnerving. He makes my flesh crawl. The rumors about him are ... are most villainous."

"One of England's finest." Brett waited, saying nothing when Brakefield paused before them and bowed slightly.

Beneath bushy brows lifted in mild inquiry, eyes of a peculiar colorless opacity regarded them, and his thin mouth twitched at both corners as if he had just heard a private jest. "Wolverton. We meet again. It's been a long time since I last saw you. Sorry to hear about your father. He and I went a long way back, what?"

"I was unaware that you knew my father in any

way but the most casual, Lord Brakefield."

"Were you? Perhaps he never mentioned it to you, but he and I had business dealings at one time. But that was long ago, and since I suffered such grievous losses in my investment, we parted company by mutual accord."

"I find it most intriguing that my father never mentioned to me any business he had with you."

"Perhaps he did not want you to know of his failures, only his successes." Northwick's eyes shifted to Barry and narrowed a little. "Ah, and Kenworth. A little surprising to see *you* here, after staying too late at White's last night."

When Barry's face reddened with anger at the earl's reference to his gambling loss, Brett intercepted with a drawling comment designed to incite immediate retaliation. "Odd, that you frequent White's instead of Brooks's, or even The Pigeon Hole, Northwick. Turning Tory on us?"

Brakefield snorted, ignoring Brett's reference to the gambling hell. "What makes you think I'm a Whig, sir?"

"Your frequent companions, I suppose. Not that I mind. Brougham and Grey are most certainly intriguing gentlemen, with connections of the highest caliber. I compliment you on your mastery."

"Do you? Odd. In these times, being a Whig is hardly complimentary." Brakefield surveyed Brett more closely, with eyes as empty of color as glass. "Didn't think you were interested in traditional political parties."

Brett shrugged. "I find it more a matter of sedition than tradition that dictates a man's beliefs. What I deem to be unacceptable, I reject."

"Ah, as the Colonies rejected England. I see. How enlightening. Shall we expect more riots, what?"

"Repeal the Corn Laws and see if well-fed people do not lose their tendency to create havoc."

"Corn Laws were enacted to keep prices from falling, and thus endangering England with a flood of cheap foreign grains. Last year's riot was foolish and futile, a mindless protest by revolutionaries with no clear idea of government laws passed for their own welfare." Lord Brakefield's bushy brows lowered over his eyes. "Are you one of those men who seek to undermine the government with loose talk, Wolverton?"

"Are you one of those men who profit most handsomely by these laws? The premise is excellent, controlling imports to keep prices high in England, but it forces manufacturers to pay higher wages, which deprives laborers of not only jobs, but the ability to pay the higher price of bread. Have you forgotten one of the key factors that brought down France's regime? If the masses go hungry, there are bound to be rebellions."

Brakefield dismissed the notion with a contemptuous flick of his fingers. "This is not France. Napoleon met his match in Wellington at Waterloo, and England reigns supreme even under the regent's rule. I find that your assertions border on the ridiculous."

"Nonetheless, the laws must be repealed one day, or there will be more unrest."

"Oh my, shall the Great Unwashed attempt to burn our houses?" Brakefield's mouth curled into a mocking sneer. "I daresay we shall know of their approach long before their arrival, simply by the stench that precedes them."

"Wolverton is right," Barry said suddenly. "I have not forgotten the outbreaks in the Midlands a few years back. The Luddite riots, when machine-breakers waged a reign of terror over the countryside. Horse-patrols were needed to hold them in check, and half the northern counties looked like armed camps for a while. Remember it well. Last riot was in 1812, I think. It was all about unemployment and high food prices. Next, it will be the colliers or weavers that riot."

"Or milliners? All armed with hatpins and lethal feathers?" Brakefield softly hooted with scorn. "I daresay, you young bucks might find it more distressing if Fribourg and Treyer went out of business and you had no snuff."

"Do not make the mistake of lumping me with the dandies of your circle, Northwick."

Brakefield looked at Brett with a quick, startled frown before shrugging casually. "No. One would definitely not classify you as a man of the town. As dangerous as it seems to be to remark upon it, you still bear resemblance to a rustic."

"Better than a libertine, I would say." Brett smiled into Brakefield's cold stare. "If you will excuse me, sir. I have another engagement this evening, and must depart."

Turning to Barry, who was gazing balefully at Lord Northwick, Brett suggested he accompany him to a card party. "My aunt will be there, as well as some of this year's debutantes. Lady Sefton is launching some of her choices for the upcoming Season."

Rather maliciously, Brakefield murmured, "By

all means, Kenworth, do find a deep-pocketed wife that can eliminate your visits to the money-lenders, what?"

"Sir, I take exception to your insolent remarks." Barry drew himself up, almost quivering with suppressed fury. "If you persist, I shall only think that you are doing it with the intention of earning reprisal."

"Dear me, do I detect a firebrand beneath that pallid exterior, young Kenworth?" Brakefield's smile was more of a smirk. "Perhaps I should remind you that I had killed three men in duels before you were out of nursery skirts."

Brett put a warning hand on Barry's arm. "Do not credit Northwick with venting his spleen wisely. At his advanced age, he has no doubt forgotten his manners."

Brakefield's brow lifted and his colorless eyes thinned to slits. "Wolverton, you do not want to make of me an enemy, and certainly not for an unlicked cub."

"What I do not want, is for you to tell me what I do not want." A hard smile curled Brett's mouth as he observed the earl's obvious surprise and anger. "I may be rustic, but I am well past the inclination to accept boorish manners as acceptable from an aging roué."

Lord Northwick stared after them coldly as they left Arthur's gaming rooms. Night shadows darkened St. James's Street, lit by gas lamps and squares of light from windows of the clubs still entertaining members of the *ton*. Kenworth was almost stuttering with rage when Brett put him into the Wolverton Town coach, his face flushed as red as the velvet squabs on which he plopped with a scowling snarl.

"Damn him for a blackhearted bastard! I should call him out, Wolverton, I swear I should."

For Northwick, Brett did not care, but Barry was still young and hotheaded enough to get into real trouble if he was not careful.

"Let it pass, Barry. Men like Brakefield eventually destroy themselves."

"Not soon enough for me." Barry's face creased into a thunderous scowl. Filtered light from one of the coach lamps slanted across his face in a hazy shaft, and in the trick of light and shadow, Brett saw more than just wounded pride in Kenworth's expression. He frowned.

"There's more to your dislike than just the evening's sharp talk, Barry. What is it?"

After a moment of tense silence and staring out the coach window, Kenworth nodded curtly. "There *is* more. While Northwick's politics may irritate me, it's his personal quirks that I find most repugnant."

"Quirks? Like wearing outdated patches to hide the scars from the pox on his face?"

"No, I mean . . . *real* quirks. Unsavory deeds. He has always been a rake and libertine, but rumors always abound about some men, and especially men who make enemies easily. Granted, Northwick has made his share of enemies, but I know that there is substance behind some of his more foul deeds." He drew out a snuffbox, started to take a pinch, and apparently recalled Northwick's snide comment about his dependence on tobacco, and put it away again. He leaned forward, ignoring the swaying of the coach over paving stones as he said softly, "Lord Brakefield prides himself on procuring young girls for his stable of whores."

"I assume you mean against their will."

"Sometimes, though there are those desperate men and women who will sell depraved fiends like him their young daughters. Ah God, I *know* what he has done, but I cannot prove it!"

"Barry, say bluntly what you mean instead of dancing around it."

Groaning, Kenworth sat back again, pressing a fist against his forehead. "Young girls, Brett—*young* girls! Children not out of leading strings yet, tiny girls with fresh faces and sweet innocence—four-, five-, or six-year-old girls have just disappeared."

Brett frowned at him. "You are speaking of a member of the peerage, Barry. Not that the title makes him a saint, but he must know he will be held accountable for his actions by someone. Would he take such a risk?"

"What risk? Buying children from impoverished wretches in Covent Garden is hardly unheard of these days."

"Yes, but for the purpose of potboys or chimney sweeps or milk-sellers, not the purposes you claim Northwick uses them for." Just the expression on Barry's face was indication enough of his revulsion, and Brett shook his head. "If what you say is true, charges should be brought against him."

"By whom? You? Me? We have no proof." He raked a hand through his hair, looking wild, his tousled locks falling over his forehead and into his eyes, giving him an absurdly youthful appearance. "There is no proof, not even . . . bodies . . . to convict him."

"How the devil do you know all this?"

Barry looked sick, and studied his hands, pale light flickering over him in erratic squares as the coach passed glowing streetlamps. His voice was low, almost a mumble. "I know, because I was there one night. It was . . . a few months ago, and I was foxed, muddled, stewed to the gills—I don't know why I was with him, but I was. It's all so vague, but I remember a little girl there. Blond. Small. Terrified. And I wanted to help her, but— ah God." He closed his eyes. "When I woke, he was gone and the child was gone . . ."

His voice trailed into silence, and Brett fought a surge of disgust and revulsion. Illegal business was one thing, but Northwick was more depraved than he'd thought. It was no wonder young Kenworth hated him so much.

"If what you say is true, Barry, a way can be found to bring charges against Northwick."

Kenworth laughed softly, a bitter sound. "He is the son of Satan, I think. No one has ever been able to charge him with anything, for he is too careful."

"Not so careful, to my way of thinking. If he was, you would not have been invited along. Men who are cautious do not invite spectators to depravity unless they are certain of their participation. Or their silence."

Barry's complexion took on a sickly pallor. He turned his head to stare out the darkened window. "I owe him money."

"So he thinks to buy your silence."

"Yes." Barry raked a hand through his light hair

again, looking slightly desperate. "He never passes up the chance to remind me of it, as you have no doubt guessed from his references to the moneylenders."

"How much do you owe him?" When Barry flushed and his mouth tightened, Brett knew it was a great deal. He asked again, harshly this time, "How much, Kenworth?"

"Fourteen thousand pounds."

"Young fool—how the devil did you get into a man like Brakefield for that much?"

"Faro." He shrugged, and his hands curled into fists atop his knees. "I was forced to give him my vowels until I could approach my father for an advance on my yearly allowance. My father refused, with a few words added to convince me that he had no intention of changing his mind and would rather see me in Tangier at Newgate before he'd give a shilling to pay more gambling debts."

"I'll give it to you."

Barry stared at him, his eyes wide and dark in the shadowed interior of the coach. "Wolverton—Brett, my God, I never meant to hint that . . . you cannot—"

"I can. I will. It is better than allowing Brakefield to hold your debt over your head. I can well afford it, though if a certain lady had her way, she would take a good share of my funds."

Stunned, Barry sat back in the plush cushions of the ducal coach and shook his head. "Damme, if you ain't managed to outfox me, Wolverton. Here I am, all done up, and you tell me you will do what my own father would not." His laugh sounded discordant and loud. "But I cannot accept, of course. It would never do, and I would soon feel as if I must avoid you because I cannot pay the toll quickly. I would rather keep you as a companion."

"I don't sell my companionship, Kenworth, not even for fourteen thousand pounds." Brett's dry tone snared the young man's attention. "I offered you the money with no terms. Take it. I assure you, the gratification that Northwick has no more hold on you will be ample recompense. It would be rather pleasant to see his face when you settle with him, however."

Barry laughed softly. "That can be arranged. Ah, here we are at my house, but I thought—there is no card party, is there?"

"Probably somewhere, but none I wish to attend."

Laughing, Barry shook his head. "Then shall we tool on down to Vauxhall? Mr. James Hook is performing tonight, and we could take a supper box."

"And pay eleven shillings for two chickens no bigger than my fist and a slice of ham no longer than my thumb? That's not enough food for a cat."

"True, but I want to see Madame Saqui, if the truth is to be known. She scales a mast and walks a tightrope right through Chinese fire, and wears only tinsel and spangles and plumes—a remarkable sight, I am told."

"I shall leave that wonder to you, Kenworth. I have a previous engagement."

Grinning, Barry nodded. "Of the female kind, I vow. Never mind. Tuesday night, then, you are to attend Lady Sefton's soirée to introduce your cousins to society, am I correct? Or do you plan to slough off on that if at all possible?"

"I will no doubt see you there, though I'd rather view Madame Saqui than endure a night of anxious mamas throwing homely daughters at my head."

"Poor Wolverton. But a man of your rank and fortune should have to suffer occasionally, so the rest of us feel better about ourselves."

Brett's reply exceeded the vulgar, and Kenworth was still laughing when the Wolverton coach pulled away from the curb. But it wasn't a woman Brett had in mind to see that night, and he gave directions to his coachman who turned to look at him with wide, dubious eyes.

"Are you certain, Your Grace? That is a particularly rough section of town, and—"

"I'm certain. There's a gentleman there who is waiting for me on the corner of Lisle Street."

Lisle Street was usually beneath the notice for the better sort of London gentleman, but perfect for Brett's purposes. When the coach stopped, a shadow disengaged from the squalor of an unlit alley and stepped to the coach window. Brett swung open the door, and a fetid odor accompanied the man who stepped inside.

"Evenin', guvnor."

"Do you have my information, Watley?"

"Do you 'ave me blunt, guvnor? A full pony, now."

Brett held out a small pouch that jingled heavily, and saw in the turbid light of the lantern a gleeful smile split Watley's gnarled face as he reached for it.

"It's all there. Ah ah. Not until you tell me what you found out, Mr. Watley."

"I ain't no chawbacon ta be cheated now, guv-nor. Not Johnny Watley. Ah, but I reckon you're good for it, sittin' there fine as a fivepence—" He leaned forward, and a sour smell wafted through the air. "You were right enough about those papers bein' sold quick-like, guvnor. Delivered to a bloody earl, they were, who snapped 'em up quick as a parson at the supper table."

"Do you have this earl's name?"

Brett's lazy drawl earned him a quick glance and shrug of the shoulders, then a wary nod when Watley looked more closely at him. "Aye—Brake-field."

"Brakefield. Are you certain?"

Watley sneered. "Ain't bloody likely to be wrong about a swell like that one, a hatchet face and gooseberry eyes—it was him, all right, in it up to his neck, he is. He's 'most dished up, deep in dun territory. Word is, he arranged for these papers to be stolen and delivered to him. Got 'em off a Colonial pirate, and he means to keep 'em. Says they're worth a fortune, though it ain't bloody likely."

Brett smiled, and lowered the pouch of coins into Watley's eager palm. "You're wrong about that. Those papers are worth a fortune to me. Can you get them?"

Watley's jaw sagged, and he shook his head slowly. "*Steal* from a dangerous swell like him? I'd be gallows-bait afore dark!"

"Not if you have enough money to travel." Brett watched him closely as greed battled with caution, and knew to the instant when Watley succumbed: "I'll pay a thousand pounds, Watley."

"Cor! Those papers must be worth a lot to you."

"They should be—they're mine. Unlike the man who now has them, I have the money to pay to get them back. Are you game?"

"Bloody hell . . . game enough, but I'll need time."

"A week."

"A week! Christ above, guvnor, I can't—"

"Two weeks, then. Can you do it?"

After a moment, Watley nodded. "Aye, guvnor, I can do it for that kinda money."

Brett smiled.

Brett stared out the carriage window at the long line of ornate carriages in front of the Sefton house and the mass profusion of lights that illuminated the road and driveway to the pristine brilliance of daylight. He swore softly, and said when Kenworth glanced at him, "I'm glad Aunt Beatrice and her daughters came earlier. This looks to be a deadly bore and much too crowded. I should have gone to White's. It would be more quiet."

"Ah, but devoid of the fairer sex. Sefton is quite gracious, not as rigid as Jersey or that frightening Mrs. Drummond Burrell, so I suppose we may actually see beauty rather than bluestockings tonight."

Amused by Kenworth's jaded assessment, Brett gave orders to his driver to wait, then followed Barry into Lady Sefton's lovely home, bowed in and announced by a uniformed footman.

"A crush," Barry pronounced, "a positive crush. Sefton will be pleased, I am sure."

"No doubt." Brett surveyed the crowded room with a sweeping gaze that was intended to discover his hostess, make his appearance to his aunt, then depart. He hated these things. Too many people, too much pretense. Hundreds of candles lit just the entrance hall, glancing off crystal, silver, and gold appointments, as well as casting glittering reflections from opulent jewels worn around necks, dangling from ears, and adorning gowns.

Impatient now to find Lady Sefton and make his excuses, he turned sharply and stepped around a huge potted palm. Just beyond, with her back against a silk wall hanging, was a slender woman surrounded by a cluster of admirers. A flash of blue, sweep of blond hair, and soft laughter commanded his instant attention, and when one of the men moved, he saw her clearly.

Kyla Van Vleet.

His jaw tightened. Look at her, the larcenous little hellion, garbed in a clinging blue silk gown that showed off the tempting swell of her breasts, with sapphires at her ears and throat, and all the manners and appearance of a lady. Only, he knew better. A whore's daughter, with the stated intention of outdoing her mother by being courtesan to only the most wealthy. . . .

Kyla was smiling, a brow archly lifted as if in mild surprise, gazing at one of the men speaking to her with less than rapt attention. It should be apparent to the object of her inattention, yet the young man continued to cajole her with a beseeching posture that grated on Brett's temper. Curse her for a beautiful, conniving witch. . . .

At that moment, she glanced up from the slender, pale young man so ardently expressing some kind of sentiment to her, and her blue-green gaze moved directly to Brett. The half smile curving her lovely mouth froze, and for an instant, panic settled on her fine-boned features. There was no doubt that she was startled to see him there. Her lips parted, her eyes widened, and when her ivory-and-lace fan dropped from her suddenly lax fingers to the floor—giving the adoring young man an excuse to offer her yet another service as he bent to sweep it up with a grand flourish—it was obvious she was disconcerted by his presence.

A faint, sardonic smile curled Brett's mouth as he met her gaze steadily, his lifted brow a mocking reminder that he knew who and what she really was, that she could garb herself in expensive silk and radiant jewels, but would still be a grasping adventuress beneath all that artifice and expensive disguise. Apparently, she read his expression accurately, for a faint flush stained her high cheekbones, making her blue-green eyes even brighter beneath her thick fan of dark brown lashes. A damnable thing, that beauty could disguise such duplicity. But it did. Nothing in London was as it seemed, the pilastered walls hiding moldy wood or crumbling brick, and the men and women disguising their corruption beneath powder and paint.

Like Kyla Van Vleet.

Staring still at Brett, Kyla allowed the young man to place the fan in her open palm. Her hand shook slightly, but she seemed to regain her composure as she wrenched her eyes from Brett to the adoring admirer. Brett could not hear their conversation, but he was well aware that she was not as attentive to the young man's words as she should be. He smiled. This might be an excellent time to reinforce his demand that she depart London.

Six

Wolverton! Here, of all places—and looking positively lethal. Why would he attend one of Lady Sefton's soirées? He didn't seem at all the kind of man who would enjoy this sort of affair . . . but then she recalled his fierce, bruising kiss, and thought that the duke was not at all like any man she had ever known. Oh dear heavens, he was coming toward her!

Blindly, she turned away, and encountered the young man who had been lingering by her side since soon after she had arrived with Tante Celeste and Lady Rushton. He was staring at her hopefully, his round face pleasant above his intricately tied cravat, his eyes earnest and shining.

"Miss Van Vleet . . . you did say you would save me a dance later?"

Kyla blinked and looked more closely at Hargreaves, who was quite nice but very young and much too earnest. But he was an excellent distraction for the moment, and she certainly needed one.

Playfully, she tapped him on his sleeve with her folded fan, smiling archly. "Later? My dear sir, I am devastated. I never thought you the kind of man who would toy with a woman's attentions so."

"Why . . . upon my word! Miss Van Vleet, I never meant—" He paused, at a loss and looking utterly bewildered and quite chagrined, and Kyla smiled.

Lowering her lashes demurely, she murmured, "I thought you wanted the next dance, sir."

"By all means! Oh yes, Miss Van Vleet, I only thought your card already full, and—please. Do me the honor." He seemed to recover his aplomb a bit, and held out his arm as he had no doubt been taught by his dancing masters, and Kyla placed her fingers atop his sleeve and allowed him to lead her onto the floor, where she hoped to be lost among the other dancers already performing the stately steps of a minuet.

Peter, Lord Hargreaves, was the son of a wealthy member of the peerage, and Lord Twilby, his father, took great pride in his only heir. Yet Peter was still so young, a year younger than she was—though it seemed as if he was much less mature—that Kyla found it difficult not to tell him quite impatiently to run along back to the nursery. He was nice enough, but far too eager and tenacious for her taste. And she was only here because Celeste and Ondine said it was *the* place to be tonight, that Lady Sefton's approval was tantamount to acceptance *everywhere*, even the much sought-after vouchers for Almack's Assembly Rooms. Already, Kyla had been named The Incomparable by some of the men, an appellation that she found more amusing than flattering, though Tante Celeste swore that it was truly a credit to her beauty and her manners, and could only help.

And now Wolverton was here. *Here*, where she had never expected to see him, and at a soirée meant to present young debutantes for their first Season. Was he shopping for a bride?

How irritating, to look up at and see him glowering at her from across the room. It left her feeling vulnerable, and strangely restless, all breathless with turmoil inside, as if he had just kissed her again. Oh, where was Tante Celeste? She had been standing there only a few moments before . . . something about a glass of punch, but even Ondine had stepped away, lost in this dreadful crush of people, leaving her quite unattended and open to scandal. Of course, she had come to further her own objects, not so much of matrimony, but of gaining access to the same people that traveled in the circles with the dowager duchess. It was Her Grace that would turn the tide in her favor, she was certain, for the duchess was anxious to marry off her own daughters and avoid any taint at all of scandal . . . surely she would find it much easier to quietly settle a generous amount on Kyla to avoid such a possibility.

Kyla smiled distractedly when Hargreaves apologized for treading on her foot, and allowed him to sweep her down the line again, her feet finding the proper steps of their own accord as she focused on greater problems.

Blackmail. It was an unsavory word and even more unsavory prospect, but at times that was what she felt she was involved in doing. But was it really blackmail, when all she wanted was for her father's family to acknowledge her rights?

And for them to give Faustine the consideration she should have had years before? *No,* she thought rebelliously. *Perhaps Maman is dead now, but if Edward Riverton's family is forced to admit that he legally wed Maman, at least then I could feel as if there has been some kind of retribution for what they did to her. . . .*

And remembering Wolverton's sneering insinuation that her mother could be mistaken about the paternity of her child, Kyla's reservations vanished. Of course it was fair for her to do what she must to achieve proper resolution. How could it *not* be, after all that had been done to Faustine?

Thankfully, when the dance ended and young Hargreaves took her back to her godmother, there was no sign of Wolverton. Kyla relaxed a bit, and gratefully accepted a glass of punch from her admirer before Celeste gave him a quelling glance meant to send him away.

"It is not at all proper for one man to devote too much attention to a lady," she observed when Hargreaves most regretfully departed their company. "Talk, you know, and at this point, we certainly cannot afford to have loose lips prattling about you when we—"

Kyla's fingers closed over Celeste's arm, startling her into silence. "He is here, Tante."

"He? Here? Who?"

A faint smile compressed her lips at Celeste's blank confusion, but she was too nervous to allow even an instant of amusement to surface, or she might burst into some kind of uncontrollable fit of laughter that would only draw attention. In a deceptively calm voice that amazed her, she replied softly, "Wolverton."

"Here? *Bon Dieu!* Not Wolverton. Oh my." Celeste spread open her fan with an agile flick of her wrist, and beat the air with painted silk and lace in quick, agitated flutters. "What shall we do?"

"Avoid him. He looks positively murderous, and I would not put it past him to cause some kind of scene that would destroy any chance I may have of achieving my goal." Kyla drew in a deep breath to calm her apprehension. It was true. Wolverton *had* looked murderous, regarding her with those silver-gray eyes like steel daggers, his handsome face sardonic and mocking and arrogant all at the same time, with condemnation written on his dark features. It wasn't natural for a man to have such dark skin and hair and such light eyes. An aberration. An oddity. Perhaps he really was the son of a native girl, as it was rumored. He could be a savage himself, for he certainly behaved like one. God. Why did she have to lose all her composure at the very thought of the man? Or the memory of his kiss? Her wits deserted swiftly when he was about, and she certainly did not need to create a scandal.

When an hour passed with no sign of him, Kyla had the hopeful thought that perhaps he had already departed the soirée for whatever evil haunts he usually frequented. In the past week she had heard a great deal about Wolverton, mostly over tea, where the women whispered the most delightfully scandalous things about almost everyone in London that mattered. Especially Breton Colby Banning, duke of Wolverton, who it seemed was a favorite topic. Rumors ran rampant about him, each more incredulous than the last.

It was reported that he kept a mistress, or had

until recently, when the lady had been presented with a most handsome little house in the country and a pleasant farewell letter.

"A dreadfully *cold* manner of ending a relationship, to my mind," Lady Warbritton had said with a sigh, "however sordid it might have been. Of course, the duke *is* a Colonial, and you know they have few proper manners, even if he was born in England and has inherited such a large property . . ."

"But of course," Amelia Lynworth had said immediately, her sharp features almost quivering with excitement, "he is so handsome, so intriguing, that it can hardly matter, can it, if his mother's lineage was less than aristocratic? I mean, it was said at the time—and she stayed here only long enough to bear the child—that she was some kind of native princess in America, but my mother always considered *anyone* from that country rude and uncouth. Not that it was said aloud, or in Colby Banning's presence, for he was not a man to insult idly. Fought more than his share of duels, you know, and now I hear his son is just like him, as hot-tempered and dangerous, nothing like the late duke, who cared more for cards and brandy than anything else. . . ."

When the conversation had turned to Edward Riverton, someone had apparently remembered that Celeste had been friends with the unfortunate Faustine, so the topic was quickly abandoned. It was just as well. Kyla did not think she could have borne listening to much more about Wolverton.

Wasn't it bad enough that he was sparing no expense in seeing that his cousins were presented this Season? Just the oldest two, for the younger girls would not be old enough for another year or two. His cousins—her half sisters. Did they wonder about her? Were they at all curious about the woman their father had abandoned? Or did they believe the lies that she was illegitimate, just another fraudulent claimant to their father's money? She tried not to think about it, tried not to care that they obviously did not want to meet her, and were not at all curious about their half sister. Perhaps that was because they had each other, and still had their mother, while she had no one except dear Tante Celeste. . . .

"Comtesse du Bois," a smooth voice purred at Kyla's elbow, jerking her attention back to the moment at hand and the elegant gentleman standing beside Celeste, "it is so very good to see you again. You have been gone from London for a time, I understand."

Celeste's fan beat the air rapidly, and her voice was stiff. "Yes, my lord, I have only recently returned after fetching my goddaughter back to England."

"Just in time for the Season, I see, what? And you have with you a most charming young debutante. Is she to be presented as well?" He was smiling, but there lurked beneath the smile and oddly colorless eyes a pervasive sense of malice that made Kyla uneasy when her godmother presented her to him.

"May I present my goddaughter, Miss Van Vleet. This is Lord Brakefield, earl of Northwick, Kyla."

"Kyla?" Northwick's brow lifted, a bushy shelf over his opaque eyes, and for a moment, there was a sharp glitter that illuminated the opacity.

"An unusual name. Most unusual, though I seem to have heard it before. . . ."

Kyla allowed him to take her hand and press his lips to the back, grateful for her gloves, for she did not think she would like his mouth against her skin. For some reason, he made her think of unpleasant things, of dark shadows and a grating voice, and a strange queasiness and sour wine.

Removing her hand as swiftly as politely possible, she gave him a civil nod and murmured greeting. A little taller than medium height, he gazed down at her with a faint, supercilious smile, his thin lips almost disappearing.

"You are exceedingly lovely, Miss Van Vleet. It must be a family trait, as your godmother has *long* been a beautiful accessory to the London evenings."

There was a taint of spite to the words and tone, and Celeste stiffened a little, her eyes growing sharp. "You are much too kind, my lord. Now, if you will excuse us, I believe Lady Rushton is still searching for us, and I must find her before it grows too late."

"Indeed." Lord Brakefield's eyes shifted back to Kyla, lingering on her much longer than was comfortable, and the faint smile still played about the corners of his mouth. "Then Miss Van Vleet must be the bright new star that Lady Rushton has been promising us jaded bachelors for the past fortnight. She swore that The Incomparable would be here this evening, and here you are."

"I do not know that I am incomparable, my lord, but I am certainly here this evening. However, if I do not make my acquaintance with Lady

Sefton, I doubt very much I will be asked to return, so if you will excuse us . . ."

This time, Northwick did not protest, and made a slight bow, but Kyla could feel his eyes on her as they walked away, Celeste holding tightly to her arm as if afraid she would be pulled back.

Kyla affected a slight shiver. "Brr! What a dreadful man. He gives one quite a turn, does he not?"

"He does." Celeste sounded grim. "I do not care for him, but it is unwise to alienate a powerful man like Northwick. He has the bad habit of seeking vengeance for slights, whether real or imaginary."

"But really, what could he do?"

"Ah, child, you have a lot to learn about what men with power can do to someone's life. My poor Faustine certainly discovered it . . . ah well. We shall not think of that tonight, for there is too much else. And look, everyone is so gay, and you must seek out Lady Sefton, for she is very kind, really, and quite anxious to meet you after Ondine has told her so many nice things about you. This could be the start of things for you, Kyla. If only you can get enough money from Wolverton to provide a proper dowry, I do believe you could choose any eligible man you like! And there are so many here tonight—oh, look—one of my very favorite young men!" Celeste squeezed Kyla's arm, indicating with her fan a tall, fair young man with a handsome face and engaging grin who stood near the doorway. "That is Barry, Lord Kenworth—not, alas, heir to his father the earl, but a delightful young man. I have always found him to be polite, forthright, and if a bit wild at times, well, young men must sow their wild oats, and one day young Kenworth will make some fortunate woman a quite decent husband. And who knows—He could become heir one day if there should be some kind of *dreadful* accident, or a venomous, highly contagious fever . . ."

Kyla laughed softly. "You have missed your calling, Tante. Perhaps you should have arranged poor Prinny's marriage for him, and then he would not be so unhappy now and the king would be less . . . strained."

"I doubt it. The prince is very headstrong, and his father uncompromising. There was bound to be disaster, but I hardly thought it would end like this, with the poor king shut up as a madman and the prince a wastrel regent. Now come, let us walk in that direction, and perhaps Kenworth will notice us. Wait until you are introduced to speak to him, remember, and pretend indifference. That always piques a man's interest."

It would not be difficult to pretend indifference, for that is what she felt. Not that Kenworth did not seem pleasant enough, but though there was no sign of him, Kyla could not forget that Wolverton was present as well. Or had he left?

But when they reached Kenworth, Celeste paused as he drew someone forward to introduce them, and for an instant Kyla thought it must be Wolverton and her heart lurched. Worse—it was the dowager duchess, and poor Kenworth was introducing them as if they had never met. Kyla looked into the duchess's icy gaze and her chin instinctively lifted at the contempt she saw there.

"Do not go on, Lord Kenworth," the dowager said in unmistakably frosty tones. "I have met

Miss Van Vleet, and regard it as a singularly unpleasant experience."

Kenworth looked appalled from the duchess to Tante Celeste, his mouth slightly open and his eyes wide.

"How unfortunate for you, Your Grace," Celeste put in calmly. "My goddaughter has been named Incomparable, you know, an honor given to only a few. Are your daughters here this evening? I've heard so little about them of late . . ."

It was a sly insult, and the duchess stiffened, hot outrage in her eyes as she glared at Celeste. Kyla stood frozen in dismay, and it was at that moment that Wolverton loomed up behind them.

"Good evening, Aunt Beatrice. As you can see, I have joined you as promised. We meet again, Miss Van Vleet." He turned to her, his eyes raking over her so thoroughly she immediately felt as if she was unclothed and had to stifle the impulse to cross her arms over her breasts.

"Yes, Your Grace, so we do." She felt Kenworth's curious gaze on them, and heard Celeste make a faint, sighing sound. "I regret that we cannot linger, for—"

"Nonsense." Without taking his eyes from her, he put a proprietary hand on her arm and drew her forward a step. "I believe your godmother has given permission for you to dance with me."

Celeste made an inarticulate noise and looked at Kyla with wide, stricken eyes. "I—I—"

"Your Grace, you must be mistaken." Kyla's heart was beating so loudly she was vaguely surprised that he heard her, but apparently it was possible, for he was shaking his head, that small, strange smile still curling his mouth.

"I would not be mistaken about that, Miss Van Vleet, for I rarely dance."

Before she could do more than stammer an incoherent protest, he had drawn her with him onto the floor, and she had little choice but to go unless she wished to risk a scene that would be quite embarrassing. Angry, and more than a little flustered, she felt his arm slide around her waist at the same time as she realized the musicians were playing a waltz. *A waltz!* Why not a minuet, or even a contredanse? Anything but a *waltz*, where she must suffer his arm around her and their bodies so close together there was scarcely room to breathe. Or so it felt, though propriety demanded that waltzing couples keep visible space between them or suffer ostracism for performing such an indecent dance. It was only recently that the waltz had been approved for polite company, while Almack's still resisted allowing it to be performed in their stilted rooms. The Regent had sealed its popularity with his sanction, however, and so it had become quite the most popular dance. The floor was crowded with couples dancing beneath hundreds of candles in the crystal chandeliers dangling from the high ceiling, so that it was hot and stifling.

Stiff, with none of the usual grace and pleasure with which she executed the steps of the waltz, Kyla kept her face averted as Wolverton swung her into the pattern. He moved easily, graceful and assured, his body an overpowering presence as he held her lightly. He wore no scent like so many gentlemen, but there was a clean smell to him, and his clothing was simple and impeccable—the very height of good style. Somehow, that only made it worse.

"Last time we met, you were much more talkative, Miss Van Vleet. Have you nothing to say tonight?"

"Nothing you would care to hear, Your Grace."

He laughed softly, a hateful, mocking sound. "I was right. Your polish is only a thin veneer. Beneath your lovely face and stylish clothes beats the heart of a wanton."

She looked at him then, anger loosening her tongue. "Do not dare speak of me as if I am one of your cast-off mistresses! I will not tolerate it."

"Will you not?" He swung her around, pulling her much closer than propriety allowed, until the heat of his lean muscled body was like a solid flame against her, stealing her breath and leaving her churning with reaction. His arm tightened warningly. "I think you will tolerate whatever I have to say. You have no choice, not if you really mean to pursue this ridiculous claim of yours. After all, if you make a scene here, Miss Van Vleet, you lose all hope of gaining your desire. I assure you, that my reputation will not suffer from it, but your goals certainly would."

He sounded angry now, and held her much too tightly, so that she could hardly breathe or think, but hung on his arm like a cloth doll as he swung her about the highly polished dance floor, the strains of Mozart filling the air. It was all such a blur, the music and scandalized expressions of people watching—oh *why* was he doing this?

Bending his head, he said through clenched teeth, "If you have any thought of using Kenworth, be warned—he is a friend of mine. I would sooner take you as a mistress myself than leave you to destroy a decent young man."

Because it was so far from the truth, and because he at once leaped to the conclusion that she would prefer being a mistress to being a wife, Kyla abandoned any pretense at courtesy.

"You pompous, arrogant ass!" she hissed. "I prefer a *man*, not some uncivilized barbarian with the crude manners of a savage. I have the freedom to choose who I want, and I can honestly swear I would *never* choose you for a lover!"

His silver eyes glittered dangerously as he looked down at her. "Never is a long time. Do not swear oaths you cannot keep."

"This is one oath I can keep quite well. Release me. I refuse to continue this farce any longer, and wish to be returned to my godmother at once."

"Very well."

Ignoring the curious expressions on the faces of those they passed, Kyla kept her head high, and thankfully the music ended just as they left the dance floor. A path seemed to clear for them, jewels winking and glittering under brilliant candlelight as people stepped back. Only Celeste still stood by Lord Kenworth, and was staring at them anxiously, opening and closing her fan with nervous little clicks of ivory and lace. She looked quite lovely in her silk gown of bottle green, emeralds sparkling at her ears and around her throat, a tremulous smile wobbling on her mouth as she waited for Kyla and the duke to reach her.

But as they drew close, Wolverton steered Kyla past her godmother and Kenworth. His fingers tightened painfully around her upper arm when she stumbled and tried to pull away, and his voice was a soft, mocking drawl:

"Cooperate, Miss Van Vleet. Unless you wish to make a spectacle for all to enjoy and repeat over their morning tea—Good evening, my lord, please allow us to pass, as my companion feels faint and in need of fresh air—thank you." His head bent slightly when she still strained away, so that his lips were close to her ear. "That was Lord Alvanley, a notorious gossip. Do you want to be a household name by morning? No? Then look faint and hold to my arm so that you may be able to keep whatever reputation you still have."

Furious, but recognizing the truth in what he said, Kyla feigned dizziness, swooning slightly so that he had to almost carry her. When they stepped out onto the verandah, where a lopsided moon shed pale light to gild treetops and huge flower urns atop the stone retaining wall, she quickly abandoned her clinging pose and turned on him angrily.

Seven

Moonlight silvered his dark hair and was reflected in his light eyes, lending a sinister cast to his face. There was no hint of compassion or concern in him, only a ruthless determination that made Kyla suddenly shiver in the cool night air and wish for a coat despite the social edict that dictated it was more fashionable for a lady to shiver than to wear a warm wrap. Oh, why must he keep staring at her like that? His fierce intensity made her hands shake and her breath come in rapid, shallow pants for air. Not for the first time, she was inclined to believe that his mother truly had been one of those primitive American savages who were said to be wild and untamed . . . Kyla drew herself up with an effort, her voice tart.

"I do not appreciate your high-handed attempt to—"

"Shut up, Miss Van Vleet."

His harsh command took her by surprise, so that the angry words on the tip of her tongue remained unspoken. His back was to the open doors leading into the house, his face lit by lanterns and moonlight as she stared up at him through her lashes, suddenly afraid of what he might say or do.

He stared back at her, his eyes narrowed and cold. "Much better. If you will remember, I have suggested before that you leave England. Now I am demanding it. I won't have you accosting my late cousin's widow in public again. Nor will I tolerate your wiles being foisted upon naive young men like Kenworth. You are too hazardous to allow you near susceptible young men who may not look past your paint and powder to the true nature beneath."

Almost stuttering with fury and shock, Kyla was goaded into reckless retaliation. "How fortunate that you wear *your* depravity so clearly, Your Grace, or I would not be able to tell you what I think of you and your ridiculous assertion. Do you think yourself so much better than I am? You have more money, certainly, but your lack of breeding is obvious to anyone who so much as glances at you! I find it most amusing that you dare question *my* parentage, when yours is—no, do not even think about *handling* me again, for if you touch me, I shall scream until all of London is out here on the verandah with us!"

Swearing softly—words that she had heard but never by a man professing to be a gentleman— Wolverton reached out for her, catching the thin silk of her gown so that the sleeve tore with a rending sound when she tried to evade him. His fingers dug into her upper arm.

"Do you think I care if you scream? I don't. But my cousin's widow might be embarrassed, and I won't have you endangering the marriage chances of my cousins any more than you already have with your stupid claims. I've warned you before, Miss Van Vleet, and you chose not to listen. Now, we'll do this my way."

She was shivering from chill night air and reaction, and he was holding her arm much too tightly, his fingers like iron bands constricting her. The faint, sweet smell of flowers filled the air, and behind him she could see the glow of lights in the house and the swirling motion of guests dancing to a melody by Liszt. Knowing people were so close, she recovered some of her composure, and met his angry gaze steadily.

"I have no intention of doing *anything* your way—" She should scream—she *would* scream, for he was looking at her so fiercely, his eyes like steel daggers, and his mouth so taut—but then she knew she had waited too late. He moved swiftly as a striking snake as he pulled her hard against him to kiss her with a ferocity that quite took away her breath. There was no tenderness in the kiss, no gentle desire, just a ruthless lust that seared her lips and left her reeling.

Feebly, she tried to push him away, but there was no give to him, just hard, solid muscle, immovable and unyielding. It was strange how the heated embrace set her aflame, yet the cool wind and her own quivering reaction made her shiver with bone-deep chill, a contradictory invasion that left her weak and dizzy. And he held her so tightly and kissed her with such savage force, his mouth burning over her lips, her cheek, then the arch of her throat when her head fell back weakly.

Ah God, what was he doing? His hands were so warm, so rough, not at all like a gentleman's smooth, soft hands, but harsh and heedless as he stroked his palms over her, pulling down the low bodice of her gown to caress her through her thin chemise. Cool air and warm hands moved on her barely covered breasts, and he raked a thumb across her taut, silk-clad nipple. Her head whirled with shock and a strange weakness that rendered her oddly incapable of moving, of pushing him away, or even offering protests to what he was doing.

Wolverton laughed softly. His mouth was still against her throat, his breath a heated caress as his head bent lower, and to her horror, his tongue flicked out over the aching peak of her breast, wetting the silk and searing like fire, making her shudder weakly and clutch at him for support.

In a faint, feeble voice that sounded oddly breathless and quite unlike herself, she managed to protest: "You cannot do this. . . ."

"I can." His mouth moved to her ear, his voice a low growl: "I will."

"No . . ." It came out more a moan than the firm protest she intended, and she tried again to push him away, shoving hard at him with the heels of her hands, then grabbing at the stone wall behind her for support when he suddenly released her. Reeling off-balance, she hung there a moment with her hair in her eyes, masking her vision, until she reached up with a hand that trembled and pushed it from her eyes, staring at him as she fumbled to pull up her gown, her gloves making her clumsy. Fierce determination stared back at her, and she shook her head slowly. "Oh no. . . ."

"Oh yes. I do not care to be threatened, and I have decided to end all danger of it." He moved aside her arm and yanked up the bodice of her gown to cover her again. "You are coming with me, Miss Van Vleet, devil take the consequences. I have called your bluff."

"Bluff?" It sounded foolish, a clumsy echo, and she shook her head. "I do not know what you mean."

"You know quite well what I mean." He retied the ribbon edging her bodice into a jaunty bow, his hands as efficient as if he did it every day. "You announced that you are for sale, Miss Van Vleet. It happens that I am in the market for a new mistress. You can refuse me, of course, but I do not think you will. Newgate can be so unpleasant."

"New—*prison*? You must be mad. I've done nothing."

"Perhaps the magistrate will see it your way, but I'm inclined to think he will believe me when the dowager duchess and I tell him how you have attempted to blackmail us. Of course, it may be a bit distressing for Aunt Beatrice, but it's much better than allowing you to continue. Turn around. My coach is waiting at the side."

Numbly, Kyla made no protest when he took her across the verandah and down the steps that led around to the side of the house. Through the shaped forms of trimmed bushes she could see carriages lined up, with side lanterns lit and the entire front of the house ablaze with lights and people and snorting horses and footmen in various livery—there was a hum of conversation and wheels crunching on paving stones, hooves scrabbling over stone, and the smell of horse and perfume and sweet flowering plants from the garden all mixed together in a chaotic assault on her senses.

But as she regained her composure, she realized as the ducal coach rolled into view and one of the footmen stepped down to open the door, just what it was the duke intended. Her confused daze dissipated rapidly. She pulled free, aghast at the implications of his proposition.

"You cannot mean—I will *not* go with you!"

Wolverton looked at her sharply, and before she could offer another protest, scooped her into his arms and leaned forward to deposit her inside the coach. Sprawled atop the luxurious cushions, it took her only an instant to regain her balance. The vehicle dipped slightly as he climbed in after her, and she grabbed at the door before it could shut behind them. Wolverton's arm clamped around her middle and drew her down, pushing her against the back of the opposite seat.

"It is your choice, Miss Van Vleet." His voice was soft and lethal. "Do you go with me, or do you go to Newgate? It would be harder on your godmother than you, I think, as she is much older, but—"

"What are you talking about?"

"Prison. Blackmail. A French emigrée conspiring with my cousin's by-blow to swindle me out of money. Need I say more?"

"No." It came out in a strangled whisper. She drew in a deep breath to calm her racing heart, evading thoughts she could not yet face. Why did she feel so much like a trapped animal? While she was not worldly, she knew enough to realize the connotations behind his threat, and that even a hint of such scandal would be enough to ruin not only her but Tante Celeste, and perhaps even Lady Rushton. Did she dare risk that? But did she dare risk going with him like this?

Then, glancing out the coach window, she saw avid faces watching them from the broad porch and knew at once that her reputation—such as it was—was already shattered.

Lord Alvanley stood on the third step from the top, his gaze riveted on the Wolverton coach. Beside him, Lord Brakefield glowered with strange intensity, a malicious tilt to his mouth.

When she turned horrified eyes to the duke, he merely lifted a brow and gave a signal to the footman for the door to be shut. It closed with a decisive snap, sealing her fate and her future as the coach jerked forward and pulled away from Lady Sefton's soirée. She sank back into the cushions and stared at his hard face and uncompromising expression.

"My God. What have you done to me?"

Her question hung suspended in the air between them, soft and appalled, a plea and an accusation. After a moment, he shrugged.

"Only what you wanted. Is this not what you were after all along, Miss Van Vleet? A wealthy protector? Now you have one. It will be all over London by morning that you are under my protection, and no one will dare approach you. If you're worried about any debts, I'll take care of them for you." He stretched out his long legs, and his knees grazed the seat beside her legs, a silent intimacy that carried a wealth of implications. In the squares of lamplight cast through the windows by the carriage lanterns, she saw him watching her from beneath the heavy brush of his lashes, a brooding regard, cynical and yet expectant. What did he expect? For her to agree? To argue? Dear God, what had she done? What *could* she do?

Shaking her head, she said in a husky whisper, "You must take me home. My godmother will be frantic."

One corner of his mouth quirked up in a humorless smile. "I doubt it. She'll be too busy counting the coin she expects to get for you."

"How dare you!" Anger rose to replace the suffocating despair, giving her back some of her strength. "Do you think Tante Celeste is some sort of . . . of procuress? I resent your inference, for I have given you no reason to think I welcome *your* advances. I do not—"

"Enough." It was said impatiently, coldly, the single word a command and a warning.

Kyla paused. He looked so dangerous, sitting across from her in the shadowed interior, his long, muscled body a lean threat. She drew in a deep breath and forced herself to silence, recognizing that it was her only refuge for the moment. It gave her time to regroup, to assess the situation and her chances of retreat. Oh, what would Tante Celeste say when she learned of her abrupt departure in his coach? He was right. It *would* be all over London by morning. Any hope she had of gaining a dowry and marrying well was ended.

Turning her head, she gazed out the window blindly, not really seeing the bright gas lamps that lined the streets, or the pedestrians and other coaches, elegant carriages and landaus, gigs and curricles and phaetons—it was all a blur, misted by angry, frustrated tears that she would rather die than let him see.

Finally, when she could speak without betraying her agitation, she said coldly, "I demand that you take me home at once."

"I am taking you home."

Uncertain, she glanced out the window, and saw now that the coach had turned in the opposite direction from Mayfair or any other familiar haunt. The streetlamps here were no longer lit with gas, and were fewer and farther between. Even the traffic had thinned a bit, and she saw nothing she recognized. She jerked her eyes back to Wolverton. He had leaned his head back against the velvet squabs, but was watching her closely through slitted eyes.

"This isn't the right direction. Where are you taking me?"

"I told you. I am taking you home—to my home. I prefer the country, and we will not be disturbed there." A mocking smile curled his lips. "You should not complain, Miss Van Vleet. It will be well worth your time to be agreeable, for I can be generous enough when I've reason to be."

While her reputation may well be ruined, Kyla had no intention of allowing him to treat her as a common harlot. Weaving as much coldness into her voice as she could manage, she scrutinized him with a lifted brow meant to quell any pretenses he might have. "You dream, sir, if you think *you* can buy me."

Without warning, he leaned forward and caught both her wrists and pulled sharply, so that she tumbled into his lap in a graceless heap, her flimsy silk skirts twisted around her legs and baring her thighs. Struggling, she tried to push down her skirts in an attempt to preserve what modesty she had left but he held her tightly. Trapped between his spread thighs, she looked up at him, panting with embarrassment and rage. There was no hint of humor in his face now, real or feigned, just ruthless deliberation.

"Make no mistake about it—I *have* bought you. And on terms you set. Did you not say you aspired to being a well-paid lady of the night? I intend to help you achieve that goal."

His gaze moved from her face downward, to where her pale thighs gleamed in the soft, shadowy light, and there was a subtle shift in his expression. Transferring both her wrists to his left hand, he still held her tightly as he reached down to drag her skirts higher.

"Lovely," he said softly, and laughed.

Shame flooded her, and mortification, and she wished now she had not listened to Tante Celeste but worn the long drawers beneath her gown as she had wanted. But it was too much, her godmother had protested, and would make unsightly bulges beneath such clinging silk, so she must wear only the thin chemise that was much prettier anyway, yes? Oh yes. It was much prettier, but it was very brief, and left her legs bare beneath only a thin silk gown and even thinner petticoat that was almost transparent. And now Wolverton was taking advantage of that, and had her skirts up almost to her waist, viewing her with such casual possessiveness that she wanted to claw out his eyes and fling them out the window!

Twisting angrily, she brought up her legs somehow, so that her skirts were bunched around her hips and her knees supported her, and wrested one wrist from his hand, losing her glove in the process. She struck out at him, her nails catching him on the side of the face and leaving long, bloody weals down his cheek. He swore again, harshly, and caught her flailing arm before she could do it again, pinning both arms to her sides with his hands as he shoved her backward, using his weight as a leverage to pin her to the edge of the seat.

"Little hellcat. This was your idea. Are you backing out now?"

It was hard to reply with him leaning against her, his body hard and heavy, a pressing weight that constricted her chest. "I . . . *never* . . . agreed to be with . . . *you!*"

"Specifically, no. But midnight ladies are not always granted the luxury of choosing their customers, or haven't you had to learn that lesson yet? Maybe not. You are still young and pretty enough to be selective, I suppose, but not this time. This time, my sweet little swindler, I have chosen for you."

Erratic light danced over them, bright bursts through the unshuttered windows followed by hazy shadows again, so that she felt as if she was in the midst of a nightmare, something that hovered between terror and rage. The demons of her childhood returned in solid form and substance— Lucifer in thin disguise, wickedly handsome and ruthlessly determined . . . danger clothed in expensive garments with hellfire and damnation in his glittering eyes . . . she began to shiver uncontrollably.

Maybe it was the dream, the dark shadows at

the far perimeters of her mind that sometimes crept into the light until she pushed them away again, but she thought she must have done this before. There was a familiar, charged tension in the coach, a heat that engulfed her, made her feel strangely expectant, as if she knew what came next. But she didn't—did she? She had never been with a man before, never allowed more than a few stolen kisses, though once, a long time ago when a French family had come to stay with Maman and brought their young son who was her age, she had yielded to curiosity and let him examine her body as she had examined his. Just touching, a kind of shy, embarrassed exploration, but they had been only seven or eight, after all. So long ago. When life had still been fresh and new.

Brought rudely back to the present by his hands on her, she blinked up at him, feeling as if she had just awakened. He caught her chin between his thumb and fingers and held her face still so that she could not twist away, but it was pointless, for her strength had suddenly deserted her. The edge of the seat pressed into her spine as he pinned her beneath him. Feeling like a snared rabbit as he held her so ruthlessly, she did not struggle when his mouth covered hers, hot and hard and demanding, his tongue plundering her mouth and leaving her trembling and filled with turbulence.

It was no dream. This was real. She must be mad, or worse. Why else would she feel this strange heat inside, this coiling flame that spun and twisted inside her, growing hotter and hotter until she could barely think? No, he shouldn't— she should push him away, tell him to stop and demand that he release her, but she could not halt the sweep of shivering response that raged through her when he kissed her, or when he touched her, or even when he pushed down the low scooped neck of her bodice. She shuddered as he caressed her bare breast, his thumb and fingers tugging gently at her nipple, teasing it into a tight rosette until she moaned.

Lantern light gleamed in his thick black hair, and he glanced up at her, a strange intensity in his pale gaze as he caught her eyes. Her breath came in short, tortured gasps. His features were sharp with desire, tension in the set of his mouth and carving furrows between his eyes. At that moment, he resembled the savage she had called him, with his feral expression and hot eyes, dangerous and terrifying.

Then his head lowered, and his tongue traced small circles over her sensitive nipple before he drew it into his mouth, tugging gently until she writhed helplessly with an urgency that she did not quite understand. Her hands were free, and fluttered upward to touch his crisp black hair, his neck, even the scratches on his cheek. Her palms cupped his shoulders as she arched into him instead of away, the desire to struggle or even protest sliding into sudden, desolate surrender.

Dimly, she was aware that the sound of coach wheels was loud, the thunder of hooves against hard-packed dirt a constant rhythm, with the creaking and swaying of the coach a rough motion that somehow added to the air of isolation, as if they were alone.

Closing her eyes, she knew she was lost, drowning in this heated sea of unfamiliar emotion and response to his mouth and hands. Just when she was reduced to quivering confusion, he sat up and pulled her onto the seat beside him and arranged her bodice and then her skirts. He released her then and leaned back, his arousal evident in his snug-fitting fawn pants. His voice, always a slow drawl, sounded thicker than usual, and almost hoarse.

"No point in putting on a show for the footmen. I can wait a little longer."

She shivered. The coach rocked and swayed, and it grew dark outside as the lights of London were left behind, so that the only light was from the small coach lanterns that were mounted high on the outside, a faint illumination that barely lit the interior. Hoofbeats pounded steadily as they raced through the dark night toward her ruin, and all she could think was that she had never known men kissed like he did, his tongue more an invasion than anything else. Worse, she had not known that her capitulation would be so swift and shattering.

Eight

Damme, Kenworth thought with horrified amazement, *he's gone and done it!* And in front of one of the worst gossips in London, too. Lord Alvanley looked positively gleeful as he flicked off an imaginary speck of dirt from his coat sleeve and glanced up at Barry. Lifting his quizzing glass with an air of indolent affectation, Alvanley peered about the room, then turned back to Barry with a languid shrug of disapproval.

"A most illuminating scene, Kenworth—Wolverton played the rogue quite handily when he lifted her into his coach. Mind you, the lady did not make a sound of protest. I daresay, the duke's heavy purse is more of an inducement than her reputation, but isn't that usually the case? Amazing, how easily some females sell themselves."

"Perhaps the lady was taken ill, Alvanley. Or you may be mistaken—"

"No mistake. Northwick was there, and he saw it as well. Mind, I've had my eye on her for a while as well, for she is a prime article, indeed. If I'd known she was up for sale instead of marriage, I might have bid, but alas, I always seem to be the last to know these things."

Alvanley affected a sigh and drew out a snuff-box and flicked it open with a delicate twist of his wrist. One of the Unique Four of Prinny's set, Lord Alvanley was still in favor, though his close friend Brummel had quarreled with the prince three years before and those two still did not speak. It was rumored that Brummel's debts were so great he might be forced to flee the country, for when he had lost favor with the regent, the bill collectors became demanding.

It seemed odd to him now, but once Barry had aspired to being included in that exclusive group. Recently, he had come to the conclusion that he much preferred remaining on the fringe. The dandies were fine in theory, but wicked company at times. Wolverton was right about that, anyway. Now he shrugged, eyeing Alvanley with less awe than once he would have done, his voice a little sharp.

"Look, Alvanley, Wolverton may be reckless, but as far as I know, he's no roué like Northwick."

Alvanley snorted in derision. "You must know better. He may be a duke, but his rustic breeding is just beneath that very thin surface of polite manners that he has cultivated. I cannot imagine why Colby Banning ever went to America, when he knew there was a possibility that one day his son would inherit Wolverton. Ah well, the excesses of some are most curious, I say. And at least Wolverton has provided us with some amusement tonight. After all, he seems to be keeping it in the family, if my information is correct."

"What are you implying, Alvanley?"

"My dear boy, don't tell me you didn't know—ah, but I see that you didn't. How droll. The latest *on-dit* is that the beautiful lady that Wolverton just carried off so high-handedly is none other than his late cousin's daughter. That would make her . . . what? His fourth cousin? Fifth? Far enough down the line to make it possible, and close enough to make it entertaining . . . excuse me. I see Lady Jersey beckoning me. No doubt, she desires to hear the tawdry details, which I always seem to know."

Barry stared after Lord Alvanley as he made his way through the crush toward Lady Jersey. Music swirled around the crowded room, but not as loudly as the whispers that were already flying thick and fast, rumors of this exciting *ou-dire* about Wolverton and what was obviously his latest mistress. Kenworth thought wryly that Brett had certainly brought down a storm of gossip on his head for a man who professed an aversion to scandal. What the deuce was he thinking, to carry off a lady in that manner? And in particular, the lady it was whispered was his own cousin's daughter? Distant cousin, granted, but now the rumor would really fly.

And it seemed that Northwick was determined to give the rumor wings, for he paused by Barry with a faint smile. "You look pale around the gills, Kenworth. Afraid your idol has fallen?"

"I do not care for your tone, my lord, nor for your insinuation. Wolverton and I are good companions, but I do not worship him."

"Yes, so you say." The earl's lips curled into a faint sneering smile at Barry's stiffness. "It would be too bad were he to be accused of something so serious as incest, do you not think?"

"I say, sir! Whatever are you suggesting? It is hardly incest to accompany Miss Van Vleet in his coach, but even if it was more intimate than that, she is not closely related to Wolverton."

"No?" Northwick's smile widened. He took a leisurely pinch of snuff, sneezed into a mono-grammed handkerchief, then clicked shut the small enameled box and tucked it back into his sleeve. "How dreary you can be, Kenworth. I thought you more astute. It is all over London by now—or soon will be, I assure you—that Miss Van Vleet is the duke's cousin. Or did you not know?"

"I heard the rumor. I do not countenance it for an instant. I am surprised that you would repeat it."

"Repeat it?" Northwick laughed softly. "Foolish boy, I started the rumor. You are such a gudgeon. I must admit that it has taken me far too long to make the connection, for it should have occurred to me when I first heard the young lady's name, but alas, it wasn't until I saw her that I knew the truth."

He shouldn't even listen to him, Barry knew, but there was something compellingly genuine about Northwick's recital and his obvious relish in repeating it, that made him stand there longer. And the earl seemed to know it, for his smile was predacious, his expression avid.

"Come, Kenworth, and I will tell you a tale from the past, a rather short, sordid little story, but one that finally has an ending. I used to won-der—but it was so long ago. Seventeen years, as a matter of fact, and yet I never knew exactly what happened to her . . . a French émigrée, lovely crea-ture, delicate and blond, and quite obliging. It seems that the man she claimed was her husband did not quite agree with her version of the story, and alas, as women often find to their sorrow, she was turned out. There was a child—a small, beautiful child named Kyla—I've never forgotten that name, for it was as unusual as the child . . . you know how I adore pretty little girls, do you not, Kenworth?"

Barry was revolted by the blatant wickedness of Lord Brakefield, his careless indifference as to what anyone else thought of him. He bowed stiffly. "My lord, the direction of this conversation offends me. You will pardon me if I do not listen to the rest of your tale."

Northwick laughed, and there was a gleam in his empty eyes like a lamp set in a vacant window. "Ah, but of course I will pardon you, for your ignorance if not your rudeness. But mark me well, Kenworth, your friend Wolverton will soon have reason to wish he had not acted so precipitately. It may well cause his downfall."

"If *you* are still accepted, my lord, I doubt seriously that any scandal caused by Wolverton tonight will exclude him from the very best homes. Now I feel the sudden need for fresh air and perhaps even a change of clothes. Good night, sir."

Barry pivoted on his heel and stalked away, feeling Northwick's eyes follow him. He had made of him an enemy, of course. At this moment, he did not care. God, the man made him sick. This entire evening had turned foul, and he was suddenly desperate to escape the crowd and murmuring voices, even the music that had begun to sound like discordant clashes of noise instead of the lovely strains of Bach.

"My Lord Kenworth! Wait!" The voice stopped

him as he reached the front door, intent upon making good his escape, and Barry turned impatiently. Comtesse du Bois hurried toward him through the crush. His heart sank. What could he say to this obviously distraught woman that would not be overly cruel or far too blunt?

An anxious frown carved deep lines beside her mouth, and her usually pretty face looked pale and haggard. "My lord," she said in a faint, breathless voice, "have you seen Miss Van Vleet? I heard—but it is impossible, of course, for she would *never* do anything so outrageous and foolish—can you tell me if you have seen her?"

Reluctantly, he shook his head. "No, I am afraid I have not."

"Then Wolverton? Have you seen him? You came together, I understand—he is still here?"

Again, unwillingly, he shook his head. "No, madam, I must disappoint you. He is no longer here, I fear."

"*Mon Dieu!*" Celeste faltered, her hand shaking slightly when she lifted it as if reaching for support, then she recovered, and straightened. "I see. Thank you, my lord. I shall find Lady Rushton. No doubt, Ondine has sent her home early, for she was complaining of the headache not long ago. I am certain that is the reason I cannot find her."

Barry bowed slightly in acceptance of this excuse for Kyla Van Vleet's abrupt departure. "Of course, it must be. I am certain you will find her at home when you arrive. Shall I call your carriage for you?"

"No, not now. I must find Ondine . . ." She looked a bit distracted, but nodded politely and turned away, moving back through the crowd with infinite dignity, ignoring the avid glances of the curious and cruel.

He went outside, where the air was much cooler and sweeter, with a faint tinge of early-blooming flowers. It had become a most disturbing evening.

The Ridgewood gates were closed and locked, and the gatekeeper was roused from his bed to open them, expressing surprise that the duke had arrived.

"No one told me," Brett heard him say as he fumbled with the huge metal lock and keys, the clank almost as loud as the impatient jangle of harness from weary horses ready for food and rest. Finally the gates swung open with a noisy creak, and the carriage rolled through, light from lanterns atop the stone corner posts flickering inside.

Brett eyed Kyla. She was huddled on the opposite seat with her face turned from him, staring out the window. There was something about her posture that invoked visions of a wild scene, prompting him to offer advice:

"Behave as a lady, and that is how you will be treated. I do not tolerate scenes in front of my servants."

Her head turned toward him. "No? What will you do if I begin to cry rape, Your Grace? Beat me? Shoot me?"

"Try it and you'll find out quickly enough." Irritated, he leaned forward. "It's not too late to back out if you're having second thoughts, but I warn you—prison can be an unpleasant home."

"You sound as if you have experience."

"Maybe I do." He laughed harshly at the quick

look of doubt she gave him. "Somehow, I think you would not fare so well in Newgate. It's cold and damp, and the only men there who could offer you protection would definitely expect more than a flutter of pretty eyelashes and empty promises."

"You realize that this is blackmail, I suppose."

"And what do you call your efforts to extort money from me for your silence? A cordial gesture? Hardly. But feel free to say what you like now. It's highly unlikely that anyone will believe you after tonight."

"I'm well aware of that."

Her abrupt reply was almost drowned out by the grating of coach wheels on crushed stone, and the vehicle dipped as a footman leaped down to open the door. Another footman swiftly mounted the stairs to rap on the door and alert the housekeeper to his unexpected arrival.

Lamps illuminated the front of the house, casting long streamers of light across the portico and steep flight of stairs that angled down on each side toward the curved drive of crushed paving stones. Brett stepped out, and turned to lift Kyla down, his hands catching her around the waist instead of taking her offered hand. She shot him a quick glare, then lifted her chin again with instinctive arrogance as he set her on her feet and released her. He wondered what her mother had really been like, if she had possessed the same innate haughtiness worn like a crown atop her small blond head. Had Faustine been the scheming harlot he'd been told? All the evidence indicated she had, yet there were moments, as now, when he had his doubts. Kyla possessed an inbred assur-

ance that most often belonged only to the aristocracy.

He recognized it, because he had it, too, at
times, a damnable tendency to be arrogant and
overbearing, riding roughshod over anyone who
got in his way. His mother had ruefully lamented
about it, but said he got it honestly from his father.
Maybe she was right. It was not one of the traits
he liked best about himself, but at least he could
recognize it as a fault of sorts.

Miss Kyla Van Vleet, standing in her torn blue
silk gown with her pale hair clubbed into a
clumsy braid that left loose wisps straggling
around her face in a most enchanting fashion,
looked as if she never had any reservations about
what she did. Only when faced with retribution
had she wavered, and now the time of reckoning
had come.

It was a little irritating to admit even to himself
that he wanted her, but he'd developed a fierce
itch for her after their first meeting, when she had
refused to back down an inch from Aunt Beatrice
but met her toe-to-toe, firing back at the old harridan like a veteran. It had been an admirable performance.

But one that was futile.

He took her arm, and drew her with him up the
stairs to the portico flanked by massive columns
like those of ancient Rome. The front door had
opened, and he saw Mrs. Wilson in the doorway,
looking a little frazzled but fairly composed. Apparently, Godfrey had gone again, as he frequently did when Brett stayed in London.

"Your Grace," Mrs. Wilson said quite calmly as

they entered the house, "we did not expect you tonight."

"I don't require much this evening, Mrs. Wilson. A fire in my bedchamber and tray of cold food will be enough for tonight."

"Yes, Your Grace. Tilly has gone up to light the fire in your room already, and fortunately fresh linens were just placed on the bed today for your return this week." She lifted one hand, and another servant scurried close, looking sleepy and disheveled but alert enough to bob her head when told to prepare a tray of cold roast chicken and cheese. "And some of the fruit that was delivered today, Susan." She glanced back at Brett, carefully avoiding noticing Kyla, as she had not been introduced. "Will that be all, Your Grace?"

It was obvious she wanted to ask if he intended another chamber be readied. Brett nodded curtly. "That will be all, Mrs. Wilson. Thank you."

"Yes, Your Grace."

If she was aware of the insult in being ignored, Kyla did not reveal it, and made no protest when he escorted her across the marble floors of the entrance hall to the wide sweep of stairs that curved upward. Potted palms and huge statues loomed in the dim light, casting eerie shadows in the faint flicker of the few night lamps. It was quiet, their footsteps echoing in the gloom of air scented with lemony beeswax and candles.

Upstairs, thick carpet cushioned their feet, and the door to his chamber was already open, light streaming out to make a bright rectangle in the corridor. At the door, Kyla jerked to a halt with a faint, incoherent sound.

"Second thoughts, Miss Van Vleet?"

She did not reply, but stepped inside, her back stiff and straight. The maid was still in the chamber, on her knees in front of the hearth lighting the fire with a spill of paper curls. It caught, and she fed it until it was a nice blaze, then arranged the brass firedogs and scuttle, being careful not to look directly at her employer or guest.

Already loosening his cravat, Brett nodded briefly when she offered a shorter version of Mrs. Wilson's welcome home, then hurried past him and out the door as if relieved to be gone. Kyla still stood just inside the door, gazing at the fire with her hands clasped lightly in front of her.

"It's warmer when you get closer," Brett observed dryly, and she looked up at him.

"Yes."

Her calm brevity was as irritating as her earlier verbosity, and he jerked his cravat from around his neck and flung it over a brocade-covered chair. A bootjack divested him of his gleaming leather boots in short order. Then he stalked past her to a small marquetry table set with crystal decanters and glasses, and poured a generous amount of brandy into two of the glasses.

"French brandy," he said, handing her one. "You should appreciate it."

She looked down at the amber liquid; its golden color reflected candlelight from a wall lamp in tiny rainbows. Her hands trembled slightly, and she sipped at it slowly, looking for all the world like a condemned prisoner.

"For Christ's sake," he snarled impatiently, "if you continue looking like a kicked puppy, I may change my mind."

"It's a relief to know there are some creatures

that warrant your sympathy." She met his gaze now, deliberately cool, provoking and seductively provocative.

"Are you suggesting *you* should? I reserve any sympathy for the deserving, Miss Van Vleet, not for extortionists."

"Your definition of deserving should be infinitely amusing to hear. I find myself curious as to just how many are on that elusive list."

"You're not one of them." He'd unbuttoned his shirt and untied his collar points, flinging the latter in the same direction as the cravat. Eyeing her with displeasure, he saw the guarded expression in her eyes, the wary waiting, as if expecting him at any moment to leap on her and rip off her clothes. It was tempting. She was particularly lovely, and enticing with her hair tumbling around her face as if she had just risen from a man's bed, loose and sensual, inviting a man to run his hands through the silky strands and watch them glitter like gold threads over his fingers. He moved toward her, and saw her eyes sharpen and her breath come more quickly. A pulse beat rapidly in the hollow of her throat when he stopped in front of her.

"I have another list more suitable for your name, Miss Van Vleet. But here, we shouldn't be so formal." He smiled at her swift intake of breath when he dipped his finger into his brandy then smoothed it across her mouth. "As we're about to become more closely acquainted, I'll call you Kyla. And you can call me Brett."

Her tongue flicked out as the brandy dripped from her lips, catching it before it reached her chin. "I don't want to . . . know you that well, Your Grace."

"But we've already decided that you shall. Unless you have changed your mind. No? Good. Here. Drink some more of your brandy, Kyla. It was an excellent year."

As she met his gaze, her hands trembling as she lifted the snifter to her mouth, the maid arrived with the tray of food. Brett waited until she had set it down and gone to the door, closing it behind her, before he moved away from Kyla. "Are you hungry?"

"No." It was faint, a whisper of sound, but when he turned back to look at her, she was staring at him steadily and there was no sign of fear in her gaze, only wariness.

"Then if not for food, maybe something else. Come here, Kyla." She did not move, and her brandy sloshed a little against the sides of the snifter, coating it with thick amber liquid as her hand shook. He set down his brandy and moved to her again, removing the snifter from her hand to place it on the table, then taking her arm to lead her toward the bed.

It was a massive four-poster draped in heavy hangings of dark blue velvet, with snowy white sheets and a thick coverlet that had been turned back. Lamplight did not reach all the way into the shadowed interior, so that the fat white pillows were almost hidden by the canopy and drapes.

When he halted beside the bed, she pulled away from him. Taking two steps back, she looked from the bed to him and shook her head. "I cannot."

"Turning hypocrite on me? You can't say you don't like kissing me. You do. It was obvious the first time we kissed, and even more obvious to-night. Or do you want to pretend you didn't kiss me back?"

"No." Color brightened her cheeks and made her eyes look more blue than green. "I did not say I didn't . . . like it. But this is not . . . I mean, I have not—there is no guarantee you'll keep any promise you make!"

"Curse you. What do you want? A contract? It's not done quite that way, I assure you. But then, most men don't choose mistresses who have tried to bleed them for money, either. All right. I'll put it in writing—after I see what I'm getting. I may not be quite so charitable later, so make your decision now, Kyla."

She stared at him blankly. "Decision about what?"

"Don't play coy with me. You've done this before. Show me what you want me to pay for, or I'll lose interest."

"You mean—*disrobe*?" Her eyes widened almost ludicrously, until for a moment he thought perhaps she had never done this before. But then he realized how wrong that was, for she began to laugh, a rather high, hysterical sound that grated on his temper.

"Enough, Kyla. I'm tired of playing games."

She nodded, her laughter subsiding. "You're quite right, Your Grace. It's time the games end." She bent and pulled off her small slippers, then turned back to look at him, seeming for a moment to flounder before she gave a brief, light shrug and began to untie the waist ribbon of her gown. "You'll have to help, of course. But I'm certain you are quite used to that."

"Do I look like a damned lady's maid?"

"You look, sir, as if you have had a great deal of experience undressing women. Here. I cannot reach the back buttons."

There were several of them, fastening a sort of short train that was designed to drape gracefully from behind, and she turned her back to him and waited. Damn her, he had no intention of playing this particular game, putting himself in the position of following her orders.

He moved to her and curled his fingers in the back of the gown and jerked, ripping it down the back and rending seams and silk impartially. In three swift motions, he had divested her completely of the gown, so that she stood garbed in a gossamer-thin petticoat and chemise, with lacy garters holding up her stockings.

Kyla whirled to face him, her eyes blazing in her pale face, but said nothing when he handed her the shredded gown without a word. She tossed it aside. "Very well. Shall I continue slowly, or do you prefer to rip off the rest as well?"

He shrugged and leaned back against the bedpost, his legs spread apart for balance, hands braced on his hips and his open shirt hanging loosely from his shoulders. "It doesn't matter how careful you are. Just do it."

Anger sparked her eyes, but she untied the thin tapes that held her petticoat around her slender waist, and let it fall slowly to the floor so that she stood in only her chemise and stockings. The silk undergarment fit her from breast to the tops of her thighs, barely hiding the shadowy triangle at the juncture, and he watched as she began to untie the garters tied just above her knees. She discarded them and rolled down her stockings, lifting each leg and giving him a tantalizing view of bare thigh as she slid them off. Then she stood in only her chemise and paused, her eyes briefly flicking over him before she began to pull down the shoulder straps.

Unmoving, Brett studied her as the chemise slid down as well to join the petticoat in a silk puddle on the floor. God, she was lovely. Long slender legs, a small waist and sweetly curving hips—her breasts were high and firm, ivory cream like the rest of her, with rosy nipples that knotted into tight buds in the cool air. She stood with chin lifted defiantly, as if it did not matter that she was completely naked, but he noted the faint flush that stained her face and throat.

Rising desire made him uncomfortable. Damn these tight pants . . . he leaned away from the hard ridge of the bedpost to move to her. She did not speak, but watched narrowly when he reached out to caress her, his hand moving over her breasts to her waist, then below to tug lightly at the springy mat of pale curls nestled between her thighs.

She gasped when he touched her there, and grabbed his wrist. "You said you would give me a written agreement, Your Grace, if I disrobed. I am disrobed. Nothing was said about touching."

"So I did." Caught between amusement and contempt, but aroused to the point of discomfort, he went to the cherry secretary against the wall and yanked it open, pulling out a sheaf of paper and a pen. He dipped the pen into the inkwell, then scrawled a few lines on the paper, blew it dry and turned back to hand it to her. "Will that suffice?"

She scanned it swiftly, then looked up at him with an enigmatic expression and nodded. "For now."

"It will have to do forever, because this is as far as I intend to be pushed." His eyes narrowed when she stepped away from him and bent to retrieve her clothing, and he stopped her with a hand on her arm. "Enough delay."

"Your Grace—"

"Say my name. I'm damned if I want to be called by a borrowed English title in bed—say it."

Her voice shook a little. "Brett."

"Better. Put that down if you want to keep it legible, or the ink will smear."

The paper fluttered to the table with a light whispery sound, and he pulled her back around and lifted her into his arms, ignoring her sudden resistance. Her skin was soft and warm, like heated satin beneath his hands, and though she squirmed and offered breathless protests, he carried her across the room to the bed and tossed her to the mattress.

She bounced once, and scrambled to her knees to stare at him in the gloom of blue velvet and white linen. "Brett, wait—"

"I've had enough delay, dammit." Untying the tapes that held his pants closed, he peeled them off in a swift motion and flung them aside. He straightened and met her gaze, reading uncertainty in her eyes, and as her gaze drifted lower, panic. He frowned. Did she intend to default now?

But then she was looking up at him, a rather dazed expression on her face even when he took her into his arms and kissed her cold, unresponsive lips. Tremors shuddered through her, and he drew the covers up over them and stroked her skin to warm her, until she relaxed enough to return his caress, a rather halfhearted slide of her hand over his chest. It wasn't until her hand slipped even lower, finding him and curling her fingers around him, measuring him with a slow stroke of her palm along his turgid length, that he forgot about her first stiff response and kissed her fiercely, forgetting everything but the sweet curves and soft skin of the beautiful creature in his bed.

Nine

Kyla tightened her fingers a little, exploring him with tentative strokes, trying to comprehend the difference between this man and the only other naked male she had ever seen. What she knew was supposed to happen between them seemed suddenly impossible. Something was wrong—but it had to be with her lack of experience. Inexperience was almost as frightening as ignorance, but thank God Tante Celeste had made certain she was educated in that respect . . . his hand curled over hers suddenly, stilling her explorations as she grew bolder, his words a harsh mutter between his teeth.

"God . . . not so fast, or this will end before it begins." He began kissing her again, hard and almost brutal this time, with fierce insistence.

Yet, as he stroked her and kissed her, surprising her by taking time to arouse her when it was obvious he was already aroused, she began at last to respond. The first fear faded and disappeared under his ardent touch, though there was a leashed violence in the way he kissed her that made her throat tighten a little. He kissed her for a long time, his mouth moving over her stiff lips in a coaxing pressure until she parted willingly for his tongue.

Still kissing her, he began to stroke her again, his hands touching her breasts, teasing her nipples until she moaned softly. He moved lower, kissing her throat, then her breasts, his tongue making hot, wet circles around her taut nipples first, then drawing them into his mouth with sensual pressure, one at a time until they were tight, aching knots. He lay beside her, his long body against her hip and thigh, and she could feel his arousal nudging against her, an insistent persuasion that made her feel a little uncertain.

With one part of her mind, she acknowledged that she wanted him to do this, that she had nothing else to lose now that she was ruined, but the other part—the logical part of her brain—told her that it would not ease her situation. Wasn't she only another conquest, a midnight lady, as he had called her earlier? A well-paid whore, though the reality could be embellished with names like courtesan and *fille de joie*. She might gain money, but she would lose all else she had held dear—her pride, her reputation, her dreams. Was it worth it? Oh, but *what* could she have done to stop him?

It had just all happened so quickly tonight, from the time he had seen her with Hargreaves until this moment, the tension and uncertainty an anguished blur.

But now, for all his previous roughness, he was being gentle and patient with her, his hands arousing, his lips and tongue teasing her nipples until she groaned with mounting excitement. And she suddenly realized that she *wanted* him to touch her like this, even if for inexplicable reasons. It was as if she was a banked fire suddenly flaring into life, into a high, hot blaze capable of consuming everything. She moaned, a telling noise in the back of her throat, a surrender and protest at the same time. Her hands moved aimlessly, fluttering over the flat muscles of his belly, up to his face, in his hair, pushing and pulling at him alternately until he took both her hands in one of his and pulled them up and over her head to pin them into the soft pillows.

"Brett . . ." Her voice sounded so strange to her, a sort of groaning whimper. "I need to tell you something—"

"Later . . ." He kissed her hard on the mouth, his tongue delving between her lips in a searing thrust, then lifted his head, his face shadowed and his eyes a pale sheen in his dark face. Holding her gaze, his face sharp with passion, he deliberately moved his hand over her, caressing her breasts, then moving lower until she squirmed. He laughed softly, and bent over her again.

Kissing her eyes, nose, mouth, and then her breasts, he brought her to fever pitch, until all the same formless sensations of earlier returned, making her ache, igniting the throbbing heat between her legs into a blaze of urgent need. She twisted beneath him, crying out when his hand moved between her legs, touching her, fingers stroking the soft damp folds with erotic caresses until she felt a strange tightening there, the tension growing taut until she thought she would explode if it was not eased.

Murmuring softly in her ear, he continued to stroke her as the world tilted awry in a heated haze and everything seemed to fade away while all her concentration was on the unfamiliar needs of her body. It came suddenly, a sweet, piercing release that spiraled through her in a rush, flooding her with a shuddering ecstasy that she had never before dreamed existed.

Brett held her as she whimpered into the curve of his neck and shoulder, and she breathed deeply of skin slightly scented with spice. She lay still for a moment, suspended in a gauzy web of warm serenity.

After a moment, he began to kiss her again, and lifted his lean body over her, nudging her thighs apart to slide between them. Still floating in a pleasant haze of release, she did not move even when she felt that rigid part of him between her legs, pressing hard against her. It all seemed like a dream, a shadowy train of events that had no connection to each other but just happened in a disjointed fashion.

Then, slowly, she became more aware, as he pushed harder against her, the first gentle pressure altering to a sharp ache. She tensed, and would have shoved at him but he was holding her hands over her head, locked in his fists, his body levered atop her as he rocked his hips forward. He slid just inside her, a brief burning invasion that did not prepare her for his sudden forward lunge. A scream lodged in her throat and her entire body arched up with shock, a movement that only brought him more deeply inside her.

Struggling, she tried to close her thighs, but of course it was too late. She only succeeded in holding him more tightly inside her. His head lifted, and in the gloom of lamp and shadow, she saw him staring down at her. She closed her eyes, suddenly too chagrined to meet his gaze. The brief sweet haze had vanished, and there was only *this* now, the harsh reality of intimacy, the burning truth of his body inside hers, and the knowledge that nothing would ever be the same again.

"A virgin." His voice sounded thick, hoarse, and incredulous. "By God—I would never have guessed it."

Bitterly, she acknowledged that truth. No, he would never think that Faustine's daughter might be innocent. And she had aided him in his low opinion of her, when all she had wanted was to restore her mother's good name. What a fool she was. . . .

She opened her eyes to look up at him. "I tried to tell you, but you would not listen."

Staring down at her, his eyes darkened, and his long lashes lowered to shadow them as he studied her. "Maybe you did. You should have spoken up, and I would have been easier with you."

If she'd harbored any thoughts that the discovery would trouble him, she quickly realized her mistake. After a few muttered words of comfort, he began to move inside her again, slower this time and not as hard, but with a steady driving rhythm that soon drowned out the pain and conjured up that hot, strange wildness again, the sense of urgency that had been there before. It was a different sensation this time, but just as intense.

And now he murmured soft words to her, some in a strange guttural language that she did not recognize, but snatches of French and English, love words and sex words all mixed together, his breath hot against her cheek and ear. He was a dark silhouette against the shadows above them, the blur of blue velvet and faint light that filled the interior of the canopied bed. Kyla wondered distractedly if this was how it always was, this compelling need to reach an elusive peak. Was it? Was it that way for him, too? Or did he even feel the same intense sensations . . . the driving need that constrained her to draw him even closer, deeper inside until the rest of the world dissolved into a blurring haze.

Twisting beneath him, her hands moved over the taut, ridged muscles of his back, sliding over his skin as she felt his muscles contract then relax, her fingertips grazing occasional ridges of old scars. Gradually, the cadence of his movements increased, and his breath came in shallow pants for air as she arched instinctively into his thrusts, striving toward the same end.

He didn't love her, she knew he didn't, yet he called her love, *amour, mi amor,* the words running together in a husky litany as he held her, his body thrusting harder and harder, until she began to shudder violently with a pleasure so sharp and potent it was almost painful. His hands tightened on her, digging into the soft flesh of her hips to hold her. He gave a final thrust that shook her and grew still, a hoarse groan coming from deep inside his chest.

They lay like that for what seemed a long time, then he moved at last, shifting his weight to one side, caressing her gently as he pulled her into the angle of his chest and thighs and held her, his arm flung carelessly over her, his breath slowing to an even rhythm. She did not move, but lay there quietly, drifting between two worlds.

It was like swimming, she thought vaguely, floating on the River Lethe, the waters of forgetfulness surrounding her, drawing her under, submerging her into blessed oblivion until there was no more day or night or pain or joy—only sweet nothing.

Morning came softly to Ridgewood, stealing through velvet curtains like a thief to lighten the soft gloom of the chamber. Trapped sunlight coaxed slender fingers through a slit in the heavy curtains over the windows, shooting a thin streamer of light into the bedchamber and across the floor. It did not reach the interior of the draped bed, but moved slowly over the richly textured carpet of deep blues and greens that covered the floor in exotic patterns.

Kyla woke slowly, startled at first in her unfamiliar surroundings, but memory swiftly returning to render her paralyzed. Oh no—it was true. It had not been a nightmare, as she had hoped . . . he was there beside her, the coverlet thrown back, his long body bare and brown and roped with lean muscle where he lay exposed for anyone to see. She stole a glance upward to his face, and saw the marks of her nails on his cheek, thin furrows like a cat's claws stitching his face from temple to jawline. *Good!* She wished she'd done more, left more marks on him, for he had certainly left his mark on her. Her lips felt bruised, and there was a faintly sore roughness between her thighs. She shut her eyes tightly, the surge of despair in her mouth and filling her throat.

When she opened her eyes again, she watched the haze of dust motes swimming in the streamer of light, unwilling to move more than her eyes to keep from waking him. How could he sleep so soundly after . . . after last night? Dear God. She must have been mad, caught up in some strange dream that seemed to have no end, no solution, and now she was here and everything was ruined. *Ruined.*

Poor Tante Celeste. She would be frantic. By now, of course, everyone in London would know of her *departure* from Lady Sefton's soirée. It would be viewed as an agreement between an available woman and a duke, not as it really had been, more of an *abduction* than agreement. She should have screamed, as she had threatened. But the gossip would still have raged, whispers of how she had gone alone with him onto the verandah, and her gown was ripped and her hair all untidy, so of course, she must have *allowed* him to handle her so—oh yes. She knew what would have been said. She'd heard it too many times, always whispered in those smug tones of satisfaction, of security in knowing that it wasn't them or their daughter who had fallen. . . .

It wasn't fair that the woman was always blamed, when the man was usually the cause of her downfall. After all, it was not as if women engaged in dubious acts alone, was it? No. Always, it was a man who led them, or at the least, was the stimulus for their fall from grace. Hadn't she seen enough to know that?

And haven't I been guilty myself of it? she thought then, a little angrily when she recalled how once she had actually thought herself attracted to Wolverton—*Brett.* A short, masculine name abbreviated from Breton, his Christian name given in honor of the land of his birth. Where had she heard that? Oh yes. Lady Warbritton. A garrulous old biddy, but quite harmless most of the time, not as nasty as some of the others could be, gabbling on about men and women, and destroying reputations without a thought, as they were no doubt doing to her this very moment over their morning tea. Those who were up, that is, the others lying abed until time to rise and eat and dress leisurely before beginning a day of constant clothes changes to make morning calls, to ride in the park, or take a short walk to see and be seen.

So many changes—carriage dresses, dinner dresses, garden dresses, morning dresses, riding dresses and opera dresses, and even walking dresses—it was essential to be garbed in a different gown each time one left the house for whatever reason. And here she was, without even a single dress to her name, her beautiful blue silk gown lying in shreds on the floor beside her pretty, lacy undergarments.

If not so infuriating, she might have been humiliated to consider her plight. *But I cannot dwell on that now,* she thought, *not when I have to think what to do next. I am ruined here, of course. It will be impossible to remain in England. Poor Papa Piers, he would be devastated if he knew that his hopes for me have been shattered. What can I do? I cannot return to India. Not when he has sent me away, and besides, word will eventually reach there of my humiliation. Oh no—what if—but surely no one will be cruel enough to mention it to Papa Piers!*

That, she could not bear. He loved her as if she was his daughter, and so many times she'd wished she truly did belong to him. But burning wishes was a child's game, and now she was a woman. And now she must take control of her fate and stop allowing people to make decisions for her. It would not be easy. It was much easier to allow others to decide, to pretend that she was satisfied with whatever happened to her, but that was not so. She was not as some of the other girls she'd known, quite content to have arranged marriages, arranged lives—no. That was behind her. As was everything else.

How odd, that Wolverton had ruined her, yet given her a new beginning. For that is what it would be. Her reputation was gone, her virginity was gone—what else did she have to lose? Perhaps, in some queer twist of fate, he had actually done her a favor. She would never have succeeded in gaining what she wanted from him, never managed to clear Maman's good name or probably even received any money from him for a dowry so she could marry some nice, dull young man and settle down in the country to rear children and fade away until she became as an empty shell, a thistle seed, puffy and quite pretty on the outside, but light enough to be tossed about by whatever wind blew.

She had once threatened him with selling herself to the highest bidder, and that is precisely what she had done. He had cynically written out a contract for her, but she no longer needed it. Now, she would make terms that needed no signature, no designation, because they would be her own, and would be whatever she felt necessary.

And really, it might not be so bad as it looked now, for perhaps she had some kind of affinity for this. Until that sharp pain, she had lost herself in his touch, in the sweeping bliss of his mouth and hands on her . . . yes, she could remain as his mistress, especially if he really paid her what he'd carelessly scrawled on that sheet of vellum, a waste of fine paper but an enormous amount of money, more than she had dreamed of getting even for her silence. Despite her angry grief at what she had lost, it could have been much worse. When he tired of her—or she him—she would have enough money to do as she wished, travel to some other country and live discreetly and quietly. Perhaps Tante Celeste would come to visit, and they could talk of Maman, or France in the days of glory. Yes. That is what she would do, once he paid her what he promised.

Blocking out the insidious doubts, the knowledge that her entire life had been reversed in the space of a single night, a single action, Kyla did not shrink away when Brett woke and reached for her, his eyes lazy-lidded, his handsome face shadowed by the heavy bed hangings.

He stroked a hand down over her face, then beneath the coverlet over her to pull it back, baring her body to the cool morning air. Despite her new vow to be worldly and brazen, a flush heated her skin and she curled her hands into fists at her side, but did not reach for the coverlet as her first reaction prompted.

A faint smile pressed at one corner of his mouth. "You're just as lovely in the daylight as you were in lamplight."

"Are you complaining, Your Grace?"

"Such formality this morning. You should warm a seat in Parliament. Although that would hardly qualify you for warming my bed."

When she did not reply, he flipped the coverlet back over her and rolled away, rising from the bed to stretch with unabashed leisure, heedless of the fact that he was completely naked. It should not matter to her, for after all she would have to grow accustomed to it, but somehow it did. It was so new yet, this intimacy with a man, and a bit frightening. He looked powerful, like a lithe-muscled animal as he moved across the room to the embroidered bell pull and gave it a sharp tug.

Studying him without being obvious, her gaze moved from his broad shoulders over the sleek muscles of his chest, to the hard ridges that rippled on his lower abdomen, then below. He looked less dangerous now than he had last night, and she was momentarily puzzled until she recalled what her godmother had told her, something about the flow of blood and being aroused, and how the obvious changes in a man were on the outside, but a woman's were hidden inside.

"Which is as it usually is, *ma petite*," Celeste had added with a soft sigh and mysterious smile, "for women are ever holding their true desires deep inside, hiding them to keep from being hurt. But a man—ah, he cannot hide what he wants. So, we have a small advantage over them that way, *n'est-ce pas?*"

Yes, it was certainly so in this case. For she could learn to hide the truth of how he made her feel, tuck it deep inside and not let him see unless it was to her advantage. Yes. She would learn to do that, for if she did not, she might end up destroyed.

Brett returned to the bed, his brow lifted as he gazed at her. "Are you all right?"

The question embarrassed her. She knew immediately what he meant, and while part of her was vaguely surprised at his show of concern, another part of her resented the fact that he only now thought to ask. Her chin bobbed in a short jerk of assent, and she tried to match his insouciance with a careless reply.

"Excellent, thank you. I fared much better than my poor garments have."

Some of his former mockery returned, and he shrugged. "Nagging already, love? Buy a whole damned wardrobe for all I care. Have the bills sent to me."

Stung by his casual assumption she expected him to buy her new clothes, she opened her mouth to tell him furiously that she had lovely clothes of her own, but stopped just in time. No, that would be so foolish. Why not let him buy her new things. She deserved it, didn't she? And it was a small, subtle way of paying him back for his callous treatment of her, his overbearing arrogance in thinking he could purchase her as casually as he would a blooded mare.

"Thank you, Your Grace."

"Kyla—use my name. It can't be that hard for you to remember."

"Yes, Brett." She smiled, but her fingers curled into claws over the satin-edged corner of the coverlet, and she thought how easy it would be to hate him.

Impatiently now, he crossed the room again and jerked at the bell pull, swearing under his breath that the service here had grown lax since his last visit, and by God, he would soon know why. He gave it another yank, viciously this time, and she could imagine the fierce ringing of the bells in the kitchen below.

In moments, footsteps sounded in the corridor outside the chamber, and Brett reached for his trousers as a knock vibrated the heavy door. Protocol demanded that the servant outside await permission to enter, but the door swung open on its hinges before authorization was given, and Kyla's eyes widened at the apparition that filled the opening.

The breath caught in her throat and her blood chilled, and if she could have summoned a scream, it would no doubt have peeled the wallpaper from the walls. Standing in the open doorway was a huge, muscular savage with long black hair down to his waist and coppery skin, clad in fringed leather garments decorated with dangling feathers. She clutched the coverlet to her chest just beneath her chin, staring at him in horror and wheezing for air, waiting for Brett to offer a violent challenge to this intruder.

But instead Brett eyed him with a mocking slant of his brow. "You're back, I see. Where is Mrs. Wilson? Or Tilly?"

"Mrs. Wilson has tendered her resignation," the man replied coolly, and Kyla was struck by his perfect diction and deep baritone. "It seems that her sensibilities have been offended by the visit of a young lady in your bed without the sanction of matrimony. I suggested she discuss her decision with you, but she said quite firmly that she has no intention of conversing with the devil, in whatever form he might take. Under the circumstances, I thought it wise to allow her to leave unimpeded. So, as Tilly shrieks at the sight of me and quivers in a corner, I was forced to prepare a morning meal for you and your guest. I trust venison will be suitable?"

"Curse you." Brett's tone belied his words, and he shook his head as he crossed to the tray of chicken and cheese still sitting on the table. He hefted a slice of cheddar in one hand and pointed with it to where Kyla still cowered under the canopy. "She no doubt takes tea. I prefer coffee. Strong and black. Send to the village for a suitable replacement for Mrs. Wilson, preferably one with less sensitive sensibilities."

Huddled in the shadows, Kyla relaxed a little, but thought that the strange-looking man was the largest she had ever seen. He looked positively savage, and was no doubt one of those American Indians she'd heard about. He certainly didn't sound like one, however, for his English was more perfect than hers was, his accent impeccable.

He glanced toward the bed then back at Brett, and began speaking to him in a language she did not understand at all, not even a single word. It sounded more like rapid grunting than anything else, but apparently Brett understood it well enough, for he grew angry, and answered sharply in the same language.

The quarrel—if it was one—lasted only a moment, then the large man withdrew, shutting the door behind him. Brett tossed the dry slice of cheddar to the tray again and turned to look at her. "You seem to have quite an effect on people. Myself included. Not that I'm surprised, for you look quite fetching sitting there with your hair all loose and tousled, looking as if you've been doing exactly what you've been doing. For now, you may wear borrowed clothes. I will send for a dressmaker as soon as possible."

"That is not necessary, for I can—"

"You can damn well do as you're told, Kyla. I have no intention of allowing you to go about naked, though the idea does have a certain fillip."

"I meant," she said coldly, "that I have no desire to wait for a dressmaker to be found, when it would be much faster to send for my own clothes. Unless you have a wardrobe full of garments stashed about, I do not relish the idea of spending several days clad in a sheet."

His eyes narrowed, and he moved toward the bed again, in that lithe predatory stride that always made her a little nervous. The mattress dipped with his weight when he put one knee on the bed and leaned over her, bracing an arm on each side of her as he said softly, "Perhaps I relish the idea of you spending several days between the sheets. Don't mistake my practicality for weakness. Sending for your own clothes would be an exercise in patience that I don't have, for I've no intention of having your godmother at my door with her hand out as well."

She almost forgot her new resolution to hold her tongue and bide her time, angry words trembling violently before she swallowed them. To achieve her goals, she must choose her battles carefully. The matter of clothes and insults was not yet one she cared to engage. Let him buy her clothes, and let him think what he wanted about Tante Celeste. He could even keep her flat on her back in his bed for several days as he threatened, but she would find a way to make him pay for every insult he levied, and she would not forget one of them, no, not a single one! Perhaps he had made a grave error in forcing her into this position, because for the first time in her life, she felt powerful.

Because he seemed to expect some kind of response, she managed the only thing that came to mind: "For your future reference, I prefer coffee to tea."

Ten

Afternoon light flooded the garden, gilding the petals of roses, hollyhocks, and delphiniums with spangled glitter like tiny wet diamonds caught in rainbow clusters. Though it had rained that morning, now the golden rays were misty and soft, shining in Kyla's blond hair with molten light. She was dressed in one of his cousin's old gowns, a bit big on her slender frame because Arabella was taller and larger-boned, but not too bad once it was cinched in tightly with the ribbon encircling her just under her breasts. Kyla reclined gracefully in a chair next to a marble-and-iron lawn table, her skirts draped from her legs and spilling onto the grass in a snowy pool of muslin.

It was hardly the sort of trait he wished to cultivate in his character, but Brett had begun to regard Kyla Van Vleet with something close to cynical amusement. Brazen little cat—did she think he would tolerate her arrogance for long? He would not, yet he found himself more lenient than he might have been with another woman's whims, for she was lovely, and more innocent than he had thought her to be.

The illusion of sweet innocence was still there, but the reality had altered to a new awareness. Perhaps that was how it was with some women, the removal of their maidenhead a prelude to sudden perception of the power they could wield with a sigh, a flirtatious gesture, even the coy lowering of lashes and a secret smile as if knowing what he wanted. Damned, inconvenient lust.

He might want her, but by God he had no intention of yielding to the disturbing temptation that urged him to treat her any differently than he had the other women who had passed so fleetingly through his life—a long line of similar faces and greedy hands, simpering moods and the inevitable tears and accusations when he wearied of constant demands and ended the relationship. Only one had ever been different, and she was dead now. Oddly, though they were as dissimilar as night from day, Kyla reminded him of her . . . absurd, really, for *she* had been nothing like this tempting little adventuress who inhabited his bed now, save for the fact that they had both been virgins when he'd taken them.

Ignoring him as if she was alone in the garden, Kyla sipped a frosted glass of lemonade, a book in her lap and her attention focused on the leatherbound volume. Her head was bent, the glass gripped in her slender, delicate fingers and held at an angle, so that the ice clinked with a light, brittle sound against the sides of the glass.

He left the flagstone terrace and strode toward her across the still-damp grass, his Hessian boots leaving a dark trail behind him, the leather glistening with transferred raindrops. "What are you reading, trinket?"

Without glancing up, she murmured, "Jane Austen's *Emma*. It is a charming little tale, though quite fanciful. One could almost believe in love."

Amused, he inserted his finger into a bright coil of her hair that dangled winsomely against one cheek. She wore it up in a cluster of curls on her crown, but several had escaped to flutter prettily around her face. She looked up at him, and in the carefully composed structure of her face, he caught a brief flicker of disquiet. It was not as easy for her to hide her emotions as she thought, for he could oft sense her tension, the waiting to see what he would do or say. He liked it that way, for he had no intention of becoming so predictable that she could maneuver him as she pleased.

Drawing his finger down, he skimmed the creamy flesh of her cheek, to her lips, then her chin, and over the slender column of her throat until her head tilted back slightly to present him with an excellent view of the tops of her firm rounded breasts beneath the demure white muslin of Arabella's old gown. A faint shadowy cleft beckoned him, and his hand moved into the valley to caress her. Her breath was an audible inhalation, but she offered no protest, not after the last time, when he had reminded her curtly that she was his, as agreed upon, as purchased and paid for until he desired to end the arrangement.

There were moments he fully expected her to launch herself at him as she had that night at Lady Sefton's, all hiss and holler, claws scratching and spitting like a cat. Yet she had shown remarkable restraint, though he could tell it cost her dearly at times.

As now, when he continued to toy with her

breast in the garden where any servant passing by could see him, his hand a possessive statement against her soft skin. High color stained her cheeks almost scarlet, yet she did not protest but sat quietly under his caress. Provoked by her composure, perversely nettled into gaining the response he knew he could wrest from her, he pushed the muslin away from her breast, baring sweet flesh and the tight pucker of her rose-tipped nipple. She quivered as his hand moved to tease the tempting bud. He twisted it gently between his thumb and finger, until at last she looked up at him, anger sparking her eyes.

"Shall I disrobe for you here on the grass? If you are so determined to make a public spectacle out of what should be private, why not be thorough about it? Odd, but I had not thought you the kind of man to do things halfway."

"How droll. A mistress who dares chastise the man who pays for services she has agreed upon performing. You are bolder than I'd thought, trinket."

"And you are more crass than I'd thought."

He laughed. "Did you think otherwise? Only because you don't know me very well."

For a moment she didn't say anything, but looked at him oddly. "No," she said at last, "I don't know you at all. Nor do I think I want to know you."

"I can assure you of that, madam. You'd best stick to reading your trite little fictions, for the reality would be far too honest for you to face."

"Honest, or harsh?"

"Either. See? I can admit the truth easily enough. I do not dwell in illusions."

She stood up, removing his hand from her bodice and letting the leather-bound book fall to the ground at her feet. "I disagree most heartily with that, sir, for you are a master of illusions."

"Am I?" He leaned against the heavy marble-and-iron table with its intricate scrollwork of entwined grape vines and ivy, and regarded her sardonically. "Tell me how that is possible, trinket, for I find myself fascinated by your opinion of me."

"You mock me, but it is true." The heightened color in her face made her eyes seem very blue, the intense shade banishing the subtle green that often imbued them with such an unusual tint. "All this—the house, the gardens, this vast estate and all your money—is only an illusion to hide what you really are."

"And of course, you intend to tell me what I really am, I suppose. You disappoint me. I thought you more imaginative than that."

She lifted one shoulder in a light gesture of indifference. "I have no intentions of telling you what you are, for as I said, I do not know your true nature. But I do know that there is something very different about you, more than just the fact that you were brought up in America instead of England. I just cannot decide exactly what it is that makes you so different, so—dangerous."

"Dangerous?" He gazed at her with detached amusement. "You flatter me, trinket. I never knew I was considered dangerous."

"Yes. You know it well enough." She toyed with the lace edging on her bodice, tugging distractedly at the tiny pink ribbon woven through the lacy folds. "It's in your eyes, the way you look at me, or at anyone who crosses you in any way. I've seen it enough now to recognize it, though you may prefer not to acknowledge the fact. After all, you act quite the aristocrat, with your practiced manners and correct clothing, just the right air of bored arrogance like all the other lords and ladies that travel in *le beau monde* of the city. It is all a sham, I think, a masquerade to hide what you really are beneath that illusion. Yes. You are, indeed, quite dangerous, sir."

"Dangerous only to annoying lace ribbons that keep me from viewing tempting treasures, my sweet. Since you've turned up shy on me, come into the house where we can be dangerous together."

Though she did not protest or offer resistance, Brett found himself forced to persuade cooperation from her with ardent caresses and lingering kisses, until her stiff surrender turned into the unbridled passion he knew she kept locked inside. It was becoming a habit, her cold resistance and martyred air, the closed eyes and lips even when she lay naked in his arms, her silent opposition gradually turning to soft sighs and moans, and quivering surrender when she gave him at last the response he wanted from her.

This was her reward for persistence, and his reward for impatience—the knowledge that she was his anytime he wanted, as long as he asked no more of her than her body, for she certainly gave him nothing else. Yes, she'd changed, that first tentative self-assurance he'd noticed in her burgeoning into a strong confidence, a certainty that aroused his unwilling admiration.

She was his to do with as he liked, but only as

he would handle a china doll. It made him even more determined to wring from her honest response, and every time he took her it was a battle of wills until she finally capitulated. Her resolve might be strong, but her passionate little body was more susceptible.

Like now, lying in the midst of the snowy linen sheets of his bed with her face flushed and her breath erratic, gazing up at him with shadowed eyes as he caressed her, aroused her until she was panting with short little drags of air. He kissed her soft trembling mouth until her lips parted for him, until she kissed him back and put her arms around his neck to hold him. Tangling his fingers in her bright hair, letting the silky strands slip over his palm, he held her head still while his mouth explored hers, then her cheek and the line of her throat up to her ear, kissing and nipping, blowing softly until she shuddered, until she was moaning. His mouth moved lower, tasting and teasing her breasts, the soft sweet fullness of them, then lower, over the taut swell of her satiny belly to the pale gold curls.

With a startled cry, she arched upward, grabbing his hair in both hands to yank hard. He looked up at her with a low growl. "Ow! dammit. What are you doing?"

Heat flushed her cheeks, and she tugged harder on his hair. "I was going to ask you the same thing."

"Maybe it's too soon ... but one day, you'll want me to do that for you, *querida.* . . ." He moved up and over her again, drawing down her arms to lock her hands in his, lacing their fingers together as he drew them up and over her head, pressing down into the pillows, levering his body over hers and watching her eyes grow wide, her tongue flick out to wet her lips in nervous anticipation.

It wasn't until he entered her, hard and swift, with determined thrusts, that she shuddered into that sweet yielding that he sought from her. Then she responded with fierce lifts of her hips into his thrusts and soft little cries in his ear, breathless urging that made him want more.

When it was over, and she lay damp and exhausted beneath him, he lifted his head to look down at her, feeling drowsy and satiated. He toyed with a damp tendril of hair against her cheek. "You should have come to me with this offer long ago, trinket. I would not have refused you then. You are worth every pound I've paid for you."

She stiffened, and the hand she'd laid against his shoulder bunched into a small fist. Her words came out in a strangled whisper: "Despite the hefty bank balance you have deposited in my name, you don't own me. You may have purchased my time, but my body and my soul are still my own."

"You're wrong, my sweet. I do own this"—his hand dragged down over the swollen nipples of her breasts, still engorged from the pressure of his mouth and hands on her—"and this. I have bought and paid for them, and they are mine."

"Are they? I think not." A light shrug lifted her bare shoulders. "They belong to me. Only my time is yours, and that only until you tire of me. When will that be? Soon? Will you soon release me, Brett, and give me my freedom?"

Staring down at her, he saw the mockery in her eyes and swore harshly. He rolled away and off the bed, angry and frustrated. She'd certainly shown no unwillingness the night of Lady Sefton's soirée, when she had gone with him onto the verandah, and maybe he had been a little high-handed about it, but there had been only the usual nominal protests before she'd yielded. The kind of protests that he'd heard a hundred times before, and the kind that had always ended with the woman in his bed.

"Curse you. This kind of conversation will certainly end our alliance, Kyla, though you may not care much for the manner. A week hardly constitutes fulfillment of our bargain."

"Do you retract your offer, sir?" Despite her calm tone and the faint smile still lurking on her lips, there was a slight tremor in her voice. "Am I to be put out without any recompense for my time? Hardly fair, I would think."

This was familiar to him, the ploy and plea, and his voice hardened. "Just when I begin to think you might be different, you prove otherwise. You cannot expect to receive more than you have earned."

She lifted to her elbows, resting on them, her hair framing her exquisite face and flushed features with pale beauty, cascading over her bare breasts in a silken screen to curl around her taut nipples. "If I have any expectations at all, they involve only my desire to keep you at bay."

"Keep me at bay—Christ. I'm not a wolf or vicious dog that has to be held back."

"That is a matter of perspective, I think."

Her cool rejoinder, delivered swiftly and with a

lift of her straight little brow, provoked him into a caustic reply: "Then you will not miss me for the next few days. I'm leaving for London in the morning to ensure the success of my cousins' aspirations, and to accept congratulations on the acquisition of my latest whore. Who knows, the public spectacle of our departure may engender great interest in you, *querida*. Shall I forward any interesting and lucrative proposals to you? The prince's brother might find you intriguing, or even the prince. And it would be a step up, in rank if not money, as they are notorious wastrels. When I am through with you, I won't mind passing you on, so you'd best consider the direction you wish to take."

Her face paled, leaving her so white her eyes were two brightly burning jewels. She said nothing, but if ever there was hell in someone's face, it was in Kyla Van Vleet's.

Eleven

It was hardly comforting that Brett slept elsewhere that night, or that he did not bother to see her before he left Ridgewood. Her first indication that he had gone without seeing her again was the sound of coach wheels on the curved drive of crushed stone beneath her window. It woke her, that and the sound of jangling harness and the coachman's whip, and she flew from the bed to the window just in time to see the black, tooled-leather coach speed around a bend in the drive and disappear behind a towering hedge shaped in a perfect boxwood triangle.

Standing in the misty light that threaded through lacy curtains behind the heavy velvet draperies, Kyla felt a sense of desertion, an oddly forlorn emotion that left her sad and uneasy. She shouldn't be sad—he was gone, and she could do as she pleased and not have to suffer his hands on her, or hear his hateful voice in her ear in the morning, waking her before first light with caresses that she always tried to resist but never could for long.

She let the dense velvet fall back over the window, plunging the room into gloom again. Brett had made her true situation quite clear. She was his whore. That was all she meant to him, now or forever, and if she chose to share her favors elsewhere, it would mean little to him.

Her bare feet padded over the thick, luxurious carpet, and she climbed back onto the high bed, sinking into the fat feather pillows to stare up at the canopy gathered in deep folds over the top. It was so quiet. The smell of burned candles and a faint scent of brandy lingered, mixing with the sharper tang of wood ash from the fireplace. No coal was to be used in this room, Brett had reminded Mrs. Lynch, the new housekeeper, for he preferred the smell of burning wood to that of something dug from the bowels of the earth.

Mrs. Lynch was a dour-faced woman with little to say, but preferable to that frightening man Kyla had seen on her first night here, but not since. Godfrey. An unusual name for a heathen, but Brett had only laughed when she mentioned it, and said dryly that she should discuss it with Godfrey if she was so curious about him.

"Don't be too rude," he'd added mockingly, lifting her hair in his hand to study the gold strands in the lamplight, "for Godfrey may decide to wear this pretty scalp at his belt if you're too impolite."

Jerking her hair from his hand, she hadn't been able to keep the edge from her voice when she observed tartly that he no doubt had engaged in such barbarous practices himself. His answer had been chilling:

"Certainly. Did you expect differently? That's odd, since the English employed that practice themselves before the American Revolution, paying hefty bounties for the scalps of Creek and Seminole men, women, even children. It is hardly new, or reserved only to the natives."

"Is that what Godfrey is? An American native?"

"He is one of the People, from a tribe in the western part of North America. Some call them Comanche." He made an odd sign with his hand, wiggling it backward, and grinned at her. "Or Snake people. I'll leave it to your imagination to come up with an explanation for that last name."

She shuddered now, closing her eyes, thinking that Brett was a great deal like a savage. Feral. Uncivilized. Barbaric . . .

But if she studied Brett's other caustic remarks, his reminder that the French Revolution had hardly been gentle and civilized, nor had the ancient Romans, nor even the English in their retaliation against the Scots and the Irish, she had to reluctantly admit to herself that atrocities seemed to know no boundaries of nationality. Did she not recall the atrocities committed in India in the name of peace? British colonization had been extensive, but not without great cost to both sides, depredations committed by English and Indian alike.

Yes, she remembered the times of unrest, when Richard Wellesley—brother of Arthur Wellesley, the now famous duke of Wellington—used the British army to crush hostile local rulers in India, and used his diplomatic skills to bring friendly rulers under British influence. She may have been young, but she could well recall the dangers, and how Maman had been frightened for her daughter even though Papa Piers assured them that as

Dutch, they would be safe from both sides. Untrue, of course, but to a child it had been comforting.

Yet, perversely, she had felt compelled to point out to Brett that it was hardly fair to compare the French time of the Terror to the crude American natives who lived in hide huts and waged sporadic battles against civilized intruders. That, of course, had succeeded in angering him, and she had retreated into the one weapon she knew she could use successfully against him—silence.

It was that method of retaliation that seemed to provoke him most, and she used it sparingly to keep its edge sharp. She would need all the weapons she could muster to withstand the approaching storm. Here, until now—she'd felt safe and insulated from censure. Perhaps the first housekeeper had given notice because of her presence, but since then there had been not even a hint of disapproval.

But now Brett was gone, her buffer between the staff and herself, and she had experience with the hierarchy of the English service class, and how unforgiving they could be to those they considered to have fallen from the place that life had ascribed for them.

Lying there in the bed she shared with Brett, she waited until she heard the familiar clink and rattle of dishes and serving tray, and then the light scratching on the door to see if she was awake. Arranging the coverlet around her, she called permission to enter, and young Susan slipped in, balancing the tray in one hand and managing the door with the other.

"Good morning, Miss." It was said brightly,

with no sign of disrespect or disapproval, and accompanied by a smile as the dark-haired maid placed the tray on a table and began fussing with thick linen napkins and china cups. "Do you prefer coffee, then, Miss?"

"Yes. Please." Kyla rose from the bed and reached for a cotton wrapper that was miles too big so that she had to tie the sash around her waist twice, a relic from one of the armoires in the other wing, Brett had remarked with a careless shrug when she asked. Unwilling to spark another conversation about clothing, she'd let the matter drop, but saw now from Susan's quick glance that she must look as ridiculous as she felt. Holding out one voluminous sleeve, she said, "I fear that both my arms could fit in this."

Susan smiled, and bobbed a quick curtsy. "Yes, Miss, it does seem that way." She hesitated, then said, "I don't want to be bold, Miss, but my aunt is very clever with a needle and thread. Would you like for me to take it to her? She could alter it for you."

"Why yes, Susan, that would be very kind. And I will be happy to pay your aunt if she could manage some other alterations for me. My clothes— have not yet arrived, so I fear that I must make do with what is here."

"Yes, Miss. Lady Arabella is much larger than you, so I am not surprised that her clothes do not fit."

"Lady Arabella—the late duke's daughter?"

"Yes, Miss." Susan looked uncomfortable, as if expecting to be scolded. "She is very nice, though, and very pretty, but—taller."

Drawn by this minute piece of information

about her half sister, Kyla moved toward the young maid, accepting the cup of coffee she held out with a slightly trembling hand. She took a sip, eyeing Susan over the rim.

"You have met Lady Arabella, then. Tell me about her. Is she—nice?"

Susan looked puzzled, but reaffirmed her early comment with a quick nod. "Yes, Miss. Very pleasant. Not at all rude like *some* people can be. Oh, not that I mind it, for I don't. After all, I'm told that I chatter too much, and take too long to do my chores, and it's very true, it is, though I try not to—" She drew in a deep breath, and her cheeks flushed. "I'm running on again, Miss. Please forgive me."

"Of course." Kyla sat down in the small chair beside the table and picked idly at a soft white roll. A pot of Devonshire cream was on the tray, and a small platter of fruit. A light breakfast, as she preferred, with none of the heavier kippers, or kidneys and eggs that Tante Celeste now preferred. An English breakfast, she'd said, laughing a little ruefully, but quite delicious once one got past the notion of devouring so much food before one was properly dressed. Of course, Celeste was quite informal, and always took her morning meal in her room, deploring Kyla's preference for coffee as uncivilized.

As she spread a liberal portion of thick Devonshire cream on her roll, Kyla looked up at Susan again, smiling to put her at her ease, wondering how to go about finding out information about her half sisters without seeming too nosy or strange. It was a mystery to her why she even wanted to know anything, for it was quite obvious they cared little for her, but she could not resist.

So as she ate, she talked quietly to Susan, and little by little discovered small, human things about Arabella, Anne, Ailsa, and Anastasia. All with names beginning in A's, and very close in age, they had once come frequently to Ridgewood.

"But that was before their father died and the present duke inherited, of course," Susan confided. "La, for a time, it was whispered that Ridgewood would be sold and we would all be turned out to seek employment elsewhere, so I s'pose it could be said that the duke died just in the nick of time. Oh! I didn't mean no disrespect, Miss."

"Yes, Susan, I'm certain of that. Ridgewood is very fortunate that the present duke was able to save it from creditors."

Susan bobbed her head. It was said all over London that he had died to escape the dun. Apparently, her father was as incapable of managing his finances as he was his personal life. Drawing in a deep breath, Kyla asked casually, as if the answer did not matter, "Did you ever meet the late duke, Susan?"

"Oh, yes, Miss, several times."

"And what did you think of him?"

Shifting uncomfortably from one foot to the other, Susan looked like a trapped mouse as she stared down at the floor. "He were . . . he were a pleasant enough gentleman, Miss, but so quiet that—that sometimes he seemed not to be here at all." She looked up, frowning a little, her brown eyes serious and earnest with the desire to help. "I don't mean any disrespect, but once I heard someone say that he was a shell of his former self, whatever that may mean. It was not explained to me, and I did not dare ask."

When Kyla did not respond, but sat gazing into her empty coffee cup and thinking about the man who was her father, Susan must have misinterpreted her silence as disapproval, for she gave a soft little whimper and said that she had not meant to be so forward, and would the lady please forgive her?

Kyla looked up, a bit startled, and smiled. "You have not offended me, Susan. It's just that I've always heard about the former duke and never had the chance to meet him. I was only curious."

"Would you like to see a portrait of him, Miss? There is one in the east wing, in a room at the back that the duchess—dowager duchess—always used when she came. That was until the duke came here from America, though, and she stopped coming to Ridgewood."

"There is a portrait of him here?" Kyla's fingers shook slightly as she placed her coffee cup on the tray again, and she rose to her feet, pulling tightly at the sash until it felt as if her breath was cut off and her lungs ached for air. "Yes, Susan, I would like very much to see a portrait of him."

Eager to please, Susan led Kyla through the long, carpeted corridors, past huge rooms furnished with massive beds and heavy velvet hangings, past gilt-framed faces garbed in garments of long-past days gazing down at her from the walls. Had these people been her ancestors? Would she find any of herself in one of these solemn faces staring down at her from scenes of pale landscapes and draped backdrops? She was related, just as Brett was related, though his claim was far more distant than hers. How odd, that he could be related by a kinship removed several times by marriage yet inherit all of this, while the former owner had been her father and she owned nothing of it. Not so much as a hand mirror or china cup could she call hers, could she say that it belonged to her in any fashion other than as the present owner's mistress.

Bitter, bitter circumstances that rendered her now, an outsider in the home where once her father had walked, where he had slept, read, played cards—even enjoyed a pipe, perhaps, in the dark-paneled library filled with hundreds and hundreds of leather-bound volumes, and a huge globe of the world that could be spun in its stand by the slightest touch of a finger . . . had her mother ever come here? Had Faustine been allowed into these halls, or was the town home all that she had ever seen of her husband's life before it was so rudely and cruelly snatched away?

It seemed impossible. It seemed even more impossible that there had ever been laughter in these halls, or in any of the 342 rooms she'd been told comprised the house. All these rooms, furnished in heavy dark furniture with equally heavy draperies over the windows and shutting out the light—from the outside, the house was impressive, built of soft pink brick that took on the warmth of the sun. It was beautiful, not as remote or forbidding as Ashleigh, but closed in upon itself.

When Susan stopped in front of a narrow door, Kyla felt suddenly afraid, as if her father was alive and on the other side of the door, waiting to meet her for the first time—but he was not, of course, only his portrait, hanging from stout cord nailed high on the wall. She moved slowly to it, each step a shaky revelation as she studied the features of the man gazing down with a faint, sad smile. It was his eyes that caught her, for the artist had used that trick of perception that made it seem as if the painted eyes followed one around the room. But that was not what caught her attention most. The color of those eyes was an unusual shade of blue-green, so familiar and yet looking out from someone else's face, from a masculine face instead of her own. She stood there a moment, hand trembling upward, then stopping before actually touching the canvas.

How foolish. It would not be warm, though he looked alive, looked as if he might speak at any moment. What would he have said, she wondered, if she had known of him before he'd died, if she had come to meet him while he was still alive. Would he have acknowledged her? Would he have wept, perhaps, and greeted her with open, loving arms, or would he do as his wife and distant cousin had, and reject her with cold finality?

Her father—she wanted to continue hating him, for it was easier. But there was such sadness in that face, such an expression of remote poignancy, that she could not at this moment find it in herself to still hate him. Not even for what he had done to her mother.

"That were made while he was still youngish, Miss," Susan offered quietly. "He looked quite different when he died, for he'd been sick. He died in the house in town and we hadn't seen him since the summer."

"He died in the winter, then."

"Yes, Miss. On Boxing Day. I heard that those in the town house almost didn't get their boxes because of it, but at the last minute, old Reade recollected that the boxes had not been given out yet, and called everyone into the kitchen to just give them out real quick-like. My cousin Becky works in the city, is how I know that. She's a parlormaid, and tells me all sorts of interesting things on her holiday—but you don't want to hear about that, Miss."

"No, I don't mind it at all. It was a very interesting story, Susan." She slowly turned away from the portrait, but the image of her father's face remained burned into her mind, his solid features, familiar eyes, and sad expression a vivid reminder of what had been lost to her. Yes, this was about much more than money, or rights, or anything else. She had been cheated of a father, and of sisters. And it was too late to do anything about it, too late for everything. Now, even if she could manage to return to London, it was doubtful that her claim would earn much more than scornful laughter from a magistrate.

Honesty compelled her to admit to herself that the chances of success had always been small, but now she had not even her reputation to sustain her in failure. It was all taken away. For her, there was only one path left, the path Brett had set her on by bringing her to Ridgewood.

Sitting in the garden later that afternoon, holding a book loosely in her lap because she could not concentrate enough to comprehend what she had read, Kyla came to the conclusion that she would *have* to leave England. But where would she go? And how could she get there? Unless she truly did become as one of those women who went from man to man for protection, she had no future here. And that, she could not abide. No, she could not bear to think of how it would all end, how people would look at her, or how she would even look at herself in the mirror after a while. She would end up alone and forgotten, tucked away in some hovel with only the memory of a bright future to haunt her.

Spain. Or even France, now that Napoleon was once more in captivity and moved to Elba. It wasn't quite the same in France, where women took many lovers without the same taint of disapproval. Perhaps Tante Celeste would go with her, and they could live in the countryside, in a pleasant little château with vineyards basking in the sun, where it was beautiful and warm instead of cold and damp. And perhaps, if she accumulated enough money, even Papa Piers could come to stay with them if he liked, where it was almost as warm as in India. Yes, that would be nice, but only if Wolverton paid what he had promised. If she left now, he would not give her a single penny, as he had so bluntly told her.

Tilting back her head, she gazed up at the lacy twining of trees overhead, the tall stately oaks that had been here for a hundred years or more, shading the garden. Ornamental statues dotted the manicured grounds, and several fountains trickled water into stone pools and spewed it from spouts shaped like fish or mermaids, a light pattering that should have been soothing but was not.

What would it hurt now to fulfill the bargain she'd made with Brett? If rumor was correct, he did not keep a mistress for very long before replacing her. It should not be too hard to stay with him for the money, should it? After all, she had nothing else to lose, as she kept reminding herself over and over when she would forget and despair about what might have been. She was free, and she could go to France to live and be quite independent, taking lovers if she liked . . . or perhaps even a husband eventually.

But first she must put from her mind the injustice that had been done her, for it would avail nothing to dwell upon it. Nor would it help to think about the curious despair she felt when she looked at Brett sometimes, or why she felt that quivery anxiety every time he looked at her, and when he touched her, and how she dreamed of him at night on occasion, but always in a different way, as if he truly cared about her, as if he loved her. . . .

She closed her eyes, blotting out the leafy intercourse over her head, blocking everything from her mind but the soothing songs of birds and the faint patter of water in a nearby fountain. Flowers perfumed the air with elusive scents that she tried to identify . . . jasmine? No, it is too early yet in this climate, she thought idly. While the days are warmer, the nights are still chilly. Flowering privet, perhaps, with the waving clusters of tiny blooms that smell so sweet—

"Excuse me, Miss."

The deep voice jerked her from her pleasant reverie and she sat up straight, her book tumbling to the grass from her lap as she stared up at Godfrey. He towered over her, his dark visage expressionless. "Y-yes, what is it?"

If he noticed her nervousness—how could he not?—he did not comment, but bowed politely, and she noticed that he was wearing fawn-colored trousers, a white shirt, and brocade waistcoat, looking rather incongruous with his long hair tied in a single braid dangling down his back.

"Do you wish to take your tea out here in the garden, or do you prefer to come into the parlor, Miss?"

"I . . . in the parlor, thank you. Is it that late? I did not realize . . . it's such a pleasant day." The words tumbled from her lips much as Susan's had done that morning, unchecked and sounding foolish and nervous, but she could not halt them. "Unseasonably warm, I think, but then, I am not accustomed to English weather in the spring, are you?"

"This is my second spring here since I was a boy. I find it pretty, but rather damp compared to the seasons I am accustomed to at home."

"At home—you mean America."

He nodded, his black eyes absorbing sunlight as he gazed down at her, and despite his deferential manner, he seemed more like master than servant. "Yes. Of course, it is quite different, for we have vast, barren plains there, but there is a rainbow of colors even in the desert areas. I have seen a place with painted rocks that is quite lovely, and cactus, for all the sharp spines that jut out at every angle, have lovely flowers that blossom."

Some of her disquiet faded, and she rose to her feet, smoothing her skirts with one hand, accept-

ing the book he bent to pick up from the grass
when he held it out to her with a flourish. "Thank
you, Godfrey. I may call you that?"

"If you like."

"But it is not your real name, I think."

The suggestion of a smile tugged at one corner
of his chiseled mouth. "No, it is not."

"Would it be too terribly forward of me to ask
your real name?"

"No, but I doubt you could understand it if spoken in my native tongue."

"Ah, the language you used with Brett my first
night here."

His gaze sharpened a little when she stumbled
and flushed at the mention of her first night, but
he nodded. "Yes. *Isawura*—Crazy Bear, in English."

"Why did you change your name?"

"I attended school in England, along with Brett,
and my name was too difficult to master. So, they
Anglicized it, choosing for me a name that they
deemed more appropriate. I rather liked it, for the
root word is God, and always makes me think of
the good fathers who were so kind to me when I
was a very small child. Shall I escort you inside
now?"

She accepted the offer of his arm, feeling awkward alongside this giant of a man with a savage
face and genteel manners, yet found him to be
quite personable. He lingered in the parlor, and
they talked of India, for he said he had always
longed to visit the country and hunt the varied
beasts that inhabited it.

"I rather fancy the idea of riding atop an elephant and shooting at panthers from a gilded box

with a silk canopy like one of the Indian princes.
How odd, I've always thought it, that Columbus
mistook America for India. We haven't a single
elephant to boast of there, though we do have buffalo herds that can cover a plain from one horizon
to the next. Quite an impressive sight, but not as
amazing as elephants."

She laughed softly. Her first fear of him was
gone, dissolving under the influence of his easy
conversation and natural manner, so that she
quite forgot how fierce he'd looked that first night.
Of course, everything had seemed frightening
then, with all that had happened. But now she
was enjoying their conversation. Godfrey was
knowledgeable and amusing, and if not for his appearance, would have been at home in any London drawing room.

"Why aren't you in London?" she asked when
there was a lull in the conversation. "I would
think you would enjoy the galleries and muse-
ums."

"Yes, but I've seen them all."

"Do you remain here because you look—different?" She flushed, then shrugged with a light
laugh. "I hope I did not offend you, but you must
know that with your hair worn in that long braid
or even loose, you present quite a remarkable
sight."

He smiled. "When I was a boy, I wore my hair
in a more acceptable fashion, but now that I am a
man, I wear it in a fashion that pleases me. It reminds me of my homeland, and my family. Brett
does not care, so I do as I please even though it
causes much comment and some consternation
when I appear in public." He lifted his huge

shoulders in a light shrug. "It is more comfortable here, where I can go hunting in the woods, or camp out if I like, sleeping under the stars and listening to the wind's song through the trees."

"You sound as if you miss your home and family very much."

"My home, yes, but my family is all gone. I am the last of my father's house."

She drew a shawl around her, shivering a bit as the sun began to set and shadows seeped into the windows to darken the parlor. Lamps were being lit in the house, providing small pools of light.

"I know what it is like to be the last one left," she said after a moment. "My mother is dead, and I never knew my father."

"Edward Riverton." When she glanced up with wary surprise, he nodded slightly. "I know, of course. And even if I had not heard the talk, your eyes give it away. You have your father's eyes, Miss Van Vleet."

A lump lodged in her throat, and she looked away. How was it that he could so easily see it but Brett denied it? And the dowager duchess? Could they not recognize her resemblance to him? No, they *would* not recognize it. Therein lay the difference.

"Wednesday," Godfrey said casually, "I plan to ride. Do you ride, Miss Van Vleet?"

"Yes, of course. But won't the duke mind? I mean—" She paused, unwilling to say aloud that servants were hardly given free use of the stables, but Godfrey obviously understood her meaning, for he merely smiled and shook his head.

"Brett and I are companions. I do not attend him as a servant, but an equal. It is a long, involved story, and perhaps one day I will share it with you. Tomorrow, the dressmaker will arrive, and it is my understanding that she will have available for you some garments that need only a little fitting to be complete. That should suffice until the rest of what you order can be completed and delivered. I shall insist that a riding habit be among the first garments completed."

"Then I will be delighted to ride with you, sir, though I am not at all certain that the duke will be so glad."

"Brett will not remark upon it, as long as you are with me."

Bowing slightly, Godfrey murmured a farewell, and left her sitting in the parlor as the shadows deepened into dusk. A most enigmatic man. It occurred to her as she sat by the cheery fire and stared into the dancing flames, that Godfrey was much more civilized than the duke. How odd. Appearances were certainly deceiving in this case.

Celeste du Bois sat with knuckles white from strain as she clenched her hands in her lap. How *dare* he! Her lips were pressed together tightly to keep from bursting into indignant protest and vile recriminations.

The duke of Wolverton leaned with one elbow propped on the mantel, looking for all the world like a predatory tiger about to spring as he regarded his visitor with hostile eyes.

"Lady du Bois, as I have said, your goddaughter went with me of her own free will. I did not drag her kicking and screaming into my coach, no matter what you may have heard."

"One does not have to be forcibly thrust into a

situation to be reluctant, Your Grace. Surely, you see my point," Celeste returned stiffly. "I came here to ask for her safe return."

"Kyla is an adult. If she wishes to return to you, she may of course do so. I do not have her held prisoner." His eyes mocked her as he added in a drawl, "She has her own money, as we agreed upon, and her free will. If she chooses to leave my protection, she may do so at any time. Forfeiting of course, the remainder of the sum I offered. Still, a tidy amount would remain to her to do as she wished. Where is the problem?"

"The *problem*, Your Grace," Celeste said between her clenched teeth, "is in the incalculable loss done to Kyla by your . . . persuasion . . . of her to leave the ball with you."

"I see. It would have been more discreet for her to meet me in a clandestine manner. That did not suit me."

"So I see." Celeste waited a moment, choosing her words carefully. "Does your preference to make her new situation so public perchance have to do with her efforts to restore her mother's good name?"

"Her mother's name could not be whitewashed with all the paint in England, and you know it." His blunt retort took her aback, and his eyes narrowed slightly. "Faustine Auberge was a paid courtesan, and that is putting it nicely. What did you both expect? That I would allow myself to be blackmailed? Kyla is fortunate I find her attractive, or she would still be knocking on closed doors with her vain attempts to extort money."

Celeste drew in an angry breath and rose swiftly to her feet. "Your Grace, I find your remarks offensive. It should not be considered blackmail to attempt to right wrongs done so long ago. *Bon Dieu!* Has your life been so exemplary that you cannot find a small bit of sympathy in your heart for those whom life has treated unjustly? Do you not have your own regrets?"

"If I do, I would not be foolish enough to share them with the world, and especially not for financial gain."

He levered his lean frame away from the mantel, and Celeste thought again how dangerous he seemed at times despite his elegant clothes and exquisite town house with expensive furnishings. She was not easily intimidated, but there was something very intimidating about Breton Banning, she thought with a mixture of despair and defiance. Still, she did not retreat, but held his gaze coolly.

"You may say what you like, Your Grace, but Kyla is not the criminal you would like to paint her. No. She is young, and passionate about injustice, but not an extortionist. The money was never the main goal for her. For me, it was, for I know what it takes to live, but Kyla thought mostly of how her poor maman suffered. Your cousin was a wicked man, and you cannot deny that."

"I have no intention of denying it. I barely knew him, but am not naive enough to pretend he cultivated any of the more noble virtues. Yet his character was never in question. It was the validity of his marriage that is doubtful, and that is what I addressed." He frowned a little, staring down at her with his cool gray eyes, then said more gently, "I know you care deeply about Kyla. I have not hurt her. When we part, I will see that she has more money than she needs."

Celeste drew in an unhappy breath. "But you will not give her what she wants most, Your Grace. Before—this—she had a chance for happiness, for the husband, children, and quiet life that she has longed for so long. She wanted to fall in love, to marry. Now who will marry her? Certainly not any of the so-called *decent* gentlemen. Not after all that has happened. Now, she is doomed to be some man's mistress all her days. You took away from her the only chance she had for dignity and happiness, Your Grace. Once more, she has been robbed of her dreams."

"Then sending her back to you will hardly restore them." His voice was hard now, and his eyes cold, but there was a tiny flicker of muscle in his jaw that betrayed some reaction. Dare she hope it was regret?

"So you say, Your Grace. I had hoped to convince you to be honorable, but I see that it is of no use."

"My lady, it would not be very honorable to return her to you ruined and penniless. At least this way, she can salvage something."

Celeste met his gaze steadily, and took a deep breath. "Would you be honorable enough to wed her, Your Grace? To give her your name as protection and restitution?"

He looked first startled, then incredulous, and shook his head. "I do not intend to marry."

"Fah, all men marry, whether they intend it or not. How else will you leave heirs to inherit your name and title?"

"My Lady du Bois, it may surprise you to learn

that I don't care a fig for this title, and the name
is borrowed. I am here because my father wished
me to be, and I am honoring his last request. That
is the only reason I am in England at all."

"Yes, so I have heard." She smiled slightly. "But
do you think that because you do not wish to
marry, my goddaughter should be deprived of the
opportunity? That is what you have done to her."

"Regardless of what you may think, it was not
a decision arbitrarily foisted upon her. I admit I
did my best to test her limits. If she had desired,
she could have refused me at Lady Sefton's ball,
and gone her own way. She chose to go with me,
and the damage was done."

"I would be most interested in hearing Kyla's
version of this tale." Celeste tugged angrily at her
gloves. *Merde! He has an answer for everything, this
one,* she thought with frustration. *How can I help
Kyla if he will not admit to any fault in the matter?*

She eyed the duke with a frown. "I suppose it
would be unacceptable were I to call upon my
goddaughter at your country home, *n'est-ce pas?*"

Wolverton smiled slightly. He took her by the
arm and turned her toward the sitting room door,
an obvious invitation to depart and indication that
their interview was at an end. "You shall soon
have the opportunity to hear Kyla's version, Lady
du Bois, for I intend to bring her to London next
week. It is time to set rumors to rest that I have
abducted her and am holding her against her
will."

Celeste turned at the door, her slippers scraping
against the gleaming marble floors with a faint
whisking sound. "Your Grace, I hope for Kyla's

sake that you will not shame her any more than has been done."

"That, my lady, I shall leave up to her."

It was not the most auspicious of interviews, and Celeste fretted all the way home that Kyla might somehow do herself even more harm. She would write her at once, a long letter that would explain matters. But she must be careful, and not put in writing anything that the duke might find offensive should he chance to read it. It was almost too much to hope that he might have a fondness for Kyla, but not beyond the pale. Ah, if only matters in England were more like in France, where it was not so scandalous for a woman to have lovers. There, one's reputation was not ruined because of an indiscretion, but often enhanced.

But this was not France. And Kyla must find a way to lessen the damage done her by Wolverton. There had to be a way.

Part II

Ridgewood Manor, England
May 1816

Twelve

As *promised*, the dressmaker arrived, and in two days time had several outfits prepared. Kyla donned the riding habit of deep blue velvet and studied her reflection in the long oval mirror that swung in an oak stand in the corner. It fit perfectly. Snug at the bosom, the sleeves were long and fitted at the wrists of the short jacket, the skirt divided with folds of material that draped most becomingly to her ankles. A white blouse boasted froths of lace at the throat, and she had ordered boots and a hat from the cobbler and milliner as well, so that all was delivered within the same space of hours.

Brett had still not returned from London, and Kyla tried not to think what he might be doing there as she met Godfrey on the front steps for their scheduled ride. It was still very early in the morning, and the dew was heavy on the newly greening blades of grass, sparkling like glittery stars on an emerald carpet. There was a fresh smell to the air, and she breathed in deeply, smiling up at Godfrey when he offered her his arm again.

"The servants will begin to talk, sir," she said with a soft laugh, and he grinned.

"That should give Brett something to think about when he returns. Perhaps he'll reconsider lingering in the city when he has a beautiful woman waiting on him here."

No mention was ever made of her true status in the house, and she was grateful. Whether it was Brett's influence or Godfrey's, not a single servant had shown her any disrespect or disapproval since Mrs. Wilson had resigned her position as housekeeper.

Soon they were mounted on beautiful, spirited horses, and loping along the wooded ridge behind the stable. Thick woods stretched a great distance, with winding paths at the very edge and patches of meadows bright with color beneath a blue sky boiling with puffy clouds skimming before the wind. They started off at a brisk pace, then slowed to a walk to rest the winded horses, ambling along a narrow track that led into the forest.

Godfrey rode as if he were part of the horse, his long muscular legs clamped around the horse's sides and disdaining saddle or stirrups. Kyla used a saddle, of course, and balanced with one leg hooked over the horn on the side and her other foot in the stirrups. She was rather envious of Godfrey's freedom, and told him so.

He laughed. "At home, the women ride as we do. It is more practical. Of course, they learn to ride when they are only small children."

"It sounds very different from what I had imagined. In India, where I spent so much of my childhood, there are extreme differences in classes, or castes. Those that are not members of one of the four castes are treated as if they simply do not exist. They are called the *untouchables*, and are considered unclean."

"Only four castes? In America, there are many different castes, only they are referred to as tribes. I am from the Comanche, but even then, we have different tribes within the main body of people. Some are from different areas, with different rules, and warring clans. Four castes sound so limited."

"Oh no, those are just the four main castes. Let's see, the *Brahmins*, or priestly class, *Kshatriyas*, or warrior class, *Vaisyas*, the merchant class, and *Sudras*, who are the laboring class. Of these, there are several thousand different castes and subcastes, based on occupations. Yet it is the family that has the strongest influence in India, for they are very large and tight-knit, and always ruled by the oldest male member. I found it all quite intriguing."

"So it sounds. Perhaps you will come to America one day. I think you would like it there. There is not the same spirit of clannish rules as in so many places, and there it is far easier to be judged by your actions rather than how you were born or the size of your fortune, once you are far enough away from what some refer to as civilization. Of course, there are always those people who want to judge others by their own set of rules, as anywhere else."

Kyla toyed with the ends of her leather reins, frowning. The wind was brisk, and the ride had chilled her face so that it felt chapped. She looked up at Godfrey, but he was staring ahead of them, his posture straight and his eyes intent. When she started to speak, he held up a hand and motioned her to silence.

Just when she began to feel the first nervous prickings of fear, Godfrey turned to her with a slight smile. "There is a treat in store for you, if you are adventurous enough to brave it. Are you?"

Uncertain, but confident that he would not risk danger with her, she nodded after a moment. "Of course. Is it as adventurous as riding elephants?"

"Almost." Godfrey laughed. "But probably less exotic and more dangerous. Come along, then."

She followed him, a little apprehensive as they rode deeper into the wooded shadows. Birds twittered and chirped, and the rhythm of the horses was a comforting sound. Then she heard the faint strains of music, an odd sort of tune, lively and exotic, sounding like nothing she had ever heard.

The acrid tang of smoke drifted toward her before she ever saw anything, and when a man suddenly appeared on the path ahead of them, garbed in rainbow colors and armed to the teeth, she bit back a sudden scream, reining in her mount so as not to ride him down. He was swarthy and grinning, and must have recognized Godfrey, for he greeted him in an unfamiliar language that sounded vaguely like Spanish.

Then his eyes moved to her and sparked with interest. He affected a deep bow, and said in thickly accented English, "Welcome, beautiful lady."

She glanced uncertainly at Godfrey, who seemed more amused by the man than anything else. His deep voice was calm. "You are a rogue, Giovanni. Better not make eyes at this one, for she belongs to Wolverton."

Giovanni heaved a great, theatrical sigh. "Always, the angels are taken before I am allowed the privilege of viewing them. Very well, come, both of you, for we have hot stew in a pot and good wine. And little Sanchia has missed you since the last time, eh?"

With a sly grin and waggle of his head, Giovanni disappeared into a clump of bushes at the edge of the track, and Kyla glanced again at Godfrey. "I know the way," he said. "They always camp at the same spot when they come this way."

When they rode into the camp, Kyla realized that these were gypsies. She had heard of them, but never seen any, and found them fascinating. The women wore brightly colored skirts and blouses, and huge earrings and colorful scarves of every hue. The men were just as striking, all dark and swarthy, most with huge mustaches. They wore multicolored loose trousers of varied patterns, stripes or plaids, or odd designs, and for the most part, shirts with blousing sleeves and open collars, covered by short vests. They all looked very exotic and as romantic as their women.

Several fires dotted the grounds, and children ran squealing about, chasing each other or small barking dogs. Someone was playing music, a rather wild, tempestuous tune.

Godfrey helped Kyla down from her mount and one of the men came up to take it, winking when Godfrey told him he expected the same animal back when he was ready to leave.

"Are they gypsies?" Kyla whispered, and Godfrey nodded.

"Spanish gypsies, or Romany. Once a year they pass this way, and Brett has always looked the other way and not run them off as so many do.

As long as they are well behaved and do no harm, he does not care if they avail themselves of some wild game and a place to rest for a week or two. They always move on, leaving it clean and unmolested. If they steal, they do not steal here."

Kyla looked around her with uncertainty reflected on her lovely face, and Godfrey thought that, at that moment, she looked very young and innocent. What could Brett have been thinking, to take her like he had? It would come to no good, but he'd told him that. Brett's succinct response was a brutal assessment of Kyla's character. Yet somehow, Godfrey could not think that this girl was as Brett thought her—a cold, calculating female who cared more about money than honesty. It didn't fit with what he'd noticed about her in the past week. She made him think of a hesitant doe at times, with a mixture of daring and fear that held no hint of docility. A most interesting young lady, this Kyla Van Vleet, and not one that Brett could use as he had others more willing to trade their bodies for a handful of trinkets or a cottage in the Midlands.

Godfrey put out a hand to Kyla and she took it, her gloved fingers small and trusting in his palm as she allowed him to lead her across the clearing to where a fire burned brightly. Several hares were dressed and roasting, and there were two pheasants plucked and sizzling on spits over the open flames. A huge cauldron, emitting delicious odors that smelled of wild onions and rich gravy, hung over one fire.

Coming close, Giovanni nudged him with an elbow, indicating the cauldron with a grin and wag of his head. "Why is it, my learned friend, that poached meat always tastes best?"

"The spice of danger, I would think in your case. You are a madman, of course. On anyone else's land, you would be burned out and hung from the nearest tree as a macabre fruit to warn other thieves."

"Ah, but you see where we camp...." Giovanni spread out his arm in an expansive gesture. "Wolverton's land, where a man can be independent and not be prosecuted for it."

"Yes. Though it's unlikely it will do any good, I must point out that you had no idea you would not be prosecuted until a very unpleasant interview with the duke last year. I remember it quite well. It was only the duke's sympathy that saved you from a swift end, you know."

"And I thought it was my wit and charm, *señor*. Ah, but this lady you have with you, she has made Sanchia very jealous, you know, with her beauty. Is she the duke's wife?"

Slipping into Giovanni's dialect, Godfrey informed him that she was under Brett's protection. "So I would not advise you to cast covetous eyes in her direction lest you wear out your welcome here much more swiftly than you would like."

"A pity." Giovanni sighed, but his dark eyes were alight with appreciation when he gazed at Kyla. "Perhaps she would enjoy our singing and dancing for a while, heh?"

"I cannot speak for the young lady, but I always appreciate your revelry."

Kyla seemed interested in the rather chaotic activity around them, and accepted with surprising eagerness his suggestion that they linger a while. "Yes, I would love it. I have never really *met* any gypsies, you know," she confided softly, "so I find this all most intriguing and exciting."

Godfrey seated her on a wood and cloth stool close to the fire and took a stance next to her, observing as the handsome young men of the group took especial interest in their lovely visitor. Several of the younger men vied to present her with the choicest morsels from the cauldron or the spit, elbowing each other with mostly good-natured competitiveness. Kyla sat like visiting royalty, accepting gravely the offerings she received as he watched over her.

Some of the men and women began to dance eventually, and the familiar wild music of Spanish peasants filled the air. Golden bracelets jingled, and bare feet stamped in the dirt around the campfire as multicolored skirts whirled and lean young men beat their boots to the tempestuous rhythm. Kyla watched, her gaze rapt as the music soared in the sun-dappled glen.

A nudge in his back made Godfrey turn, and Sanchia stood behind him. She gazed up with brown eyes that flashed in anger. "So, this is your new love? A woman who pretends she is a lady? I thought you said you preferred fire to ice, *mi puto!*"

Catching her hand, he smiled a little at Sanchia's obvious rage and jealousy. "*Gatita*, do not leap to conclusions, for often it is an exercise in futility."

"Speak plainly, *rojo!*"

Amusement tugged at the corners of his mouth more strongly, and Godfrey held Sanchia's hand tighter when he saw Kyla half turn to glance at them curiously. "You are creating a scene, *gatita*. This is not my woman."

"No?" Sanchia cast a brief, scathing glance of doubt at Kyla's averted head. "Yet you bring her here, where none but you come—you have never brought a woman here, never!"

"Precisely my point." He pulled gently, and Sanchia moved closer to him, some of her rage dissolving into a pout that told him she was willing to be coaxed from her anger. "If I have never brought a woman here, why would I do so now? She is Brett's woman, and he is gone, so I thought when I saw you were back, that it might interest her to meet you. And, I admit, I longed to see if a certain fiery-eyed little cat would still be with Giovanni, or if she had perhaps married and gotten fat in the past six months."

His teasing cajoled her out of her sulks into a smiling temptress again, but still Sanchia cast a dubious glance over her shoulder. "She is milk-faced and too pale, as interesting as cooked cabbage."

"All women pale in comparison to you, my fiery beauty."

Sanchia's smile was genuine now, and she lifted to her toes to press kisses along his jawline. "It has been too long, *querido* . . . come with me now."

"I cannot leave her. Later this evening, I will return once she is safely back in Ridgewood."

The beginning of a pout pursed Sanchia's red, ripe lips, and when she turned her head to look at Kyla again, the tiny bells that formed her dangling earrings danced and jangled. "Then perhaps we can amuse her while she is here, and she will not miss you so much, yes?"

Before Godfrey could stop her, Sanchia wrenched free of his light clasp and planted herself in front of Kyla, hands on her hips and her bright, patterned skirt swirling around her bare legs. "I am Sanchia," she announced. "We have good food here, and good music. Do you dance?"

"Why . . . yes, of course. But not as they are dancing."

"It is easy. Come. I will show you."

Sanchia pulled Kyla unceremoniously to her feet, then took a step back to gaze at her critically. "Your clothes will not do—you must wear something that moves with you, no? Come along, for I have something that will fit."

"Sanchia." Godfrey moved forward, frowning. "I do not think it would be wise to involve her so quickly."

"Involve her in what? A dance? Pooh, you have become an old woman since last I saw you. It is a dance, and nothing else. And she looks so bored just sitting there—you would like to dance with us, would you not, *señorita*? Ah, I thought you would. . . ." Sanchia kept her hand on Kyla's arm, urging her along toward one of the painted wagons that served as shelter. "We are close to the same size, I think, but you are a bit more . . . supply? Equip? Ah, the word does not come to me, but I have a blouse that should still fit you. . . ."

Kyla cast a helpless glance at Godfrey, but there was no fear or resentment, only a kind of amused tolerance in her eyes that made him hold his tongue. Perhaps this would be just the thing to distract her from Brett's indifference and absence. And it might be just what was needed to give her back the spirit that he knew existed in her, instead of her mute acceptance of whatever Brett did and said. If she did not show him her claws, he would never respect her. He knew Brett, knew that meek, mindless females were soon discarded with little more than a handful of baubles for their time.

Somehow, he felt that Kyla Van Vleet was different. The Spirits had shown him another path for Brett, not that his friend fully believed in those things though he gave them lip service. No, Brett was not a true believer in the Old Ways. But he was, and he had read in the smoke and dreams that this girl was entwined in their future, that she was a bridge between two cultures. He did not understand it all, but he was not meant to know everything. It would all be shown in time.

In a few minutes, Sanchia returned with Kyla in tow, and Godfrey had to stare at the transformation. She looked like a golden gypsy, with bare legs and flowering skirt, her hair loose and tumbling around her shoulders in a seductive spill of gilded silk. . . . Godfrey straightened, suddenly wary of what he might have allowed.

The music paused, and it grew still, with the laughing chatter of children all that broke the sudden quiet as the adults turned to gaze at Kyla. She looked uncertain, lovely and untried, standing with her chin lifted in a gesture of shy defiance, gazing back at those staring at her.

Lifting one hand in a clattering jangle, she smiled. "Do I look like one of the Romany now?"

Sanchia laughed aloud, but there was a note of honest appreciation in her husky voice when she said, "You are far more lovely than I had thought you would be. I think I shall watch you very closely, *niña*."

Yes, Godfrey thought ruefully, *it may be necessary to keep a close eye on her, after all.* . . .

Apparently, he was not the only man there with that thought, for three of the young men rushed her at once, all clamoring to be her partner. Before he could intervene, Sanchia took charge, and announced tartly that they sounded like geese gabbling, and to move away "Before I take out my sharp little knife and prick you so, heh? Now come with me, Kyla—I may call you that, yes? Good. I shall show you a few steps, then *I* will choose your partner for you, so that you will not be bothered with silly boys who stumble over your feet—you should not wear shoes, of course, but I do understand that you are not accustomed to the ground as we are, so—move away, Marío!"

With a threatening gesture at the impatient young man crowding them, Sanchia led Kyla to the center of the camp, where dirt had been packed down hard and boards laid atop to form a floor of sorts, smooth and worn by hundreds of feet over the years. Sanchia herself was a marvelous dancer, supple and sensuous, her timing perfect, and she started off slowly, leading Kyla, teasing her a little at her first clumsy efforts, then picking up the rhythm.

Guitar and fiddle began, with a single horn as accompaniment, playing the old dances of Spain, the peasant dances that were unrestrained and joyous. Sanchia danced the way the music intended, with abandon and grace, soon forgetting her pupil in her involvement in the dance, and Godfrey recalled again why he found her so fascinating. Long black hair whipped about her dusky face, and her sloe eyes gleamed with alternate lights of passion and invitation, of taunting promise and teasing rejection, until every man there felt as if she spoke to him with her lithe body and graceful gestures.

Faster and faster she whirled, until her skin glistened with dewy moisture and her black hair stuck to her damp cheeks, until the music rose to a final crescendo and peaked, ending with a flourish as did Sanchia, going to one knee and bowing so that her hair fell about her face to drape on the wooden platform. Kyla clapped enthusiastically with the others amid the shouts of *"Olé"* and flung scraps of bright cloth and a few flowers.

"Marvelous," she enthused, her blue-green eyes alight as she turned to smile at Godfrey, "simply beautiful! I have never seen such grace and spirit combined in dance."

Obviously preening at the unabashed praise heaped on her by the girl she had considered a rival, Sanchia abandoned her first resentment and coaxed Kyla to the floor again, this time taking real effort to teach her the steps. Godfrey felt stirrings of disquiet at the quickness of her pupil, for Kyla watched intently for only a moment before picking it up, mimicking almost perfectly Sanchia's steps. The music began again, slower this time as Kyla found her rhythm.

Sanchia had chosen the flamenco, urging her to improvise if she wished, but above all to "Dance with your heart instead of your feet . . . as if you dance for your lover, no? *Sí*, that is how it is done, *niña.* . . ."

And indeed, Kyla performed well. Her feet moved over the boards with precision at first, the slow-bending curve of her body an innocent posture, her arms at her sides and her fingers snapping with indolent rhythm, until as the music began to quicken, so did her feet, toes to heels to toes again, a quick snapping of her feet and graceful twist of her body until she began to blossom before their eyes from a neophyte to virtuoso.

Spellbound, by her beauty as much as her performance, Godfrey found himself watching her as if he had never before seen her. Where was that shy, reserved girl he had observed in the garden primly reading a book and picking bright blossoms? Gone forever, it seemed at the moment, absorbed into the sensuous, seductive woman before them, tossing her hair, holding out her arms, eyes and parted lips gleaming and teasing, a faint mysterious smile curving her mouth and beckoning to an invisible lover to join her . . . sunlight had grown thin and low, and torchlight and firelight gleamed in the gold lushness of her hair as she tossed her head, her eyes a smoldering invitation beneath the tangled strands.

Faster and faster the music swirled, and so did Kyla, and one of the young men joined her, his lean body a counterpoint to her slender loveliness, his movements timed to match hers perfectly as they alternately invited and rejected with eyes and steps, heels clicking against the wooden floor. Turning, swaying, moving close then far apart, they danced as if only for each other, faces intent and glistening.

Godfrey watched with conflicted emotions, admiring and dismayed at the same time. It was just as well that Brett was in London. This was not something he would understand, for he wasn't at all certain he understood it himself. From the chrysalis had emerged a butterfly of startling dimension, spreading her wings for what seemed the first time, as breathtaking as the Creation.

Caught up in the spectacle, Godfrey turned only when he heard a familiar, drawling voice behind him, and saw with a sense of fatalism Brett Banning leaning against a slender oak with his arms crossed over his chest, watching Kyla and the young man dance. After a moment, his eyes moved to Godfrey and his brow quirked up in that cynical way he had, the manner that always indicated extreme irritation.

"What a lovely sight, if a bit surprising, to find my expensive mistress in the arms of another man."

It was just the sort of comment Brett would make, designed to provoke response, and Godfrey waited with grim resignation for the results.

Thirteen

At first, Kyla did not know why her partner came to a sudden stop, or why the music crashed to a discordant finish. Her blood thundered in her ears so loudly she could hear little else. She stood panting for breath and damp with perspiration despite the cool breeze in the shadowed woods, a little puzzled. It wasn't until she glanced around and saw Brett that she understood, and knew from the sardonic curl of his mouth that though he stood there with surface calm and mocking amusement, that he was really quite angry.

It was something of a surprise, therefore, to see her partner move from her angrily, his eyes flashing as he ignored Giovanni's attempt to stop him as he approached Brett. "It was only a dance, *señor*. Surely, you do not begrudge a dance, or is it that you fear you will lose her?"

Brett looked amused. "Do not flatter yourself. A woman like this one has no intention of deserting money for love—or even lust."

His crude assessment of her brought heat to her already flushed face, and Kyla curled her hands into fists at her sides. How dare he! But of course, he dared what he liked, for was he not the owner of these lands? Yes, and he could send these gypsies fleeing for safety in the night if he wished, or even hang them, for no English magistrate would lift a finger to stop him. After all, they were considered a scourge in the land, and though it might not be a completely undeserved judgment, nothing had been done to warrant retaliation in this case.

With a low hiss of anger, the young gypsy started toward Brett, but a sharp warning word from Giovanni stopped him before he'd gone more than a step. Brett looked only mildly amused at the young man's reaction, but Kyla noted a tense wariness about his posture that was ominous.

"Your Grace," she began, and at a swift dark glance from him, steadied her racing heart with an effort, "I trust you have not misunderstood."

"Is there something to misunderstand, trinket?" His soft drawl and amused curl of his lips did not soften the underlying menace in his tone. "Don't tell me—you have a sordid confession to make."

"Don't be idiotic." She caught back the rest of the words on the tip of her tongue. It would be unfair to risk the gypsies when, after all, no one had done anything wrong. Brett was quite capable of misunderstanding deliberately, for hadn't he chosen to do so with her? Oh yes, and was incapable of seeing past his own assessment to any sort of truth that might lie beneath the misconceptions.

Managing a smile that felt stiff on her lips, she lifted her shoulders in a light shrug. "I was merely dancing."

"I could see that, trinket."

More sharply than she intended, she snapped, "Don't call me that!"

"What—trinket?" He levered his long body away from the tree trunk behind him, moving toward her with a casual, graceful stride, a threat and a promise in exquisitely cut clothes, making her think again of a prowling panther. He caught her by the wrist and lifted her hand to his mouth, his lips cool against her heated skin as he pressed them against the back of her hand. "It is an endearment only. Does it annoy you?"

Feeling slightly foolish, she jerked her head in a short nod. Everyone was staring at them, or had been, for when he turned his attention away from the young man who had been her partner, some of the tension eased and they began to drift cautiously away. Godfrey, she noted from one corner of her eye, remained still and silent while Brett spoke.

"But why does it annoy you to be called trinket? There are other, probably more suitable and less flattering names that I could use, but trinket seems so innocuous."

She snatched her hand away. "I am not a trinket; therefore, I do not care to be regarded as one, or called by that name."

"Ah, but you are mistaken." Brett took her by the arm, and walked her away from the small clearing that was lit by late-afternoon light and campfires, past Giovanni and a garishly painted wagon with huge wheels, taking her toward the growing shadows beyond the camp. She noted a new horse, slightly lathered, waiting patiently, and was not surprised when he steered her in that direction. He turned her, pushing her back so that her spine was pressed against the heaving, damp sides of the animal, and the derision in his eyes was easily visible in the diminished light.

"Trinket is a pretty bauble, an ornament or a trifle of meager value—a trinket is you, Kyla. Lovely, decorative, and easily replaced." His finger drew along the slope of her cheek down to her angrily quivering lips to trace them with an idle caress. "So you see, it is an apt name."

She knocked his hand away from her face with the side of her arm. Drawing in a choked breath, she hissed at him, "Curse you!"

"I've been cursed for many years, trinket. You are not, alas, the first to heap more abuse on my head. Now come along, for it grows late and it will soon be too dark to see the path."

Without giving her a chance to refuse, or to coolly walk away as she longed to do, he lifted her with both hands around her waist and flung her up onto the back of his horse. By the time she regained her balance, he was mounted behind her, and reached around to take up the reins. Kyla pushed at the loose hair in her eyes, hardly mollified to see Godfrey watching them from only a short distance away. She stared at him with faint hope.

"Godfrey—"

"I shall see you both at the house, Miss Van Vleet."

It was a rejection and a symbolic washing of his hands, and Kyla recoiled. She had thought, briefly, that the tall, voluble man who had frightened her at first, might become a friendly presence in her days. It was obvious she was quite mistaken.

Godfrey said something to Brett then, in that strange language they shared that she thought must be Comanche, and Brett's reply was sharp and guttural, sounding more like a snarl than a complicated dialect. Then he turned the horse down the path that wound through the trees, while slender saplings like twisted figures loomed at the narrow sides, not friendly as they had been before, but menacing now. Kyla was far too conscious of Brett so close to her, of the heat of his body against her and his gaze lingering on her thighs revealed beneath the short hem of the gypsy skirt she wore. God, her clothes, left behind in the huge wooden wagon that smelled of spices and smoke, while she was garbed now in this short flowing skirt and thin blouse that barely covered her.

For a moment she saw herself as he must have seen her, clad in a cotton blouse gathered at the neck with a drawstring to allow it to ride loosely on her shoulders, the thin skirt that moved with her every step, and of course, no undergarments, save for her boots and stockings. Yes, it was possible to think her provocatively clad, but cold logic had no place in such suspicions. Would she have been foolish enough to flirt under the very nose of Godfrey? It hardly seemed likely, yet Brett obviously found it feasible. Or perhaps he was just using her actions as an excuse to be angry, to take out some other frustration on her.

She began to think she must be right, for there was a tightness to his movements that betrayed him. Long shadows stretched across the path, dissected ahead of them by a wide swath of mellow afternoon sunlight. She squinted when they rode into the warmer light, blinking a little at the brightness after being in shadow. His voice was mocking when she tilted her head away from the glare and tugged at her skirt.

"Too late for modesty now, trinket."

She yanked at the reins, but his hands tightened so that her efforts to wrest free were futile. She glared at him, angry that he was being so stubborn and contrary. "Let go of me!"

"No."

His arms were like iron bands around her middle, cutting off her breath until she stopped struggling and managed a careless shrug. "How brutish. I suppose it makes you feel superior to behave like an animal."

"After eight days of learning intriguing information about you, trinket, I already felt superior."

There was a raw edge to his tone that warned her it wasn't just finding her dancing that angered him, and she retreated into cautious silence. Until she knew exactly *why* he was so angry, she had no intention of antagonizing him with futile resistance.

The soft breeze of earlier had grown quite cool with the lowering of the sun, and Kyla's thin blouse and skirt and bare legs were no protection. She shivered, and he laughed softly.

"Coward. Have you no curiosity? Don't you even want to know what I've learned about you? Or do you already know, *querida*? Of course, you must. Why else would you be so sullen and silent?"

"I prefer to think of it as being mysterious."

Her cool reply seemed to take him aback, and after a startled instant of silence, he laughed again, not meanly this time, but with real amusement. She stared down at his hand in front of her, so dark in contrast to a spill of white shirt cuff beneath his jacket. Capable hands. Strong hands. A man's hands, not like those of so many Englishmen that were pale, with long slender fingers and smooth as a girl's. *There is something,* she thought, *so telling about a man's hands. It is indicative of his nature, perhaps. Soft hands, soft life—harsh hands, harsh life. But is that true of Brett?*

It certainly did not seem so, for he was wealthy, one of the aristocrats despite having lived so many years abroad. If he was regarded as an outsider in some ways, he was definitely included in the most important customs. Not like she was, a pariah, excluded from everything, even marriage.

"What a nimble tongue you have, *querida,*" he murmured in her ear, his breath warm against her cheek and sending another shiver down her spine. In response, he tightened his arms around her even more, as if to warm her. "You should be dressed more appropriately. I know the dressmaker has arrived by now. Where are your proper clothes?"

"I . . . Sanchia insisted that I could not dance in my riding habit, and loaned me her garments." It sounded silly said aloud, but he did not laugh at her, merely shrugged in displeasure.

"If you persist in trading expensive velvets for cheap calico, I'll be forced to allow you another protector much sooner than I planned."

Irritated, not so much by his words as his casual assumption that she would willingly acquire another man as protector, she turned sharply in his arms to glare at him.

Late-afternoon sun glinted in his eyes, caught in the gray opacity by a trick of light and mirrored like twin flames that reminded her of a wolf's yellow stare. Just now, with his dark visage struck by sunlight and his mouth curled into a faint snarl, he looked far too dangerous and feral to provoke, so she settled for a curt, "I resent your implication, sir."

"The implication that you need more than one healthy purse to afford you? Beautiful women have rarely come cheaply, even novices. I have my limits."

"Then I am to understand that you would not mind if I were to look elsewhere. How convenient. Perhaps you can point out the most affluent to me, so that I will not waste my time with those men who can afford only to look instead of touch, Your Grace. It would, after all, save all of us so much more inconvenience, don't you think?"

"What I think is that you don't give a damn for convenience, *querida*. If you did, you would not have been showing off your charms so blatantly in the woods to men who can offer you only a quick tumble in the weeds. Am I to understand that you have gone from virgin to venality so quickly?"

"Ooh! You horrid beast—stop this horse and put me down at once. As if a man like you could comprehend innocence! I refuse to go another step with anyone as despicable as you, or to allow—"

His arm tightened again, this time cutting off her flow of angry words and her breath, squeezing against her rib cage with threatening force. "Enough."

The one word was said softly, but the underlying menace was loud enough to curtail her rage and remind her that if she was to overcome this predicament, she must tread carefully. She took a deep breath when he relaxed his grip, and clenched her bottom lip between her teeth.

Brett's laugh was a harsh gust of sound that was hot against the back of her neck and her cheek. "You can still be roused to a temper, I see. And just when I'd begun to think you'd forgotten how to be a hissing little cat."

"Had you? Dear me, I find it so awkward to admit that I had not forgotten for a moment how insufferable you can be."

"Careful, princess—You might be starting something you can't handle."

"You're the one who started all this, Brett Banning! You might claim that you don't like being here and that you don't want to be a duke, but your actions are contrary to such empty claims. You're a fraud—a cheat." She squirmed in his increasing grip, almost breathless from anger and his tight hold, but managed to turn enough to face him.

He was staring at her coldly, his jaw clenched tightly so that a muscle leaped beneath his dark skin. Who was he really, she wondered with a tinge of curiosity coloring her anger. He puzzled her as much as he enraged her. In the past weeks she had grown almost as familiar with his body as she was with her own, and yet she knew so little about him, about what he really wanted, and why he stayed in England if he wanted so badly to return to America. It was more than marrying off his cousins. She knew that. Brett Banning was not the kind of man to care about that sort of thing. He would let the dowager duchess handle the details, and stay out of it. So why was he still here?

Instead of asking him, she said crossly, "Must we ride so fast? You should have let me get my horse—"

"So it sounds."

She might have thought of something else cutting to say, some remark that would reveal the depth of her contempt for him, but he nudged his mount into a faster pace so that anything she might say would only come out in disjointed sentences because of the jogging of the horse. It was annoying enough that he thought so little of her, had come to drag her away from Godfrey as if she was a willful wanton, but he had been gone over a week and all he could drag up to tax her with was what could only be stale information. He knew everything about her, knew almost everything about Faustine. It was no secret that his barristers had been ferreting out information ever since she had first contacted them, so what else could he have discovered that was so dreadful?

There was nothing, of course. It was only his grating habit of throwing out snide comments meant to hurt her, for whatever reason he had. It was as if he blamed her for his abduction of her from Lady Sefton's ball. But didn't she have good reason to want what should be hers? From what she had seen of Brett Banning, he was certainly the kind of man who would go after what he considered his. It should be no different for her just because she was a woman.

It was almost too tempting to tell him that, and she held hard to her resolve to be cool and composed even after they arrived at the house and he nearly flung her from the horse at the front doors, telling her shortly, "Go inside and wait for me."

Oh yes, it was so tempting to say something rude, a crass vulgarity such as she'd overheard the servants make to one another. "Stubble it!" would feel so good on the tip of her tongue right now. It was probably the only thing a man like Brett would really understand, but unfortunately, it would put her on the level he already thought her, and she needed to keep reminding him with icy reserve that she was *not* one of those women!

Yet as she ascended the steps with as much dignity as she could muster, ignoring the wide, curious gazes from Mrs. Lynch and even Susan, she could not ignore the niggling worry that perhaps she really was one of those women. Perhaps not by choice, but certainly by circumstances. Oh God, was this something she would always have to contend with, this *judgment* directed at her? *No wonder poor Maman had fled England. Life as an indentured servant must have looked preferable to suffering the shame of scorn from those who had once been her friends.*

The calico skirt fluttered around her calves as she passed the marble statues in the entrance hall and mounted the wide staircase, her spine stiff and straight as if returning to the house in such odd garments was normal. Once, Tante Celeste had remarked that a lady could get by with almost anything as long as it was done with elegance. It was not as true as she might wish it to be.

But that did not mean she would allow Brett

Banning to intimidate her more than was necessary to survive. He might be the duke of Wolverton, but she had her pride and her limits.

When he returned, she was sitting at the small dressing table brushing her hair, and looked up, her eyes meeting his in the mirror facing her. She tugged the brush through her loose hair in a leisurely glide, listening to the strands crackle in her hands like fine silk, curling wantonly around her fingers. She focused on her hair instead of his face. Why must he look at her so? So—coldly? It made her uneasy, and she had to keep the upper hand, had to retain her self-control and composure. It was all that was holding her together right now, for she felt as fragile as an empty eggshell.

He came toward her, moving quietly across the thick carpet with the smooth, catlike tread that made her so nervous. Damn him, he was *trying* to fluster her. Well, she would not let him. No, she would feign indifference, no matter what he said.

Yet it was not so easy, not when he caught her eyes finally, a strange expression on his face as he drawled in that soft, husky voice, "You should have told me about Lord Brakefield, Kyla."

She stared at his mirrored reflection stupidly. "Lord Brakefield?"

Her clumsy echo was hardly from her mouth before his hand closed with casual cruelty in her hair, tugging her head slowly backward so that she was forced to look at him instead of his reflection.

"Yes, Lord Brakefield. Earl of Northwick. Or are you pretending you don't know what I'm talking about? Christ. Do you think it wouldn't have made a difference?"

There was a savage undertone to his words that warned her how deeply affected he was by this information, though she was still mystified. "I recall being introduced to Lord Brakefield at Lady Sefton's, but I am certain I do not know how this can possibly affect me now."

Brett's fingers wound tightly around a long strand of her hair. It brought her head back even more, baring her throat to his caressing hand, to fingers that were so rough textured, and at this moment, inexplicably gentle. "You should have told me, Kyla."

"Really, Brett, I have no idea what you are talking about. Told you what? That I found Lord Brakefield to be a rather unsettling man with gooseberry eyes and a ravaged face? That is the truth of the matter, though I cannot imagine why you seem to think there should have been any conversation about him between us."

"Perhaps not, but it would have been less surprising to hear from you about him than to be faced with it in public." He abruptly moved away from her to stand at the side, leaning his shoulder against the wall next to the mirror to gaze at her with a brow lifted in that hateful, sardonic way he had. "Not, I suppose, that you care about appearances."

"What on earth are you talking about?" Confusion shifted to irritation, and she gripped the handle of the hair brush tightly in one hand, glaring at him.

"Brakefield and your mother, the infamous Faustine Auberge, whore to the rich and ready— is it true that she sold you to him, my sweet, or is it only another baseless rumor, such as your parentage and modesty?"

Fourteen

Even as angry as he was at her for keeping it from him, it was a crude blow. He saw immediately by the rapid paling of her face and dilated eyes like bruises that his words were a harsh shock. Dammit, she looked too pure and innocent, but was she? He found it difficult to equate with the young woman now sitting in his bedchamber what Northwick had said and others had verified. Was she what they had hinted? Northwick's depravity was a well-known secret, and Faustine Auberge had been desperate. Had she sold her daughter to the earl for enough money to leave England as Brakefield claimed? It was feasible, even probable, and for some reason, it left him with a sick feeling in his gut.

Northwick—a lecher, a thief, his sworn enemy—a desperate man who was trying to ruin him and would think nothing of destroying a young woman as well. Kyla was the weak link in the scheme unfolding around him, and the most vulnerable. *Christ.* How did it get so involved?

She half rose, then sat slowly down again. A drift of her perfume wafted toward him. Jasmine.

Sweet, heady, potent. As intoxicating as the mysterious lady wearing it. She was nothing she seemed to be—not innocent. Yet not the immoral baggage he had first thought her, either. Goddammit, which *was* she? Shy, naive young woman? Or the picture Northwick had painted of her—as a childish participant in perverted games that no child should ever suffer?

Brett watched her closely. Her agitation was visible as she looked away from him. "Is that—what is said of me? That I was Lord Brakefield's—*plaything*?"

It was said with such loathing, spat out as if bitter, and his eyes narrowed slightly. "Yes. Of course, I know certain facts about you that he apparently does not, but there are ways men like Northwick have of defiling a person that could not be detected. Did he touch you, Kyla? Did your mother sell you to him?"

She gave a harsh little laugh that sounded strangled, and her mouth twisted. "Is it so important to know that, Brett? I wonder. It cannot make any difference to you what was done to me in the past, can it? After all, you have done so much more in the past two weeks. . . ."

"Goddammit, it's not the same. You're a woman now, not a helpless child."

"Yes. That is very true." She rose to her feet with fluid grace, shaking her skirt free of wrinkles with one hand. "I am a woman now, and the past matters only if one allows it to—but you have made it quite clear that the past is of no consequence in regard to my parentage, why quibble about sordid details now?"

"I have my reasons."

"No doubt. I can only imagine what they are."

"Are you protecting him, Kyla? Christ! I think you are." He stared at her, angry and frustrated. High spots of color brightened her face, and her mouth was set into a mutinous line that he'd come to recognize. Several suspicions flicked through his mind, and after a moment, he said deliberately, "No, you are protecting your *mother*. She sold you to that perverted bastard, and you're protecting her for it. . . ."

He wasn't prepared for Kyla's furious reaction, or the way she flung herself at him, screaming that he was wrong, that her mother would never do anything like that, her hands flailing at him like windmills as she tried to slap him, scratch him, until he was forced to grab her wrists and wrench her arms behind her. Pinning her between his body and the edge of a table, he held her until she began to quiet and her struggles faded. Panting, her hair a bright tangle in her face and puddling like loose silk on the table's surface beneath her head, she glared up at him with wet, glittering eyes.

"Let me go," she said between clenched teeth. "Now."

"Promise not to swing at me and I'll let you up, Kyla. I don't want to hurt you. No—swear you'll behave."

"I swear." It was said sullenly, after a long pause, but he released her and straightened slowly, keeping a wary eye on her as she twisted from the table to stand erect.

She pushed at the hair in her eyes, her face averted, and he felt suddenly sorry for her, an emotion so unexpected and unfamiliar that he didn't quite know what to do at first. He stood awkward and scowling.

Kyla looked up at him, and her voice was calm. "My mother did not sell me as you think. It was nothing like that. I would remember if it was. But Northwick—he must be the man from my dreams. My nightmares." Her laugh was a little hollow. "I was very young, you see, but I remember small things. Bits and pieces like broken glass . . . his eyes and his voice. Perhaps that is why he sounded so familiar, why I felt so—so *unclean* when he looked at me that night at Lady Sefton's ball. I wondered."

Tears had pooled on her lashes in spiky clumps. Some of Brett's cynicism faded. She sounded sincere. Either she was a much better actress than he'd given her credit for being, or this was genuine emotion. It left him unsettled enough to want to know the truth, whatever it was. Damn her. He'd thought by leaving her at Ridgewood he could forget her, forget himself in the arms of other women. And at first, he had almost succeeded, joining Kenworth at Arthur's one evening for cards, and from there, to haunts he sometimes frequented on his more debauched forays into London's seamier areas in Pall Mall or Covent Garden.

There had been a slender blond at one of the houses with the kind of voluptuous curves Kyla had, long legs and a thick mane of hair like scented silk—he'd had almost enough to drink not to notice the small differences. It wasn't until later in the evening that he'd noticed coarser features, the vulgarities in her speech, and her cheap perfume. It had been enough to make him lose any spurious interest.

This wasn't at all what he'd wanted to find when he returned, Kyla dancing like a gypsy in the woods, clad in seductive clothes with her hair loose as if she was just up from a man's bed—all of Northwick's nasty comments and innuendos seemed true. A born flirt. Sold at a tender age for the pleasure of men—for Northwick.

Kyla lifted drenched eyes to him, and in her gaze was an expression like that of a lost child. He felt suddenly inhumane, as if he had kicked a small puppy. It should not matter to him what she had done or been before he'd known her, save how it affected him, but it did. *Christ.* It did matter. He'd wanted to kill Northwick, inexplicably and blindly furious at the thought the roué had even touched her. Not just because no man should harm a child, but because that child had been Kyla. Beautiful, scheming Kyla.

It was obvious Northwick would use her to provoke him into overplaying his hand, but he had no intention of being so obliging. He had his own methods of reprisal.

"Tomorrow, my pet," he said softly, "we shall go to London. It's very lively this time of year, and there are some of my acquaintances who want to meet my new ladybird. I think you will find it diverting."

She just stared at him, her alabaster skin tinged with only the faintest blush of color, and most of that reflected from the glow of the lamp. He cupped her chin in his palm, watching closely as her lashes quivered downward to hide her eyes, then bent and kissed her lightly on the mouth. Her lips were cold, like a statue.

It took effort not to attempt to wring a response from her. Instead, he released her and stepped away, keeping his voice light and indifferent, as if none of this mattered.

"Sleep well, my pet. We leave early in the morning."

As he shut the door behind him, it occurred to him that she had never really answered his questions.

Impatient, he went downstairs to the small parlor, sipping brandy as he waited for Godfrey's return. No doubt, it wouldn't take him long. For some reason, Godfrey had grown far too protective of Kyla, and would hurry back to be certain she wasn't harmed.

His expectations were correct, as Godfrey soon returned and found Brett in the parlor, shutting the door behind him to come and stand before the hearth where Brett sat in a wingback chair with his second snifter of fine French brandy.

"I trust Miss Van Vleet is resting comfortably now."

"Really, my friend, you are far too transparent." Brett placed the snifter on a japanned table and rose to his feet to lean back against the mantel, regarding his friend and blood brother with a frown. "Why should you care if she is resting comfortably, or if I have treated her as she should be treated?"

Godfrey's dark-hued face was impassive, but there was an edge to his voice. "If you treated her as she should be treated, she would be in London with her godmother. Must you involve her in this?"

"How do you know I am? Maybe I intend to return her to the illustrious comtesse du Bois."

"No, you do not. Your early return can only mean that things did not go as you wished, and that you intend to enlist Miss Van Vleet as bait. Am I correct?"

Brett smiled slightly, shaking his head. "You really are astute, my friend. It wouldn't surprise me to see you rise to the highest level of government, if you weren't so basically honest."

"If you're through insulting me, please answer my question."

"Yes, I intend to use our lovely little guest as *bait*, as you so crudely put it." He rubbed a hand across his jaw, staring thoughtfully at Godfrey. "In a manner of sorts, anyway. She won't be hurt. When I've accomplished what I must, I will pay her well and return her to her godmother. Will that suffice to make you happy?"

Godfrey's shoulders lifted in a shrug. "Will it make you happy?"

"What the devil do you mean by that?"

"Only that you are not as inured to the lady's charms as you might wish to be."

"Devil take you. She's a means to an end, and a way of killing two birds with one stone, as the saying goes. I can rid myself of her insistent claim, and rid myself of a threat at the same time. A perfect plan, as it has turned out."

"What did you discover in London?"

"Just what I expected." His jaw tightened. "Northwick has the deeds to my silver mines, all right. The bastard must be wearing them next to his heart, because my sources couldn't find them. Goddamn him—if he files them with the deeds office, I may never get them back. Or if I do, it will take years, and with ownership tied up in the courts, all that silver will just sit there. *Christ!* How he knew about them is still a mystery. They shouldn't have been on that ship. Someone in my trust has betrayed me, and when I find out who . . ." He let the sentence fade. Godfrey knew well enough what would happen when he found the informant who had sold those deeds to Northwick. If the man was lucky, he would die quickly, but by God, he was tempted to kill him slowly, as the Comanches might, begging for death long before it came—He glanced up, and saw in Godfrey's eyes that he understood full well what Brett was thinking.

Shrugging, Brett looked into the fire. "First things first. When I have the deeds back in my possession, I will deal with Northwick before I go back to deal with whoever betrayed me."

"I pity the guilty man when you find him." Godfrey met Brett's uplifted gaze with an impassive expression. "Is it an accident, do you think? Or did Northwick set out to steal them?"

"I'll find that out when I find the man responsible. I've discovered some most intriguing things about Lord Brakefield of late. Apparently, theft is among his lesser deeds. He has a penchant for young girls—*young* girls. It may be that sin that brings him down, if I can arrange it."

"You know this for a certainty?"

"An eyewitness is willing to testify. It should make Northwick's death much more plausible, I think."

Godfrey's mouth tightened at one corner. "I see. you have thought all this out thoroughly, it seems. Would the witness be Miss Van Vleet, perchance?"

"No. But she was once one of his..." He paused, unwilling to say it aloud, and finished grimly, "victims, if my information on that score is correct."

"Ah, so now there are two reasons to exact vengeance on the earl. I see."

Brett eyed him for a moment. "Yes. I think you do, but don't read more into it than is there, *haitsii*. My only concern for Kyla is that Northwick preyed upon her as a small child."

Godfrey smiled, and Brett's eyes narrowed with irritation. Damn him. He would think what he wanted, as always, but that did not matter. What mattered was dealing with Northwick.

City lights glittered alongside the streets still wet from a recent rain, reflecting blurred rainbows as the ducal carriage came to a stop. Kyla held hard to her composure. It was difficult, more difficult than she'd thought it would be in the face of Brett's insistence that she accompany him. Why was he doing this? What did he hope to prove? It was unnerving enough that he had been so polite since they had returned to London. There was a hard, brittle edge to his courtesy that set her teeth on edge and made her nervous, however, for behind the banked embers of his restraint, she sensed there was an ultimate purpose. No doubt, it would not be something she liked.

She stole a glance in his direction. Brett stared out the window. His dark visage was silhouetted by the lamps outside and the shadows of the coach, more remote and unapproachable than ever. He had not touched her since they returned to London. While she was grateful—or told herself she was—she was uneasy at his reserve. This was certainly not the Brett Banning she'd grown to know, the hard-eyed autocrat who had swept her from Lady Sefton's ball under the noses of everyone, including her godmother, without a thought. Now, there was a barely controlled edge of violence to him, simmering just below his surface but visible nonetheless. And tonight, he seemed even more on the edge than he had during the past few weeks.

Frowning a little, she held out one hand and examined her soft new gloves, wiggling her fingers. Gloves, marabou trimmed capote, slippers from R. Willis at 421 Fish Street sewn from brocade and adorned with tiny ruby chips that imitated the delicate necklace of rubies and diamonds around her neck, clocked stockings and exquisite garters of satin and lace, were but an accompaniment to her gown. Fashioned of sheer silk over satin, it seemed to float about her when she walked. The high waist was caught just under her breasts with lavishly embroidered trim of gilt and tiny rubies. At first, staring at her reflection in the long mirror, Kyla had thought she could not *dare* wear such a gown out! For though she was quite covered, the sheer crimson silk over pale beige satin gave the illusion that she was entirely naked beneath.

It was only when Brett had come to an abrupt halt in the doorway and stared at her with narrowed eyes, that she realized it was just what he expected her to wear. To argue with him would have been futile, so she had merely shrugged carelessly and said it was a very lovely gown.

"Shall I dampen the skirts so that it's transparent? After all, one has to look *closely* to see anything."

"No, you're showing quite enough without that." Brett ignored her biting tone and shrugged, but there had been a hot light in his eyes that told her he meant it. Why then, did he want her to even wear such a gown?

Now, out in public, she felt naked and exposed, and knew that she looked like exactly what she had become—a courtesan. Oh, what would Tante Celeste say when she heard about this? She would be so hurt, so disappointed. She did not blame Kyla for what had happened, but there was a definite undercurrent of sadness, of disillusion in her warm words and discreet offers of support once she left Wolverton's protection. Their brief reunion had been awkward and uncomfortable.

Idly, Kyla scraped her fingers over her blurred reflection in the coach window, staring blindly at the misty streets. Was she to lose everything?

"We have arrived, Kyla. Try to stop admiring yourself for a moment, at least until there are others to do it for you."

Brett's caustic remark stung, and she glanced up at him angrily, tugging hard at her gloves. "Since it would suit you best if I were to look haggard, Your Grace, you should not have gone to so much expense to ascertain that I wear such a revealing gown. It seems to me that you wish to advertise my position tonight, not disguise it."

His eyes narrowed slightly. "You are more astute than I guessed. How inconvenient. Perhaps I only want to drive up your price. Keeping you has become damned expensive. The footman waits, my pet. Shall we go inside the opera house?"

It was difficult not to curse at him, but already she could see a few curious glances from those outside King's Theatre. Good God, there were so many people! Lines of carriages and a glittering array of jewels and elegantly garbed *ton* choked Haymarket. Not until she stood in front of the huge auditorium with Brett holding her arm, did she dare acknowledge the trembling in her knees and the nervous flutter in the pit of her stomach. She willed herself to hold her chin high. No one would see how nervous she was if she could help it. Why give them the satisfaction?

Oddly, Brett was her bulwark at the moment, fending off the curious stares directed at her. She clutched the edges of her capote more closely around her, glad it half concealed her daring gown, wishing she was anywhere but here. Beside her, Brett was a solid, warm presence, his tall frame clad in black evening clothes, a meticulously tailored coat with waistcoat and trousers. Snowy white linen formed an elegantly tied cravat at his throat, emphasizing his dark good looks. He was arrogantly handsome. A man who earned his share of looks, mostly sly glances from behind fluttering fans or artfully lowered lashes. If he wasn't so hateful, perhaps at one time she could have even fallen a little bit in love with him.

After all, he made her feel breathless with anticipation on occasion, especially when he looked at her with his eyes half-closed and his mouth slanted in that particularly appealing smile he could wear so easily . . . and at times, when he touched her, murmured soft words in her ear, she forgot they were only sex words, and almost let herself believe for the moment that she really was his love, that he really cared about her. Of course, it was foolish, and she knew it, and when he had left her or gone to sleep, she always acknowledged the truth; but still, there were those brief moments of blinding hope for a better life that often left her restless and uncertain. And—yes, she admitted it—angry.

Nothing in her life had happened like she'd once thought it would, as she had dreamed when she was a young girl prone to floating on her back in the river and dreaming of her future. That was a lifetime ago. Another world, perhaps, certainly another girl. Here, she was adrift on unfriendly seas, lost in the maelstrom that had become her life, not knowing whom to trust or how to move forward.

"Your Grace," a feminine voice murmured, and Kyla turned to see the countess of Grenfield smirk. "I did not know you enjoyed opera."

"I have varied tastes, my lady." Brett tugged on Kyla's arm until she moved closer, so that light from a tall lamp fell across her face. "Have you met Miss Van Vleet?"

For an instant, Kyla's eyes met those of Lady Grenfield before the countess looked away, her voice and gaze cold. "No. Excuse me, Your Grace. Perhaps I shall talk to you again another time."

It was an obvious snub, cold and lethal, and Kyla's face flamed. The cat. They *had* met before, though it had been nearly three months, and then Lady Grenfield had been very cordial. How infuriating. The countess did not have a sterling reputation herself, being considered a bit "fast" by some of the more staid dowagers of the *ton*, and for her to cut Kyla so directly was outrageous. Like Lady Melbourne, the countess had a number of children by different fathers, yet she *dared* snub her like this!

Lady Grenfield was not the only one to cut her that night. Not one of the women who had formerly been her companions at soirées, hostesses at teas, or guests at Lady Rushton's home, would so much as speak to her. After the first shocked glance, it was as if she did not exist.

The men, however, had no qualms about speaking to her, but she would almost have preferred they did not. The sly glances and remarks were enough to keep her tense and wary, so that she acknowledged their greetings without really looking at them, letting their gazes and words roll over her without heed.

It seemed to take forever to reach the box Brett had subscripted, an elegant enclosure draped with heavy velvet and fitted with plush chairs to view the opera on the stage below. He pulled back the drapes, and steered her into the carpeted area that smelled of candlewax and stale perfume. Deep shadows filled it toward the back, and she stood a moment as her eyes adjusted to the absence of bright light.

Wolverton's box was almost close enough to reach out and touch the stage. The lower of five tiers, it had the distinction of being the best box in the house. In the shape of a gigantic horseshoe, the auditorium boasted the claim that it was the largest in England to be used for opera, and she could well believe it. Besides the five tiers of expensive boxes and the lower pit, there was a huge gallery that seated an amazing thirty-three hundred people. So many crowded into this one building, all glittering with jewels and titles and there to see and be seen as well as attend the opera.

The high ceiling was painted with diverse scenes, plastered and ornately gilded. Below in the orchestra pit could be heard the abortive sounds of violin and horn, some false starts, a few riffs, then silence again, all mingled with the low chatter and hum of conversation and laughter. Brett nudged her forward, and she moved into the lit area with a self-conscious lift of her chin as she sensed stares in their direction. Despite her sudden grip on the edges, Brett gently removed her capote and draped it over a chair, leaving her garbed in her daring gown.

A rustle of silks and satins heralded the turning of people to look, the sudden absence of laughter and the crescendo of whispers signifying that there were those who found her appearance at King's Theatre most entertaining. This, after all, was her public debut since Brett had so publicly taken her from Lady Sefton's ball, and no doubt, was the subject of intense speculation and rumors.

She wished she had not come, wished she had never met Wolverton, and most of all—wished that she was safely out of England. Back in India, perhaps, with Papa Piers. She didn't care if they had no money or she had no decent prospects. If she had remained there, at least she would still have her self-respect, and the respect of others. Now look at her—the subject of malicious gossip at so innocent an outing as the opera.

And Brett had known she would be, of course, or he would not have brought her here. Why was he torturing her like this, damn him! What did he hope to gain?

Then she thought she must know the answer to that question as she heard a deep cough behind them, and a rather ebullient voice ring out a demand for an introduction to the lovely creature to have the dubious fortune to be with Wolverton.

"I say, Wolverton, you have the damnedest luck, finding such exquisite beauty, heh? Is this the beauty I've been hearing so much about of late? The one you stole from Lady Sefton's ball? I say, she's quite a sight, heh? Lovely, yes goddamned lovely, I'd say. Look at her—splendid *form*, Wolverton, splendid."

With cheeks already flushed from embarrassment, Kyla turned angrily, and was introduced to His Grace, the duke of Cumberland. The fifth son of King George, the duke was considered by most to be a vile, uncouth lout. If not for his royal blood, he would no doubt have been considered beneath regard. Yet he was the king's son and the regent's brother, and so was tolerated, however reluctantly.

Kyla's smile felt stiff and unnatural, but she was not about to allow anyone to guess how she felt. Especially not this dreadful duke, with his battle-scarred face and single eye that peered at her so closely. His gaze seemed riveted to her breasts, where crimson silk fluttered so sheerly over the beige slip dress beneath, yet left little to the imagination. Aware of Brett watching her with a lifted brow, she managed a cool nod of greeting.

"Your Grace, I am honored to meet you."

"Damme, but she's delightful, Wolverton!" Cumberland slapped his thigh, seeming to Kyla more rustic than any man she had ever met, and certainly not indicative of what she had thought the prince regent's brother would be. "Yes, I see what you find in her," he was saying, "and m'brother will no doubt find her just as fascinating. But of course, I've a notion you are aware of that, heh?"

It was a surprisingly shrewd remark, and Kyla caught the undercurrent in his casual words and looked up. Brett was smiling, urbane and unruffled, looking for all the world as if he belonged in this set. A counterfeit duke, she thought suddenly, angrily, usurping the title when he did not care about it at all. Oh yes, she had heard his disparaging remarks about it, his comments to Godfrey that he wanted to return to America. She wished he would go, would leave her in peace, instead of drag her out like this to—to *display* her! What did he intend? She knew there was something behind this, knew Brett had an ulterior motive for bringing her to the opera. Did he think she would sit like some mindless puppet and allow him to pull the strings? If he did, he would soon find how mistaken he was in that hope.

Kyla snapped open her fan of ostrich feathers, waving it with negligent sweeps so that the feather tips brushed against her nose and cheeks. She smiled when Cumberland glanced at her, and saw his eyes light with appreciation.

"I say, Wolverton, you don't mind if I remain in your box, do you? It's the best in the house, y'know. Mine is not nearly so suitable. Deuced awkward, but then, you've the blunt to pay fifty thousand pounds a year for an opera box, I hear."

Brett's reply was an expected approval that Cumberland barely heard as he leaned closer to engage Kyla in trivial conversation. Several minutes passed while she verbally fenced with the duke, aware of Brett watching and listening, his dark brow lifted with sardonic amusement. He knew what she was doing, of course, and obviously thought her amusing. Would he think her so humorous if she acted upon the duke of Cumberland's sly suggestions? She was almost tempted to find out, but that would be going from the pan into the fire, and she had no desire to risk greater aggravation. Especially when it seemed as if Brett was waiting on someone else to arrive. His casual glances toward the corridor beyond the curtains were too obvious.

Until she heard him behind her, heard others greet him and the whispers grow louder, she did not guess who else was expected. But when the regent swept into the box with royal aplomb, looking padded and stuffed and oddly elegant in his black silk breeches and bright yellow waistcoat, his hair carefully casual and his plump face ruddy with good nature, she knew at once that it was he whom Brett had been awaiting. The affable prince, she had heard him called, and indeed he was. He greeted his brother with some surprise, then Brett, before turning an admiring eye on Kyla.

There was none of Cumberland's jocularity or crudeness in his voice or words, but a rather kind, warm greeting that sounded honest and much too practiced at the same time: "It is very nice to finally meet the lovely lady I have heard so much about, of course. Miss Van Vleet, I am honored to make your acquaintance."

With another man, it might have sounded mocking, and there was no doubt George, Prince Regent, could be cruel when he chose, but tonight he must feel kind, for he smiled on her quite graciously, flattered her, even put his slightly damp hand on her elbow to escort her to one of the cushioned chairs.

"I say, Wolverton, you have the best fortune," the prince remarked, smiling at her while he talked, "for she is a breath of fresh air. You must bring her with you next week to Carlton House as well. I am giving a grand affair, and will not take no for an answer, of course. My dear, you will come, won't you?"

She found herself smiling at him, much more at ease than with his brother. "If you command it, Your Highness, I can do nothing else but wish it myself."

"Aha! What a delight. As I said, a breath of fresh air. Is it true that you have spent time in India, my dear? I have heard that you did, what little Wolverton will divulge, for he can be close-mouthed a fellow as you have ever seen when he desires to be. Now tell me all about the elephants and tigers, for you know I have a passion for unusual things of beauty, and find them most intriguing. I've spent some time and effort enlarging the menagerie, you know, as well as *trying* to beautify this city with decent parks and buildings where all can enjoy the beauties of the past. Like the friezes of the Acropolis in Athens, despite Lord Byron's denouncement of Elgin for removing them—but that is another complaint, and I hear the music beginning. Perhaps later we can have more lengthy conversation... I have it—a drive in the park tomorrow. I can show you some of the more lovely spots, and it will do you good to be about, do you not think? A shot in the eye to some, and enjoyable to boot."

"I... I am certain that it would be most enjoyable were I to drive in the park with you, Your Highness. But I am not at all sure it is advisable, as I—"

"Tut. Wolverton will come along, if you like. Is that what bothers you? Oh, no one will dare say anything to either of us, I assure you." He leaned close, and the strong scent of rose water filled her nostrils as he confided in a soft, conspiratorial tone, "See those boxes on the second tier? Those women dressed so beautifully? Women of the town, here looking for protectors. When I've a notion, I choose one of the lovelier bits to take with me in my phaeton. It's of no consequence to anyone but myself, of course, and quite commonly done. Do not answer until you have thought about it, will you? Besides, Wolverton may prefer to renew his acquaintance with the fair Catalani before he must introduce me, do you not think?"

Winking, he turned to glance at Brett, who merely lifted his brow in that annoying way he had, while Kyla sat suddenly still and frozen. Was this the introduction Brett had threatened her with? The protector to be the prince? And Brett—with the fair Catalani. She should have known!

Fifteen

As the regent rattled on, completely ignorant of her sudden tension, Kyla managed to focus on the parts of his relentless dialogue that required replies, while her mind was spinning in convoluted circles that kept returning to the same theme: Brett and the fair Catalani, the opera singer who was to perform tonight. Was Catalani the real reason they were here? Did Brett intend to *renew* his former acquaintance with the opera singer and fob *her* off on the prince or Cumberland or whoever wanted her?

Damn him . . . and oh God, how long must she sit here like this, enduring the lascivious gazes of men staring at their box, and the no doubt vicious whispers of rumor that she could hear rippling through the crowd like the sibilant hiss of a snake? She was tempted to escape, to rise from her chair and push aside the velvet curtains and leave the theater and prince and Brett behind. . . .

But that would be admitting fault, and she refused to be so cowardly. None of this was her fault. Not entirely. She noticed a bit angrily that Brett seemed oblivious to any repercussions. Why should he not feel the same tension she endured? How could he ignore her as he was doing, when he was behaving as no more than a . . . a *procurer!* Oh, if only she had somewhere to go, someone else to turn to.

Tante Celeste would never turn her away, but she could not risk hurting her any more than she already had with all the scandal. No, it was much too late for that comfort to be accepted. She could not put Celeste's comfortable existence in jeopardy.

It seemed as if the night would never end. Kyla sipped champagne and pretended to enjoy the opera, while the regent gave rhapsodic sighs of bliss at intervals, openly admiring the beauty of the dark-haired Italian opera singer as she performed *Il Turo in Italia*. Below, no one else seemed to be watching the opera, but rather each other, and occasionally there was such a commotion that it was near impossible to hear the music. Laughter and crude jests filled the air, and in the boxes the prince had pointed out to her, she saw men visit the flirting ladies who waited there.

It was maddening to sit there and watch, to know that the rather vulgar and cowlike Lady Jersey—who had been quite civil to her only a month before—was seated in her box not far away, pointedly ignoring Kyla as if she no longer existed. And really, for all intents and purposes, she did not exist for those people. Not in the sense that she might once have done.

Deliberately, ignoring Brett's frowning gaze, she took yet another glass of proffered champagne. Anything to escape the tedium and scalding glances. What did she care if she became a bit too gay? Besides, it was rather pleasant seeing Brett's jaw grow rigid with suppressed anger when she leaned close to the prince—*very* close—when he remarked on the opera. Did Brett care? Or was it only his silly male pride that was wounded because she was enjoying herself?—Or pretending to.

The murmur of conversation that had never ended during the act grew louder as the lights grew brighter, and Kyla realized that it must be intermission. Heads turned, the buzz of talk increased in volume, and necks craned and lorgnettes lifted as those in the audience strained to see those about them. The prince leaned close to Kyla again, wafting the strong scent of rose water toward her. A barrage of whispers rippled around them.

"Miss Van Vleet, you are not at all what I expected," the prince murmured with a smile. "No, not at all!"

"Am I not, Your Highness?" Kyla smiled at him over the gold-edged rim of her champagne flute. "What, if I may be so bold as to ask, did you expect?"

For an instant, the prince looked flustered, and the glance he shot toward Brett was a bit guilty and confused. Then he recovered with a shrug and a wide smile. "Never anyone so lovely, of course, or so intelligent."

"Is Wolverton in the habit of keeping company with only plain simpletons, then?" She pressed the lip of the gilded flute against her lips to hide her smile when the prince looked at her with an appalled expression.

"No, no, of course not! Ah, I see what you are

about, you sly baggage. Making a bit of fun with me. Naughty of you, y'know."

"I beg your pardon most humbly, Your Highness."

The prince smiled. "I've a notion you do nothing of the kind. But never mind. I am certain that I like you, and my approval will open all the doors for you that you could ever want. Is that not so, Wolverton?" He glanced over his shoulder at Brett, who inclined his dark head.

"As you say, all doors open for princes."

The prince snorted. "You would say that, of course. Yet we know it is not true. Here I am, wasting away my years as regent while my father's advisers refuse to allow me to be king. Damned impertinent of them, I say, for all know that I run the country—it's Pitt, of course. But, here we are at a lovely outing, and I shall not ruin it with my problems, not when I have such a lovely, attentive young lady smiling at me. Damme, Wolverton, you're a lucky dog to have won the heart of such an incomparable creature. She reminds me of my own lovely Maria, gone to me now—ah, the inequity of the world!"

To Kyla's astonishment, huge tears welled in the prince's eyes, forming silvery tracks down his cheeks and making furrows in a light coating of powder on his face. It looked as if he might at any moment break into sobs, but Brett diverted him as tactfully as if the prince was a child, pointing out that Catalani was coming near their box.

"She knows of your interest in opera, Your Highness," he added with a faint smile, and the prince was at once diverted from Kyla and his lost love to the stage.

Brett took the opportunity to grasp Kyla by the wrist, his fingers digging into her tender skin. He leaned close, his mouth against her ear. "I think you've had quite enough champagne tonight, *querida*. It makes you more lively than you should be."

"Does it?" She pulled away, and saw the quick flare of anger in his eyes at her defiance. That made her reckless, that and her fifth glass of champagne. She laughed softly. "But I enjoy being lively, Brett. And the prince does not seem to mind."

Brett's eyes narrowed. "The prince is otherwise engaged for the evening, if that is your hope."

"Don't be beastly." She tilted her glass and drained the last of champagne, then held it out to him. "I would like more, please."

Brett wrenched the empty glass from her fingers and set it aside. "You've had more than enough for the evening."

"Here now, Wolverton," Cumberland protested with a sly smile, "don't be such a Turk. Give the lady more champagne if she likes."

Kyla smiled. "You have my thanks, Your Grace. I find it most refreshing to meet a gentleman who does not think he must behave brutally in order to impress his will upon others."

For a moment, Kyla thought she had gone too far. Brett looked positively furious, and she would not put it past him to cause a scene, not caring a fig if the prince or his brother minded. But when the duke turned to look at him, Brett merely smiled and sat back in his chair with a careless remark that it was not he who would have the headache the next morning, and the moment passed.

Yet Kyla was not fooled. He would make her pay for her reckless behavior once they were alone. She had not forgotten for a moment how swiftly he could change from urbane gentleman to ruthless barbarian.

Just before the climax of the opera, Anjelica Catalani moved to the edge of their box and gazed at them with dark gleaming eyes. It was as if she was singing directly to Brett, and Kyla's attention riveted on him as she watched him smile back at her. Then as the song ended and a thundering of applause rose into the air, Catalani flung a long-stemmed flower into the box. Brett caught it deftly and rose to his feet, sweeping her a bow of acknowledgment for her effort. Another burst of applause and laughter greeted this byplay.

"Well done, Wolverton!" The regent laughed, clapping in admiration, "Well done! I do believe the fair Catalani still has a tendré for you, heh?"

"We are only old friends. I met her a long time ago, in Italy." As Brett turned, his eyes met Kyla's in a brief glance before she turned away.

Kyla burned with resentment. It was obvious there was something between them, for no woman looked at a man as Catalani had looked at Brett unless there was. But why did he bring *her* here tonight if he wanted the opera singer? Why force her to watch?

When it was over at last, and she was bundled into her wrap and still holding an empty champagne glass, the regent offered to escort Kyla safely home should Brett have other plans for the evening. Dismayed, Kyla froze, and saw Brett's wicked grin. *No, surely he would not!* she thought furiously. Her heart thumped so hard against her ribs they felt bruised as she waited tensely for his reply.

"Your offer is most generous, Your Highness." Brett smiled slightly, then drawled, "But I have promised Miss Van Vleet special entertainment after the opera tonight. Perhaps another time."

"Yes, yes, another time. Tomorrow, perhaps, a ride in the park." The prince lifted Kyla's cold hand in his and pressed a kiss on her knuckles, his mouth damp and warm against her skin. There was a definite note of regret in his voice when he sighed and murmured that the opera had ended too quickly. "But, I shall call upon you soon, Wolverton, damme if I don't. I have not forgotten your promise. Neither of them, matter of fact."

"Your presence is always a pleasure." Brett's response was as smooth as Kyla would expect it to be, but apparently the regent saw no reason to doubt his sincerity. The prince accompanied them from the box and down the carpeted stairs, pausing in the corridor to converse with those who sought him out, and Kyla recognized a few of the gentlemen as influential men. One name caught her attention, and she was introduced to the rather austere Robert Stewart, Lord Castlereagh, the foreign secretary who had attended the Congress of Vienna and was instrumental in Napoleon's downfall.

"I am honored to meet you, my lord," she said when he bowed briefly to her.

"And I you, madam. You are the goddaughter of the comtesse du Bois, are you not?"

Kyla's cheeks grew warm, and she nodded. No doubt, a man in his position would have heard the gossip, of course.

"Yes, my lord. Do you know her well?"

"A charming lady." A faint smile curved his mouth, and softened his stern visage. "We have had occasion to meet at several functions, and share an admiration for Paris, of course. She was of great assistance to me in recommending the Bains Chinois when I was in Paris last autumn. I remain in her debt, and am most pleased to meet the goddaughter of whom she has always spoken so fondly."

Kyla returned his smile. "The pleasure is mine, my lord."

There was a shrewd glint in Robert Stewart's eyes when he turned to Brett and extended an invitation to join him at his club the following week. "I believe we have some of the same interests and goals in mind, Wolverton."

"Do we, my lord? I was unaware of the fact." Brett smiled slightly. "I try to stay out of politics as much as possible, as my interests lie elsewhere."

"Ah, but this has nothing to do with politics."

"Then I am intrigued."

"Yes, I thought you might be. Next Wednesday? I shall send you my card as a reminder."

"I am at your service, my lord."

The prince immediately engaged Castlereagh in a spirited discussion of the Greek friezes the earl of Elgin had brought to England, which he was trying to persuade the House of Commons to purchase for the British Museum. Brett took the opportunity to move Kyla to one side, his grip on her arm tight.

"Little fool," he muttered in her ear, "unless you truly wish to find yourself lying under the prince, you'll stop that damned flirting and behave."

Kyla fluttered her feather fan and regarded Brett with a lifted brow and slight smile. "Why, Your Grace, dare I hope that you are consumed with jealousy?"

"It's obvious that you dare anything." His fingers tightened on her elbow with painful intensity, and her feather fan stilled abruptly. There was a steely glitter in his eyes that made her stomach tighten. "Don't push me, Kyla. Not tonight."

"Why is tonight different from any other night? Is it because the prince is here? Are you afraid everyone will learn what a . . . a bully you are?" She pulled away, aware of Cumberland's arrested gaze on them, and suddenly aware that Brett was powerless to stop her if she tried to leave. It was so public here, and all she had to do was walk away from him. Did she dare hope that Castlereagh might help her? He spoke highly of Tante Celeste—but no. What could she say? That she was being held prisoner? If she was a prisoner, it was her own fault for being too cowardly to leave what protection Brett offered her.

"If I were you, my pet," Brett said coldly, his voice low and tight, "I would worry more about tomorrow than tonight. And I don't give a damn what people think of me, in case you haven't noticed."

"I've noticed." She pried his fingers from her

arm. "Do not touch me again, please. I've been mauled enough lately."

"If you've had enough mauling, I suggest you curb your tendencies to offer your wares so unwisely, madam. There are those men here who do not take refusal lightly, if at all."

"Like you?"

"If you're implying that you offered me any refusals, you might reconsider. I don't recall hearing one from you."

She flashed him an angry glance, but already his attention was diverted, and she followed his gaze to the woman approaching through the crowd. People were applauding, and it took a moment for Kyla to realize that it was Anjelica Catalani, the dark-haired opera singer who had near mesmerized the regent. Flamboyantly adorned in a glittering diadem and scarlet tunic hung with tassels, she moved through the crowd as if royalty and they parted for her without comment. When she reached them, she moved directly to Brett, who took her offered hand and pressed a kiss on the back as if she was, indeed, a queen.

Dark eyes flashed above high cheekbones and a long nose, and her lips were thin and painted bright red. Her brow rose, and she burst into a spate of Italian.

Grinning, Brett did not stop her when she rose to her toes and pressed a kiss directly on his mouth, ignoring the shocked glances from some of the ladies present. Instead, he seemed to kiss her back, while Kyla stood rigidly beside him and wished he would go to the devil. After a moment, he disentangled himself, and turned the opera singer with a hand under her elbow, letting his sardonic gaze slide over Kyla as he introduced Madame Catalani to the prince.

Catalani curtsied gracefully, and the regent spoke with her in Italian while she flashed her dark eyes at him and her red lips smiled. She was dusky of complexion, reminding Kyla somehow of Sanchia, and though she laughed and spoke with the prince, her dark gaze kept straying back to Brett.

Kyla stiffened. *The cat! It's obvious that her true interest is in Brett, though she's prudent enough to give the regent a generous share of her attention... but I don't care. Let her have him if that's what he wants... then I can be free!*

Brett took Kyla's arm again, and said something to the regent and Catalani that generated immediate protest from her and smiling approval from the prince.

Laughing, Brett shook his head, and said in English this time, "You have made a conquest, *signora*, and I dare not risk my prince's ire by outstaying my welcome. There will be another time for us to relive old memories."

Catalani looked directly at Kyla, and her dark brow lifted. "She is lovely. Bring her with you when you come to visit, Brett. We can talk of old times."

It was obvious she meant nothing of the kind, and Kyla turned to the duke of Cumberland, who still hovered at her side as he had most of the evening. Her laughter sounded brittle even to her own ears when the duke murmured that his brother's tastes had always ranged to the vulgar.

"Not that I mean anything ill of the fair Catalani, of course," he added wickedly, "though her conquest of dear Prinny seems certain at this moment. Rumor has it that she's a fickle creature, and her heart belongs only to her husband. Yet the latest *on-dit* is that she lends it out on occasion. . . ."

"Really, Your Grace," she replied lightly, "you put too much faith in idle gossip. There are those who have little else to do but foment unfounded rumors."

"And those who have too little faith to ignore them." The duke's smile twisted his ruined face. "But you are closely acquainted with such, are you not? No, do not retreat, beautiful lady. It is of no consequence to me, or to any man of intelligence, for the world is such these days that any person with a grudge and a sharp tongue can ruin another. Pity. There are those who do not deserve it."

Kyla stood stiffly, her champagne haze dissipating rapidly. "So I understand, Your Grace."

"Yes, better than most, I imagine. I never thought of Wolverton as a fool until tonight— would you care to join us, madam? Oh, not alone. Do not misunderstand. I am not so big a fool as to think Wolverton would be tolerant of such a breach—he will escort you, of course. And I mean nothing by the invitation other than a desire to tweak my brother's nose, perhaps." One corner of his mouth tightened. "He has never appreciated my interference."

Kyla hesitated, her head spinning a little. She should not have had that last glass of champagne . . . Brett was laughing at something the opera singer said, and even the prince looked fatuous and utterly delighted. It was not until Brett said something in Italian that sparked soft laughter from Catalani that Kyla turned to the duke with a smile that felt taut and accepted his invitation.

"I am certain that if *you* ask Wolverton, there is no question of refusal, Your Grace."

"There rarely is."

Yet incredibly, Brett refused the invitation. Politely, of course, but firmly. Cumberland looked a little nonplussed and annoyed.

"No? Damme, Wolverton, no need to go home so early when your lady wishes to remain, is there?"

Brett's cool gray gaze shifted to Kyla, and she met his stare with a defiant tilt of her chin. "I'm not as tired as I was earlier, Brett. Maybe I would prefer staying out longer."

"Would you?" The harsh slant of Brett's mouth curled into a slight smile. "I would not." When Kyla would have offered more protest, he cut her off by turning away from her to Cumberland. "You were speaking to me earlier of your recent investment in the East India Company, I think, Your Grace. If you would still care to discuss the selling of shares, I would be interested. It is my understanding that you are involved in several intriguing enterprises lately."

"Am I? Yes, yes, s'pose I am, Wolverton, I s'pose I am. How awkward—but of course, gentlemen can discuss business anywhere, do you not think?"

Brett's smile looked more predatory than reassuring, and Kyla frowned when he murmured that gentlemen could do almost anything as long as it was done civilly. "Do you agree, Your Grace?"

Cumberland looked first startled, then wary, but bobbed his head in assent. "Of course. Civilized—less trouble that way. I take your point. Shall we discuss the merchant trade?"

It was the perfect topic to divert Cumberland, and Kyla saw at once that the duke was far more concerned with greed than the tweaking of his brother. Not surprising, since the princes were notoriously reviled as financial millstones around the neck of government. Only a discussion of politics would have been more diverting to Cumberland, as Brett certainly must know.

Fuming, she stood stiffly still and tried to pretend that the rapacious stares from men and women alike did not matter. What did she care what they thought? These members of the *haut ton* were no different from her, save that they were usually more discreet than she had been. But that was not all her fault, either.

It didn't matter what she had done, or what they thought she had done. She was *not* like them, nor like those painted, preening women selling their wares so openly. Her head hurt, and her throat ached from the effort of holding back angry words, so that she felt only relief once they were in the coach again and moving away from the opera house. But to her dismay, Brett gave the footman directions to a gaming house at Number 10, St. James's Square. She glared at him as the coach lurched forward.

"I thought you would rather return to your town house," she could not help snapping at him. "I'm tired. The evening was dreadful, and I cannot bear another moment of saying what I don't mean and smiling when I don't want to."

"My my, a little testy, are we?" Brett's mocking smile grated on her temper. "You certainly seemed to be enjoying yourself. Or are you upset because I would not allow you to go with the regent? Sorry, *querida*, but I'd made Anjelica a promise, and meant to keep it."

"Anjelica—!"

"Signora Catalani knows of Prinny's fondness for the arts. I would venture to guess that she can wheedle whatever she likes out of him soon enough." He sat back against the squabs, gazing at her in the dim light with that enigmatic expression she had grown to hate. She glared at him.

"I think you are making that up. She was far more interested in *you* than the prince, and I daresay she would not hesitate to ask you for whatever she wants."

Brett laughed softly. "Anjelica doesn't ask. She expects. And she usually gets."

That rankled. Kyla turned to gaze angrily out the window of the coach. "Take me home, please. I do not feel like enduring any more insults for the evening."

"Insults? You charmed the prince, my pet, and his brother as well. How is that an insult?"

"Don't regard me as a fool, please. I am well aware of your intentions this evening. First, you garb me in this gown, then you parade me around on your arm like some kind of prize and subject me to snubs and insults, and finally present me to the prince and his odious brother as a possible plaything. No, not an insult at all! I should be pleased, I suppose."

Silence fell, and when she looked over at him, he was gazing at her thoughtfully. To her surprise, he nodded. "Yes, I imagine it did seem like that. It cannot be helped, Kyla. There were some things that I had to establish tonight, and unfortunately, there are those people who will do and say what they think."

"I don't understand."

"No, I can see that. Never mind. You will."

He stretched out his long legs, looking for all the world like a lithe panther in his black evening clothes. Unsettled, Kyla turned to stare blindly out the window again, at glistening gas lamps reflected like a blur in shop windows they passed. The sound of carriage wheels over paving stones was a loud rumble, with accompanying creaks and squeaks of leather and iron as the vehicle swayed through the streets. She curled her hands tightly in her lap and tried to think of nothing.

"Kyla, you needn't look like a damned martyr." His voice was a low growl, and she turned to look at him. Despite the faint glow of carriage lanterns, his face was shadowed. He looked so dark, so— dangerous. When he leaned forward, lamplight illuminated his grim expression. "You've managed to capture the eye of the prince, as you no doubt set out to do."

"Isn't that what you wanted?" She tapped her fan irritably against her gloved palm. "Why else would you have brought me with you tonight? It's obvious that you have tired of me, and wish to *renew* your acquaintance with that opera singer."

An amused smile curled his lips. "Now who sounds jealous. Is that why you flirted so outrageously? Don't you know it's dangerous to flirt with princes? Or do you intend to accept his proposal."

"I hardly think an invitation to ride in the park is a proposal for intimacy. Unless, of course, he prefers your less than subtle method of forceful ravishment."

Brett's eyes narrowed. "Little fool. I'm trying to warn you. Once the regent sets his mind on a lady's affections, he can become quite insistent. And annoying. In your position, you may be asking for more trouble than you can handle."

"Don't bother to warn me about trouble, when I'm already ruined. What more can happen? Didn't you *see* those people tonight? Or did you even bother to notice that I was cut by ladies who once welcomed me into their homes? It's as if I no longer exist."

Her voice was trembling with anger, and Brett regarded her with sardonic amusement. "Those ladies only welcomed you because of your godmother and Lady Rushton, Kyla. If not for their sponsorship, you would never have been invited to so much as laundry day at their homes. It's a cold business being a member of the social set, and you should have thought of that before you came back to London to blackmail me into giving you money. Why complain now? You have money, don't you? Isn't that what you really wanted?"

She glared at him angrily. "You know that's only part of it. I wanted what should have been my mother's—the respect she was denied."

"Might as well ask for the moon. You're more likely to get it."

The blunt cruelty of his reply took away her breath, and she stared at him as light and shadow flickered erratically over his face. He was right.

There was no denying it. She would never have the respect she wanted. Not now. Not here. It was a daunting admission.

When the carriage stopped at last, Brett gave her a funny look, a faint smile tucking in one corner of his mouth. "Since you're so tired, go home. I'll have Burton take you."

"Do you mean—"

"I *mean, querida,* that you're free to sleep alone tonight."

She glanced out the window at the shabby facade of a building, then back at him. He wanted to be rid of her. Of course. He meant to meet the opera singer. *Damn him!* How dare he shame her like this? First, taking her as he had, and now so publicly making it obvious that he was tired of her! By God, she would not stand for it. If he thought to escape confrontation, he was sorely mistaken. No, she would not be one of those women shuffled off with a house in the country and a cold letter of farewell . . . but he was already stepping down from the coach and giving Burton directions to take her home, as carelessly as if he had not done everything possible to ruin her life.

It wasn't until the coach jerked forward again that she knew what she would do, and Kyla rapped sharply on the door to engage the footman's attention.

By God, Brett Banning would soon regret treating her this way—if nothing else, he would never forget her!

Sixteen

Kenworth looked up and recognized the ducal coach that rolled to a halt in front of the doors of the gaming house. Finally, Wolverton had arrived—and good God, was that the delectable Miss Van Vleet with him? It was . . . and looking more beautiful than he remembered her to be, clad in a clinging silk over satin, with a magnificent ruby-and-diamond necklace that glittered against her creamy skin in the dim light of the coach . . . No good pining after what would never be his, but damme, if she wasn't an angelic creature!

Gleaming blond hair was piled atop her head, dangling from beneath a hooded capote in small curls on each cheek, and her exquisite profile held character in the small rounded chin with a hint of a cleft in the center. She looked wary, her eyes turbulent as she turned to stare out the window of the coach.

Barry started when there was a movement beside him, and Northwick stepped from the shadows beside the door. Revealing light slanted across the earl's ravaged face as he gazed at the coach with something akin to alarm. Barry had been so intrigued with the lady that he had not even noticed the earl behind him, and his mouth tightened with dislike and an irresistible urge to provoke Northwick.

"Excuse me, my lord, but you are blocking the door."

Northwick turned slightly, his bushy brows lifting in sardonic amusement. "Dear me, it's Kenworth as well. What a pity you cannot seem to stay out of the gaming hells, m'boy. It would save you so much. But now that you are paid up, you want to risk shooting the cat again, I see. How droll."

"Save your humor, my lord. I find it objectionable."

Scanning him with narrowed eyes, the earl pursed his mouth thoughtfully. "Too bad we do not see eye to eye more often, Kenworth. I fear that you may annoy me too greatly soon. Are you certain you wish to stay? I may feel it may be necessary to ask you to leave if you are too annoying."

"I quiver with anticipation at the prospect. Now, if you will excuse me, I am being beckoned."

As he moved past Northwick, Barry heard him murmur, "By all means, be a toad-eater, my boy. Wolverton still holds your chits."

Because it was true, and because he could not deny it, the words rankled. He wheeled around, but Northwick stepped inside again, disappearing into the shadows of the dark doorway. Curse him. Thank God he no longer owed the bloody earl money, for Wolverton had lent him the blunt to repay. At least Brett was gentleman enough to accept his vowels, and to shrug carelessly when offered collateral.

"I do not need collateral from you, Barry. Your word is enough for me."

Those simple words had cemented Kenworth's already high admiration for Wolverton. His father referred to it quite nastily as hero worship, but it was nothing of the sort. He only admired the man for his supreme self-confidence and cynical wit. Brett was no dandy, but he had seen how the man commanded respect and admiration from those he encountered. It was something done so casually that Barry found himself frequently studying Wolverton to see how he managed it. And why not? Should he be like his father? A dullard, though respected enough, he supposed. Yet Wolverton had been many places and done many things. There were even rumors that he'd dabbled in piracy, though Barry discounted those as envy. Why would a man of Wolverton's wealth bother to pirate what he could easily purchase?

It was that air of reckless adventure that lured him to Wolverton in a way, for if ever there was a man capable of piracy, it would certainly be Brett. He'd seen him engage in two duels, coming out the better man in both. One duel had been under the oaks at dawn, with swords as the weapon of choice. The last had been with pistols, and Brett facing his sweating opponent with a cool head and accurate aim definitely designed to rattle any man.

It was a skill that Barry admired and feared at the same time. If he possessed Wolverton's cool head, he would not have had to endure Northwick's months of insults. How humiliating to admit even to himself that he was lacking, but it wasn't in courage. No, he hadn't Wolverton's skill with a pistol or sword, damn the luck.

But after tonight—yes, if all went well, perhaps the score with Northwick would be settled to satisfaction. He moved from the shadows to greet Brett once the coach lurched away from the curb and rolled down the street.

"Any problems?" Brett asked in his soft drawl when he joined him at the door, and Barry shook his head.

"Nothing but Northwick's usual sarcasm. Curse the man, he certainly seemed unhappy to see you arrive. If—"

"Let's go inside." Brett's swift interruption conveyed his wariness, and Barry nodded, following him down the dark, shadowed hallway into The Pigeon Hole, as the den was aptly named, for plucking plump pigeons who thought to beat the house's odds.

It was crowded, as usual. But this gambling den did not require expensive membership as did Arthur's, so catered to a class of men rougher than was seen at many of the other London clubs. Many here were greenhorns out for a lark, up from the country with a bit of money in their purses. *Fat pigeons indeed*, Kenworth thought.

"It is rumored that Northwick is a partner in this establishment, you know," he murmured in Brett's ear. "I don't suppose he's the abbot of a nunnery, as is the Mr. Seaton who owns a half interest here and is said to be worth near a hundred thousand at best."

Brett laughed softly. "If Brakefield had that much blunt, he wouldn't need my money."

"No doubt, but there are some men for whom there is never enough." Barry paused, thought about his own wastrel habits and silently vowed a change that even his father would approve. But now, he had a debt of another kind to pay, and by God, before the night was over, he intended to see it settled.

Brett moved to a Hazard table, his attention on the roll of the dice. Only a careful observer would note that he surveyed the room more than the game, his posture lazy and his eyes half-slitted in his darkly saturnine face.

"Crabs," one of the players said in disgust as he lost, and looked up at Brett across the green baize. "Are you in, sir?"

Shrugging, Brett paid in. *"Facilis descensus Averni,"* he observed lightly, and Kenworth gave a soft laugh.

"Descent to Hell is easy," Barry translated when the player looked puzzled. "It's a quote. Virgil said it first and best, I think."

The man shook his head. "I'm not acquainted with Mr. Virgil, but he must have been a regular client here. This is the third night in a row I've been cleaned out by the children in the wood."

Brett smiled slightly, juggling the wooden dice in his palm. "Perhaps Hazard isn't your game."

"None of them are my game." The man shrugged and moved away from the table, and the play continued.

Brett was up by fifty-two pounds when there was a small stir at the door, and he glanced up, tension in his face and posture. Then he swore harshly, and Barry turned to see the cause, tense himself with expectation that it may have begun.

A shock rippled through him—Kyla Van Vleet stood at the door, quite alone and demanding to be granted entrance. Good God, was she mad? What was she *doing* here? And tonight of all nights! Surely, Brett could not—

But it was quickly apparent that Wolverton had no intention of allowing her in, for he abandoned the play and moved swiftly across the room to the door to take her by one arm. Barry followed, alarmed that everything might be ruined by this unexpected turn of event.

"What the hell are you doing here?" Brett demanded harshly, and Kyla met his gaze with a coolly lifted brow that elicited a certain admiration from Barry for her courage if not her good sense.

"Perhaps I came to gamble. That does seem to be what you're doing here."

"What did you think? Never mind. I know what you thought—" Brett paused, scowled, then said more calmly, "I'll have Burton's head for this. Is my carriage still here?"

"Yes, of course. But I have no intention of leaving now."

"That's too bad." He turned her around and pushed her toward the door, then stopped as it swung toward him.

Behind them, Barry could not see the reason for Brett's sudden halt, until he heard a familiar voice murmur a surprised greeting: "Why, Miss Van Vleet. How delightful to see you again—and quite astounding, what? Wolverton, I did not know it was your habit to bring your lady along with you to such—diverse—entertainments. Do you take her to Amy Wilson's house with you as well?"

"Here here," Barry protested heatedly, "low blow, Northwick! Not in front of the lady, at least."

Kyla turned her expressive eyes toward Barry, and he saw a glint of appreciation in them mixed with the hot light of anger. "Thank you, Lord Kenworth. It is most rewarding to see that there are still *some* gentlemen left in London. I had begun to despair."

Northwick laughed softly, and his thick brows lifted with sardonic amusement. "I believe she has you there, Wolverton, what? Let her stay. I fancy a bit of beauty this evening. Far too many rough faces around me of late, and she is such a lovely distraction, do you not think?"

"This is no place for her, nor for any woman." Brett turned her toward the door as it swung open again, but Kyla pulled back, jerking free of his grasp to whirl on him with anger sparking her eyes.

"Excuse me, but I do not care to be pulled this way and that as if I have no mind of my own. I am quite capable of deciding what I want, and I have decided to remain. Unless, of course, you have some *other* reason for sending me away?"

Brett's jaw clenched, and his voice was tight. "This is no place for you, Kyla. For once, make things easier for yourself."

"No, you mean make things easier for *you*. I prefer to stay, thank you."

"Good God, Wolverton, is it you?" a voice exclaimed from the open door, and the duke of Cumberland strode into the main room, blinking a little at the smoke and gazing from Brett to Northwick, then his gaze shifting to Kyla. "I had not expected to find you here, of all places—and with Miss Van Vleet. What a charming surprise."

"Nor did I expect to see you, Your Grace." Brett managed a tight smile, cursing inwardly at Kyla's abysmal timing. Her arrival could very well ruin everything, and now the duke was here, hard on her heels. Had he followed them? It was becoming plain that he had suspected the wrong prince of being aligned with Northwick. Sending Kyla away might arouse Cumberland or Northwick's suspicion, and he could ill afford to put them on their guard. Dammit. What the devil was keeping Watley? "There was a change of plans, Your Grace," he said smoothly, and tugged on Kyla's arm to bring her closer to him.

"Yes," Northwick said with sardonic glee, "and it seems that Miss Van Vleet has seen fit to change them for you, Wolverton. Teach her to play, won't you? It should be a most entertaining distraction for all of us. Come in, Your Grace," he said then to the duke, and Cumberland looked rather uncertain as he moved past Kyla and Brett to Northwick. The earl smiled, a thin curl of his lips that lent a sinister cast to his expression. "I've not had such an expansive group of notable company here at my little establishment in some time. Faro, Your Grace?"

As Cumberland moved toward the Faro table with the earl, Brett moved Kyla away from the door, steering her toward the Hazard table. "If you're going to stay," he snarled in her ear, "then you'd damn well better do what you're told."

"I don't—Brett, you're hurting me!"

His fingers dug into her arm with brutal intensity, and his mouth moved against her ear as if he was whispering endearments that made her shiver. "This is not a good time to assert your independence, damn you. No—don't try and pull away. Listen to me, you little fool. There will be trouble here tonight, and whatever I tell you to do, do it. Do you hear me?"

She nodded silently, and he was satisfied to see her glance nervously around her, as if suddenly aware that this was hardly the type of place she should visit. It was too late to consider that now, especially after Northwick and Cumberland had already seen her. It was obvious the earl hoped she would be a distraction.

Brett halted in front of the Hazard table, still holding Kyla by one arm. "As you can see," he said softly, you have garnered the attention you so obviously desire. Is this what you wanted?"

"Brett—"

"Oh no." His grip on her arm tightened as he cut her off, frustration giving a sharp edge to his temper. "Since you insist upon staying, you will do as you're told. It should be a welcome change—ah ah, *querida*. Do not be so foolish as to resist unless you relish being embarrassed even more than you should be. There's not a man here who would stop me were I to treat you as no more than a Covent Garden whore. After all, this is hardly the sort of place decent ladies visit."

She was trembling, and her chin quivered slightly as she slanted her eyes toward him, and he was only slightly satisfied at the apprehension in her gaze. Then she shrugged, a careless lift of her smooth shoulders as if totally indifferent to what he might think. "I should not have come, I suppose, but I thought—not that it matters. Perhaps I should leave now."

"No. Not now. You're here, and by God, you'll stay for the moment. I'll teach you to play, as Northwick so conveniently suggested I do."

The dice tumbled onto the table with soft clacking thuds, and one of the men groaned, "Crabs. Thrown out. Just my luck." He looked up, saw Brett, and grinned. "Just as well, now that you're here, Wolverton. You play too close a game to suit me."

"It's all in mastering the odds, Pemberton." Brett swept up the dice. "Do any of you gentlemen object to allowing the lady to try her hand at it?"

Kyla looked startled, and one of the gentlemen scowled, but none offered a protest. Yet, as Brett instructed Kyla in the throwing of the two dice, they drew a small crowd, Northwick among them. The earl's previous composure was restored, his manner as confident as always. But now Watley had arrived and was across the room mingling with players around a Faro table. Brett smiled a little, and focused on Kyla.

"You're the caster, Kyla. You must score five, six, seven, eight, or nine. The first die is the main, the second thrown die, the chance. If your second score equals the main, you've nicked it and won. If you throw crabs—two, three, eleven, or twelve— you've thrown out and lost."

Kyla rolled the two dice in her palm, beautiful despite her obvious confusion. She worried her bottom lip between her teeth. "And if I do none of that?"

"You continue casting the dice until you either

equal the main and lose, or hope your second score nets you a win. It's a game of chance, hence the name Hazard, but the real skill is in betting the odds."

Frowning, she shrugged her bare shoulders, and the ruby-and-diamond necklace around her pale throat glimmered in the lamplight. "As long as I'm playing with *your* money, I don't mind giving it a try."

"Naturally." Brett's tone was dry, and he glanced up at Barry with a wry smile. "Shall we hope our pigeon flies?"

It was a double entendre, and Barry grinned his appreciation. Kyla tossed the dice and lost. On her second try she did better, and with only a little coaxing began to gauge the odds rather well. By this time, the small crowd of men around the table had grown larger. Drawn by the novelty of a beautiful woman in their midst, most came to watch, but a few more joined the play.

It wasn't long before Northwick entered the play, his colorless gaze riveted to Kyla from across the table. She fumbled a little when he first joined them, but Brett reassured her in low tones and she grew more confident again. There was a tension in the air now that hadn't been there before, and he wasn't the only one who felt it. Two of those observing drifted away.

Brakefield played safe, betting little and cadging the odds, but Brett sensed the rising tension in the earl. He watched him with all appearances of idle curiosity, while focusing on Watley and his hand-picked crew of confederates. The men ranged through the room at different tables, arriving at staggered intervals so as not to arouse suspicion.

Good. None of them looked out of place, but resembled the others crowded around the gaming tables.

He glanced at Kyla again and saw the look of fierce concentration on her face as she studied the green baize tables and tumbling dice. She won, a small amount, but enough to make her face flush with pleasure, lending a most becoming color to her creamy cheeks.

With her sheer gown and the luster of jewels at her throat, she was a most captivating sight. Mirrored in the eyes of many of the men around the table were images of Kyla as she leaned forward, the rounded swells of her breasts straining against thin silk and satin as she tossed the dice. The low neckline barely restrained her, and the promise of exposure was imminent enough to rivet more than one man's eyes to her gown. Northwick could not keep his eyes from her.

"Nicked it," someone said in admiration, and Brett saw that Kyla had won again, another small sum but enough to keep that becoming flush on her cheeks. She laughed, a light tinkling sound like small silver bells, and he found himself looking at her again instead of Northwick.

Excitement made her eyes gleam, or perhaps it was only the glasses of champagne she had consumed, and her mouth was curved into an eager smile as she rolled the dice in her small palm. Her gloves were gone, discarded in the coach, he thought, and her long slender fingers toyed with the wooden die before she leaned forward again to play. The soft thud of a die hitting green baize was followed by another, and Brett looked away from Kyla to the earl.

He was staring at her as if mesmerized, his mouth slightly open, and his pale eyes slitted beneath the bushy brow like a furry strip knotted over his long thin nose. Once he had been a handsome man, Beatrice had said, but his years of lascivious life were reflected now in his harsh features.

Smoke drifted in thick layers over the tables, and across the room two men lifted their voice in sudden quarrel. Northwick glanced from Kyla in that direction, and started to move away just as Brett saw Watley slip from the main room toward the narrow hallway.

"My lord," Brett said with deliberate sarcasm, "do you not play Hazard with women?"

Northwick turned back and paused, his thick brows lifted. "All play with women is hazard, Wolverton."

Brett acknowledged the acid pun with a slight smile. "So it is—but you would know that better than most."

"Ah, but I defer to you in that regard, Your Grace. It is said that you take more than your share of chances." A tight smile curled the earl's thin lips. "How else could one explain the apparent abduction of a young lady in full view of two hundred guests?"

Brett felt Kyla stiffen beside him, and heard her indrawn breath as she threw out and lost the toss. He put a casual hand on her shoulder, his fingers toying with the loose tendrils of blond hair dangling in front of her ears.

"Abduction, my lord? She does not look a prisoner—do you, my pet?"

Kyla shot him a narrowed, angry glance, and

her flush rose even higher. "A prisoner of circumstances, perhaps, as are most of us."

Neatly done. Brett smiled appreciation as his hand caressed the bare skin of her shoulder, and saw from the corner of his eye how Northwick watched closely. Slowly, deliberately, he drew his fingers lower as if toying with the diamond-and-ruby necklace around her throat, the edge of his hand skimming the tops of Kyla's breasts. She grew still. Her lower lip quivered slightly as if holding back angry words, and her long lashes lowered to veil her eyes. Her hand clenched into a small fist against the baize-covered table edge.

Brett damned her for coming, for putting herself into what could be a most dangerous situation. But at least she was serving to distract Northwick, an unexpected advantage in the evening's plans, because the earl could not keep his eyes from her. Was he thinking of her as a little girl he'd once known? Or just as an alluring woman? Damn the bloody bastard—it was all Brett could do to keep from calling him out, but that would be disastrous. No, he had to get back those deeds, and this seemed the only way to do it without publicly accusing the earl of having stolen them. As a Colonial upstart, he would certainly be hard put to convince anyone of the truth of accusations against a member of the peerage. Northwick might be a slimy bastard, but he was one of them, while a Colonial duke would be viewed with displeasure and distrust.

If this was Texas, he would already have confronted Northwick with a pistol and demanded the return of his deeds. But in England, things were done differently, with adherence to an implicit code of conduct. Satisfaction was obtained by calling a man out, but that would do him no good if he could not get his deeds back first.

Brett removed his hand from Kyla only when Northwick moved away from the Hazard table and toward the Faro table, where Cumberland was—as usual—betting heavily and losing. It was quite crowded now, the smoke a thick haze in the room and the play growing louder as men swore at cards and dice.

Barry sidled close, his eyes worried and his voice a low murmur. "Do you think they will still do it tonight? I mean . . . are you sure your informant is right about this? If Cumberland is involved . . ."

"How better than to do it right under our noses?"

Kyla lost again, and one of the men offered slyly to take his winnings in trade, a remark that earned him an angry gasp from her and a swift upward glance from Brett. Just the threat in his face served as warning, and the man laughed and protested that he was only jesting, of course.

"Just a joke, guvnor, that's all. She be a looker, and I meant to 'ave a bit of fun is all."

"Stick to Hazard for amusement, my friend. It's less costly."

Someone jostled him, and Brett saw from one corner of his eye that Watley had returned and was giving him the signal. Northwick and Cumberland were no longer at the Faro table, and Brett leaned close to Kyla and unfastened the diamond-and-ruby necklace around her throat. He tossed it carelessly to the table and smiled.

"High stakes, gentlemen. Just to make the game more interesting."

"Brett—!"

He took her chin between his thumb and finger and pressed a swift, hard kiss to her mouth, ignoring her angry exclamation. "If you lose it, *querida*, I'll buy you another," he said against her parted lips. He drew back, eyeing her flushed face. "And if you win, I'll buy you two. That should be enough incentive, don't you think?"

"I don't know why you're doing this, but if you want to throw your money around so carelessly, I'll be more than happy to take it," she shot back at him. She rolled the dice in her palm, her brow lifted and her gaze angry and uncertain.

"Just concentrate, Kyla. These gentlemen look quite determined to have it off you."

Still uncertain, she glanced back at the table, then shrugged carelessly and leaned forward to roll the die. It should suffice to keep her busy and the room diverted, he thought as he moved away from her a few steps. Across the room, Barry edged toward the darkened hallway near the rear exit. The play on the Hazard table intensified with the high stakes drawing fierce competition, and in the press of men crowded around the table Brett slipped away.

He felt someone come up behind him, heard Watley's rough accents in his ear: "He's this way, guvnor."

It was dark, and farther down the corridor was a musty smell like damp earth and rotting wood. Two men lay still and sprawled on the floor in the shadows, no doubt from Watley's attentions. Ahead there was a low murmur of voices, and in the shadows he saw Barry turn toward him and his eyes glisten palely in the murky light.

"Northwick and Cumberland," Barry muttered, and jerked his head toward a small door set into a brick wall.

Christ. High stakes, indeed, for the king's brother to play if he was involved in something so shady with Northwick. Too many scandals would hardly sit well with Parliament.

Pausing outside the door, Brett glanced behind him to be certain Watley's men prevented anyone else from stumbling into the hallway. Three men were silhouetted against the light through the doorway, and Watley gave a confirming nod as he saw the pistol in Brett's palm.

"Just as you ordered, guvnor. No guards, and my men will hold the doorway."

Brett's fingers curled around the solid chill of the pistol and he edged forward. The door was closed, and the murmur of voices grew louder. It was locked, and Brett stepped back against the wall opposite to use it for leverage as he lifted his foot and kicked. Watley lent his weight to the effort, and the door gave way with a resounding crash.

Cursing, Northwick turned toward the doorway, then stopped short when he saw the pistol Brett had aimed directly at his chest. His mouth twisted. "Well, well, Wolverton, you have reverted to barbarian completely, I see. Just what the devil do you think you are doing barging in on a private conversation? I daresay, Cumberland will be most put out with you, what, Your Grace?"

"Indeed," Cumberland put in angrily, but behind the bluster there was a set tension to his mouth and his eyes that betrayed his nervous guilt. "What is the meaning of this, Wolverton?"

With the barrel of his pistol, Brett indicated the papers Cumberland held. "I believe you know full well the meaning of this. Those are stolen papers. If you have bought them from the earl, you have been cheated, for they are mine."

"Stolen?" Cumberland shook his head. "Not at all, sir! Do you *dare* accuse me of stealing?"

"No. That accusation I'll save for Northwick. But you are aware, Your Grace, that those documents you hold are lawfully mine, not the earl's. It would be a shameful involvement, if it was to be made public."

Cumberland scowled, and glanced at the earl. "These are lawfully yours, am I right, Brakefield?"

"As you can see, Your Grace, these papers bear the signature of Colby Banning assigning me his share of the mine we both owned in the Americas. It has taken me some time to find these documents, but they are, indeed, now mine." He met Brett's stare coolly, and shrugged. "A pity you were not aware of it, Wolverton, but then, that's the toll one must pay for not being thorough, I suppose."

"You're a damned liar." Brett stepped forward and held out his hand, keeping the pistol trained on the earl as he did, and Cumberland hesitated only slightly before relinquishing the papers to him. Brett studied them, and saw his father's signature scrawled across the bottom of the deed. At the top, attached to the deed, was a codicil designating the Santa María Mine to Carlton Brakefield, Viscount Erby and future earl of Northwick. The date was nearly twenty years old, and bore his father's name and signature as well. He looked up at the earl, and saw his triumphant smirk with mounting rage.

"This is a forgery, Northwick. My father would never have left the mine to you."

"My dear Wolverton, as shocking as this must be for you, I fear it is true."

"If it's true, why the devil have you kept it secret? Why have the papers stolen if they are authentic? No, I don't believe it for a minute, and neither should you, Your Grace." He turned to Cumberland, and said brutally, "I doubt you have the funds to purchase a silver mine that is worth a fortune—it's well-known that you are up to your ears in debt."

"Ah, so you think my brother may be the real money behind this purchase?" Cumberland's mouth twisted, and his single eye narrowed slightly. "No doubt, that is the reason you made certain he would be—entertained—this evening, I suppose. How foresighted of you. But you are wrong, Wolverton. George has no idea of this, or he would be planning to spend it on more marbles or some of that god-awful architecture he favors. Nor do I intend to share with the bloody government. This is my doing, and mine alone, and my partners are my business. Do not forget who you are dealing with, sir. My father is still king, and I am still regarded with some wariness if not respect."

"No doubt, but not even the king can steal and escape unscathed. Do you have any idea of the character of the man you are bartering with, Your Grace? How do you think the king—or Parliament—would accept the knowledge that along with your other known vices, you keep company with a lecher—a man who preys on children."

Cumberland shifted uneasily from one foot to the other, and turned to look at Northwick. The earl glared at Brett and denied it hotly. "Dear me—you must be mad! Or is it that you just wish to justify the fact that your current mistress once belonged to me? No fault of mine, dear boy—her mother sent her to me, and what else could I do but give the poor child shelter?"

Kenworth stepped forward from the shadows behind Watley. "There are those who would disagree with you, my lord," Barry said quietly, and Northwick looked startled when he recognized him. "I know firsthand that you prey on young girls bought in Covent Garden. You cannot deny what I saw, and even if you do, the scandal will be enough to ruin you."

When Cumberland made a small sound, Brett moved forward into the small pool of light cast by a lamp upon the damp brick wall. "I intend to see you brought before the magistrate upon grave charges, Northwick, and not even your connection with Cumberland can save you from that."

"Damn you, Wolverton. You cannot prove anything. It is all hearsay. My word against yours— a crude Colonial who is not really English at all. And you, Kenworth, you foolish young pup— what will you say? That you witnessed such rumored depravity but did not report it? How will that look? And who would take the word of an unlicked cub known for gambling away his allowance?" Northwick's laugh was unpleasant. "I am afraid, gentlemen, that you have concocted wild tales for nothing. They will not fly. Once my ownership of the mines in America is discovered, it will be known that you are trying to discredit me in order to gain control of the Santa María. Hardly credible."

Furious now, Brett heard Barry mutter something under his breath, and Cumberland frowned. He turned to the duke. "Is that a risk you're willing to take, Your Grace? I have nothing to lose, because I don't give a damn about what people think. I have no one to answer to but myself. You, however, have much more to lose. Are you willing to risk it?"

After a moment of tense silence, Cumberland swore fervently and wheeled around to face Northwick. "He's right, you know. I cannot take the chance. Enough has been done to discredit me through my own efforts. I cannot risk more."

Northwick shrugged, but there was a hard glitter in the gaze he turned to Brett. "No matter. There will be another willing buyer for my deed. Perhaps you, Wolverton? Or could it be that without the silver mine, you have no fortune to spend? How daunting."

"Don't be overconfident, my lord. I have the deed in my hand, and am not likely to return it to you. At this point, I can afford to undergo a lengthy legal battle much more easily than you, so think twice about protesting to a magistrate. I don't think the duke will be able to confirm your claims without endangering his own welfare, so it seems that for the moment, you have no alternative."

There was another moment of sizzling silence, then Northwick executed a small stiff bow in Brett's direction. "Very well done, Wolverton. You have me in check at the moment, but do not think the game finished."

With a contemptuous glance at Barry, Northwick pushed past Watley and out the door into the hallway. When Kenworth protested, Brett shook his head. "Let him go for now. He has no place to hide from the law."

Folding the deed, Brett slid it into his inner pocket while Cumberland cleared his throat, and said awkwardly, "No harm done, then, I suspect, hey Wolverton?"

Brett did not reply, but eyed the duke coolly until he flushed and looked away. "Dammit, Wolverton, I do not want this to get about."

"Is the prince involved?"

"No. Actually—I was commissioned to purchase the deed from Brakefield by a firm in New Orleans. Offered to settle my debts if I would buy it and stake my claim. They felt that few would argue with a prince of the realm." The duke's mouth twisted with derision at this last.

"And the name of this firm?" Brett tucked the pistol into his waistband out of sight beneath his coat, then glanced again at Cumberland. "Your Grace—?"

"Damned fine mess—very well. But I want no scandal about this, you understand, nor do I want it put about that Northwick dallies with children. Too many people know of our occasional association, and I've no desire to be tarred with the same brush, by Christ. Is it a bargain?"

"Brett, no," Barry protested angrily. "You cannot let Northwick escape unscathed again!"

"There are other ways to handle that, Kenworth. It is a bargain, Your Grace. Who contacted you?"

Cumberland took him aside, away from Watley and Barry, his voice low as if afraid of being overheard. "Señor Javier Aguilar y Portillo—ah, I see you recognize the name."

Brett stared at him. "Javier Portillo? Are you certain of this?"

"Yes, of course I am. He sent his secretary to me in the guise of goodwill ambassador, one of those damned French exiles that are so arrogant. A detestable man. Remember, you agreed not to divulge what I have told you."

"I will remember."

Brett turned abruptly away and left Cumberland in the small shabby room, then pushed through the door ahead of Watley and Kenworth. Javier Aguilar y Portillo—his mother's brother. Why had he not seen this coming? And here he was in London, while Javier had free rein and was no doubt scheming to take away everything Colby Banning had managed to accumulate through the years. Goddamn him!

Rage filled him, seeped into his veins to course with icy determination throughout his entire body. He had to return to Texas. But first, he must end things here. There was still Kyla to deal with, and God only knew what he could do with her.

Kenworth caught up with him just as he entered the main room, his voice rough. "I say, Brett, you aren't going to let Brakefield get away with this, are you? Is it true that he—and Miss Van Vleet? Good God, man, if it is, how can you justify letting him go? After being so vile as to even *touch* a lovely creature like her? It's an outrage, and I cannot stomach the thought of her being at the mercy of a man like Northwick! She has already been shamed enough, I think!"

Impatient and frustrated, Brett turned on Barry, and saw the honest outrage in the young man's face. He stifled a harsh retort, and instead drawled, "Then perhaps you would like to make an honest woman of her, Kenworth."

Barry stared at him with incredulous eyes, stammering a little. "D-d-do you mean m-marry her? *Christ*, Brett!"

He hadn't really meant it, but the thought suddenly struck him that it might be the best thing for both of them. Why not? Kyla needed a decent husband, and Barry certainly needed money—Celeste du Bois was right. She had berated him for ruining her goddaughter and he had. Yes, it might be the answer, to marry her off to Kenworth, or someone like him.

But when he arrived at the Hazard table where he'd left Kyla, she was gone. One of the players looked up, a smile of satisfaction on his face as he dangled the ruby-and-diamond necklace from one hand.

"Not bad for an hour's play, wouldn't you say, sir?"

Brett paused. "Where is she? The young lady who owned that necklace—where is she?"

"Gone off with another swell, maybe one that won't wager her jewelry, heh?" He laughed, then took two swift steps back when Brett started toward him. "Here now, don't be lookin' at me! I ain't had nothin' to do with it, save that I won when she threw crabs . . ."

His protest ended in a frightened gurgle when

Brett grabbed him by the collar and shoved him up against a wall. "I don't give a damn about the bloody necklace. Tell me who she left with."

It was no big surprise when the man gasped out, "I don't know his name but he was playin' here earlier—a swell like you, with bushy eyebrows that go all across his face—that's all I know!"

Coming up behind him, Kenworth muttered, "Brakefield. *Dammit!* Now he's got Kyla."

Seventeen

Kyla shivered, muddled as much by the swift manner of her departure from the gaming room as the last glass of champagne she had drank. She should not have taken it, should not have allowed Northwick to give her anything! Oh, why wouldn't this pounding in her ears go away? It was as if she was in a well, with voices and light and vague impressions whirling around her in a constant, blurred flow of hazy impressions . . . she blinked, frowned, and tried to lift a hand to her head but could not.

It hurt so. And she was cold. Oh, it was all so confusing, the way voices seemed to come from nowhere, out of shadows, drifting around her in formless patterns that only made her certain she should make sense of them. But any attempt to do so was useless. Nothing made sense.

Where was Brett? Why had he left her? He'd been there one moment, then gone the next, and now—oh now she could not think without her head hurting.

One of the shadows detached from the darkness and moved toward her, the voice a low familiar purring, like that of a large cat, an ominous grating that made her shiver again.

"Cold, m'dear? Never mind. You shall be warm soon, what? Yes, I shall see to you, as I should have done from the first moment I recognized you." An unpleasant laugh mingled with the man's words, and she blinked up at him, desperately trying to see through the fog.

"North . . . wick." Her voice sounded strange to her, far away and lethargic.

"Yes, m'dear. You're coming out of it a bit, are you? Very good. I want you to feel everything, to hear everything." Again the unpleasant laugh that sent chills up her spine. "No, no, pretty child. Do not struggle. It will do you no good, as you will no doubt learn in just a moment. I have you quite secure here . . . lovely little slut. You have a beautiful body, though a bit overblown for my usual tastes. But then, you know that, don't you? I remember you as a child, you know. So blond, so pretty, so perfect . . . an innocent. Untouched and untarnished—awaiting the awakening. Unlike now. Now, you have become as all of them do—dirty from the touch of so many hands on you, a slut for any man to take."

Slowly, his words sank into her like heavy stones, and she looked up, perceiving through the misty haze in front of her eyes the nature of her danger. She blinked to dispel the fog, then put out her tongue to wet her dry lips. Her voice was an unfamiliar croak: "No . . . I am . . . not."

"They all deny it." There was the sound of boots on something rough, then Northwick's face loomed directly in front of her, terrifying in its close proximity, chilling her with the glint in his colorless eyes, like empty windows reflecting light. His hand cupped her chin, not roughly, but compelling her to look up at him when she tried to twist away. "You may deny it with words, but your body will betray you. All women deny it until they must at last acknowledge the true evil of their souls. You will be no different. But remember—I tried to save you from what you have become. If your bitch of a mother had not taken you away when she did, I could have salvaged you. . . ."

His voice trailed into a silence fraught with meaning, and Kyla shuddered. "What do you . . . intend . . . to do with me?"

"Save you."

It was said simply, the two words devoid of inflection, but the implication behind them pierced Kyla to the marrow. She tried to think, groped for a way to stall him for time until she could think more clearly, and her head fell back, striking something hard and solid. A wall, damp stone behind her, her hands tied at the wrists but her legs left free—could she manage to flee? If he left her even an instant's opening, perhaps she could find a way out. But where was she? It was so dark and shadowy, the only light coming from candles flickering on low shelves around the chamber. She blinked again, and drew in a deep breath of fetid air, like that of a burial chamber. The comparison made her shudder again.

"My lord—do you mind? My wrists hurt where they are bound so tightly."

"Yes, we will do something about that. But not now." Northwick rose to his feet, looming over her again, and as her vision cleared, she saw him now as something more substantial than a hazy shadow and opaque eyes. He was moving away from her, and she turned her head to survey her surroundings. They were in some kind of a room resembling a wine cellar, but there were no casks of wine or racks of bottles, only empty shelves and a feeling of dampness.

Her wrists hurt, and her head ached, and she was cold, so very cold. What did he intend? And where was Brett and even Kenworth? Northwick had obviously drugged her, but why?

The answer soon became chillingly clear, as the earl returned to lift her into his arms and carry her across the room. Gently, he placed her on a cold rock shelf lit by candles; it looked to Kyla like a sacrificial altar. She shuddered at the thought, and tried to twist from the earl's grasp. He laughed softly and held her down, pulling her arms over her head to bind them to an iron circle set into the stone.

"Foolish child. Do not try to escape your destiny. This is meant to be, though late by some years."

There was an odd lilt to his voice, a soft purring note that terrified her, and she began to struggle more fiercely. "Damn you, let me go! Brett will kill you for this. . . ."

"Will he? I doubt it. Even if he should discover your absence, it will not be in time. No one knows of this place save for those I trust. Those I do not trust, rarely leave."

Half-sobbing, Kyla strained against her bonds, but they were too tight. The stone was ice-cold beneath her, and her gown was no protection against the damp chill of the cellar. God, what did he intend?

"You look so frightened, m'dear. Do not be. I intend to release you from this world of sin. Though you have lost your innocence, you are still so beautiful, and I remember the sweet pure child that you once were. . . ." His voice trailed into incoherence as he loomed over her, eyes wide and so pale and colorless in the dim, turbid light of candle-gloom and shadow.

"You . . . you're mad," she whispered through stiff, icy lips, feeling terror seep into her bones as he stared down at her with a fixed expression. It was as if he was carved from wax, only his eyes betraying any sign of emotion, and those so cold. "Why are you doing this? I have never done anything to harm you. . . ."

"Have you not?" His hands were surprisingly warm against her skin as he slowly drew her gown up to bare her legs, and when she tried to kick him, he caught her in a harsh grip. "You force me to truss you too tightly, when if you would only understand, you would accept it."

Kyla caught back a terrified sob, her throat aching with fear and apprehension as Northwick bound her legs to more rings set into the stone. Then he loomed over her again, while above and behind him long, distorted shadows flickered on the high walls and ceiling like the capering monsters of her childhood. Only this was no nightmare, this was real and dangerous, and she must keep her wits about her to survive.

It was obvious Northwick was mad, beyond reason and intent upon her destruction. She must find the weakness in him, must appeal to that small chink in some way, or she would die here in this dreadful, dank tomb.

"My lord . . ." She paused, licked her lips and forced her quavering voice louder, "My lord—perhaps you do not need to tie me. Tell me what it is you require, and I will not be so frightened."

"I require submission." Northwick smiled, his voice a husky grating as he stared down at her. "Complete submission, like that of an obedient child. It is soothing, really, how children can be so docile and receptive. It is only when they grow older and they learn . . . learn how to be coy, hateful creatures, deceitful and manipulative—ah yes, I see that you are beginning to understand me now."

While he talked, he began to pull away her garments, the silk and satin rending with soft destruction beneath his careless hands, and Kyla tried to ignore the awful sensation of his hands on her, casually stroking her while he removed her clothes, talking to her all the while in that peculiar, eerie voice. She shivered at the cold air on her bare skin, and clenched her teeth when Northwick began to explore her body with light, intrusive touches. She was completely exposed to him now, the shreds of her clothes beneath her, his eyes avidly devouring her while he caressed her breasts, belly, and thighs.

Huskily, the earl muttered, "I wanted you so badly then, the pure, unsullied daughter of a whore—mine to mold, to form into whatever I wanted you to be, sweetly pure and acquiescent . . . but she refused me, the bitch. That golden-haired French whore . . . I vowed that I would have you one day. And then she took you away from London." He looked up, his face contorted with fury. "I looked for you for weeks, until I discovered her treachery. Damn her—I would not have hurt you. I only wanted to save you from becoming what she was, from becoming a slut like all the other women who walk this earth tempting men . . . do you know that I would have given you anything? I only wanted to hold you, to touch you . . . ah, lovely purity—so fresh and innocent with such beautiful blond hair. There has never been another like you, though I have looked and looked through the years, searching all of London for another child as perfect . . . but now that I finally have found you, Wolverton has ruined you. *Ruined* you . . . but he shall pay for that."

As his voice faded, she wanted to shrink away, but forced herself to remain calm and quiet beneath his hands, sensing that any attempt to resist would only meet with more deadly force. Was this why he preferred children? Perhaps it was easier to terrify them into silence for his perversions . . .

Her arms ached from the strain of being tied over her head, and the humiliation of being so exposed was almost as overwhelming as the effort it took to lie still while he touched her in the most intimate of places. It still was not clear to her exactly what he expected other than her compliance, for he made no effort to rape her, only touch her. His expression was taut, raptly intent as he stroked her, murmuring almost indistinguishable endearments while his voice became more strained and guttural.

Quivering beneath his exploration, Kyla tested the strength of the cords binding her arms over her head, and began to worry one of the knots with her fingers. She was so cold that it was difficult maneuvering her hands into a position to enable her to tug at the looped silken cord. It might be her only chance, and if she could just free even one hand, perhaps there would be a moment when he would be off guard.

Taking her by surprise, Northwick bent to kiss her suddenly, thrusting his tongue between her lips. She nearly gagged, but forced herself not to resist, squeezing her eyes tightly shut as he kissed her. If this depraved earl preferred innocence, any move she made that might be misinterpreted as response would certainly enrage him. Had he not said that all women were sluts? She must be as the child he once lusted for, must be as docile and frightened but obedient until she could somehow escape.

Yet it was so difficult to remain still when she was repulsed by his hands and mouth on her, touching her in places only Brett had done . . . Oh God, *where* was Brett? Why had she been so foolish as to insist upon remaining in the gambling hell after she had seen the rough element there? Her jealousy, her foolish jealousy at the thought of Brett meeting the opera singer had catapulted her into such idiocy. Irrational, stupid reaction . . . it wasn't as if she loved him, after all. Why should she care if he was with someone else? Oh *why* had she followed him like some—some betrayed *wife* instead of the casual mistress that she really was?

Northwick kissed her again, the smell of sour wine and smoke mixing with the damp stench of the cellar. She closed her eyes against him, trembling while he moved lower, his mouth wet on her throat, the chilled flesh of her breasts, then her belly. Oh God, she could not stand this, could not bear it if he violated her any more than he was doing now. . . .

There was a rushing sound in her ears, like that of the sea, and she focused on it instead of what the earl was doing, shutting out everything but the intense desire to be somewhere else. Desperately, she forced herself to retain control, holding tightly to that small part inside that warned her that to react violently would only provoke Northwick. She must stay strong, must concentrate on freeing herself. There was no one else to help her. She had only her own wits to extricate herself from this madman who held her.

But how? How could she manage it when she was tied so tightly? She must find a way to persuade him to release her arms, at least, but it was such a fine line to walk. Carefully, slowly, she opened her eyes to look up at the earl, and he lifted his head to gaze down at her with eyes glazed as if in a trance. He was mad—truly mad, and she was at his mercy. God help her. . . .

The earl straightened, and Kyla caught the feeble glint of metal in his hand as he moved away from her. She held her breath, icy fear paralyzing her as she realized he held a knife. Stepping back, Northwick held up the blade and regarded her from beneath the shelf of his brow for a long, tense moment.

"Are you afraid?"

His soft voice sounded almost tender. She nodded, eyes wide and fixed on the sharp blade. "Yes. . . ."

"Sweet child. I only mean to help you. The world has grown so evil, so full of wickedness . . ." He drew the flat of the blade over the bare skin of her thigh as if a caress, and she stifled a scream. He smiled. "I promised I wouldn't hurt you. I won't. It's almost like going to sleep . . . a small sting, just a tiny prick on your wrists, and all the corrupt blood will drain away, so slowly that you will not even feel it . . . oh no, do not struggle. That makes it happen too quickly, and we must have time, time to purge ourselves of the sin of lust."

This time Kyla could not stifle the scream that erupted from her throat, and it sounded much too loud in the vaulted cavern, bouncing from walls and ceiling as if a hundred tortured souls screamed their terror with her.

Calmly, Northwick moved to where her wrists were bound to the iron ring. Kyla tried to evade the sharp edge of the knife, but he held her still and there was a quick, stinging pain that began to throb.

"No! Oh God, please don't do this . . ." She hadn't meant to beg, but she heard herself as if it was someone else, another woman lying on this bed of stone and pleading for her life, while Northwick ignored her. It came to her then, that this was her funeral bier, this slab of stone with the candles arranged around it, just as Maman had been laid out in the parlor in India. Only Maman had been dressed in her favorite gown, her face serene in the scented glow of dozens of candles around her. There was no peace in this, nothing but stark terror.

"See, Kyla? Only a small sting, like I told you." The earl smiled down at her, candlelight reflected in his pale empty eyes like the fires of hell. "You will be at peace soon. As will I."

Kyla sobbed softly, despair slowly conquering hope as she felt blood seep from her wrists. It was so cold, and she could not stop weeping, tears flowing as freely as her life from her veins. The roaring in her ears grew louder, and Northwick's murmured words of comfort and condemnation grew distant. So many memories, so many regrets, and they all revolved around her in an endless whirl like a child's toy, brief images to haunt her, a collage of confusing impressions from her past that began to meld into one another . . . poor Tante Celeste. She would blame herself, somehow, as she blamed herself for not being there for Faustine. If only she could tell her it was not her fault this had happened—but the bright colors were melting into one another now, dissolving into hazy images, and oddly, there was Brett Banning in the center of it all, a darkly handsome face, mocking and yet so elusive . . . why did he not love her? She could have fallen in love with him, could have loved him if only he had wanted her.

And now she would never know if it could have been. Now, she was to die, alone in this terrible place with the deranged man of her nightmares, and would never know what it was to be truly loved.

Dying may not be so bad, she thought hazily, while the world whirled around her faster and faster. If only this loud buzzing in her ears would stop . . . even Northwick was only a blur now, his droning voice so distant . . . why was he yelling at her? *Isn't this what he wants? Yes, he wants me to die, and I am. Why is he shrieking so?*

There was a loud noise, like the cracking of a whip, then another, the sound reverberating from walls and ceiling in endless waves, crashing around her like the roar of the surf, threatening to engulf her.

Something hot splashed over her, then a heavy weight, and she tried to keep her eyes open but could not. It was all so confused—and as the darkness crept closer, she was a little surprised and yet comforted to hear Brett's voice come from the shadows, so familiar and strong, telling her that it would be all right. Then the weight was gone, and her arms were free, and she felt herself being lifted and held . . . warm hands were on her, pulling her up, but it was too late. She only wanted to sleep, to slip into that beckoning world where there was no pain.

Yes. It will be all right now. . . .

Eighteen

Voices again, sounding much closer. And she was warm at last. Was she dead? Kyla wanted to open her eyes but was afraid of what she might see. No, better to lie here and listen than to risk what might await her once she opened her eyes . . . was it Brett? It sounded like him, and the urgent voice with him sounded like Kenworth. Were they dead, too? No, of course not. Then perhaps . . . she struggled for a moment to make sense of it, her fingers uncurling to test the smooth surface beneath her. Linen, not rock. She must be in a bed. Alive, then. She had not died in that dank cellar with Northwick.

Relief swept over her, and she opened her eyes a tiny bit. Subdued light illuminated a room she recognized as the one in Brett's town house. Yes, there was the rose-hued lamp on her bedside table, filtering through half-drawn bed curtains draping each side of the high bed. Soft pillows cradled her head, and she turned slightly, wincing at a sharp throbbing pain in her arm.

Another voice rose, tart and female—Tante Celeste. "I will not have it, Your Grace! I do not care what you say, she must be protected from more scandal. You've done enough to her, and—"

"I agree." Brett's reply was calm. "I fully intend to protect her from more scandal. With Northwick dead, no one need know about what happened in that cellar. Only Barry and I know what he did to her."

"Well . . . that helps, but *bon Dieu!* it is not enough! You have ruined her. Her name has been smeared over all of London by now, and because of you. How can you rectify such a disaster?"

"Seeing her properly wed will do the trick, I think."

There was a moment of silence, and Kyla held her breath, hardly able to believe her ears. Did he mean to wed her? Oh God—perhaps he did love her, after all. She closed her eyes again, a little dizzy at the thought. But was she certain *she* loved *him*? There was no rhyme or reason to it. Certainly, she felt something for him—an unwilling attraction, she'd thought until a few days ago. But then, when he had returned from London, she had been foolishly glad to see him despite his silly reaction to her dancing in the gypsy camp. Now— oh, it was all so confusing, her emotions in such turmoil where he was concerned, that it was exhausting to think about it.

But as she slipped back into the escape of sleep, she dimly heard Tante Celeste say: "It's about time you realized that, Your Grace."

When she woke, she was alone and the room was deep in shadow, only a small lamp burning atop a mahogany chest across the room. She blinked, and lifted one arm, a little surprised to see the wide white swath circling her wrist before

she recalled the gashes Northwick had cut into her
skin. She shuddered weakly. He had near killed
her. Was it true? Was he dead, or had that been
only part of some wild feverish dream? It was all
such a blur that she wasn't certain what was real
and what was imagined. What really mattered
was that she was alive and safe—and that Brett
Banning had told Tante Celeste he would marry
her.

Kyla struggled to a sitting position. She was
thirsty, and there was a crystal carafe of water on
a table beside the bed. When she reached for it, a
wave of dizziness threatened to send her crashing
off the edge of the mattress, and she cried out with
alarm.

Almost instantly, a shadow loomed up from the
gloom beyond the bed, and her cry this time was
terrified, a high, wild shriek torn from her parched
throat. A hand clamped down on her shoulder,
holding her when she would have wrenched free.

"Hush, Kyla. You're safe now."

"Brett—it is . . . is it really you?"

"Yes." His hand shifted, this time moving to
press against her forehead. "Your fever has broken. Are you thirsty?"

As the pounding of her heart slowed again, she
sank back into the pillows and nodded, almost
shy now when she recalled what she had overheard. Brett poured water into a glass and held it
to her lips, his other hand slipping beneath her
back to lift her so that it would not spill. It seemed
odd for him to be so efficient at this, but then, it
seemed odd for him to be here with her. Did he
care about her? Or had he only agreed to marry
her because Tante Celeste insisted? She would ask

him when the time was right, for she had to know.

But for now, she was content just to lie against the fat pillows cushioning her, grateful still to be alive. She plucked idly at a piece of loose thread in the satin coverlet over her, then looked up. Brett still stood beside the bed, his face partially in shadow, his darkly handsome features half-hidden from her.

More to ease the moment than because she needed to know, she asked about Northwick: "Tell me about the earl. Is he dead?"

"Yes. Did you think I would let him live after what he did to you? Someone should have killed him long ago. I should never have let him leave The Pigeon Hole alive."

She frowned slightly. "But you weren't there. I looked for you, and you were gone. He—the earl—said you'd left me there. Did you?"

"No. Of course not. Christ. Do you think I'd leave you in that den of thieves?" He sounded irritated, and set the half-empty glass of water back on the bedside table with a thump. "Why in God's name did you go with him? Because you thought I'd left you?"

"I didn't mean to go with him. I thought you had sent him for me—that's what he said, but when we went into the back and I did not see you there, he said you'd left me and I must go with him."

"Did it occur to you to refuse?"

Brett's sardonic drawl stung, and her fingers tightened around the satin edge of the coverlet. "Of course I did! But he'd put something in my champagne, I think, because I got so dizzy, and then I must have passed out for a time. When I awoke . . . when I awoke, I was tied up and in that . . . that *awful* place—oh Brett! I thought he had killed me. . . ." Her voice broke despite her best efforts to remain calm, and the mattress dipped beneath his weight as he perched on the bed beside her and took her hand.

"He nearly did, princess. If Barry hadn't remembered where the earl had once taken him, we might not have found you in time. As it was, we were almost too late."

After a few moments, she looked up at him, still holding his hand as if for courage. "How did he die?"

"I shot him. There was no time for anything else, though I would have preferred to turn him over to Godfrey for some amusement rather than let him die quickly. The Comanches are rather talented at that sort of thing."

She shuddered at the grim malice in his voice, and a quick upward glance at his ruthless expression convinced her it was no idle comment. Brett squeezed her hand.

"You should rest. I'll let Celeste in to see you now. We've been taking turns sitting with you the last few days."

"Few days! How long have I been asleep?"

"Six days. The physician said you lost too much blood and needed rest, so he gave you something to make you sleep." He rose to his feet, and she saw then that he had a heavy beard shadow, and his eyes were dark with strain. He managed a faint smile, one side of his mouth kicking up in a parody of his familiar cynical smirk. To her pleased surprise, he bent forward and pressed a light kiss upon her cheek, then drew back quickly as if embarrassed to express any tender emotion. "Rest now, princess. I'll call Celeste to come and sit with you."

"Brett?"

He paused and looked back at her, his face in the shadows again. "Yes?"

"Did—will you come to see me again?"

"Of course. Sleep now."

Kyla nodded, ignoring the pounding in her head as she leaned back against the pillows. When the door closed behind him, she laced her fingers together, a little irritated that she was too cowardly to ask him if he meant what she had heard. Later, when she was stronger, he would tell her about it, would make a formal proposal of marriage. She closed her eyes, opening them again only when she heard Celeste enter.

"Ah, *ma pauvre petite*," Celeste said softly as she moved to the bed, "I have failed you so badly."

"I knew you would think that, but you have not, tante, truly you have not. What happened was my own fault. Oh, it's all been such a mess—"

"Shush, *ma chère*. Rest now. It's all behind you. Soon, this will all be as a bad dream." Celeste's cool hands stroked her face, trembling slightly with emotion as she caressed her, and she spoke to her in a mixture of French and English, assuring her that all would be well, that she must only regain her strength so that she could be like her old self again. "And then we shall walk in the garden, or take a drive in the park, yes? Of course, and you will be happy soon, *chère*, I think you must be."

"Oh, Tante Celeste—do you really think I will

be? It's been such a nightmare—everything that has happened since I left India and Papa Piers. I think I was wrong to come here, to—"

"No, no, do not say it. You were not wrong to want to make things right for your maman's memory. Perhaps we went about it the wrong way, but what other way was left to us? And you are right to want what is rightfully yours, what was denied you by the treachery of others. No, *ma belle*, you were not wrong. I think, perhaps, the duke understands this now."

"Do you?" Kyla smiled sleepily and yawned as the drug in her system reclaimed her, and her eyelids drooped with exhaustion. "The duke... maybe he does know that I never meant harm to him, that I only wanted... to be accepted."

"Yes, he must know, *petite*, or he would not be so patient with you now. Sleep, *ma bébé*, and let your poor body rest now. Sleep like the sweet innocent you are, and I will watch over you."

With Celeste's soothing litany in her ears, Kyla drifted again into sleep, this time a restful slumber without the nightmares that had marked her restless slumber of the past days. Celeste sat beside her while the lamp burned low, and thought of Faustine Auberge and Edward Riverton, and their doomed love.

So long ago, so many regrets. What would Faustine say now if she saw her daughter lying so pale and fragile in the bed where once she had lain? Yes, so many years had passed since Edward had betrayed her, had allowed his parents to rip apart their life. A curse, he had once called his title, a curse and affliction that he must bear because of his birth. It was a curse that had the power to still haunt his daughter, and it was a curse that had taken him to his grave a changed, broken man, just as it had changed Faustine from the sweet girl she once was to the courtesan of many.

Celeste sighed and closed her eyes, and the steady ticking of a clock on the mantel marked the passing of time as she sat beside Kyla and reflected. If there was a way to help Faustine's daughter, she must do it. Yes, she could not allow Kyla to become what her mother had been, to die as her mother had done. But Wolverton had said he would see her properly wed, and she could only hope that he meant it.

In the past six days, Brett Banning had rarely left Kyla's side, often gazing at her with a brooding expression that Celeste hoped meant he cared for her more than he would admit. Could it be? Could it be history repeating itself? Would Kyla become the duchess of Wolverton as her mother had been so briefly? It would be a twist of fate, one of those vagaries of life that could be so ironically appropriate. This duke was not a man to be manipulated by title or by expectations as had been his predecessor, and if he married Kyla, it would be because he wanted her. But did he?

Certainly, he had taken her from Lady Sefton's, and made it obvious he wanted her in his bed. But there was so much more to it than that, she mused with a faint frown. If not, would he have taken such care to keep Kyla's involvement in Northwick's death a secret? The discovery of the earl's body had caused some stir in London, with damning diatribes written in the papers condemning the lawlessness that allowed a member of the realm to be so brutally murdered in the streets.

No mention had been made of Kyla, nor of Wolverton, and the hunt for the murderers proved futile so far.

Perhaps the outcry would have been greater if the earl had not been found in a particularly notorious section of the city, where only the most dangerous—or depraved—were known to frequent the haunts. Northwick was known to have his vices, and it was said rather cynically among the *ton* that he had no doubt met his match in some way there in the stews.

Kyla was safe from speculation, her part in the affair unknown—as was Brett Banning's. Had he done it for her, or to hide his own involvement? There was more to the incident than she knew, though she was certain he must have his own motives for hating Northwick that had little to do with Kyla. Did he care for her more than he would admit, perhaps?

Ah, he must. How could he not? Celeste sighed, and gazed at the young woman sleeping now so peacefully. Yes, he must care for her a little, at least. Yet she wondered what Wolverton really thought, for he revealed nothing by word or expression.

Nineteen

It had been a month since Northwick had near killed Kyla, and during that time Brett set all his London affairs in order. With the recovery of his deeds secure, he arranged the needed financing for the purchase of a mine in South Africa, as well as completing the sale of two of the less productive mines Colby Banning had acquired in South America. Now, he tended to a less complicated but far more unpleasant task by visiting the home of the dowager duchess of Wolverton.

She received him in her morning parlor, exquisitely garbed as usual, sipping tea from thin china and regarding him over the rim of the cup with a disapproving stare. "I suppose you've come to inform me of your decision regarding the amount of the dowry to be settled upon my daughter?" she murmured at last, and he looked up from the brass firedogs that reflected bright dancing flames.

"Unseasonably cool this year, don't you think, Aunt? I've never known such a cold, wet summer, even in London."

"Yes. Quite chilly."

He smiled slightly. The ice in her tone matched

the cool weather. Leaning back against the mantel, he crossed his arms over his chest. "I have given my approval to the prospective match for Arabella with Lord Sebring."

"Sebring!" China rattled in the saucer. "While I agree that he is a young man of good birth, he has limited funds, I understand."

"Arabella prefers him. And it is a match that is more than suitable, as I've settled a comfortable amount on her that will give my cousin a generous income for life."

"Arabella is rather headstrong. It is not up to her who is the most suitable. I told you that I much prefer the suit of Lord Havering. He stands to inherit a duchy."

"Only if he resorts to homicide. He has an older brother who is rumored to be quite healthy. This is not open to discussion, as I have already come to terms with Sebring's father."

"Of course. Why should I be consulted? I am only the girl's mother, after all, while you care nothing for her best interests."

"On the contrary. Arabella came to me and said she much preferred Sebring, that they are in love. It's the least I can do for her."

"I agree—the least, indeed!" Fire flashed in the dowager's eyes as she carefully placed cup and saucer upon the tray in front of her, then sat back, regarding him with that cold condemnation that he'd come to expect. "She is the daughter of a duke, not some upstart nothing who must settle for any offer. She can do much better."

"She's no raving beauty, after all," he said quite bluntly.

"Unlike your current tart, I suppose! Really,

Brett, you say the most awkward things." Drawing herself up, Beatrice sniffed haughtily. "All of London is agog with the rumor that she is staying with you in your town house. Can you not be more discreet?"

"Why should I be? You'll be gratified to learn I intend to leave England before long."

"Delighted is more like it. And your tart? Will she be traveling with you, or do you intend to pay her off as you have all the rest? I cannot understand why you must continue to see her, when it is so obvious she is nothing but a greedy adventuress. The influence of your American roots, no doubt."

"No doubt, which is why I consider myself fortunate. But as regards Miss Van Vleet, my plans are private, and not open for discussion."

An expression of surprise flickered over the dowager's face, and was quickly replaced with suspicion. "Do not tell me—you have developed a *tendre* for this creature!"

"I'll tell you nothing of the sort because it is not the least bit true. Good day, madam."

Irritated, as much by allowing Beatrice to know she pricked him as by his reaction, he was in only a slightly better mood when he arrived at his town house. What he felt for Kyla was too complicated to sort out at the present. He wasn't sure what he felt for her, besides guilt at almost getting her killed as well as at being partly responsible for all that had happened since the night of Lady Sefton's ball. During the last month since her brush with Northwick, he'd kept his distance from her as much as possible, but now he went in search of her. She would eventually hear of his planned departure, and he preferred she hear it from him.

Kyla was sitting in the small garden off the terrace when Brett found her, and he paused to study her a moment before alerting her to his presence. She was thinner now, her features more defined from her loss of weight but no less beautiful. Wrapped in a warm shawl, she sat in the rare sunlight that filtered through heavy oak branches to dapple the grass and flower beds. Golden light bathed her in a shimmering aura, highlighting her hair and the pure line of her profile.

There was color in her cheeks now, and he thought of how he'd seen her there in that cellar with the life dripping from her wrists, lying in the midst of the tattered remnants of her clothes, and felt another unwelcome pang of guilt. He thought of how he'd almost lost her, how he'd almost caused her death with his selfishness, using her to trap a prince—the wrong prince. Godfrey was right: His arrogance had almost cost him—and her—everything. The ultimate price for his arrogance. It should humble him, teach him a lesson about using other people, about playing with their lives. Didn't he hate to be used, and he hated it when he *had* been used, when Kyla had tried to manipulate him? Yes. And yet he had done the same—no, worse. Much worse, to her.

Now he must try to rectify the wrong he had done her, make it right somehow, and give her back the life that he had taken—nearly taken completely away—leaving her nothing, lying dead on a stone altar in that dank wine cellar beneath the city streets of London.

For an instant, he almost regretted leaving her behind. He'd grown accustomed to her warm curves in the bed beside him, still enjoyed slipping inside her with long, leisurely strokes and hearing her soft breathy moans in his ear. It was a pleasure he had not denied himself, with the reasoning that he would more than compensate her for her time.

Kyla looked up then, her eyes widening when she saw him, and smiled a welcome so that he moved forward and sprawled into a chair opposite her.

"You have finished your business for the day?" she murmured as she closed her book and leaned forward to place it on a low table. The movement caused her shawl to slip, and afforded him a generous view of the swelling mounds of her breasts pressing against the square neck of her white muslin bodice. Scowling, he looked away.

"Yes. Most of it."

"Good. Are we to go for a ride in the park again today? It won't take long for me to change, if you still wish to go."

"Did I say we'd go for a ride in the park?" He knew he sounded churlish, but what he had to say weighed on him, and he found it difficult to be pleasant in the face of her quiet contentment.

Kyla's brow lifted. "Yes, you did. But if you have changed your mind—"

Abruptly, he rose to his feet. She looked up at him, a faint frown marring her creamy features and the sunlight gilding her long lashes like spangled gold. Damn her. He did not need to feel this way, did not need these feelings of guilt for doing what he must.

"You should rest. You've not regained all your strength yet."

She rose from her chair in a graceful twist, pulling her shawl around her. A wave of sweet scent wafted toward him. "I hardly think a ride in a carriage will exhaust me, but that's not really what is troubling you. What is it, Brett?"

He started to tell her, to say bluntly that he was leaving and she was free, but once the words were said there would be no turning back. Instead of telling her, he reached out and jerked her to him, his head bending and his mouth crushing against hers as her shawl fell away. He felt her small start of surprise, then her arms rose to curve around his neck as she leaned into him, yielding to his kiss and his tight embrace. Curse her, he wanted her, wanted her beneath him, naked and willing, meeting his passion with her own.

His hand tangled in the knot of hair on the nape of her neck and freed it from the tidy coil so that it tumbled down her back and over her shoulders. It flowed like silk through his fingers, soft and fragrant and so inherently feminine . . . he lifted her into his arms and held her against him as he strode from the stone terrace into the house and up the staircase to their chamber on the second floor. If he was to leave her, he would put off until he must the inevitable scene. There was always a scene, and it did not matter that there had been a mutual agreement between them.

A maid scurried from his path as he entered the bedchamber, her eyes wide with alarm. Brett heard the door shut behind her, and smiled grimly. Servants carried tales, and no doubt this one would be all over the house within a half hour. Not that he cared. She was his, was she not, this golden-haired, gypsyish woman in his arms? Willing, beautiful Kyla, who haunted his dreams at night and his thoughts during the day, tormenting him with the knowledge that he had almost caused her death.

It was a knowledge he wanted to forget, to wipe out with her sweet body beneath his, the taste of her on his mouth and the feel of her soft flesh beneath his hands. He lay her back on the bed and leaned over her, kissing her lips, her closed eyelids, the slope of her cheek and the slender arch of her throat, his hands tangling in the loose strands of her hair, curling it in his fists. She made him forget his best intentions, his decision to leave her fading for the moment as he lost himself in her.

Damn her. He wanted her—why not admit it? He would keep her with him as long as he could, until he must finally let her go before he left. It might only be for a little while, but she belonged to him completely now and he meant to sate himself with her, immerse himself until he could finally put her out of his mind and out of his life forever.

His hands slipped beneath the loose dressing gown she wore, tugging at the laces that held it closed until he grew too impatient and tore them free. Her skin was so soft, like silk, a potent lure to his exploring hands to caress her, to memorize every inch of her by touch and taste and sight . . . he sat back, pulling the dressing gown away and tossing it to the floor, surveying her flushed face and heavy-lidded eyes with a sense of satisfaction and futility. She wanted him, too. It was evident in her eyes, in her parted lips, and the faint smile that curved them as she gazed up at him. Her breasts rose with each breath she took, a little faster now as he drew his hand down over the sweet, tempting mounds, fingers kneading the taut nipples until she moaned.

God, how he loved that sound, loved it when she arched up under his touch as she was now, her body a silent invitation to him to take her, to lose himself in her. Was that what made her different from all the others he had known? Her unselfish offering, a mixture of desire and need that mirrored his own? Perhaps, or perhaps it was a sly trick of fate that made him want the woman who had tried to ruin him. Whatever, he could not deny that he did want her.

Frustrated, with her and himself and above all else, with his own weakness, Brett kissed her half-parted, quivering mouth, shoving his tongue between her lips in a stabbing desperation to ease his torment. And when she opened for him, he groaned, sensing that he was losing himself in her again, drowning in that mindless maelstrom of desire that threatened to ruin everything.

He took her then, ruthlessly, ignoring her soft cry of alarm as he shoved apart her legs and entered her more roughly than he intended, the exquisite thrust and drag of his body inside her taking him to release. Then, half-ashamed of his roughness, he kissed her more gently, arousing her again and taking his time now.

"Sweet Kyla," he muttered against her throat, the words almost lost in the faint hollow where her pulse beat in a steady thrum against his lips.

"Brett..." Her hand slipped down his back, under the unbuttoned shirt he still wore. "Ah God, Brett. I never dreamed it could be like this ...so sweet, so ... sweet ..."

He stopped her words with his mouth, closing his eyes and his ears to her soft endearments, the damning words like accusations against what he knew must come. He brought her to the edge of release again, teasing her with his body, suckling her breasts, caressing her until she was panting and squirming beneath him, broken sentences a plea for him to continue. Lifting himself above her, he dragged her thighs apart to drape her legs over his shoulders while his hands moved to her breasts to torture her nipples. She stiffened and cried out with shock but he ignored her as his mouth found her, tongue exploring her hidden softness.

Her body writhed, sobs mixed with increasing moans, and then her fingers caught his hair and held him, tangled in the thick strands to pull him closer as she arched beneath him.

"Oh God, Brett . . . oh God. . . ." Her soft, helpless cries grew frenzied as he seared her body with his tongue, until she shuddered and sobbed, soft guttural sounds of ecstasy. Only then did he stop, sliding his body upward and over hers, slipping inside her hot, wet body again in a heated glide that made them both shudder.

"I told you . . . that you would like it," he muttered thickly, the words coming out in a sort of groan as the hot, familiar friction brought him too close to the edge. It was as if he could not get enough of her. The elusive summit he sought stayed just beyond his reach, though he took her again and again, until they were both too exhausted to move and the light through the open draperies had faded to night.

Kyla's eyes were closed, one hand bent beneath

her chin, her lips slightly parted in a faint, satisfied smile. Brett stared up at the draped canopy over them that was lost in deep shadows, the fire in the grate having burned to just faint red embers now. It was doubtful any servant would be coming to stoke the fire until he called, but he delayed. Rather cynically, he considered that the exorcism he had attempted had failed significantly. She still consumed his thoughts, filled him with feelings of guilt and an unwilling affection. Maybe Godfrey was right. Maybe he did have some sort of conscience after all. A damn fine time to discover it, after all these years. Not that the discovery would solve anything.

If he did what he should, he would release her. It was the only unselfish way to make amends. A quick, clean severance would be the least painful way for both of them. It was just so goddamned hard to do.

He thought of the last woman he had loved, and how she had died without him, alone and afraid, her life slowly draining away as she bled to death from having their stillborn child. The two graves were still fresh when he'd finally returned, the memory still raw of how he had failed the sweet girl who had been fool enough to love him. Yes. It would be kindest to leave Kyla to find a man who would always be there for her, who would love her as she deserved to be loved.

Finally, he slept, holding her while she curled in fatigued contentment against him.

Twenty

A *clock* ticked loudly on the mantel of the downstairs parlor, and Barry Baylor paced impatiently, glancing at it again and again. Where the devil was Brett? Damme, if this was another one of his convoluted intrigues, he would refuse. Hadn't they barely escaped unscathed the last time? Except for Kyla, of course. She had been nearly killed, and the memory still had the power to make him tremble when he recalled how pale she had been lying there on that stone shelf, her blood dripping from her to pool in a crimson puddle, looking near death when they had found her. It had been so close—*too* close.

His desire for vengeance against Northwick had vanished even before Brett had taken careful aim and pulled the trigger of his pistol, even before Northwick had jerked, turning toward them with wide eyes and gaping mouth, then pitching over into a lifeless heap.

Not even moving the earl's body to that alley had sufficed to make him feel better about it. He felt as if doom hung over his head, like the sword of Damocles, waiting to fall.

Dammit—where *was* Brett, and why had he summoned him if he meant to keep him waiting? Impatiently, he turned again, then his head snapped up as he heard the door open.

Brett filled the doorway, looking as suave and coolly composed as ever, just as he had looked after those duels, and even after killing Northwick. It was only when he had gone to Kyla and seen the blood flowing from the gash in her wrist that he had evinced any emotion, and that more anger than fright. It made him seem less than human, somehow, an impression that disturbed Barry.

"Sorry to keep you waiting, Kenworth." Brett tugged off his gloves as he strode across the room. "That fool groom I just hired nearly sold the wrong horses. I had to stop him before he cost me more than just money."

"Selling off all your cattle, are you?"

"No. Just those I won't need. Pemberton's been after me for a while to sell him those matched bays, so he finally came up to scratch on the price. But I didn't ask you here to talk about horses, as I'm sure you've guessed by now."

"Yes." Barry eyed him curiously as Brett strode to the fire burning in the grate. He looked distracted, despite his air of calm, and there was a certain tension in the set of his shoulders and his expression. "What's the latest? Not something about Northwick, I hope."

"No. I don't think the earl is greatly missed, though I wouldn't put it past Cumberland to have guessed as to the cause of his early demise." He turned with his back to the fire, staring so intently at him that Barry began to feel uneasy. "This is about Kyla, Kenworth."

"Kyla? Is she well? I thought the physician said she only needed rest and—"

"Her health is fine. Much better. That is not what concerns me. I'm leaving England for a time. Before I go, I'd like to be certain Kyla is well cared for. Do you recall that night at The Pigeon Hole?"

"Yes, of course I do. I could hardly forget it, though I've tried hard enough." Barry frowned. "What has that to do with Kyla's welfare now?"

"You mentioned marriage to her. I'm prepared to settle a handsome dowry on her, enough to see you set for the rest of your life if you stay out of the gaming hells. Are you interested?"

Stunned, Barry could not answer for a moment. The clock sounded much too loud, ticking and ticking while he struggled for composure. "Are you serious?" he asked finally, and saw Brett smile. Flushing, he added, "I know I sound a bit green, but you've just asked me if I want to wed your cast-off mistress. Hardly a normal question, you must admit."

"Yes, but not so unusual. Men marry their mistresses every day, especially wealthy mistresses."

"But she's not my mistress. She's yours."

"A mere question of timing. Or semantics. Kyla needs a husband. I do not intend to marry. You need money, and I'm offering twenty thousand a year and my country estate as dowry."

"But . . . why me? I mean—has she said something about me?"

"She likes you, but if you are asking if I act on her behalf, no. She is not yet aware of my intention. Look, Barry, I'm leaving England. I don't want to leave her here without some kind of protection. You can give her your name, make a life with her. You're just the kind of man she once wanted to marry, decent and kind—you would never hurt her."

"And you will."

"Yes."

"Damme, Brett!" Barry raked a hand through his hair, feeling at a loss and a little undone. He laughed, and it sounded a bit shaky. "It's not that I don't like her—hell, what man wouldn't? She's beautiful, and sweet, and I've never been one to care a fig about rumors, but it's not me she's in love with. It's you."

"She's not in love with me. She has had little choice about being with me because I gave her none. I took her virginity and offered nothing in return. She deserves better."

Brett sounded cold and brutal, and Barry winced at the truth of what he said. He thought of his father and what he would say if he married Kyla. There would be a protest, he was certain, but after all, it was true that men usually married for money, and twenty thousand a year and a landed estate was ample inducement.

He looked up and Brett met his gaze calmly. Slowly, Barry nodded. "If she is willing, I will marry her."

"Good."

"But you must tell her about it. If you've not yet discussed this with her, I don't want to be the one to break her heart."

"I don't think it will do more than put a small dent in it, believe me." Brett's mouth tucked into a cynical smile. "Most women are adaptable enough to a change in circumstances."

"Somehow, I don't think Kyla Van Vleet is one of those women, Brett. I think you've misjudged her."

"Possible, but unlikely."

Barry bent to gather up his gloves from a table, then turned back to Brett. "If you don't mind, I'll give you time to discuss it with her. Tell her that if she needs me, all she has to do is send for me, and I'll come."

"See, Barry, I knew you were the kind of man who would be reliable."

Kenworth smiled crookedly. "I'm not at all certain that is a compliment."

When he left, he looked back, thinking wryly that he would never hear from Kyla Van Vleet. Only a blind man could have missed the way she'd looked at Brett since that night, and he had seen far too often the soft glow in her eyes when she gazed at Wolverton. How had Brett missed it? He could not have. But Barry could have sworn that he felt the same, that he had seen Brett look at her with something close to genuine emotion in his face. Obviously, he was mistaken. If Brett cared for her, he would not leave her behind.

Kyla did not move, but gazed at Brett as if seeing him for the first time. She could not have heard him correctly. It must be a mistake, some residue of her recent ordeal that caused her hearing to be faulty. She cleared her throat.

"Will you repeat that, please?"

"Certainly." Brett sounded brisk and business-like, his tone calm and matter-of-fact. "I've arranged a marriage for you with Barry Baylor. He's only a viscount but a decent enough man, and I think you like him. You'll have your own income so be relatively independent, and after a time, I think you'll find that life will be what you once wished for. He can give you a home and children. I've settled Ridgewood on you as part of your dowry."

"I see." There was a peculiar ringing in her ears, and the chill she felt had nothing to do with the unseasonable weather. Numbly, she walked to stand in front of the fire, staring at the dancing yellow-and-orange flames. It smelled of oak and pine, fragrant and smoky. She turned, her back to the flames again as she regarded Brett. He was watching her from beneath his lashes, a narrow, watchful gaze for all that he seemed so casual. Dressed in a white shirt and black pants, with his knee-high riding boots, he looked as if he had just come from a brisk ride. "Has this only just occurred to you, Brett, or is it all arranged?"

How calm she sounded, when inside she was shrieking with disbelief.

"I spoke to Kenworth yesterday. He has agreed, if you will have him."

"I see." Why did she keep saying that? She did *not* see! Why wasn't she screaming at him, howling her rage and pain at him? She looked down and took a deep breath, a bit surprised that she still stood there so calmly. When she looked up again, Brett was frowning slightly, his dark brows lowering over the gray eyes that had gazed warmly into hers only that morning after making love to her. She had thought—really thought—he meant to marry her. What a fool she was, a stupid, ignorant, lovesick fool. Men like Brett did not marry their mistresses. They married them to other men, or set them up in houses of their own, or even cast them off with some trinket like a diamond necklace. *Trinket.* Yes. He had called her that, and she should have realized then that was how he saw her. A worthless bauble, meant to be used and discarded.

"Kyla?"

She blinked. "Yes. Forgive me. I was just thinking. Do you mind if I consider this? I'm certain you don't require an answer right now, and this comes as a bit of a surprise. I had not expected you to choose my next lover for me quite so quickly. Silly of me, I know, but I had thought I would be required to find my own. Please." Her voice had risen a little and he moved toward her, halting only when she lifted a hand to stop him. "Don't. I would like to be alone. No. I think I shall go to see Tante Celeste. Please have a carriage brought around front, will you, Brett? I won't be long, and when I return, I will give you my reply."

She moved past him, still amazed at how composed she was, when she longed to rake his arrogant face with her nails and rail at him like any Fleet Street harridan. Even in the carriage on the way to Tante Celeste's she remained calm, though she kept hearing his emotionless words over and over in her head, echoing loudly enough to drown out the noise of the city.

"*Ma petite*—are you well?" Tante Celeste greeted her with alarm, rising from her chair and coming toward her across the small morning parlor. "*Mon Dieu!* What has happened to you?"

"Nothing. Everything. I . . . I don't know. Oh

God—oh God I don't know what I will do. . . ."
She collapsed in her aunt's arms, her composure
crumbling to shreds as she began to sob wildly.

Celeste soothed her, speaking in French and English, rocking her as if she was a child again. Kyla
wept until she was drained of tears and energy,
sagging against Celeste as they huddled on the
settee near the fire. When she had calmed, Celeste
straightened and gave her a dry linen handkerchief to wipe her face.

"Now. We will do what must be done, *ma chère*.
This Kenworth—do you wish to marry him?"

"Of course not. Oh, he's nice enough, and I like
him as a friend, but—but I never considered that
he would offer to marry me." Her voice grew bitter. "I suppose Brett is paying him a great deal to
take a used mistress off his hands."

"Brett Banning is an arrogant fool. But that is
no longer our concern. What we must do is make
arrangements for you. Do you have access to the
money he settled on you?"

She nodded numbly. How odd, that she should
be here discussing this with Tante Celeste, when
only yesterday she had dreamed of the rest of her
life with Brett.

"*Bien*," Celeste was saying as she rose and
crossed to a small cherry secretary against the far
wall. "I will do what must be done. You cannot
stay in London, of course. There has been too
much talk. Ah, if only this were France. It is so
silly, that everyone takes lovers and no one talks
about it . . . but discretion is not always so discreet. Now come. I have friends still in France. Do
you think you would like to go there?"

"No—oh, I cannot." Tears threatened to flow

again, though it seemed impossible that she had any left. Kyla shook her head, wincing at a stab of pain. "It's too close to England—I thought I might return to India, perhaps, and stay with Papa Piers."

"Impossible, I fear. Besides, there are so many English there it would be almost like being in London. Oh wait—I know. Caroline Dufour. Of course—but it is so far away, and I cannot abide another sea voyage. But there, it is almost like France, I hear. Until a few years ago, it belonged to France, and Caroline has written begging me to come and visit. I would, but the sea, oh the sea— would you like to go to America, *ma belle*? Caroline Dufour and I were friends in France many years ago, and she knew your maman very well. They were great friends, and I know she would love to see Faustine's daughter again. Shall you go?"

"To America?" Kyla hesitated. It was so far away, but wasn't that just what she needed? Yes, to be far away from Brett and England, never to have to hear his name or see him again, never to have to know when he took another woman as mistress or eventually married—She looked up and nodded. "Yes."

"*Bon!* Then you shall go. I shall arrange all. But Kyla—do not tell Wolverton. I think it best that you leave as soon as I can make the arrangements, and tell him nothing. He thinks he knows what is best for you? He thinks to marry you to one of his friends? No. Let him think what he likes, and let him wonder. It will do him a world of good to discover that it is not so simple to try and order the life of another person so arbitrarily."

"But I don't know what I will say to him. . . ."

"You will say nothing, because you will not see him again. We must act swiftly before he can guess what we intend. I will send my steward with you to the bank, and you will take out all the monies he deposited for you. They are in your name, yes? Good. He has made it easy for you to leave him, then." Her mouth tightened, and her soft brown eyes hardened. "I warned him once not to be so arrogant as to think he could treat you badly. Now, this duke will see that he has misjudged us both."

Kyla felt as if she had been suddenly swept into a storm, as Tante Celeste acted with uncharacteristic efficiency and swiftness. By nightfall, Kyla was bundled aboard a ship docked below London, and ensconced in a tiny cabin that reeked of exotic spices and musty wood. Dazed, she bid a tearful farewell to her godmother, and some time after midnight, the ship slipped from port and sailed slowly down the Thames toward the sea.

Part III

New Orleans
September 1816

Twenty-one

The ship dipped through whitecapped waves in a dizzying drop, and a warm wind filled canvas sails with a loud popping sound that overrode everything else, even the rush of blue-green water around the keel, the constant strain of creaking ropes, and the incessant thud of men's bare feet against wooden decks worn smooth through time, sun, wind, and use. Kyla leaned against the rail. It was familiar to her now, the endless cacophony of noise that filled her days, and even her nights. She was grateful for it at times, a distraction from the painful assault of memories that intruded far too often. Oh yes, it was better, *far* better, than remembering what must be forgotten, what she must push to the distant recesses of her mind and never think of again, those horrible hours with Northwick.

Yet, at times, even when she tried her hardest, a sharp memory would return to gouge her so that she must take a swift deep breath and will herself to think of nothing, or focus on the world around her instead of London—and Brett Banning. She closed her eyes and gripped the ship's rail tightly, holding on as if to keep from pitching over the side and into the frothy green waves rushing past so swiftly beneath the ship, carrying her away from England, away from the pain and the shame. Oh, the memories were still so intense, still had the power to render her almost immobile, so that, at times, she grasped at any distraction to free her from their grasp.

"We should reach New Orleans early in the morning, *ma chère.*"

Kyla's eyes snapped open and she took a deep breath, then slanted an irritated glance at the man who came up beside her. "I have told you, Monsieur Renardeau, that I do not appreciate your familiarity. Please be so kind as to be more discreet."

Raoul Renardeau, not a whit abashed by her reproof, grinned. "Discretion is so boring, and takes far too long, *Mademoiselle Van Vleet.*" His teeth gleamed whitely in the late-afternoon sunlight that washed over the ship's deck and glittered in his fair hair. He was quite handsome, with that careless charm so common to many Frenchmen, and especially common to exiled French aristocrats, and he was quite persistent in his pursuit of her. Now he bent his head to one side, eyes narrowed against the press of sunlight. "Am I to pretend not to admire you? That is not discretion—that is foolishness."

Exasperated, yet amused by this brash man who had pursued her ardently on the voyage across the Atlantic, Kyla could not help a small smile at his arrogance. His attention was an admitted sop to her vanity, though it did not ease the despair and *grief*—yes, she admitted to it—at leaving Brett

Banning. Despite her vow not to, she could not help but wonder—did he think of her? Did he miss her, or was he too angry at her deception and escape to care that she was gone? Yes, it would be the last that mattered most to Brett, she thought angrily, for he had never indicated by word or deed that he cared for her more than as a warm body in his bed.

Ah God, *why?* Why had he thought that marrying her to another man would be acceptable? Damn him. Damn all of them. No, she would not be bartered, nor would she be given away as carelessly as a piece of jewelry. A trinket.

"*Ma chérie?* Are you listening to me?" Raoul moved closer, and the wind whipped at his long fair hair, dashing it over his forehead and into his brown eyes so that he pushed at it impatiently. "You have gone away again," he reproached, speaking loud to be heard above the noisy wind that flapped canvas sails and made rigging creak and groan. "Where is it you go when you have that so sad look in your eyes, *hein?* I cannot bear to see you desolate, *ma chérie*. Tell Papa Raoul what you fear."

"You are much too imaginative, Monsieur Renardeau. I fear nothing other than more of your tedious questions."

Her tart reproof made him laugh. Kyla smiled a little. Really, he *was* quite handsome, especially when he laughed as he did now. And his ardent attention was as balm to her wounded vanity. At least *he* found her lovely and desirable, and told her so again and again, a comfort in one way, for she had left England feeling as if she was unworthy of love or admiration. And why not? Certainly

Brett had made it plain that he found her unworthy to be his wife, or even to be loved. So—she had flirted with Raoul occasionally, but only when it suited her and only a little bit, just enough to encourage him and amuse her, and enough to keep thoughts of Brett Banning at bay. It would do for now, though she was not ready yet to be seriously involved with another man.

Not yet—maybe never, she had told herself many times, and repeated it silently again as she tilted her head to one side, holding the blue ribbons to her fashionable straw hat firmly under her chin to regard Raoul. An exile like Tante Celeste, he had been born to comte de Sayre in the province of Nantes near the Loire; but that was before the Terror, of course. His parents had been slain in that fearful bloody revolution, and he had barely escaped the same fate. It had given them a bond of sorts when he revealed his past, and so she had told him about poor Maman, and how she had suffered so during that terrible time. Raoul was a bit more fortunate than some, having escaped with some valuables and his head intact—as well as his inbred arrogance.

"You are a beast, Monsieur Renardeau," she said firmly, but a slight smile took the sting from her words. "I do not know why I even talk to you."

"Because there are only sour-faced Puritans aboard this ship, of course." Raoul took her hand, still grinning. "I was the last resort, *n'est-ce pas?*"

"Perhaps." She removed her hand from his grasp and ignored his exaggerated sigh, turning back to the rail to stare over the billowing waves toward the promise of unseen land. "Five weeks aboard ship is long enough for anyone to endure. I yearn to feel solid land beneath my feet again."

"As do I. But you still have not answered the question I asked you last night, *ma belle*." He moved closer, so that she could feel the warmth from his body next to her, a vivid contrast to the sharp bite of the wind crashing over the ship's decks. "Will you allow me to court you when we reach New Orleans?"

She smiled. "You will forget all about me once we arrive. I am told that New Orleans is very gay, and has many beautiful women."

"Ah, but none as lovely as you, *ma chérie*. Your golden hair, your eyes the mysterious color of the sea off the isle of Crete, and your alluring curves—" He kissed the tips of his fingers with a flamboyant Gallic gesture that made her press her lips together tightly to keep from laughing. "You are exquisite!"

"You are impertinent, monsieur. Your masquerade is far too exaggerated for anyone to believe that you are only a French citizen instead of a count."

He grinned. "Once we reach my beloved New Orleans, you may refer to me by my proper title, if that will impress you enough to agree to see me again."

"Titles do *not* impress me." She looked away from his surprised expression at her suddenly fierce reply, and took a deep breath. Foolish, to be so sensitive. But why allow everyone to know how badly Brett Banning had hurt her? More to cover her sudden turmoil than because she wanted to know, she asked, "Why were you in England if you prefer New Orleans?"

"As I told you, I had business there. London is a cold place, much too cold for me. Fortunately, my business did not take long, and so I am able to return. And even more fortunate for me, I am on the same ship as a most beautiful woman with remarkable eyes and a most lovely smile, a woman who does not care if a man possesses a title, yes?"

"I told you—I do not."

Raoul shrugged, and turned slightly to lean on the rail next to her. Silent now, he reached out and put his hand over hers where it was curled over the smooth wood of the rail, and held it quietly for several moments before he murmured softly, "I am glad, *chère*, that titles do not impress you. It is the man that matters, yes?"

Her answering smile felt wobbly. "Yes. It is the man who matters."

"Then let me be that man. You intrigue me, with mystery in your eyes and your sad smile . . . ah, do not pull away. I did not mean to distress you . . . I shall call on you even if you do not give permission, for I am not a man who accepts defeat, *ma petite*. And I know your friends, for they are acquaintances and will invite me into their home anyway, so you cannot escape me. *Hein?* You think you may?"

Half-amused, half-angry, Kyla shook her head. "You are far too persistent for me to believe that. Do not be too disappointed if you do not get what you want this time, Monsieur Renardeau. I am not the fool I was once, and I do not surrender easily."

Rather than daunting him, her words seemed only to encourage Raoul, and a bit irritably, she took her leave of him. His protests rang in her ears as she descended the steep ladder to the stuffy cabins below deck.

The walls seemed to close around her as she entered her cabin and shut the door. A small round porthole let in greenish light, but was shut tightly against any air or encroaching ocean. Fetid smells of past occupants were suffocating in the heat and humidity that reminded her of India.

She removed her straw hat and tossed it to the narrow bunk against one wall. The voyage had not been bad, with only a few storms that had been frightening, but for two weeks now the heat had begun to press down on the ship and at times, left it becalmed. Now, thank God, they were almost to New Orleans. She was weary of this ship, and of Raoul. Really, he was much too persistent, when she had hoped to have a quiet voyage in which to consider her future.

A small, tarnished mirror hung on the wall over a washstand and cracked bowl and pitcher, and she leaned forward to peer into the smoky glass. Her reflection was distorted, a collage of pinched mouth, unblinking eyes and a complexion that looked much too pale. Did she always look so colorless? It must be the uncertainties she faced.

What lay ahead for her now? Would it be too much to hope for a new life in the new world she had heard so much about from Godfrey, the young country that was rumored to give second chances to those who wanted them?

Kyla stretched out on the bunk and closed her eyes, while the ship rocked and the groaning sound of rigging and creaking wood provided an unending melody. *Dear God, let it be so . . . let me start over again. . . .*

* * *

That hope lingered when she disembarked in New Orleans, and was accompanied by Raoul Renardeau as she made her way down the steep pitch of the gangplank to the stone dock. It was much noisier here than even in India, she thought in amazement, a little surprised at the crowded bustle in a city she had considered primitive until now. But here—there was an air of civilization, so exotic when she had imagined it to be crude and uncivilized.

"Ah no, *chérie*, New Orleans has become very civilized." Raoul held to her arm, and for the moment, she was grateful for his presence. He waved an arm toward the spires of a church rising ahead, and to a wealth of warehouses and long buildings laced with iron balconies. "You see, of course, the Spanish influence everywhere, for it once belonged to Spain, and to France, but now it is the *Americaines* who have acquired such a lovely city. A pity. Soon it will lose its quaint charm and European sophistication, and be nothing but a brash overblown town filled with noisy, vulgar Americans. But now, it is still charming. I will show you about once you are safely ensconced with your friends, yes?"

"Really, Monsieur Renardeau—"

"Ah no—Raoul. Please."

She managed a faint smile that felt stiff, and held to the brim of her hat when a sultry wind threatened to sweep it from her head. "Very well. Raoul. Yes, you may call on me once I am settled. I am certain we will see one another again soon."

"But they have not sent someone to meet you, no?" He scanned the crowd of carriages juggling for space next to dray wagons, while the crack of carters' whips and shouts of stevedores filled the humid air. "I do not see the Dufour carriage."

"They do not know when I will arrive, of course. I can find my way, I am certain, for—"

"Ah no, I will not hear of it! You will allow me to see you safely there, *chère*. I insist."

Despite her vague protests, Raoul soon had her in a carriage and the arrangements made for delivery of her baggage. Kyla was glad that her straw bonnet sheltered her face from a sun that was so bright here! It made her think of India and her childhood, and Papa Piers. She had written him of her decision to travel to America, and hoped he understood. How could she admit that her attempts to set things right had failed so disastrously? She could not, and it was bitter that she was in no position now to offer him any assistance.

The carriage dipped with Raoul's weight as he climbed into the open hack, and he smiled warmly at her. Faint beads of perspiration dotted his forehead and cheeks, but he seemed as coolly composed as ever as he turned to her. "I have sent word ahead that you are to arrive, so that they will be prepared. *Tout bien?*"

"Yes. Yes, of course. You are too kind, monsieur, and I do wish you would not take on so much for me."

"Ah, but it is my pleasure, you must know. Of course you do. I have not made my feelings secret."

Kyla frowned slightly. Must he be so forward? It made her uncomfortable, and she wished now she had not decided to assuage her wounded vanity by flirting with him so much.

If he sensed her reticence, he did not show it, but instead sought to entertain her with an endless stream of conversation, pointing out areas of interest and informing her about New Orleans.

New Orleans was nothing like she had expected, but exuded old world charm mixed with an energy that could only be peculiarly American. Spring and summer rains had turned the streets into quagmires or washed them completely away, and scores of dark-skinned men toiled in the hazy sunlight digging ditches. Oddly, the men seemed perfectly content, singing in deep baritones as they swung picks and scoured the earth with shovels, light glinting from muscular torsos that were shiny with sweat in this humid climate.

"It is the new canal that is being built," Raoul explained with a dismissing wave of one hand at the working men. "So distasteful—the smell is dreadful, and I thought that the waters would never recede. I was glad to leave for England and abandon the open sewers here." He drew out a small perfumed handkerchief, smiling. "Never leave home without one. It is a must in this fetid air, I fear."

"Are they building a new canal for ships to use?" Kyla accepted the perfumed square of fine linen and lace, noting the embroidered silk with his initials—RR.

"No, it's—ah, I cannot recall exactly. Driver, what is the reason they are digging this ditch?"

Sharp, acrid scents of sluggish canals filled the air, and their driver turned in the seat of the carriage to explain.

"We have bad flood this spring and summer, monsieur." He pointed with the end of his buggy whip at the huge mounds of raw earth and drenched grass. "All the water have to be pumped out from a crevasse at Macarty's Point before we could build the dam here, but it is a good job to have, no?"

Kyla observed the workers as the carriage rolled past swiftly. They seemed cheerful enough, working with alacrity and good humor, singing and laughing as they toiled. She sat back against the cushions and glanced up at the flowers spilling over iron balconies in a bright profusion of color. Perhaps it would not be so bad here. It was certainly warmer than England, though not as hot as India.

"There is the Orleans Theatre, completed only a few years ago," Raoul said, pointing down a street where she could just see the top of a gable and an American flag fluttering in the wind. "It is impressive, I think, with three floors and the colonnades. And on Canal Street between Baronne and Dryads, only last year a new charity hospital was completed. We are very civilized here, do you not agree?"

"So all the reports I heard of marauding pirates frequenting New Orleans are false, is that right?" She laughed a little at his sudden start and scowl, and leaned close to put a hand on his arm. "I am teasing you, I fear. Do not be aggrieved with me. It was an irresistible opportunity, you must admit."

Raoul relaxed, and smiled. "Yes, so it would be. But you must not put stock in rumors, *chère*. Pirates have long since left New Orleans behind since the American government sent so many gunships after them. Not even Lafitte dares enter the city anymore."

"No? Yet I heard that he supplies the entire city with whatever pirated European delicacies it requires. Oh, stop scowling at me so fiercely, monsieur, or I shall think the rumors are right and you just do not wish to admit it."

"Ah well, you tease me too much." He took her hand and lifted it to his mouth, gazing up at her while he pressed his lips against her wrists. There was an intensity to his gaze that slightly unnerved her, and she frowned. He lowered his eyes, kissed the tiny faded scars, then straightened and glanced around them. "We are on Condé Street, where the Dufours reside. We will be there much too soon, and our charming interlude will be ended. Promise you will see me again, *ma chère*."

"I am certain our paths will cross." Kyla looked away from him as the carriage rolled to a halt, her attention focusing on the two-story house of brick with iron balconies festooned with flowers and vines. Now that she was finally here, she was nervous. Would the Dufours accept her? Had they heard of all that had happened in London? She prayed they had not. After all, Caroline Dufour had known Maman so well, and though it had been years, they would remember Faustine with fondness.

Raoul murmured something under his breath, and Kyla drew in a nervous breath as the front door of the house swung open even before the carriage came to a complete stop. A young girl with dark hair and bright eyes swept down the narrow walkway and to the carriage, smiling up at them.

"You must be Kyla Van Vleet, Faustine's daughter. Oh, Maman will be so pleased when she learns of your arrival. She has talked of your mother so often, you know—please. I am sorry to greet you so impulsively, but when the comte's note was delivered saying you had arrived, I could not believe my eyes. It is very kind of you, Comte de Sayre, to escort her all the way here. Papa will be—pleased—to hear of your assistance."

There was an odd tone to the last, and Kyla felt Raoul stiffen beside her, but then he was helping her down from the carriage and she was being swept into such a warm hug from the young girl whose name she did not yet know, that she thought no more of it. It was overwhelming, this enthusiastic delight with which she was greeted, and quite comforting.

"Please, call me Esmée," the girl said, tucking Kyla's hand firmly into the bend of her arm, "and you must tell me all about India, for I know that Maman went to visit you there long ago, though I was too young to go with them. My brother went, though. Perhaps you remember him—Antoine?"

"Antoine! No—that is your brother?" Kyla laughed, a little embarrassed, for she recalled the young boy with whom she had experimented so many years before, more a touch and tickle than anything serious, an innocent childish curiosity about the differences in their bodies. "Yes, of course I recall him. But we were only children then."

Esmée laughed, then turned back to Raoul. Her eyes cooled a little. "I am certain that we will see you again soon, monsieur le comte."

"But of course." He swept an elaborate bow, and as he straightened, looked straight at Kyla. "I have an excellent reason to visit again very soon."

Kyla managed a faint smile, though she was a little embarrassed by his obvious admiration and attention, and hoped that she was not thought a flirt her first day in New Orleans. Fortunately, Esmée seemed to forget about Raoul, as she escorted her into the house and rang for tea to be served in the garden.

"Maman will be here quite soon, and will want to see you at once. Would you like to freshen up first?"

"Yes, please. I feel so rumpled, for it was cramped in my cabin, with no place for a proper bath."

"Of course. Here. I will show you to your room at once. It is always ready for visitors, though it needs airing a bit as it is so warm during the heat of the day. It's been cooler than usual this summer, not so hot as it often is, so you should be quite comfortable."

Rather dazed by Esmée's light chatter, Kyla murmured an abstract reply as she was led up a winding staircase to a second story. Ornate iron balconies flanked all four sides of the house, with the long corridor opening onto them at each end, long doors flung open to allow in cooling breezes that smelled of the river and exotic scents. Netting draped a huge four-poster bed set in the center of the room, and filtered light through slatted shutters hung over the windows made small bright slivers on the floor. As she chattered, Esmée motioned for the light-skinned servant girl to open the shutters, and the comfortable room was quickly flooded with light and the sweet smell of jasmine.

"Tansy will see to your needs while you are here," Esmée said with a smile. "If there is anything you need, just tell her. I will inform Maman of your arrival when she returns."

Suddenly exhausted, Kyla managed a faint smile in return, and after a moment, Esmée departed, leaving her with only the efficient Tansy. The pretty maid bustled about, automatically closing the shutters to darken the room again, but leaving the windows and doors open to allow in cooling breezes. "You might want to nap, mistress," she said in a soft, accented voice that indicated a Caribbean island heritage. "It is hot in the middle of the day."

"Yes. Thank you, Tansy."

Alone, finally, Kyla moved to the wooden shutters and peered between the slats. Below, the garden walls were covered with ivy and tropical blossoms, and a huge tree grew in the midst, shading the flagstones of the terrace. She could hear the distinct patois of the Creole accents, a soft exotic sound that drifted up as lazily as the sultry breeze through the shutters. Here at the back of the house, the sound of carriage wheels was distant.

Perhaps it would be pleasant here. She thought of Tante Celeste, seeing again her tear-filled eyes as she'd bidden her farewell, and wondered if she would ever see her again. Dear Celeste, so fiercely loyal—had Brett gone to her to find out where

Kyla had gone? Or did he even care that his mistress had abandoned him before he could cast her off?

Suddenly weary, Kyla turned to the bed and slipped beneath the netting, pulling it closed as she stretched out on the cool sheets. She was comfortable here. Safe. Surrounded by all her things that had arrived soon after her. She must stop thinking of Brett.

She slept uneasily, despite being completely exhausted and drained of energy after the past twenty-four hours of physical and mental strain, the wondering if she would be accepted. It was dusk when she awoke, embarrassed that she had been so rude as to sleep away the day when a guest in the home of her mother's friends. What must they think of her?

She hurriedly changed into an evening dress and brushed her hair, not taking the time to call a maid to help her, and was grateful when Tansy knocked softly at the door and came in to lace up her dress.

"Oh dear, I'm afraid I've committed a *faux pas* my first night here," Kyla muttered with a sigh, and Tansy laughed.

"You will find that it is not so very formal here most of the time, maitresse. This family is very unlike many others, in that they are easy in the way they live. Do I say it right?"

Kyla smiled. "I hope so."

"There. You have such lovely hair. It is like the sun, all bright and gold. I hear Miss Esmée say that you are most pretty, and she is almost jealous of your hair."

As Tansy finished sweeping up her hair and

binding it with small jeweled combs, Kyla bent to pick up an ivory-and-lace fan, holding it nervously as she left the room and went downstairs to meet the Dufour family.

"But you are so beautiful!" Caroline Dufour exclaimed with all sincerity when she greeted Kyla with open arms. The opened letter from Celeste crumpled in her hand, and she drew back, smiling. "In her letter, Celeste did not say how lovely you are, only that you are her beloved goddaughter, and we are to care for you as if you are our very own, heh? But yes, of course we shall, for you shall stay with us as long as you like and be one of our little family. Now come, for it must have been a most tiring voyage all the way from England. I came here so long ago it is as if I was born here, you know, but have not been back to France since I left—but Celeste must have told you all of that, so I will not weary you with more prattling."

Dinner was not, as Tansy had said, a formal affair, but eaten on the terrace, where a cool breeze rustled palm fronds and green leaves and the sweet fragrance of jasmine and magnolia scented the air. Fish, fresh vegetables and fruit were the main courses, a light repast accompanied by glasses of wine and lively conversation.

"Papa," Esmée said over a dessert of fruit ices topped with drizzles of thick brandy, "the comte de Sayre escorted Kyla from the ship today."

Pierre Dufour looked up from his dessert. A handsome man in his late forties, he regarded Kyla quizzically. "Oh? Do you know de Sayre well, my dear?"

"No, I only met him on the ship. He was returning from England on business, he said, and when he learned I was to visit with you, mentioned he knew you."

"Yes. That is so. We have had business dealings in the past."

Nothing else was said, but Kyla wondered if Raoul Renardeau was as well acquainted with the Dufour family as he pretended. Not that it mattered. She doubted if she would see him again. Shipboard friendships were usually short-lived.

Twenty-two

A stagnant breeze drifted through tall bunches of sawgrass and cypress, carrying the stench of the swamps to the men in the pirogue. It was quiet in the shadowed recesses beneath ancient cypress trees and gnarled roots sticking up from brown water like knobby knees. The pole dipped into the water again, moving the small, flat-bottomed boat over the surface like a huge water bug skimming the river's edge. Dusky shadows seamed the line of water and sky closer together as night fell.

Upriver, the city rose from the swamp in a blur of lights strung in a pattern like a diamond neck-lace in the distance. Masts swayed in the distant harbor, a forest of ships docked at the edge of New Orleans.

Here, at the mouth of Barataria Canal, the illicit market set up to sell merchandise smuggled up the coast from plundered vessels was doing a lively trade. Music enlivened the night, and bon-fires lit the dark with leaping flames and smoke.

Godfrey leaned hard against the pole, and Brett worked the tiller to steer the small pirogue to shore through the swirling currents. They had been greeted earlier by a negligent wave from one of the privateers running the market, and admitted to the thin rivulet of the back bay area without challenge.

"We fly a flag of different colors every time we come here," Godfrey commented. "It seems to make no difference to these ruffians."

"Or to me." Brett stood up, legs spread for balance, then stepped over the side of the pirogue to the shore, deftly tying up the small craft with a few loops of the line. The heavy *thrrrrump!* of bullfrogs was a constant cadence in the murky shallows beyond. Swarms of mosquitoes buzzed loudly, and he swatted at them impatiently as he turned to wait for Godfrey. "You'd think these cursed pests would rest for the winter."

Godfrey shrugged. "It is too warm here, even for an October that is colder than normal. One of the men aboard ship said that he believes the reason for our unusual weather has to do with the eruption of a volcano in the Pacific. It spewed ash and rock for miles into the air, and the sun was blotted out for weeks."

When Brett did not reply, Godfrey smiled to himself. He had been surly for the past three months, ever since Kyla Van Vleet had disappeared from London. What did he expect? That she would wait to be bartered away? No, not from the little he knew of her. She had spirit, that one, and despite all that had happened to her, she was not the kind of woman to allow Brett to run roughshod over her. Perhaps that was why he could not forget her, why he was so angry that she had foiled his plans by doing what she wanted instead of what she was told.

Of course, any attempt to point that out to Brett had been met with hostility, and that icy stare that was intended to freeze a man to the bone. But he had known Brett too long for it to work with him, and not been in the least intimidated. No, this was something his friend would have to work out himself, would have to accept or change but not ignore as if it did not matter.

Brett strode ahead of him by several paces, and one of the men around a fire detached from the group and came to meet them, a wide grin bisecting his swarthy face. "Ah, so you come again to Louisiana, *mon ami*. It is good to see you, and your so fearsome companion. Do you stay long this time?"

"Long enough to take care of some business, *capitaine*." Brett was grinning, too, accepting Jean Lafitte's proffered bottle with a nod. "Caribbean rum, I suppose?"

"Only the best. Or worst, depending upon your point of view. Come, *mon ami*, and sit by the fire where the smoke will drive away the pests for a time. We have missed you in Barataria. And your merchandise. Do you still traffic?"

"If I did, I would not tell you. Your prices are too low when you buy, and too high when you sell."

"I am wounded that you would think so!" Lafitte put a hand to his chest, but his grin was still amiable as they followed him to the group of men gathered by the fire. It was a motley group, composed of pirates, outlaws, runaway slaves, and men of dubious character, in Godfrey's opinion. They were French, Spanish, American, and English for the most part, with a few Cubans in their ranks.

The conversation turned eventually to trade, as it usually did. Jean Lafitte's brother Pierre remarked morosely that things were not as good now that America and Great Britain were at peace. "During the war, ah then we made much money! Then, the people came in droves to buy our contraband. But now there are those customs import duties, and we cannot sell in the French Market our goods." He lifted his shoulders in a melancholy shrug. "Now we must depend upon private citizens to support our little market."

"You've forgotten the federal officers who purchase for the army," Brett pointed out dryly, and Lafitte grinned.

"Sometimes it happens that a ship will fall into our hands, and then, of course, we happen to have the supplies that the army needs for sale. It is odd how that occurs so frequently."

Leaning back against a fallen log for support, Brett stretched his arms along its length and laughed. "Very odd. But you men are regarded as heroes now after the American war against England, are you not? You came to General Jackson's rescue at Chalmette, and saved the army of the United States from being annihilated."

"Americans seem to have short memories when it comes to gratitude, and long memories when it comes to piracy." It was Jean Lafitte who commented on Brett's observation, and he was frowning. "It is Chew, of course, who has taken offense to us. He is the collector of the port of New Orleans, and gives us much trouble."

"It is my understanding there is a vast difference between piracy and privateering," Godfrey said. "In a state of war, naval acts are regarded as acts of war. In times of peace, the taking of foreign vessels can be construed as acts of piracy. If you will choose only those vessels that have incurred the wrath of the American government, you should be safe enough."

"But that is so tedious, *mon ami*." Lafitte smiled. "And at times, the temptation has been too much." He tilted the bottle of rum, then lowered it after a moment and wiped his mouth, eyeing Brett. "You have come back to Barataria for a reason, I think."

"Why do you think that?"

"If you had not, you would have visited me in New Orleans instead of here." He swept out an arm to indicate the swamp and stacks of plundered goods. "It is private here, and men do not take away tales from this place. I think you do not wish for anyone to know you have come to me."

A faint smile touched one side of Brett's mouth. "Perhaps. We will talk later."

Godfrey was half-asleep and the fire burned down to gray ashes and red embers when Brett rose to his feet and moved some distance away to speak with Lafitte. Their voices were low murmurs mingling with the steady thrum of bullfrogs and slap of water against the muddy banks. Closing his eyes again, Godfrey slipped back into that half-world between sleep and vigilance, ever-watchful in strange surroundings.

It was early, before the sun had done more than cast a faint pearly glow in the eastern sky, when he rose to go with Brett, and they slipped the pirogue back into the river and steered toward New Orleans.

"Did you discover what you need to know?" Godfrey asked when they entered the city. It was midday, and the pirogue had been left in an inlet below the city, the final miles to New Orleans traveled by foot up a track through tall grasses and muddy slopes.

"I learned who I need to ask." Brett shaded his eyes from the bright sun overhead and grimaced. Noise from the French Market was loud, and they went almost unnoticed among the bustle of vendors and shoppers, both of them resembling some of the men who brought in furs to sell, or fresh meat or fish. A little ruefully, Brett remarked upon their appearance. "If we don't bathe soon, we will be mistaken for Creole fishermen."

"You, perhaps, but I am too distinctive."

Brett grinned. "And you called *me* arrogant. Come. After a bath and hot food, we will both look and feel better."

It was dark when they left l'Hôtel de la Marine. The Café des Exilés was in a tall building at the corner of Royal and St. Anne Streets, only a short walk from the hotel. Brett wasted no time once inside, but went directly to a distinguished gentleman at a table near the front.

"Monsieur Sauvinet?"

The man turned, gazing at him politely. "Yes. I am afraid you have the advantage, Monsieur—"

"LaPorte." Brett smiled as recognition lit Sauvinet's eyes.

"Of course. Our mutual friend must have sent you to see me."

"He did."

"Please. Be seated, you and your tall friend."

They took seats at the table, and Brett eyed Sauvinet for a moment before saying, "I am looking for someone."

"Yes, so many are these days. A man, or a woman?"

"A man. I do not know his name, but he does business with Javier Aguilar y Portillo."

"Ah." Sauvinet sipped his brandy silently, then looked up at them both. "There are many who do business with the firm of Portillo and Poydras. Perhaps you should go there to find the man you seek. Mention the name of the chevalier de Touzac. The man who answers will help you."

When they took their leave, Godfrey gazed curiously at Brett. "Do you think Don Javier is involved in the revolution in Mexico?"

"More than likely. It stands to reason that if he succeeds in driving Spain out of the country, he will be able to seize any disputed property he wishes."

"Then the deeds may do you no good."

Brett looked up, his voice suddenly fierce. "The mines belong to me, and I keep what is mine." Godfrey said nothing, but lifted a brow, and Brett muttered an oath under his breath. "You're right. Spain may have granted my father the rights to mine silver, but I have no guarantee that the rebels will not seize them. All I have now are pieces of paper signed by Spanish viceroys. Worthless unless the revolution is a failure."

"Then Don Javier has pinned his hopes on a tentative prospect. It is likely that the Spanish will succeed and the rebels will fail. They are led, after all, by a patriot-priest with a ragtag army of men. The odds are on your side."

"And therein lies the rub." Brett lifted his shoulders in a brief shrug. "If not for the fact my mines lie in territory now claimed by Spain, I would be on the side of the rebels in their fight for independence."

Godfrey lapsed into silence, and after a moment, Brett shook his head. "If Texas territory belonged to the United States, it would be a lot better for me. But for now, I must do what I can to stop Javier from taking what does not belong to him."

"As your mother's brother, he no doubt feels that he is entitled to lands that were her dowry."

"They belong to me, as her son. And I intend to keep them."

"Odd," Godfrey remarked thoughtfully as they crossed the narrow banquette to the street, "that you have this stubborn desire to hold what is yours, yet let your most precious possession slip through your fingers."

"If you think you are being oblique, you are not. I know perfectly well that you are referring to Kyla, and I refuse to be drawn into that argument again. It was her choice to go."

"And now she is here in New Orleans, and so are you. A rather fortuitous arrangement, do you not think?"

Brett halted and swung around to stare at him coldly. "I came here to find my uncle, and to find the man who betrayed me."

"Yes. So you say."

Cursing, Brett swung back around and stalked away, and Godfrey smiled a little as he followed.

There were times it was best to cause a small irritation, then let nature take its course. As it would, as it certainly would, he was quite certain.

Kyla slowly fanned herself, warm despite the chill of the evening, and slightly out of breath from dancing for the past three hours. Musicians played in the huge ballroom of the house belonging to the French consul. The chevalier de Touzac had fought in the American Revolution under Baron von Steuben, and in the more recent fight between the United States and England. The house was filled with distinguished guests from America, France, and Spain, and she had danced with many of them since she had arrived earlier with Esmée and Caroline Dufour.

Now Esmée joined her on the balcony, breathing hard and fanning herself, her dark eyes alight with pleasure. "So many handsome men here tonight! There are too many, and I do not know which I prefer, the so gallant *capitaine* of the Spanish dragoons, or the *very* handsome French cavalier with the bright epaulets. Which do you think, Kyla?"

Laughing, she shook her head. "Both. You are too young and too pretty to choose only one man. Enjoy yourself with many before you must decide."

"Ah, you say that only because you have already made your choice," Esmée teased, taking Kyla's fan and sweeping it in a slow arc so that the small ringlets on her forehead shifted under the currents of air. "And I see that he is so jealous when you dance with another man. But when will you set the day to be married? Poor Raoul. He complains that you are too aloof, that you make him plead for every kiss."

Kyla managed a stiff smile. "That is because he is too impetuous. I'm not even certain—"

She stopped, and Esmée looked at her sharply. "Not what? Certain that you wish to marry him? He is very rich, you know, with houses and a huge plantation out on the river road, and many slaves to tend the fields. What makes you uncertain, *petite cousine*?"

It was an affectionate term between them, this fictional bond of blood, and Kyla smiled a little at her use of it. She shrugged her shoulders, and said in a helpless, soft tone, "I don't know. It's just that I don't think I am ready, Esmée."

"Not ready? But you are twenty-one now! Almost an old maid! Why, girls here get married at fifteen, and by your age have several children."

Kyla made a face. "If you are trying to make me feel bad, you are not succeeding. Despite your comforting words, I just wonder if I am doing the right thing."

"Because of the man you left?" Esmée laughed softly. "Do not deny it, Kyla. It is so obvious to me, and I may be young, but I am not blind, no? It must be another man you love, or I would not see that faraway look in your eyes at times. A lost love . . . I am right, I know it—see? You cannot deny it but must stand there staring at me as if I have two heads!"

Gathering her composure, Kyla forced a smile that felt like a grimace. "You are very imaginative, and should stick to your novels instead of think what is not true. There is no *lost love* as you so dramatically put it. Ah, I see your Spanish dragoon coming toward us. Quick, pinch your cheeks to put some color in them and go with him. He looks very determined to dance with you again."

As Esmée left, laughing with her dragoon, Kyla thought that she must be very transparent at times if even this young girl could see her disquiet. Why did she ever even think about *him*? It was ridiculous, and not at all true, of course, but she could not help remembering things, wondering if—ah, she felt much older than she ever had before. While it was true that she was not ready for marriage, it had nothing to do with Brett Banning. She simply still had some reservations, as she had from the first. But Raoul was so insistent, and even Père Dufour said that he seemed very sincere and certainly seemed to have a great deal of money to spend on a wife, so that she had been worn down in the past few months. Only a few days ago, she finally had said yes to another one of Raoul's proposals, and he had already told nearly all of New Orleans.

Quite a contrast, she thought wryly, between here and the life she had endured in London. Perhaps Tante Celeste would be pleased to hear of her marriage, and not feel that she had somehow failed her. Ah, it was another world now, another life, and it seemed so long ago instead of only six months. Had she really been here that long? Since arriving in New Orleans she had even become acclimated to the climate. It was pleasant, with warm days and cool nights, and if it rained a bit too much, it was, after all, something she was used to. Even in India there had been months of rain during the monsoon season, solid sheets without relenting for weeks and weeks. At least here the rain paused on occasion, and the sun would appear again and the air would be sticky and humid, pressing down on the citizens of the city and sending them indoors to their gardens and open windows.

She looked up, and saw Raoul searching for her through the throng of guests, his bright hair reflecting light from hundreds of candles in crystal chandeliers, and she thought suddenly how stifled she felt. Impulsively, she slipped along the balcony to the spiral stairs that wound down in a graceful curl to the terrace below, her skirts lifted in one hand as she descended. Silly, to run from him, but he was so possessive of her, so jealous as even Esmée had seen, when she danced with another man, even an old soldier like Colonel Devereaux.

Carriages lined the streets outside the chevalier's home, and uniformed servants waited patiently for the return of their masters, tending restless horses. She avoided that direction, and turned instead toward the back of the grounds, where she saw a string of lights and heard the sound of lively music. A fire blazed in the midst of a patch of cleared ground, and torches formed an oval where men and women danced.

It wasn't the *voudous* that she had once witnessed, a native dance of some secrecy, where the participants were part of some native ritual, but a form of peasant dancing being conducted by Creole servants. It was a mixture of French and Spanish music that was wild and primitive but intriguing, and she stopped to watch.

A young woman with long black hair to her waist and bare feet stood in the center of the oval ring of torches, and two guitars and some horns began to play a melody that reminded Kyla of the Spanish gypsies she had met in England. The music rose into the air and the girl began to dance, eyes half-closed and her arms at her sides, fingers snapping to the rhythm slowly at first, then faster as the tempo increased. Her ankle-length cotton skirt whirled around her brown legs higher and higher, and she tossed her head and held out her arms, alternately pleading and teasing a young man watching, then whirling away from him in a blur of red skirt and flashing legs.

Fascinated, Kyla watched them for a while, standing back in the shadows beneath a huge oak tree. She should return, for Raoul would be looking for her, and she did not want to worry Esmée or Caroline, but it was so free here, the dancing so exuberant and unrestrained, while in the consul's house it was rather stilted and stuffy, that she lingered far too long. Smiling, she swayed as the music rose higher and others joined in, envying them their freedom as they laughed and danced, and passed around a small jug wrapped in dried palmetto leaves.

"You should dance, maîtresse," a voice murmured behind her, and she turned with a swift gasp, faltering a little as the lithe young man smiled at her. He indicated the dancers with a tilt of his head. "I saw you tapping your feet in time to the music. You dance the *malengua*? The *jarabe*?"

She shook her head, not recognizing the names, and he smiled more widely.

"I think you do, maîtresse, though you may not know it. Come. We are all friends here, and no one will hurt you. I will dance with you, if you like."

Kyla found herself allowing the persuasive young man to coax her forward to join the others dancing in the packed-down dirt of the clearing. No one even glanced at them, though she was hardly dressed as they were, wearing a gilt-trimmed satin gown instead of plain cotton skirt. There must be liquor in the bottle that was being passed around, for the music had grown wilder and the dancing more uninhibited.

As she lost her self-consciousness Kyla found the rhythm, and followed the steps of the others without much difficulty. Perhaps it was her restlessness that helped her lose her constraint, and she threw herself into the primitive tempo of the music with abandon. Somehow—had she done it?—her hair had come loose from the combs Tansy had secured it with earlier that evening, and tumbled around her face and over her shoulders.

I'm free, she thought once, a fleeting thought that was quickly gone as she concentrated on the fast beat of the music, the deeply thrumming guitars that sobbed and soared into the shadows lit by torches. Someone passed her the bottle and she drank from it as she had seen the others do, tilting back her head to take a long swallow, then passing it on. The liquor burned a fiery path down her throat and into her stomach, leaving her light-headed. Now her body seemed to move of its own volition, her feet taking her into the steps of the Spanish *corrido*, body twisting, her head flung back and eyes half-closed with the hypnotic movement of the dance.

The young man looked up at her with admiration and appreciation. *"Merde!* You dance so beautifully, maîtresse!"

"Do I?" She smiled dreamily, enjoying the way he stared at her, not as if he owned her like Raoul did, and not so cynically as Brett had done, but with genuine admiration. It was pleasant, and she liked it. This was much more fun than being in the ballroom upstairs, where it was so crowded with dignitaries and elderly women who stared down their long thin noses at her if she laughed too loud, or danced too long with one man. Now, she did not feel old, did not feel as if her life was over before it had really begun. It would end too soon, she knew even while she danced, and she would have to go back before they missed her, but for now, it was far too pleasurable to leave.

Laughing, she danced in the very center of the crowd, losing herself in the music and the hot, lusting eyes of the men who watched her, not caring what they thought, not caring what anyone thought as she moved in sinuous abandonment.

That was how Brett found her, her blond hair and gleaming white body standing out among the dark-haired Creoles as she danced with utter abandon. He halted, not certain he believed his own eyes, and beside him heard Godfrey's muffled snort of laughter.

"I believe that she does not miss you at all, *haitsii*. Do you not think so?"

"Shut up," Brett growled, and pushed his way through the crowd to Kyla, reaching out for her and snaring her by the wrist to jerk her to a halt.

A protest died unspoken on her lips as she pushed the hair from her face and her eyes grew wide, swallowing light like a mirror as she stared up at him. "Brett?"

"Christ. You're making a spectacle of yourself, dancing out here like some damned gypsy. What the hell do you think you're doing?"

His words seemed to snap her out of her shock, and she scowled at him, wrenching free of his grasp and lifting her chin in the familiar gesture that he remembered as defiance. "I am doing exactly as I please, and you have no right to stop me."

"The hell I don't."

"No!" She put a hand on his chest when he reached for her again, and this time anger sparked in her eyes and she sounded breathlessly furious. "I am betrothed to another man."

Inexplicably angry himself, he glared at her. "Then you need to be with him instead of out here throwing yourself at the servants."

Without warning, she slapped him, her hand flashing up to crash against his cheek before he could guess her intention. He caught her wrist in a tight grip, deadly furious now. "I warned you once what I would do if you ever hit me again. . . ."

Her breasts rose and fell with her angry breaths, and she twisted her arm in his grasp. "Let me go."

"And if I don't?"

"If you don't," a cold voice said behind him, "I will put my sword through your back, monsieur. Release my fiancée and turn around to face me so that I may call you out properly."

Brett released her and turned, a little surprised that Godfrey had not warned him, but then saw why: Raoul Renardeau stood facing him, his face

contorted with rage and his eyes spitting hatred.
Renardeau—the man who had betrayed him, the
man who had stolen the deeds and given them to
his uncle.

Twenty-three

"*Really, chère,* you have the most abominable timing," Raoul said softly, his words directed at Kyla but his eyes still on Brett. "Must you choose tonight to be gracious to the servants when the other guests are famished for your presence? Please, go to the house now. Mademoiselle Dufour has been searching for you everywhere."

Brett did not glance at her, and was not surprised when Kyla refused: "No. I wish to stay here, Raoul."

Apparently, Renardeau was not accustomed to being refused, for he swore harshly in French and motioned for a servant to escort Kyla from the area. She was led away, offering another futile protest that went unheeded.

Brett watched her go, a little amused, and it must have shown on his face, for Raoul Renardeau took a step forward before checking himself. He bowed stiffly. "You may have your choice of weapons, monsieur. Name the time and place."

"Don't be a fool, Renardeau. You're making this too easy."

Raoul's eyes narrowed slightly, and he regarded Brett with a thoughtful gaze for a moment before shrugging. "Easy or difficult, I challenge you. Do you refuse?"

"No."

"Very good. I will have my seconds call on you at your convenience." He bowed stiffly again, his gaze flicking up and past Brett to Godfrey, then pivoted on his heels and stalked away.

It had grown still and quiet, so that the only music now came from the house beyond the oak grove, the faint strains of a waltz drifting through the air and sounding innocuous in the constraint of the moment. Slowly, people began to drift away, and Brett looked at Godfrey.

"She doesn't waste much time between men, I see. But Renardeau was right—she has abominable timing."

Godfrey followed him, and Brett decided not to go back to the house, where no doubt Raoul was being treated to a sizzling diatribe from Kyla. Damn her. Seeing her here was the last thing he had expected tonight, and he would not have been here himself if he had not been told that Renardeau would attend. Now Kyla was betrothed to him, and would no doubt think Brett had killed her fiancé because of her instead of the fact that he was a treacherous bastard.

"Have you decided yet?"

Brett glanced at Godfrey. "Decided what?"

"If you will tell her the truth about why you must kill the man she wishes to marry."

"There are times that you are far too perceptive for your own good," Brett commented sourly.

"I've been told that before, I believe."

"I don't doubt it. Yes, I suppose I will tell her, if she'll allow me close enough."

Godfrey smiled. "She will. I'd place a wager on it."

Shadows deepened as they left the sprawling house of the French consul, and behind them Brett could hear the unmistakable sounds of someone following them. He did not have to look to know that Godfrey heard it, too; the man was uncanny when it came to sensing things most men never noticed. It was his heritage, the years of living on the plains that no amount of beatings from an English schoolmaster had been able to eradicate, that wild streak of Comanche blood that had saved both their lives too many times to count.

As if planned, both Brett and Godfrey simultaneously parted as they turned a corner out of sight of their pursuit, immediately stepping back against the opposite sides of an alleyway. The footsteps grew louder and closer, a little faster now as the man lost sight of them. He was only a few steps past where they stood waiting when Godfrey moved, as swift as a striking snake for so large a man, his huge hands flashing out to cover the man's mouth with one palm, his other hand around the throat as he jerked him backward into the alley.

Brett reached for the knife in his boot, and held it up so that a faint glimmer of light from a lantern across the street gleamed along the razor edge of the blade. "Now, my friend," he said softly, and saw the terror grow in the man's eyes, "you shall tell me what I want to hear. . . ."

*   *   *

It was late, and the house had finally grown quiet. Kyla lay in her bed, wide-awake and still quivering with uncertainty. Brett, here in New Orleans! Good God, how had he found her? And *why*? He had not wanted her six months ago, did he want her now?

Not that it mattered to her, for she would not have him now. He had hurt her too badly, treated her as if she was nothing, and she would not allow him to do it again. Yet, inexplicably, she found herself remembering how tender and gentle he had been after he had rescued her from Northwick, and how he had been so patient, holding her up to give her water, wiping her brow with a damp cloth—it was hard to reconcile that Brett with the Brett he had become, or the man she had first met. But why was she surprised? He was a chameleon, changing in front of her eyes at times, melding from gentle to vicious in the blink of an eye.

No. She could not risk it. *Would* not risk it. So why did she keep thinking of him? She would marry Raoul. Yes, she would marry him quickly before she changed her mind, and then she would never have to think of Brett again. At least Raoul was consistent, possessive and a bit overbearing, but not overly cruel or demanding as Brett had been.

Restless, her mind spinning from one possibility to the next endlessly, she tossed and turned while the shadows cast by the courtyard tree flickered across her wall. The lamps in the garden below were lit at night for safety, and at times kept her awake. Now, she was grateful for them, for the wind had picked up and begun to blow, rattling the wooden shutters and billowing the draperies.

She slept finally, easing into slumber, when she heard the first small drops of rain begin to strike her window pane.

Slept, only to be jerked from sleep by a hard pressure across her mouth, making her arch upward in terror and begin to thrash.

"Be still," a familiar voice grated in her ear, "or so help me, I'll throttle you. Will you be quiet?"

Brett. Of course. She knew then she'd been expecting him, expecting just this to happen, and looked up at his dark silhouette looming over her and nodded. Slowly, he withdrew his hand, and she sat up, pushing irritably at the hair in her eyes.

"What are you doing here?"

"I'm glad to see you, too, *querida.*" Even in the faint light she could see his mocking grin, and that irritated her even more, especially when he did not move away but remained beside her on the bed, his weight a warm, heavy presence that reminded her far too vividly of things she'd tried too hard to forget.

"I suppose you've come to tell me you're glad to see me again," she said tartly, lowering her voice at his warning motion. "Well, don't! Just leave me alone. Can't you see I'm happy now?"

"Are you?" His shoulders lifted in a slight shrug. "Then you won't welcome my news. Did your beloved tell you that he challenged me?"

She grew still, staring at him as her eyes adjusted to the absence of light and she could see him more clearly. "No. He did not. Do you mean to a . . . a *duel?*"

"You're perceptive tonight. Yes, of course."

"Did you—will you fight? Oh, Brett! Don't! Please, don't fight Raoul. . . ."

"Would you be sad if he killed me? Or if I killed him? Which is it, *querida*? Tell me. Just for the sake of satisfying my curiosity, of course."

"Promise me you won't fight him . . . I don't think I could live with the knowledge that I caused the death of anyone, not after . . . after what happened in London."

"As if Northwick didn't deserve it. But don't fret unnecessarily, my pet. To be truthful, I have intended to kill Raoul Renardeau for several months, though I wasn't sure until today exactly who he was."

"God, you're insane!" She put up a hand to stop him when he reached out to cover her mouth, shaking her head. "I'll be quiet," she said in a hiss, "but why are you doing this? Why do you want to kill him?"

"I have my reasons. And they have nothing to do with you, so don't be too flattered." His voice altered, growing husky as he ran a finger along her arm up to her shoulder to move aside a long strand of her hair. "Though I wouldn't mind slaying a dragon or two for you if you needed it."

"Now I know you've run mad." She knocked his hand away, shivering from his touch, her entire body throbbing with reaction to having him so close to her. How did he do it? He had only to touch her, and she melted like hot wax in the sun. "How did you get in here, anyway?"

"A little late, but you're finally curious. Up the tree and onto the balcony, then a simple matter of finding out which room is yours. I was lucky. No one woke up but you, but then, you're the only one I wanted to wake. Faithless little Kyla—why did you run away?"

As his hand closed with casual cruelty in her hair, holding her head still when she would have twisted away, she met his eyes, and saw the anger in them despite his careless words and tone. "Why shouldn't I have left England? You intended to marry me off to the first man who would accept whatever you offered him for your used goods."

"Yes. I was willing to pay much more than you're worth."

She gasped with anger, and tried to push away his hand, but he was immovable, holding her with easy force. "Damn you for a black-hearted bastard, Brett!"

"You're not the first, *querida*...." His thumb slid along the side of her jaw in a light stroke, then shifted to press against her throat. "But you're the most persistent. I find it more annoying than I do amusing lately, but then, I haven't been in the best of moods."

"How unfortunate." She swallowed as his hand moved again in a light caress over her throat, fingers like iron bands as he held her in a clasp that could have been thought gentle if it was any man other than Brett Banning. She watched his face, half in gloom, but with erratic light illuminating it when the shadows of the tree shifted with the increasing wind. In the distance, thunder growled, and a sudden flash of lightning lit her room to the brightness of noon for a brief instant. In that instant, Brett's face was clearly defined, with temper showing hotly in his eyes. He was *angry*! Why?

Because she had refused to allow him to direct her life? Damn him—*damn him!*

Taking him by surprise, she shoved hard at his chest with both her hands and he released her throat to grab at her arms. She eluded him, her hand flashing out and up, but he caught her wrist before she could manage to strike him again, and twisting her arms behind her, pushed her back on the bed, holding her down with his weight.

"Oh no," he said softly. "I have no intention of letting you hit me again. You're far too prone to that, my pet, and it's liable to get you in real trouble one day."

She could scarcely breathe with his heavy weight atop her, his body pressing her deeply into the mattress, his legs straddling her to hold her down when she tried to heave him off. Anger and frustration filled her, and she thrashed futilely beneath him, her breath coming in harsh pants for air as she raged and sobbed her hatred of him, her fury that he had come into her life again.

"I hate you, oh God, I hate you, Brett Banning!" The words sounded weak, erupting between sobs and in dissonant notes that were torn from her throat, filtering into the gloom between them. "You're nothing but a sham, a fraud, pretending to be a duke when you're only a . . . a half-breed, a cross between a savage and an *American!*"

Breathless, panting, she felt his weight shift over her, and he levered his body upward slightly to stare down at her through narrowed eyes, the familiar mocking smile curling his mouth. "You say that as if it was a curse, my sweet. Too bad it doesn't bother me. I'd rather be American than English, and only wish I could claim to be Comanche. Unfortunately, my mother came from a long line of Spanish *gachupines*, more arrogant than even the English. So you see, I have inherited my birthright quite naturally, a true product of English infallibility and Spanish arrogance."

"You mean cruelty." She twisted beneath him, but he did not relent. "Let me up, Brett. Damn you, let me up or I'll scream until they come and shoot you, so help me I will!"

He laughed softly. "If you were going to scream, Kyla, you would have done it when you first saw me. I think you like this, that you wanted me to come, despite your vows of hatred."

Half-sobbing, she arched upward in an effort to free herself from his weight. "I do hate you, God help me, I *do* hate you, Brett Banning. . . ."

"Do you? Show me. Show me how much you hate me, my little blond gypsy dancer . . . you've learned much since last I saw you. Do you dance for your new lover like I saw you dancing earlier? Do you dance for Raoul wearing only something like this sheer gown you have on now? No wonder he is so determined to keep you, determined enough to try to kill me rather than risk facing me in a duel . . . ah no, my pet, don't even try that."

His voice hardened when she managed to free her hand and lash out at him, and when she opened her mouth to scream he jammed his lips over hers in a bruising kiss that was more violent than tender. Tangling his hand painfully in her hair, he held her head still as his mouth crushed her lips. She felt his tongue invade her mouth, a hot brutal possession, and his hand moved to her breast, rending the thin silk of her white gown with a soft sound. She struggled but it was no use, and felt his thumb and finger close over the taut bud of her nipple, rolling it in an erotic motion that ignited a steady, throbbing pulse in the pit of her belly and between her legs. Oh, why was he doing this?

Writhing, she felt his hands roam her body freely, touching where he willed, caressing her with lingering strokes, moving from her breasts to her belly, then along the soft inner skin of her thighs until her breath came in swift harsh pants and she realized dimly than he had stopped kissing her mouth and moved to her throat, then her breasts.

"Brett... oh why are you doing this to me? Stop—I don't want..."

Her words ended in a gasp when his hand shifted from her belly lower, sliding between her legs in an invasion that made her arch upward as his fingers slipped inside her. When she would have cried out he kissed her again, his mouth stifling her incoherent protests as his hand moved between her legs in arousing strokes that made her shiver with response.

Distantly, as if it were someone else, she heard her sobbing moans, her vows of hatred and Brett's soft, mocking laughter. "Hate me like this, then, *querida*...."

"Ohh—" She wanted to remain aloof, to show him that he had no power to affect her, but it was useless. She knew it even as he did, that she was lost, lost in this heated haze of passion and yearning, in the waves of pleasure that he summoned with his mouth and hands and body... and then there was no time for rational thought, as everything around her dissolved into a rush of such fiery ecstasy that she was clinging to him with shuddering tremors and sobbing his name over and over, a litany of hope and despair.

Outside the thunder crashed and the very house seemed to shake with the reverberations; and as if in a dream, she felt Brett over her, saw him in disjointed flashes of lightning as he leaned over her again, his hard-muscled body dark against the pale drift of mosquito netting around her bed, saw the fierce intensity of his expression as he entered her, moving slowly and steadily against her while her treacherous body arched up to receive him, awakening again as she moved up greedily to take him inside her. It was as if she was possessed by more than just this man, this silver-eyed devil who had haunted her dreams for so long.

"Put your legs around me," he whispered huskily, and even as she did, lifting her legs to wrap around his lean waist and hold him deep inside her, she knew that whatever came next, she could not lose him again.

And then it didn't matter, nothing mattered as he moved against her, increasing the rhythm of his movements and sweeping her into sweet oblivion.

Twenty-four

The rain had left the air sweet and clean, washing the stones of the terrace free of dust. A few scattered limbs and leaves littered the courtyard, also remnants of the storm, but servants swept them away as Kyla wandered out onto the terrace. She felt so strange this morning, her body sensitive and her eyes heavy. Did it show? Was it obvious that she had spent most of the night with a man? It had been near daylight before Brett left her, kissing her lightly on the mouth before dressing and leaving the way he had come—out the window.

It was late, well past the hour for breakfast, but she had not woken until Tansy opened the shutters. The young servant had looked at her curiously, but said nothing, even when she retrieved Kyla's torn gown from the floor beside the bed.

God, what must she have been thinking? Kyla put one hand to her head, frowning. Nothing had changed, except that she had made a fool of herself again despite vowing that she would never allow Brett to get close to her. There had been no promises between them, no words of love, only that wild joining of their bodies. At least there was that, though it was small comfort. How could she marry Raoul now? Yet—did she dare be foolish enough to think Brett cared for her as more than a willing mistress? Hadn't he made it quite clear in England that he did not want her? Good God, he had even tried to marry her off to his friend . . . yes, she would be a fool, indeed, if she allowed him to deceive her again.

"Maîtresse? You have a visitor."

Kyla turned, a little startled because she had been so lost in thought she had not even heard Tansy come up behind her. "Who is it?"

"A Monsieur Banning, duke of Wolverton. Oh, a duke, maîtresse! Here to see you . . . Shall I show him out here to the terrace?"

Brett . . . so soon. God, she wasn't ready for this, did not know what she would say—what she *should* say. . . ."Yes, show him out here, please. And bring more coffee."

It was foolish to be so nervous, like a schoolgirl, she chided herself, but still it was difficult not to feel this way, especially after last night. How would he act? Would he smile at her with that lazy, knowing mockery that always set her teeth on edge and pricked her temper? Or would he be as he had been those few weeks in England, sweet and considerate, a prelude to the final betrayal . . . how could she trust a man who would do that?

The thoughts chased endlessly through her head, but she managed to appear serene and cool as Tansy showed Brett onto the terrace. Sunlight filtered through the branches of the oak and gleamed in his dark hair, the blue-black color of his Spanish ancestors. Perhaps it was not so far off the mark that his mother had been rumored to be a native of America, for in a way, she had been. New Spain, this part of the country had been called then, belonged to the Spanish first, then the French.

"You look tired," Brett said as he strode toward her, and deviltry glittered in his eyes as he took her offered hand and bent over it. "Did you not sleep well, Miss Van Vleet?"

She jerked her hand away, irritated and a little nonplussed by his teasing nonchalance. "It was a restless night. The storm . . ."

"Ah yes, the storm." He looked so handsome, garbed in an immaculate white shirt with elegant neckcloth, his coat perfectly fitted and his snug trousers skimming over long, muscled legs into the tops of knee-high leather boots. Why did he have to come today, when she was still so unsettled by the night before? And he was much too close, so that she could almost feel the heat from his body. But he was moving away then, accepting a cup of steaming black coffee from the servant, gazing at Kyla over the rim of the thick cup with an appraising stare until the servant departed and they were alone. "I suppose you wonder why I have come to see you today."

She cleared her throat, pleating folds of her shawl between her fingers as she looked up at him. "Yes, as a matter of fact, it did occur to me to wonder why you would visit today after the scene at the chevalier de Touzac's last night. Is it about my fiancé, Monsieur Renardeau?"

Brett's eyes narrowed fractionally. "In a manner of speaking, yes. When last we met, I neglected to mention a few things that I thought might be of interest to you."

"Oh?" Kyla reached for her coffee with a steady hand, avoiding Brett's sharp stare. "What could you have to say that would possibly interest me, Mr. Banning?"

Deliberately dropping his title, she saw the quick flash of amusement in his eyes before he said wryly, "You do not seem the least surprised that I know him. Would you mind telling me why?"

His question took her a little aback, and she frowned as she sipped her hot, strong coffee, stalling for time. "I suppose because Raoul has so many business acquaintances. Really, it did not occur to me that he knew you or not. I do hope you both have settled this ridiculous affair of the duel by now, and that you have come to tell me of it."

"It's quite settled, thank you." Brett set the coffee cup down with a slight rattle, and the expression of idle amusement was gone from his face when he moved toward her. "Dammit, tell me the truth, Kyla, and stop evading the question. How much do you know about Renardeau's business dealings?"

"I cannot imagine why you think I would know anything." She slammed her cup down on the small table beside her chair, rising to face him. "You are a guest here. Do not make a scene, or you may find yourself escorted to the street. Why would I know anything about his business other than the fact that he imports merchandise from France and Spain? And why would it matter to you?"

"Because I am curious about several things, especially when they pertain to me and to my own holdings. It seems odd that you would arrive on my doorstep in London claiming to be Edward Riverton's long-lost heir, and then I discover that important documents were stolen from my offices and sold to Northwick—a man obsessed with you. Now, I find you here in New Orleans, engaged to marry the same man who is responsible for stealing those documents in the first place. The connection is a bit obvious, don't you think?"

She stared at him. "I don't know what you're talking about."

"I think you do."

He said it softly, deliberately, and there was none of the mocking amusement she had heard in his voice the night before, nothing but cool accusation. She stiffened.

"Shall I have a servant show you to the door, or do you think you can find the way on your own?"

"I found my way in, and I can find my way out."

She was shaking, and pulled the light shawl more snugly around her. "Good day, sir."

"Oh no, *querida*, you don't get rid of me that easily. I'll leave when I'm damned good and ready, and unless you feel like explaining just how well you know me to your hosts and anyone else who asks uncomfortable questions, you'll be smart enough to answer my question—did you conspire with Renardeau?"

"No! Are you satisfied? I never even met him until I boarded the ship to come to New Orleans, and even if I had known him, I would never have *conspired* to do anything. All I ever wanted was my mother's rightful heritage. She was married to your cousin, whether you choose to believe it or not, and by all rights, should have been allowed to stay with him, though I don't know why she would want a man who was too cowardly to defy his own parents for her. I am ashamed he was my father, and glad . . . *glad* . . . that my mother was as brave and determined as she was—I'd be dead or worse if she had been less than so courageous, for she risked everything for me . . . for *me* . . . and I cannot even tell her that I know, that I appreciate it and realize the sacrifices she made to keep me from that horrible Northwick, to keep me from what she had to endure because of my father. . . ."

She was sobbing, her voice a ragged, hoarse whisper and her throat raw with emotion as she dragged in painful breaths and blinked hot tears from her eyes. Brett had not moved nor spoken while she railed at him, and after a moment, he said quietly, "I do believe you, Kyla."

Using the edge of her shawl to wipe away her tears, she tilted back her head to look up at him, her voice unsteady. "Do you? It's about time."

"Yes, I imagine it is, but I've always known that your mother was legally married to my cousin."

"And you never admitted it? You could have cleared her name, and then people would know the truth, and—"

"And what? Would it bring her back? Would it change the gossip? No. The marriage was annulled. I told you that. And I told you the truth when I said your father left no money behind. He didn't. Christ, Kyla, it wouldn't have changed anything to drag all that sordid mess out into the open again. Maybe I should have believed you from the first, but you must understand that you were hardly the first scheming claimant to show up with a demand for part of Edward's estate. Most of them were his creditors, but there were some who tried to present false claims for what they thought he had left behind. A common enough occurrence when a prominent man dies, but damned irritating."

"So you lumped me with the rest. How gratifying. I suppose that justifies the way you treated me, how you threatened me and *ruined* me. . . ."

"No. I don't have an excuse for that, and I won't try and invent one. I wanted you. It's that simple, and I didn't think past your threat to become a courtesan."

"I see."

"No, I don't think you do. But that's not really why I came here this morning, or even last night."

"Why *did* you come?"

"Because I had to know the truth, had to know if what I've been thinking all this time was true. Kyla—"

"Well, I hope you've found out what you wanted to know. Now go away. And please— don't come back here. I never want to see you again. You've done nothing but ruin my life, and I wish to God I had never met you! Oh, just *go*!" She could not look at him, could not bear the thought that he did not care for her, could not endure hearing him say good-bye. It was easier this way, if she said it first. At least she could keep some shreds of dignity and pride.

When she looked up, he had gone, leaving so quietly she had not heard him. The terrace was empty except for her and the empty coffee cups, and she thought that the pain was too great, that she would never be the same again. It wasn't until Esmée came onto the terrace that she managed to move again, crossing to the small fountain in the center and perching on the edge of the stone, dragging her hand through the clear cool water that still had bright fish swimming in it.

"Was that the duke who was just here?" Esmée asked, coming up behind her. "The same man who is to fight Raoul in a duel?"

"Yes."

"It is true then. . . ."

Kyla looked up, but instead of censure, she saw sympathy in the girl's eyes. "I don't know what you mean, Esmée. . . ."

"I think perhaps you do, *petite cousine.* Servants talk, and there were many who saw what happened at the chevalier de Touzac's last night. Already, my maid has reported that this duke, this Brett Banning, had eyes only for you while you danced, that it was so obvious he wanted you. And now here he is—*voilà!*—on our doorstep the next morning, and after being challenged to a duel by your betrothed. So, it is not so impossible now, I think."

"Your thought processes amaze me, Esmée." Kyla smiled despite the fact she felt more like weeping.

"Do they not? I am perceptive. So—what will you do now?"

"Marry Raoul, as I have planned."

"*Quoi!* When you love another? Why would you do this?"

"Why do you think I love another? Really, Esmée, you have far too wild an imagination."

"No, it is not my imagination. I can see that you love him, for there is so much pain in your eyes, that if you did not care, you would not be so distressed because he came to you. Or is it because you fear Raoul will kill him that you weep?"

"Oh God—the duel. They must not go through with that, I must stop them . . . I will demand that Raoul withdraw his challenge."

Esmée laughed softly. "I think you may be too late for that. They are to meet under the Oaks at noon today, for I heard Papa say he is going to watch."

"Noon! But it's nearly that now . . . oh, you must help me, Esmée, you must. Do you know where this is? Can you take me there?"

"Perhaps, but if Maman were to hear—oh, do not despair, I will take you there. I cannot refuse you when I see how much it means, and if Maman is angry, she will recover. Come, we must fetch heavy cloaks with hoods so that we are not recognized."

By the time they arrived, it had begun to rain again, a cold December drizzle that turned the roads to a thick mudlike gumbo that sucked at carriage wheels and slowed the vehicles to a crawl. Kyla was frantic that she would be too late, and before their carriage came to a halt behind a long line of carriages wet and shiny with the rain, she had leaped down and was stumbling across the road, her cloak billowing behind her.

Huge, sprawling oaks spread heavy limbs out over a large expanse of grass, and it was there that the men had gathered, a large crowd flanking the two men standing in the midst of the winter grass.

Kyla recognized Godfrey's tall frame, but did not see Brett and for a moment wasn't certain to·be relieved or terrified. Was she too late?

But then she knew that she was not, for she saw a white flutter of a small scrap of cloth at almost the same instant that she saw Brett. He stood several yards from Raoul, and as the cloth drifted to the ground both men raised their arms and took aim. There was the sound of simultaneous explosions, and orange-red spurts of flame stabbing into the gray mist. Brett spun around, but not before Kyla saw the crimson stain on the front of his white shirt. There was a loud buzzing in her ears, and she wanted to scream but could not move, could not make a sound.

"*Mon Dieu!*" Esmée breathed behind her, and clutched at Kyla's shoulder. "We are too late. . . ."

A long sigh shuddered through the crowd, as if collective breaths were being released, and then Kyla saw Raoul stumble and step forward, his face contorted as the pistol fell from his hand and he pitched forward onto the wet grass and lay still. There was a crowd gathered around Brett, and men ran toward Raoul. Kyla did not know she had moved until she reached Brett, until she was grabbed by someone and held back, and looked up and saw Godfrey staring down at her with a frown creasing his rain-wet face.

"Godfrey—is he—is he dead?"

"You should not be here." Godfrey turned her around and pushed her firmly away. "Go home. It will only make things worse if anyone recognizes you."

"I don't care! Tell me if he is dead, or if—"

Relenting slightly, Godfrey shook his head. "He

lives. Now go, before someone sees you."

With that small scrap of comfort, Kyla allowed Esmée to lead her back to the carriage, and it wasn't until they were home again and Tansy was helping her take off her wet clammy garments that she thought about Raoul.

She turned, and saw Esmée staring at her. "Raoul is dead, *petite cousine*. And now the authorities say they will arrest your handsome duke for murder. There is a great scandal, Papa says, and all of New Orleans is talking about it."

"Arrest Brett? But it was a duel—"

"Duels have been outlawed since New Orleans has become American. They are uncivilized, it is said. So, now they hunt for Brett Banning with a warrant for murder, and if he is caught, he will be hanged."

"My God." Kyla shuddered, then realized exactly what Esmée had said. She looked at her again. "He is gone?"

"Yes. Though he was wounded, he has wisely decided to leave New Orleans. Ah, this will soon be forgotten, for though the American government is quite serious about halting the duels, here it is not so important. A man's honor means much to the French, and after all, New Orleans is still very French despite the flag that flies above the square."

When Kyla said nothing, but gazed into the flames of the fire dancing cheerily on the hearth, she heard Esmée murmur with sympathy, "I am sorry, *petite cousine*."

Kyla didn't know whether to laugh or cry. She thought she must look silly, standing silently with her hair wet and hanging about her face in limp strands, saying nothing and not even crying when her fiancé had just been killed by her former lover. But of course, Esmée did not know that detail, only that Kyla loved the wrong man ... yes, she supposed it was true, or she would not feel so dead inside, would not feel bereaved because it was Brett who was gone from her life while she could not summon more than an abstract sorrow for Raoul. But she had never loved Raoul, had told him so over and over, had only agreed to marry him because it seemed as if she would never have what she really wanted.

How could she admit to that? How could she tell anyone that she had been so foolish? And now she was alone again, truly alone.

Twenty-five

It was already hot, though it was only April. Kyla sat beneath the shade of a tree, fanning herself slowly. She should get up from this chair and get ready to go the soirée at the Sauzerac home this evening, but she didn't really want to go. She was only attending because Esmée had pleaded so with her, and Caroline had been so worried about her since all that had happened.

Funny, but it was as if it had been years ago instead of only four months. She rarely thought of it now, and though everyone thought she was in mourning for her dead fiancé, Esmée knew the truth. It remained an unacknowledged secret between them. Allowances were made for her, for the grief that she must be feeling, and she did not bother to tell anyone the truth.

It had come out in all the papers, how Raoul Renardeau had stolen the deeds to silver mines belonging to Brett Banning, and attempted to sell them in England. There were a lot of rumors about all the details, about Brett's uncle, Javier Aguilar y Portillo, who was behind it all, who wanted the mines for himself so that he could finance a rev-

olution in Mexico. It was Don Javier who had paid
Raoul to go to England and convince a proxy to
purchase the deeds. It was so involved, the duplicity and schemes behind the efforts to control
the mines, involving princes and revolutionaries
as well as Spanish authorities. Not that it mattered
now. The revolution in Mexico had all but ended,
with Spain retaining control of the country, and
Don Javier fleeing for his life when his schemes
collapsed.

"Come, *petite cousine*," Esmée came to say, her
voice bright as it usually was when she wanted to
coax her out of her reflection, "we must get ready
if we are to be the most beautiful women there
tonight!"

Kyla glanced up, smiling. "I think I prefer staying home tonight, Esmée. This heat has given me
a headache. Will you forgive me?"

"Of course, but don't you think it is time you
forgot all that has happened?" Esmée bit her
lower lip, and her face screwed into an expression
of concern. "I mean, it has been almost five
months now, and you cannot spend the rest of
your life hiding in this house."

"Perhaps I should leave. Oh, do not look so distressed. I have money of my own, you know, and
it's time I was independent. Your family has been
so kind to allow me to stay so long, but I must
think of the future."

"But to live alone! It would be a scandal. You
are not married, and—"

"Ah, it is only a thought. I will not mention it
more now. Please—go to the soirée tonight and
make my apologies to Madame Sauzerac for me."

Kyla would not be budged, and finally Esmée

gave up pleading with her to go. When they all left, the house was quiet again, with only the servants as they performed their evening duties. Kyla wandered outside again, restless in the unusual heat. A full moon gleamed overhead, brightening the stone terrace and masses of bright, fragrant flowers in the garden. Her silk dressing gown trailed behind her on the stone path as she wandered the garden, listening to the faint murmurs of birds and the distant sounds of the city. It was so quiet and peaceful here, but she meant what she'd said to Esmée. She had been a guest too long. It was time she lived her own life, time she thought about more than just getting through the day.

But what would she do? She still had most of the money she had brought with her from England, the money Brett had settled on her. Perhaps she should visit Tante Celeste, and maybe Papa Piers. She had sent him some of the money, an investment, she'd said in her letter, so that he could make a success of his plantation.

Idly, plucking a deep pink camellia from one of the bushes along the garden path, she held it to her nose, brushing it over her face, letting the soft petals tickle her cheek. The moon was so bright overhead it was almost like day, but there was a quiet stillness in the garden that shrouded her like a cloak.

It was peaceful, comforting, and she sank down to the cool surface of a stone garden bench, closing her eyes and letting the night wash over her in a soothing tide. Time passed slowly as she sat there, and the peace she felt began to subtly change, altering to a strange anticipation, as if she expected something else. But what?

Opening her eyes, Kyla looked about her. Nothing had changed. The garden was still bathed in moonlight and shadows, serene and quiet, with the flower beds silvered with misty light and silence broken only by the sound of her breathing. Not even a bird rustled in the trees, and the wind had died. She shivered, and rose to return to the house.

But as she moved down the path, one of the shadows beneath a tree shifted, and before she could flee, a hand grasped her by the arm. Her scream was quickly muffled by a palm over her mouth, and the camellia dropped to the garden path at her feet as she struggled.

"Quiet, dammit."

Instantly, she grew still. Her heart pounded and she waited, not daring to believe—after a moment, the voice next to her ear said softly, "Don't scream, and I'll move my hand."

Nodding, she felt his hand move, and turned slowly, believing now as he loomed over her. Silver light glittered in Brett's dark hair and illuminated his face, and she saw the same silver light reflected in his eyes as he stared at her a little narrowly.

"Hope you don't mind my dropping in unannounced, but it seemed the best way to see you without letting all of New Orleans know I'm here." The familiar drawl sounded the same, soft and a little husky, and faintly amused. "You weren't at the Sauzerac's soirée tonight, *querida*."

"Oh, were you invited?" It came out all wrong. She'd meant to sound just as careless, just as nonchalant, but there was an annoying tremor in her voice that betrayed her emotion. Brett laughed softly.

"No. But when I saw you weren't there, I thought you might be lonely. Are you?"

"What are you doing here, Brett? Not only in New Orleans, but *here*? What if someone sees you?"

"What if they don't. I came to see you, *querida*. I had the idea you might have forgiven me by now, and be glad to see me."

"Where have you been? I thought you were wounded. I thought—I thought you were gone."

"I had business in Mexico, but it's all straightened out now. They were having a small revolution down there, and I had some ... family ... affairs I had to see to before I could get back. But you must have known I would come back, didn't you?"

"Damn you—you're a madman. If the authorities find you, they're liable to hang you."

"Then come with me."

She stared at him. He looked the same, but there was something different in his voice, a note of intensity that she had never heard before. His mouth tucked in at one corner in the familiar mocking smile, but his tone was gentle when he murmured, "I've missed you, Kyla."

She could not answer, could only stare up at him, hardly daring to believe that she had heard him right as her eyes searched his shadowed face in the darkness, studying the faint glow of reflected stars in his eyes. Then he reached for her, and pulled her against him, his muscles tensing beneath the hands she put against his chest as he kissed her.

And then she fell into his embrace, and the tears ran down her face and into their mouths as they kissed, tasting of salt and relief and love. He murmured endearments in her hair, his hands moving over her, touching her face, her lips, her loose hair where it cascaded over her shoulder, and he told her that he loved her, that he was a fool and worse, and that he wanted her with him.

"Will you come with me?" he asked.

"Where?"

He laughed, softly, pulling her against him again and holding her with fierce intensity. "Does it matter?"

She shook her head. "No," she replied truthfully. "I don't care where you go."

"What if I told you that I'm no longer a wanted man?"

She drew back, staring at him. "You're not? But why—I thought they wanted to hang you for murder."

"Oh, I'm sure they did, but that's all been changed now, with the help of a very good lawyer and a few salient facts that were overlooked. Suffice it to say for now, that I've been pardoned, and by the efforts of no less than President Monroe. He is very grateful, it seems, for my part in a certain affair between the United States and England a few years back."

"You have the look of the devil," she said tartly, and he grinned.

"So I've been told. Well? You'll like Texas, I think. It may even remind you of India."

"Texas . . . your home."

"Our home, if you want. I have a hacienda on a river, Kyla, and I've sold my interests in the mines to concentrate on raising cattle—a great help to the national budget of the United States, though it certainly did irritate some Spanish officials. America is growing, and one of these days, there are going to be Americans living in Texas, too. Mexico can't keep them out forever, though they'd like to try."

"Then how do you manage to stay in Texas?"

"My mother was Mexican. But I already told you that. Do you think you could stop asking questions long enough to answer mine—will you come with me?"

She hesitated. Did she dare risk being hurt again? Did she dare risk loving him? But what else was life but a series of risks, she thought then, with only hope and love to make it all bearable ... she looked up at him, saw his eyes narrowed and realized that for the first time since she had known him, he was nervous and uncertain. Somehow, that gave her the courage she needed, and with a soft, trembling sigh, she nodded.

"Yes, Brett. I'll go with you. For as long as you want me to stay."

"Maybe I should warn you that I don't ever mean to let you go again, *querida*. I've been a fool in the past, but being without you these past months taught me a painful lesson, and I have no intention of letting you get away from me again."

"I intend to hold you to that, so be careful what you say, Brett." When he bent and swooped her up into his arms, she clasped him around the neck, laughing softly. "Are you abducting me again, sir?"

"Yes. But this time, I'm taking you straight to a priest and we're getting married. You're not getting another chance to escape me." His voice lowered, rough with emotion as he held her tightly against him. "I love you, Kyla. God help us both, I love you. Will you marry me?"

And she did not have to say she loved him, too, though she knew he had to see her answer in her eyes. As the moon shone with soft light on the garden, Brett held her in his arms, and Kyla knew that it did not matter to her where they lived, not as long as she was with him.

Epilogue

Texas, 1818

Winter sun seared the air and baked the ground, wafting up around Kyla in an enveloping cloud as she relaxed on a cushioned longue on the stone terrace. Brett had been right: She loved Texas, loved the climate that reminded her of her childhood in India and loved the easy, carefree nature of many of the people.

In the distance, cattle roamed land that rolled in gentle hills to the blue haze of the mountains that formed a boundary of sorts between Mexico and the United States. It was peaceful here, as the recent revolution had not reached the Santa María Rancho, Brett's home. It was named after his mother, whose family had once owned thousands of acres in New Spain. There was even a mine named after her, though it was sold now that Brett had decided to focus all his energies to raising cattle. It was the future, he'd said with a slight smile. America was expanding, and the need for meat would always be profitable. Perhaps he was right. None of that really mattered to her right now.

Oh, it was all so different than she had thought it would be, living with Brett—they had wed in a tiny mission chapel, their vows said in front of a priest with Godfrey as the only witness. Had it really been over a year now? So long, and yet so short a time, filled with happiness and yes, adjustment.

It wasn't all serenity and bliss, but it was worth it. Kyla smiled and tugged at the brim of the broad straw hat she wore to shade the sunlight from her eyes. Yes, it was definitely worth it. She splayed one hand on her swelling abdomen and sighed. A child, soon to be born, anticipated and yet feared—would the baby change things between them?

Oh God, there were moments she wondered if she could ever be a proper mother. And Brett— he treated her as if she was made of glass and would shatter if left alone for even an instant. It was Godfrey who had explained Brett's reasons, telling her about the girl he had once loved:

"My sister, Morning Light, loved him as do you," Godfrey had said with a sad smile. "But among my people there are always struggles. The Apache came when the men were out hunting the buffalo and caught the village unaware, taking women and horses and cattle. Morning Light managed to flee, but alone in the hills she went into labor. She and the child both died, and Brett felt responsible because he was not with her. It has always been on his mind, I believe." Godfrey paused, and then said softly, "But she was not strong like you. You have the strength to do whatever is necessary, and you will."

It was true. Kyla thought about all that had happened in the past two years. Faustine had left her the best legacy of all, something that Edward Riverton, duke of Wolverton, could never have bequeathed: strength. It was that strength that had enabled her to survive so much, even Northwick's attempts to kill her, even her grief at Brett's betrayal. Knowing now some of the reasons for his deception, she could understand why he had avoided admitting even to himself that he loved her.

Still, at times, he retreated into the remote shell that had been such a part of him, the familiar mockery he used to put distance between them. But it was never for long, because she would not tolerate it. No, there would be only truth between them now. She smiled, closing her eyes against the bright press of sunlight that warmed the winter months and her soul. Yes, he loved her, and she would not allow him to deny it for even an instant.

"You'll turn into a prune if you lie in the sun too long, *querida.*"

Kyla opened her eyes, and Brett crossed the verandah to her in three long strides. He looked reckless and a little dangerous, wearing pistols and a long knife stuck in his belt. There was none of the elegance she had first seen in him apparent now. Here, he looked more at ease, as if he belonged in this wild, raw country instead of London drawing rooms.

"You smell like a horse," she said tartly when he sat beside her on the longue, and he grinned.

"Never satisfied, are you? That's what I like best about you, your sweet temper."

"You'd be bored by a woman who always said

what you wanted to hear." She dragged a finger-tip over the smooth surface of his buckskin shirt, idly flicking the row of fringe across his chest. "Admit it."

"Freely. Not that I have to worry about you ever agreeing with me on any given subject. How do you feel?"

"Like an overripe fruit." She grimaced but smiled when Brett put a large brown hand protectively on the swell of her stomach. "Rosita says it must be a boy, because I am so large in my seventh month."

"I hope so. Though if a girl were this large, I would never have to worry about some man taking advantage of her."

"That would certainly be poetic justice, I think." Kyla laughed at the outrage in his eyes, and after a moment, an unwilling smile slanted his mouth.

"You're much too saucy for your own good, wife. By the way, the mail was delivered today. Godfrey ran across Pablo Gomez on his way back from the coast." He pulled out a large envelope and gave it to her, smiling when she cried out with delight at seeing Tante Celeste's familiar handwriting. "I thought you might be glad to get it. She should arrive soon, you know."

"Here? Oh Brett—Tante Celeste is coming *here*?"

"I was afraid it would be a little difficult convincing her to board a ship, but I promised her that this time of year the seas are not so rough. She should be here to help you with the baby, I think."

Tears welled in Kyla's eyes, and Brett looked a little chagrined. "Dammit, *querida*, don't cry again.

This is supposed to be a pleasant surprise."

"Sorry." She dabbed at her eyes with a corner of the shawl around her shoulders. "I can't help it lately. Oh Brett, I cannot believe that you managed to convince her to come . . . it will be almost like having my mother here."

Brett's large hand curved around hers, and he smiled though he did not reply. He understood the needs of her heart but would deny being considerate. How typical of his nature. Kyla drew in a shaky breath. She thought then of Faustine and how she would have approved.

"Isn't it odd, Brett, that though my mother was denied her rightful place as duchess of Wolverton, it has come to me? I have my inheritance, though nothing is at all as I had once thought it would be."

"Complaining again, *querida?*" Leaning over her, Brett captured her mouth with his in a lingering kiss. She put her arms around his neck, yielding to the almost painful press of love that welled up in her. After a moment, he broke away, breathing hard, a rueful smile on his face as he shook his head and muttered that it had been too long since they had made love. Then he pressed his forehead against hers, shoving aside her wide-brimmed hat, filling her world with his face.

"It doesn't matter how it happened. I'm just glad it did. I cannot imagine my life without you, *querida*. Do you think it will last?"

She took his face between her hands and whispered, "*Toujours . . . para siempre*—always and forever, my love."

Brett's slightly mocking smile faded and the light in his eyes was real, his voice tender with emotion when he echoed her words: "Always and forever . . . *vida mía, mi alma de mi corazón—eres toda mi vida. . . . "*

Yes, and he was her life as well, for now and always, forever—*toujours.*